KING LUDD

Also by Andrew Sinclair

FICTION

The Breaking of Bumbo
My Friend Judas
The Project
The Hallelujah Bum
The Raker
Gog
Magog
A Patriot for Hire
The Facts in the Case of E. A. Poe
Beau Bumbo

NON-FICTION

Prohibition: the Era of Excess
The Better Half: the Emancipation of the American Woman
The Available Man: Warren Gamaliel Harding
The Concise History of the United States
Che Guevara
The Last of the Best
The Savage
Dylan: Poet of His People
Jack London
John Ford
Corsair: the Life of J. P. Morgan
The Other Victoria
Sir Walter Raleigh and the Age of Discovery
The Red and the Blue
Spiegel: the Man Behind the Pictures

DRAMA

Adventures in the Skin Trade (play)
Under Milk Wood (screenplay)

TRANSLATION

The Greek Anthology

KING LUDD

a novel by

Andrew Sinclair

A John Curtis Book
Hodder & Stoughton
LONDON SYDNEY AUCKLAND TORONTO

British Library Cataloguing in Publication Data

Sinclair, Andrew, *1935–*
  King Ludd.
  I. Title
  823'.914[F]

  ISBN 0-340-48556-6

126782

TO SONIA

with whom this book was finally written

The Albion Triptych

While the novel GOG deals with 1945 and the mythology and the history of the struggle of the people against power in England until that year of the victory of the Labour Party, and the novel MAGOG deals with the history of power and its corruption in England from 1945 to 1968, the last novel of *The Albion Triptych*, KING LUDD, deals with Gog's version of the history of the Luddites – the machine-breakers between 1800 and 1987 – and the mythology of communications from the age of the Druids to the dominion of the computers.

Contents

THE GOGAM SCRIPT KEYBOARD

PROLOGUE

The True History of King Ludd

(as submitted to Professor Maximilian Mann,
King's College, Cambridge, on June 14th, 1936)

Nottinghamshire, 1811

The mills marched across the Pennines on stilts. From the hills and the villages, the tall chimneys of the new factories looked like the peg-legs of the mummers who danced, comic giants in the streets, at the guild festivals and on holy days. Above the chimneys, black gross bodies of coal smoke were puffed over the fells, until they were bloated into monstrous Gargantuas of cloud that put all the cottages of Nottinghamshire and Lancashire into their shadow. There were days of sun when no sun was seen, only an orange trim on the edge of the swollen smoke. Sometimes Hell seemed sent to Heaven, the old world topsyturvy, wrong become right. And there was no outwork.

The hand-looms in the cottages were silent, the weavers also silent. They did not understand. The laws of God and man were as clear as the sky had once been. A man worked for his trade in his own home or for a master who looked after him, body and soul, if the second item were not a private matter. The new brick halls of Mammon that belched out the sooty air and fouled the mill-streams were evil. They mired men and women and children in slums round the power-looms and set them to work in herds for unfair pay. This black industry spoke for freedom, for free trade and free markets, but it did not speak for the freedom of the villagers. They were bound now to leave their homes or to beg. Bound to mass in Birmingham or Manchester instead of in their houses by the green. Bound to lease out their wives and children to wrinkle quickly and starve slowly at the spinning-jennies and the iron mules. Bound by need and want as surely as if they were bound in chains for poaching and transportation to the new Australia of the factory towns. Bound for life to be convicts in a chain-gang at the machines. Bound for bread and wages. Bound, bound, bound. Man was now born unfree, and everywhere must break his chains.

"Enoch," Ned Griffin said. "Enoch's the master." He swung the great hammer against his anvil so that the clap of

11

it shook the smithy. A drizzle of sparks spurted and went out. "I'll take my Enoch to them. What's a Crompton with his mule or an Arkwright to my Enoch? What men have put together my hammer can put asunder."

The man who called himself Doctor Miniver among a multitude of names, sat in Griffin's smithy. He was wondering why the smith should engage himself in the quarrel of the weavers against the factories. Shoeing horses was a trade that would always need a strong man and hot iron and money on the nail. Still, that was the village for you, tight as Cheddar, thick as honest men. Miniver had spent ten years scurrying through the Midlands under an alphabet of aliases, trying to find out where the other Republicans were. His life was to whisper and suggest, to connive and remember, through the seasons of dust and mud. They were the only two seasons on the English road until the tarmacadam came, which it never did.

"Beware the redcoats," Miniver said. "They're not all with Wellesley in Spain. And there's the barracks Pitt put near the factories for the yeomanry. Clever little bastard! Said it was to keep the Jacobins quiet, not the weavers. Always something foreign, Ned, always some foreign devilry said to be at back of it. Always the red cap in the air, not the British bonnet, when we get up and say – Enough. Bread or blood. Enoch or fair wages."

"Enoch'll smash a hussar's head just as soon as a loom," Ned Griffin said. "Happen the soldiers'll join us. Local lads, some of them."

The agitator Miniver looked at the huge Griffin, easy as only giants can be, thinking his hammer was enough to settle the doubts and the debts and the ills of society. What of his own ten years of rabbiting about, slipping the government's snares, burrowing down when their spies were close on his tail? He knew himself to be little and scared and tenacious, able to organise and never to lead, waiting to incite the hungry men to riot at the right time, which also never came. If he could strike, if he had the arm and the bottom for it . . .

"You're right, Ned," Miniver said. "This is a good time. The men are ready to break the machines, to take the power into their own hands. But where's our leader? Who's to set the hour?"

"They're all in London," Griffin said. "Cobbett and Orator Hunt. Fine-spoken too. Always count your ears after you listen to a gentleman. They may be lifted off your head. You don't really know what you've heard." He paused. "When the time's here, we'll know. People know."

"There has to be a leader," Miniver said. He rose and stood by the branding-irons that hung on their hooks on the smithy wall. He hoped for Griffin to brand him as the leader, not to brand him for what he was, the man without a mark, never there to take the consequence. Yet if there were no leader, perhaps even a Miniver . . .

"Hood," Griffin said. "We need Robin back in Sherwood again. Happen the Sheriff of Nottingham would shit his britches, if Robin came again."

"Hood." Miniver fell in with the false great name. "We could call our leader Hood, whoever he was. A code. A banner. We march for Robin Hood and Old England and our rights."

Griffin turned the head of his hammer in his hands, so huge that they could cradle even its dented weight.

"There's older than Hood," he said. "The first Hammerer. The Thunderer. Thor."

"Foreign agitator, they'd say," Miniver said. "We'd prove them right. We'd be led by a foreigner, an invader."

"Gog," Griffin said. "The old giant of England. Gogmagog. We'll be led by Gog."

"He was beaten," Miniver said. "He was dashed to pieces, some say. And others say he was chained up in London. A loser, Gog. No good. We need an old name like King Arthur. But he lost too, in the end."

Griffin looked at his hammer.

"London," he said. "Ludd's town. King Ludd built London, the old books say. And he built it from the country people's work, so that it was the fairest city in the land. We have to have London with us, to take all England like Oliver Cromwell did. No London, and we'll not chop off the King's head again. So we'll call our leader Ludd. City and country, all together, we'll smash that mad old King George and fat Prinny. Let the people rule. With King Ludd."

Miniver considered the name for a while. It was blunt, heavy. It sounded like a blow.

"Ludd," he said. "I like Ludd. But King I don't like. What about General Ludd, like Cromwell? When there was no king of England, the Lord General ruled the Commonwealth. So General Ludd."

Ned Griffin swung his hammer as a pendulum, loosely in his hands. Its head grazed the tops of his boots as if it foretold the time to strike by slow arcs in air.

"Some as hate generals as they do kings," he said. "What be Ludd's first name?"

Miniver looked at the huge Griffin, larger than life, bigger than a figurehead on a man-o'-war, stout enough to wallop Tom Cribb, champion of England.

"Let's call him Ned," he said. "Like you."

Miniver had meant it as a joke, but the gravity of the giant man's face made the remark serious.

"Aye," Griffin said. "Ned Ludd. That's the job."

He raised his hammer and brought it down on the anvil.

"Ned," he said.

The clap of the iron on iron boomed away in dying reverberations in the smithy.

"Ludd," he said, and brought down the hammer again.

When the knell had sounded in his ears, Miniver had to go. He had two other Republicans to visit that day, each in a different village. Agitators never stopped.

"Ned Ludd," he said. "King and general and plain Ned. That should appeal to all parties. But who is he? We must have a leader."

Griffin gave one of his rare smiles. He seemed to pity Miniver, an urchin in his presence.

"When the time comes, the people will know," Griffin said. "We'll send the summons from Ludd. And people will find him. They always do, when they need him. That's one thing always forgot. The led matter more than the leader. Ludd is who's with him."

"Bloody cut-ups," the stockinger said, looking at the knit on the wide loom of the machine. "That's not bloody stockings.

That's cut-up and bodge ten pair from one knit. Split at the seam they bloody do."

He swung the blade of his scythe and slashed at the cloth in the frame. Criss-cross, criss-cross, he marked the cloth.

"There's work for ten stocking-frames come back," he said, "if you'll give him your Enoch, Ned."

Swing the great hammer for Ludd, for King Ludd. Smash at the timbers of the frame, split them into splints. Swing again for the Redeemer, the Grand Executioner. Break cog, scatter bolt, fly nut, fall pin. And a third blow for Ludd, to crown it all. Mess of cloth and fibre, shatter of wood and iron.

Then the Scamp running up with the lard, dropping the lumps on the weave.

"Fire." Listen. "Fire."

The torches are falling on the grease and the waste, as the Luddites smash the machines by scythe and hammer and flame. A hundred men stamping and shouting at the joy of the destruction. Down, Mammon! Moloch, thy glory is departed! The gig mill's alight, and no salvation will douse it. Sing, sing for the fire that will be the beacon for Old England:

> Sing no more, sing no more of old Robin Hood
> His feats I but little admire.
> Sing for the power of General Ludd
> Now the Hero of Nottinghamshire.
> Though bayonets be fixed, they can do no good
> If we keep to the rules of our General Ludd . . .

Out along now, as the flames eat the bricks, crack of straw in hard clay, and the beams catch the sparks as they pitch and toss, somersault to the roof. Out along now, the mill's a furnace, hot bowels spewing out the village men, the croppers and the stockingers, the puddlers and the hodmen. At their head, Ned Griffin, his mighty hammer over his shoulder:

> Great Enoch still shall lead the van!
> Stop him who dare, stop him who can!
> Press forward every gallant man
> With hammer, scythe and pick . . .

15

Ahead of Griffin, the Scamp runs, bearing a man of straw in a cocked hat like Boney's. "Ludd, Ludd," the men shout, laughing. Ludd is here, Ludd is there, Ludd is everywhere that men are marching against the machines, everywhere that the red scarves are flying in flags for the flame that will burn the mills in this black night of tyranny.

The military will be there in the morning, fresh from the putting down of the Irish, bog-perfect in the slap and the bruise and the question. For each shearing-frame broken, ten Ludds will have their bones broken. For each factory burned, ten Ludds will have their necks stretched. But not if they don't talk, not if they holy hush. Home, Ludds, each man of you, home and not a whisper. Hammers under floors, muskets up the chimneys, picks in the coal-face, scythes to the harvest. Then King Ludd's back to Sherwood and Robin's Oak, where he won't be seen for the trees.

"It's a good scythe," Ned Griffin said as he tested the edge with his thumb. "Sheffield. Bound to be Sheffield."

"Aye," the travelling Man said. "Happen to be work round here?"

The smith looked at the Man's hands. Too soft for the trade he carried on his shoulder. That one had not worked in the fields for a while. No farm labourer he, no gaunt Father Time with a scythe, no Grim Reaper with only stubble to harvest. A middling Man with an accent from another valley.

"I once saw where blades as this were made," the smith said. "Abbeydale, it was. Four big water-wheels drove tilt-hammers, they beat the blades out. They had a Huntsman crucible to melt the steel on side. More than I can do. It don't bother me. Takes no work from me. Better scythes, better harvest, I say."

The Man looked a little down in the mouth.

"I'm hungry," he said.

"You don't look it," the smith said.

"Is there no work?"

"Not enough here," the smith said. "You'll be passing through."

"Not that work," the Man said, eyes roving round the smithy. "Ludding. That's the work for me."

16

Ned Griffin laughed.

"Ludding," he said. "I've heard tell of that. But not round here, not round these parts. You can ask any one of the lads. They'd all say same. No Ludds round here."

The Man seemed weary. Not a wall that wasn't blank in Nottinghamshire.

"But I'll tell you," the smith said, "if you want the General himself, King Ludd . . ."

The Man hid his interest in a yawn.

"He's hid in a scarecrow, I heard tell," the smith said. "In a scarecrow on the way to Sherwood Forest, where he lives with Robin Hood. He's Robin's son, did you know? Though Maid Marion won't answer for him."

"You like the old stories, don't you?" the Man said. He picked up his scythe and turned to go on his way.

"You like telling the new ones," Ned Griffin said. "Good-day."

The military and the uniforms would not leave Ned Griffin alone. Any man with an Enoch, even by way of trade, was on their list. But when they came for him, the word ran ahead of the trot of the horses, and Ned was gone to the forest, his hammer in his hand.

For years, not a man heard a true word of Ned Griffin in Nottinghamshire. Some said you could leave your horse unshod in Sherwood Forest with a crown piece on the sward. Come back in the hour, you'd find it with four new shoes cold-hammered on its hooves. Some said, when the clouds shouted with thunder and lightning cracked the heavens, that Ned Griffin was at his forge, casting the cannons for the rising to come. Yet as he stayed away, more people said, "Ludd, Ned Ludd, yes, we know him. He's gone to be King of the Other People, the General of the Wood."

PART ONE

Cambridge, June 1937

1

Gog is left out.

Sitting in his Trinity attic on a summer Saturday, Gog knows that the brilliant and the best and the beautiful are elsewhere. In fact, up King's Parade. There in the rooms of Maynard Keynes, the Cognoscenti are acting as they have acted for a hundred years, making an art of clandestine conversation for their mutual delight. The swallows gliding over the Wren Library in the copper evening, the far faint shrieking of girls skittering on the Backs, the low light pinking the yellow stone of Nevile's Court – no sight or sound can console Gog's excluded heart. He is left out. Too awkward, too lumpish, too blurting, too banausic, too strange. Not to be trusted.

There is a knocking on Gog's oak.

"Come in."

Putney Bowles appears round the door, his fair hair flopping forelock over his white brow, the skin so delicate that the bone seems to be pushing through it. All the blood from Putney's face has drained into his lips, chopcherry chopcherry ripe within, so that they appear to be waiting for kisses or humiliation. They are pursed in anger as Putney looks at his odd friend. Never say people have odd friends, Putney once explained to Gog. You are always somebody's odd friend.

"Putney," Gog says. "I didn't expect to see you on a Saturday."

"I'm not going there ever again," Putney says. "You don't mind me barging in on you?" He surveys the carpet, its holes covered with open books and sheets of paper and chips from the wooden runes that Gog is carving. "I can see you're doing your thesis." Putney swings the turn-ups of his flannel bags away from the open tin of baked beans on the floor. "At least, you can hear yourself think in here. Or read. Not all that bloody chat till your mind's not your own."

"Sherry?" Gog asks. "I've got some port, too. That's it."

"Sherry," Putney says. He thumps the hole in the seat of the empty armchair, then sags into it. "I won't go back in there, you know."

"I never heard of an apostate from the Cognoscenti," Gog says.

"Judas," Putney says. "Though I feel like bloody John the Baptist, refusing to be tempted, I don't think they'd butcher me and serve my head up on a silver salver as long as they're sure I won't betray them. Anyway, if you think Salome was Rupert Brooke . . ." He laughs at his own conceit as Gog gives him Amontillado in a toothmug, then he fixes Gog with his intent blue eyes. "You're not meant to know, Gog. But I know you do."

Gog sits on his old chaise-longue, five springs pressing their metal curls into his bottom.

"Anyone's got the right to ask where the brilliant and the best minds disappear every Saturday evening," Gog says. "Secret societies can't be very secret when they always meet at the same time and in the same place."

"Here's hoping," Putney says, raising his toothmug.

"What for?"

"Hope."

Putney drains his sherry in one swallow and murmurs, "Cleanses as it burns." Then he gazes at Gog again. "I haven't had too much hope lately. It's not the international blues. I'm not like the others. I couldn't give a damn about the rise of Herr Hitler. Or the decline of bloody England. I'm depressed about me. And what they're doing to me."

Gog is silent. Putney has to confess. For that, sympathy is more effective than torture.

"Always coming to me, James and Anthony, who has made an art of dialectic. Will I, won't I, will I, won't I, join the Party and the dance? It's a dreadful mixture of chic and dialectic. Brotherhood with only the right people, naturally – none of them are workers. Snobbery with a dash of buggery. An irresistible proposition, only there's something in me . . ."

The words fade into pause. Gog makes suggestions.

"Old-fashioned," Gog says. "Don't worry. Fashion changes. The old doesn't. There's nothing wrong with being old-fashioned. It'll be the new fashion for the next world war."

"It's already begun," Putney says, "in Spain."

"That's a civil war."

"I don't think so," Putney says. "But the next world war

is what we have to avoid now. Russia must have the time to arm – and the democracies, of course. If and when the world war comes, we have to be on the right side. Or on the wrong side. Right or wrong, but *not* my country."

"Ah," Gog says, "do you mind if I ask you, Putney? Have you ever joined the Party?"

"Do I carry my little red card?" Putney does not answer himself. "We're not meant to tell that either. We may be needed where we're least noticed." He pushes out his toothmug. "I hope you've got another bottle of this drain fluid, Gog. The one which goes round the bend. I need to get drunk."

Gog fills the mug with the rest of the sherry and some port, then settles again on his fakir's couch.

"You don't have to join anything," Gog says. "The Cognoscenti are an aesthetic club, not a recruiting agency for the International. I don't understand. I thought it was all Old G. E. Moore's Almanack, the *Principia Ethica*, as interpreted by Bloomsbury. No more righteousness and duty as per Queen Victoria. Just intense friendship and the pursuit of pleasure, intellectual and sexual. Not the greatest good of the greatest number. Just the greatest good of the happy few, chosen by the very few as the last examples of civilisation."

"You were suggested as one of them," Putney says, "but they didn't want you in. Though I can see you would want to be out. You seem to understand them so well. But not all of them. There are cells inside the club. A petty Comintern among the dandies. A King's Kremlin in the beauty parlour. I know. They asked me."

So Putney confesses the evening away. The approach is made to him because of his good looks, his brains and his impeccable connections. His face is a Bronzino after barbering; he took a First in Classics in his second year, just right for the Civil Service; his father is high in the Treasury, his uncle a general in India. Would Putney like to join the Cognoscenti who ask only the best? They will aid one another through advice and influence for the duration of their long lives. They are the eminent and the nascent. The economist Keynes and Trevelyan the historian, the writers Morgan Forster and Lytton Strachey, the philosophers Bertrand Russell and Ludwig Wittgenstein, the art critic Roger Fry and Leonard Woolf and everyone who passes for male in Bloomsbury, and all blessed by the shade of the glorious martyr, Rupert Brooke, who has stopped the clock at Grantchester always at ten to three.

The flattery is irresistible, the oath of initiation inescapable. Putney has to hold up his right hand and swear more lurid than a Mason that his soul will writhe in torment for hell and hereafter if he whimpers a word about the Cognoscenti to anyone who is not a holy member. The phrases are terrible and risible. They would curdle milk, not blood, like a nursery curse or the irrelevant echo of the alchemists or the Carbonari. More awed by the distinguished company than the dread oath, Putney is now included in the conversazione every Saturday, the youngest of the elect. He is in the Society which the Provost calls, "Simply heaven on earth, dear boy."

The sherry finished, the port is low and midnight past as Putney reaches the seductions. They are emotional as well as intellectual, spiritual as much as physical. Appeals to brotherhood with the poor and the oppressed through personal feelings for the cultured and the committed, who are his Cambridge chums – though comrades never, never, never shall be mates. The idealism of changing the world rather than accepting it, warts and unemployment and all. The principle of sharing rather than greed. The victory of serving, not saving self. And finally, the laying on of hands, the anointing through caresses, the release in the body beautiful as only young men's bodies can be beautiful in their passing strength and grace, Plato in Marx, Alcibiades in Engels, Adonis for Moscow and love of the masses.

"The trouble is," Putney says, "our generation, we're still virgins. Perhaps not you, but most of us don't dare get girls into trouble, even if we prefer them. As for contraception, it's a joke. Who wants to sleep with a woman with a rubber sock on his cock, or penetrate a sponge or a fizzy douche? There's no romance in that. And passion with a woman, that's not on with most of the Cognoscenti. It's a form of obscenity best kept out of that society."

"Where else do you have to go?" Gog asks.

"Right here," Putney says, and laughs.

"Not much of a place."

"It has its values."

"Nobody can understand why you come and see somebody like me."

"Begging for praise, Gog?" Putney is instantly repentant. "I didn't mean that. You know what you have. A dogged belief in people, even in the people. A loyalty to your friends, though I don't think you'd put them before your country. Even your patriotism isn't perverse or reactionary. It's there without making a fuss about it. And a thesis on the Luddites, *praising* them – with a supervisor like Max Mann." Putney laughs again. "If I didn't know you better, I'd say you were perverse, or loved to lose."

"Max Mann isn't my examiner," Gog says. "And if I can prove I'm right, he'll see it."

"Oh yes, the dons at King's all have intellectual integrity, or they wouldn't be there. Who am I to destroy your illusions?"

"I presume Max is one of the Cognoscenti."

"Does that matter?" Putney rises. "I must climb out and then climb back in. Walls do not a prison make, but they certainly make a college."

"Spend the night on my sofa."

"Not your bed?" Putney grins at the shock on Gog's face. "Oh Goggie, you are too straight to be true. That's why I love you. No, I'll climb out. The port will give me wings over the spikes. And thanks for being a good ear. You won't mention . . ."

"Not a word."

"I don't want a trial. The bitterness of losing friends. As long as I can talk to you from time to time." Putney smiles with his loose mouth. "You're a damn good ear."

"Why don't you leave them? Lock yourself in. Sport your oak. Fade out."

"They wouldn't let me. And I'm too far in." Putney goes, high-stepping with the delicacy of the drunk. "And I do love one or two of them, you see."

"Treason? Luddism has nothing to do with treason? The labourers, they were trying to protect their way of life."

Gog is protesting to Maximilian Mann. By the windows of his rooms in King's, the don stands, tall and larded into his striped suit like a barber's pole. He contemplates the pricking pinnacles of the chapel as if he would like to impale the stupid mind of the lank graduate student behind him. Then he turns his dark brown skull, the hair wavy with false youth, and shows his face to Gog, who can study the wide brown eyes under the dark lids and the indirect lips, moving to sneer or strike.

"You would call treason, Griffin, a deliberate attack on the good of the state?"

"The Luddites weren't doing that. They were trying to save their jobs."

"So your retrograde piece of historical fiction claims, which I have read with the full attention I would give to Edgar Wallace. You appear to sympathise with your Ned Ludd. Marx did state that man was a tool-using animal, but you seem born with a wrecking-bar in your infant hand."

"My grandmother Maria, sir, she always told me . . . Ned Ludd was her father."

"Griffin, you are too credulous to believe." Maximilian chuckles in little peals, but Gog is defiant.

"As Ludd's true identity is unknown, he could as well be my great-grandfather as anyone else's."

"So you elect him to be? Because he was as muddleheaded as you are? Backwardness may run in your family – but there is no need to choose to add to it."

Gog is baffled. He knows he should dissemble or Maximilian will never recommend his thesis to the examiners. Yet how can he conceal anything from the finest mind in Cambridge bar Wittgenstein. So Maximilian's friends declare, with his consent. He is not only too clever by a whole. His brains have gone to his head.

"I still don't think wrecking machines is treason, sir. It might be in a war . . ."

"Not by definition," Maximilian says, "although the government did hang Luddites for breaking those first power-looms. England was fighting the French Revolution. And it's worse now. When man depends totally on the machine, when the machine is the means of production, when the good of the state is owning the means of production for the good of all. Once treason was to attack the king and the penalty was an axe in your neck. Now treason is a spanner in the works."

"That's sabotage."

"Treason, my dear Griffin. An attempt to halt the inevitable. Treason against the masses, who will demand a greater penalty than treason against the king."

There is a knock on the oak door leading into the room. Without waiting for an answer, an angel appears in worker's clothing. Wearing a shiny brown suit, baggy and patched, and a dirty red shirt suffering from too many late nights or revolutions, a slim gilt figure with downy fuzz on his rounded chin lounges into view.

"Busy, Max? Shall I pop in later?"

"Do stay, Rupert. I'm just finishing with Griffin, whose got a bad case of the Ludds. To solve unemployment – bury Birmingham and carve your own wooden spoons."

"Better than a bad case of the Trots."

Gog now recognises the red angel. Rupert Fox, his halfbrother's idol at Eton, come to King's on a Classical Scholarship, the prize of the left and the smart, Rupert the Second, not to be sacrificed in another world war. Incredibly, he seems to know Gog.

"Griffin?" Rupert enquires. "Aren't you related somehow to my friend Magnus Ponsonby?"

"We have the same mother," Gog says. "Merry. He's in the Civil Service. Ministry of Defence."

Gog sees Maximilian give a slight smile to Rupert, then show a sudden dismissive interest in his graduate student.

"Perhaps you should rework the first of your Luddite papers, Griffin, into something more meaningful – significant for these times. What you have written might have been relevant for the Druids of Boadicea. But in this day and age, when we know the dialectic of history, you must make it relevant."

"The Picts and the Scots," Rupert says, "are now Marx and Lenin. It's easy to change your essay. For woad, read class throughout."

Maximilian laughs again in a carillon of delight.

"Rupert, my dear, wit will be your firing squad. It's straight subversion, and Stalin won't stand for it."

"Not in the bourgeois state. It's straight promotion. Wit will get you everywhere."

Gog cannot intervene. He feels as clumsy and thick-headed as he appears to be. He rises.

"I must be going, sir," he says. "I'm off on a long walk to clear my head."

"Oh, a reading party," Maximilian says. "With Harold in Fiesole? Or is it to join a new hunger march to Westminster?"

"I'm walking on my own," Gog says. "First a long hike across Cambridge – to wear my boots in."

"Kicking the proletariat?"

Gog ignores the interruption.

"Then a real long march, kicking off at Tolpuddle –"

Maximilian's laugh rings out for the third time. He shakes his head.

"How too incredible. You – the last unreconstructed individual left in the modern world – going on a pilgrimage to the village of the trade-union martyrs."

"It might help me redraft my Luddite piece, sir."

"You write with your feet?"

Rupert smiles at Maximilian's insult, but his eyes look kindly on Gog, blundering on.

"I think it'll help me see what you said, sir. At the beginning of the Industrial Revolution, breaking machines was a kind of treason."

Rupert is highly amused.

"Treason?" he asks. "What's that? A bad word invented by bad governments to terrorise those who need to get rid of them. As all the poets say, success eliminates treason. Almost all our present governments are institutionalised treason, bureaucratic conspiracies against the masses." He assumes a sonorous and mocking tone to show that he is quoting Dryden. "'Treason is not owned when 'tis descried. Successful crimes alone are justified.'"

"While they are successful," Maximilian says. "Mussolini is a successful criminal and presently the whole Italian state. *Il Duce ha sempre ragione.* But for how long? They may hang him upside down by his heels. Rupert, it's good of you to drop in on that bit of business . . ."

Gog can take a hint when it is as subtle as a hammer. He moves towards the door. His arm is patted *en passant* by Rupert as regally as if he were being touched for the King's Evil.

"Don't worry," Rupert says. "You too will have your consciousness raised in time. And anyway, for Magnus's sweet sake, I'll love the brother while I hate his betrayal."

2

Gog sprawls in the sun and on the grass of the Backs; he is casting runes and arranging twigs. Up the Cam, baggy undergraduates push punts with long poles that they have to lower like pikemen to pass under the arc of Trinity Bridge. The other side of the cultured river, the pink-and-yellow block of the Wren Library lies complacent in its rational structure of stone and plan. Its serious harmony confronts the vagaries of Gog, seeking enlightenment in the mysteries of the North.

He has carved his own runes in small circular blocks of different woods. First, the runes of his nickname:

$$\times \quad \Diamond \quad \times$$

spelling Gog, but possessing the magic powers of the symbols of the slanting cross and the standing diamond. The woods on which they are carved are ordained by the ancient Celtic alphabet, ivy wood for G and furze stem for O. To these three runes, Gog has added three more: ᛗ twice over, signifying M and wrought from the branch of the vine: and ᚱ , the rune for A and hacked from a silver fir. These runes add to those of GOG and make up MAGOG, the nickname of Gog's younger half-brother. The second runic M denotes majesty or king and is the symbol for king as in King LUDD. The last four runes make up the name of LUDD: ᚱ for L, sliced from the rowan tree; ᚲ for U, made from root of heather; and ᛈ two discs of the butterfly D chipped from old oak. These are the seven symbols that dominate the images in Gog's mind. As he scatters the wooden counters on the grass, he scrutinises them for prophecies of peace or war. These are the rumours of the time.

The first casting is not auspicious. The double rune ᛗ is paramount, its cross and hurdle and crowned might heading the runes of GOG and LUDD with only one oak rune foretelling a winged victory for the people after long endurance. Gog now begins to arrange the augury in its order in his twig alphabet, his version of the old Celtic Ogam script that survives in scratches and notches nicked on the ancient stones of Northumbria and Wales. A long twig slanting over a short one makes up the M; two short twigs upright on a horizontal twig is the D; then various combinations of twigs set down or up or aslant to the number of five twigs for each letter lay out the remainder of the runes as cast on the grass.

Two shadows fall on Gog at his arrangements.

"Get out of my light," Gog says, then he rolls back to see a black rune against the sun, two tall figures with linked arms, the M of the game of divination.

"Ah, Diogenes," Putney Bowles says, but does not move his shadow from Gog's face. "Meet my friend Ludwig as in Wittgenstein."

The left upright of the black rune squats by Gog and considers the twigs and the wooden counters, how they align on the ground.

"Ah," he says, "I see from the symbols and the digits that you are refuting Bertrand Russell. So am I. The twigs do not run to infinity. The symbols only describe, they do not prove. The *Principia Mathematica* is rubbish. We do not discover principles in mathematics, we invent them."

"They are runes," Gog says. "And the twigs are the Ogam script of the Celts and the Druids."

"As reinvented by Gog," Putney Bowles says, lounging down alongside the counters. "I'd call it the Gogam script. A personal invention that my friend wishes to describe as antique."

A small noise erupts from Wittgenstein, more like an explosion than a laugh.

"You know language is games," he says. "You also know language is pictures. That is more than most of these serious young men know. Stalinism. Dialectics. As if such proofs of the so-called science of history had anything to do with statements or information in practice. The sound of a sentence – the order of words – they do not give connections of signs any meaning." A forefinger as long and gnarled as a dried root prods at Gog's twigs. "There are no rules in strings of signs or letters, unless they serve a purpose. My purpose? Your purpose? His purpose? The question is: Does it make sense to arrange things so?"

Now Wittgenstein pushes six of the twigs into the shape of the rune O, the middle letter of GOG, which contains the X that signifies the rune G which makes up Gog's whole name. He makes this shape:

Then he adds two twigs more to form two diamonds end to end, and he drops the two runes made of ivy and the two runes made of oak within the diamonds. To Gog, the pattern now looks like this:

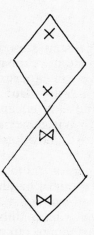

"Imagine the geometry of those four-sided diamonds," Wittgenstein says, "if they were drawn to learn about the living conditions of spirits."

"I can imagine it," Gog says.

"But does that mean it is not mathematics?" Wittgenstein asks, but never stays for an answer. "Even arithmetic is invention. Let us count as we look at the figure on the grass. If we say one rune counter and one rune counter inside a diamond are two, we can see two plus two are four."

He picks up four more twigs in the fork of his finger and puts them in a diamond across the other two diamonds to enclose a rune disc from the top and from the bottom diamonds. Now the pattern looks like this:

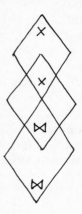

"You can see," Wittgenstein says, "that two plus two plus two are four. Counting is only probable. We cannot prove, we cannot calculate. We can experiment. We can decide to accept a statement as a proof. But to prove is to make a statement that may be false. You can count on it."

Gog laughs along with Wittgenstein, a low grumble to the philosopher's snort of mirth, now joined by Putney's rippling chuckle.

"An unlikely meeting of minds," Putney says, while Wittgenstein pulls a lace out of his shoe. "The wild Luddite Gog, the new Druid and symbolist agrees with the philosopher from Vienna. Meaning is only pictures in the mind. They are based on the names our words give to objects. Shuffle and deal the symbols. Cast runes. Arrange lines. As long as you can get some use from it, even if you can't make any sense of it."

Wittgenstein is arranging the twigs above and below his shoe-lace, stretched in a straight line across the grass. He makes a pattern from the horizontal strip of cloth and vertical pieces of wood:

"The top line of verticals above the shoe-lace," Wittgenstein says, "makes a pattern, eighteen lines on the left side, thirteen on the right side. If you count the whole top row, it makes thirty-one lines. But does it prove 18 plus 13 equals 31? Isn't it queer to call a pattern a proof? Two divided lots of thirty-one twigs represented by two numbers, 3 and 1?"

Gog is excited by this question of the meaning of mathematics. He has his own meanings to give. So he says,

"In the Ogam alphabet –"

"The Gogam alphabet," Putney suggests.

"There are five letters made up of groups of vertical lines running up from a central line. They are B, D, G, R and T. And the vowels in the alphabet run across the line in crosses like plus-marks in maths – A, E, I, O and U. And then there are five more consonants made up of vertical lines below the central line, F and L and N and P and S. So you could look at your arrangement, Professor Wittgenstein, in a different way."

"I do, I do," Wittgenstein says. "I have not begun my description. It is meant to illustrate the perils of dividing and the folly of decimal points."

"In my version of the Celtic lines," Gog insists, "we only use dots and dashes for representing numbers. But looking at your pattern as an arrangement of symbols for letters, we can find a message in it." Gog makes small spaces between the twigs, flicking away those that do not serve his purpose. "One twig up equals G. Two lots of three crossed twigs, a double O. Two twigs up, a D. Our first word is GOOD. Then five twigs down is S, four cross twigs is E, four twigs down is N, then the twig lines for S and E again." Gog finishes rearranging the twigs in a variant of Wittgenstein's pattern. "There. Now it spells GOOD SENSE."

Wittgenstein smiles and shakes his head to see the new pattern of shoe-lace and slivers:

"Good sense makes nonsense," he says. "How can sense be good? As a statement, it has no meaning."

"This is a mystical alphabet," Gog says. "Each letter means a tree with all its virtues and properties as well as just a letter. Good sense means something to a Celt in Celtic lines, while it means nothing to a Roman in Roman script."

"It is pictures," Wittgenstein says. "I do not say no to any series of pictures or to any sense that can be made of them. But actually I set out the lines to disprove the logic of mathematics and numbers. Now in your new pattern, you can see one line and three lines and three lines and two lines and four lines and four lines on the top row, making seventeen digits of one. Then you have the long cross line of division and below it, three lines and three lines and five lines and four lines and four lines and five lines and four lines. So the total of the digits of one in the bottom row is twenty-eight. If we accept that these two series of lines can be counted, we get 11 divided by 28, which is expressed as a decimal, 0 or nought point three nine followed by a series of numbers said to run to infinity because they do not divide exactly." A fingernail stabs the grass at the end of the shoe-lace, digging out four small holes. "If we end the division with the mathematical convention for an infinite series of numbers, we see four holes or dots." Wittgenstein lifts his fingernail to his lips to scrape out the dirt on his bottom teeth. "Another meaning." He spits out an invisible mite of earth. "Meaning nothing."

Putney Bowles reaches across and rakes his fingers over the twigs and the wooden rune discs. He picks up the shoe-lace and returns it to Wittgenstein, who puts it in his pocket, leaving the uppers of his left shoe agape. A choir at practice begins to sing distantly somewhere within Trinity College, and a splash sounds as an undergraduate forgets to lower his punt-pole while passing beneath the bridge and is plucked by counter-force into the Cam. In the air, the strangulated word, "Bugger."

Putney Bowles rises and helps Wittgenstein to his feet. Gog starts to rise, but Putney pushes him down, saying, "Go on with your forecasting. Construe your lines, Gog. I'll send someone to see you. Our friend Colin Graveling. He loves cryptology, the words hidden in lines and dots."

Once more Wittgenstein stands between Gog and the sun. Out of the black that is his body and the symbol for the question mark (?) in Gog's alphabet derive statements.

"Language is pictures. Calculus is symbols. If there were a calculating machine that could decode the ciphers we call mathematics, could we conceive it? And if we conceived it, could we read it? Stay with the signs that serve your purpose. Call them letters or runes to suit yourself."

3

Gog has sported his oak for days. Nobody can enter his rooms beneath the roofs of Trinity. The wooden outer door leading from the top of the stairs is closed. If Gog wants to relieve himself, he climbs out of the square dormer windows on to the lead roof above Nevile's Court and salutes nature in the gutter, watching the stars above the Wren Library. He must not be disturbed. He is designing the keyboard for his new Gogam typewriter that will convert Roman letters and numbers back to the lines and dots and arcs which the old gods gave to the Druids through the language of the trees. He has filled in the last of the numbers, and his oak door is open for a meal to be delivered.

A college porter does not come through the door, but a shambling, hairy, squat figure wearing bristling tweeds and ferocious locks and black moustache awry. He glares at Gog and says nothing. Gog stares back, also silent. Now the porter clumps through the door, carrying a wooden tray on his head and forcing the stranger farther into Gog's room. The tray is swung down on to Gog's table – a bottle of Chablis, roasted pheasant and vegetables under silver covers, and *crème brûlée* with thick sugar glaze, Trinity's greatest contribution to human felicity since the fall of the apple and Isaac Newton's discovery of gravity.

"Thank you," Gog says, as the porter stumps off with the stranger looking angrily after him. "He's a refugee, you know, not a slave. Out of Germany. We take in porters at Cambridge, not only philosophers and physicists."

The stranger turns on Gog.

"Having a meal like that carried on somebody's head to your room," he says, "is degrading. For him. And decadent for you."

"I haven't been out for two days," Gog says. "Working on something. I'm starving. This is convenient. Have a glass of wine."

"No, thank you," the stranger says. "I'm a beer man.

Putney said I should see you – a primitive binary system. Wittgenstein was impressed, though it may well be one of his jokes."

Gog rises and pours himself a glass of wine, then puts more wine into his toothmug, which he gives to the stranger.

"Pretend it's beer," he says. "It's alcohol in a mug. The same thing, bar the taste, and who can see that?" He picks up his drawing of the Gogam script keyboard and gives it to the stranger. "That's my version of the oldest written language we have in this country. It's meant to be the Celtic version of the Scandinavian runes, but I'm sure it's the other way round. The runes are copied from it, so I've put them in the bottom corners of the Celtic script. That came from the Druids. It was based on a Druid reading of the trees and a tree alphabet. Its numerals are a system of notation for use in astronomical observations from stone observatories like Stonehenge and Callinesh. Very early mathematics and signs from a time before the tyranny and false logic of Roman letters and numerals."

The stranger looks at Gog's keyboard and takes a swallow from the toothmug in his hand. He sees the strokes and points and semicircles that Gog has depicted. He does not laugh.

"This is really based on historical truth?"

"In so far as history is ever true. I can show you ancient stones that these lines are carved on."

"I'm a mathematician. Colin Graveling. I wouldn't say history is bunk, but it's irrelevant." He studies the keyboard with its symbols. "It looks more like a code than a language."

"The people who used that script and the runes also used ciphers. They scrambled the symbols in patterns to make them more difficult to interpret. The symbols also had magic significance. You could cast them and read them differently, depending how they fell."

"So if you made a typewriter with this keyboard," Graveling says, "a runic machine – and you typed at random – any symbol you liked in any series – you would still get a message you could read or decode."

"Yes," Gog says, "that is the point. Hazard or fate, the ways the signs fall – that is the message. And the prophecy."

Graveling laughs and takes another swig from the toothmug.

"I like it," he says. "Putney said you were crazy, but interesting." He simulates the drawl of their mutual friend. "An insane perspicacity permeates Gog. Like summer lightning. Perfectly useless flashes of inspiration jaggedly connecting two totally disconnected points in air. Utterly meaningless, but visible all the same. And simply lovely, except for the intellect."

Gog laughs.

"It's a fair description of my working method," he says. "But how can this script interest you at all?"

"You could make a good cipher from the letters and scramble them easily," Graveling says. "All those strokes and lines. But as a mathematician, I'm much more interested in the numbers. They run 0 to 12, I see, not 0 to 9. Is that the Druids?"

"Yes," Gog says. "Everything was in twelves – the months, megalithic yards, feet, inches. It's much more efficient, isn't it, than that damned limited metrical system? Like the French language, only a quarter the size and meaning of ours. A metrical system can only be divided into 5 and 2 and 1. But a system to 12 can be divided into 6 and 4 and 3 and 2 and 1. More precise, really."

Graveling shakes his head.

"Don't go into mathematics, Gog. Stick to the symbols and signs. Why I like your Druid numerals is that they suggest early means of communication. That 3, for instance. Dot, dash. It's like an early Morse Code, the first electronic message system. Your numerals are all in dots and dashes, though above each other like the sign for 'equals', your 4. That's not true of your 8 and 9, which look like the triple crossbars you draw for a game of Noughts and Crosses. But I think that 0 is prophetic, four dots – the modern mathematical sign for a series of numbers to infinity. And the Druid 10 and 11 and 12 . . ." Graveling points at the last symbols on the keyboard, ⊙ and ·| and ·||. "They suggest extraordinary possibilities for something I am working on. A calculating machine."

"Impossible," Gog says. "Have some cold pheasant, colder potatoes and frigid greens."

They share the meal, eating off the same plate put on the stained carpet. It takes nine taps of a silver spoon to crack the sugar ice on the *crème brûlée*. Gog reheats some coffee still standing in its metal pot on the ring by his gas-fire. He has boiled his breakfast egg in the coffee that morning. Eggshell residue – he has read – is good for human bones. Graveling does not notice how bitter and stale the coffee is, as he tries to define his theory about a calculating machine. A friend of his in King's has written a paper on computable numbers. These numbers can be fed to a machine which could work through processes involving rolls of paper printed with symbols from 0 to 1 and 10 and 11 and 100 and 101 and 1000 and so on. If the correct data for a problem can be put on the rolls of paper and be fed through a machine that previously has been given other memory rolls of solutions for millions of mathematical problems, the machine can find the right answer in minutes. A mathematician will take months. The machine may not think, but it may become the fastest tally clerk in all the world.

"Speed before illumination," Gog says. "How are you going to print the rolls of paper?"

"Pierce them," Graveling says. "Put holes in them. Dots and dashes like the Morse Code or your Druid 11 and 12."

"That might work," Gog says. "But it will never get near the human mind. It can't forget. It doesn't rely on the random. The magic of the Gogam script or the runes doesn't signify."

"I can incorporate a random element. The machine can have a roll punched with a random series of figures. Why not dots and dashes in equal quantities? If this roll was included with all the other memory rolls, you would have a random factor."

"Very contrived," Gog says. "Hand-carved chance. Rational fate. And anyway, how are you going to get the machine to think quick enough?"

"Mercury, I suggest."

"Quicksilver?" Gog laughs. "You convince me at last. You're into alchemy – and ancient medicine. Quicksilver used to be the only cure for the pox. They used to say: *One night under Venus, a lifetime under Mercury*. People once took so much mercury to cure the clap that they sweated silver drops. It killed them, but then it also killed the clap."

Another figure comes through the door, the radiant Rupert Fox in his worker's clothing, the fair down of his light beard completing an aureole round his ram's head with its glittering curls of red gold. He seems to irradiate the rough Graveling, who takes on a glow as if struck by a ray of light.

"Rupert," he says. "Why are you here?"

"You should be with me, Colin, in King's. It's conversazione time." He smiles at Gog. "Another club, Gog, not the one you think. Ever since dear Peter Kapitsa was snaffled back by Stalin three years ago, the best and the brightest of the maths and scientists have languished on Thursdays. There's been nowhere to go since Peter dear gave up his rooms in Trinity for some Lubianka laboratory in Moscow. So I and a few friends have tried to keep that spark alive. Openly."

"It was exciting," Graveling says. "I wasn't there when Chadwick found the neutron or Cockcroft spoke of splitting the atom, but I remember the buzz. We knew we were changing the world."

"And the language," Rupert says. "You should have heard Peter's prose. He got all his words wrong and his theories right. That's why we sent his laboratory after him to Russia. He can get the theories and the words right over there."

"We sent his lab?" Gog asks. "What was he working in?"

"Low temperatures," Graveling says. "The magnetic properties of matter in very strong fields. And splitting the atom, of course. It's rather shaken up our views of matter."

"Not enough yet," Rupert says. "It will. But come along, Colin. We're late."

Graveling rises. "How do you know Gog, too?"

"Everyone does," Rupert says. "Sort of. He's Magnus Ponsonby's brother."

"That man who wants me to work on a death ray?" Graveling snorted. "Absolutely absurd. Buck Rogers, if you ask me."

"Absolutely classified," Rupert says, and gives Gog a wink. "Anyway, it's invisible beams now. Radar, to give it a spurious Greek derivation. It is not meant to destroy the nasty Nazi Stukas and Dorniers in the air, but to detect them early. You can't object to that."

"We're not at war yet," Colin says.

"We are in Spain."

"Only if we think we are," Gog says. "Our government doesn't officially think we are. And if you think we are, Rupert, why don't you volunteer for the Ebro and defend Madrid from Franco?"

"Some of us are going," Rupert says. "And some of us should stay. To mobilise opinion. Raise consciousness. I'd rather fight, but I'm told my place is still here."

"Who told you?"

"A little bird in my ear," Rupert says. "One of your ravens of prophecy." He puts an arm round Graveling's shaggy shoulder. The mathematician trembles as if touched by majesty. "On our way, dear. It's David Champernowne, who swears you can play chess by numbers. And Grey Walter, who promises he can make a perpetual-motion tortoise which can defeat the hare over infinity and win the race and solve the perennial paradox." He pauses and looks back, linked to his hirsute comrade. "Sorry, Gog, you can't come. Maths simply isn't your forte."

"I don't know," Gog says. "I see lines and connections that you can't see. I'm going along a ley line next week. The old lost straight track. The underearth forces. Of course, it's crazy, but then, by Merlin's Second Law of Geodynamics, only the unseen exists, only the buried is."

4

On Wormwood Hill, Gog stands. He looks down the rough grass broken by elms to the slope which rises ahead towards the great circular hill-fort of Wandlebury. Beyond the hump, the spires and fringe dwellings of Cambridge. In Gog's hand, a letter cut from *The Times* of June 12th, 1936, and signed by Lethbridge, the excavator for the Cambridge Antiquarian Society. It runs:

Sir,

Gog Magog Hills

Gogmagog, or Gourmaillon, was undoubtedly responsible for the name of these hills. His figure cut in the downland turf, either inside Wandlebury Camp itself or on the hillside close beside it, was still visible in the middle of the eighteenth century, as the following extract from the manuscripts of William Cole, the antiquary, shows: "In a quaint book by Bishop Hall in 8vo., printed by Edward Blount and William Barrett, called the *Discovery of a New World or a Description of the South Indies*, with the running title, The description of Tenter-Belly, and subscribed the Cambridge Pilgrim, at p. 44, is this:

'A Giant called All Paunch, who was of an incredible Height of Body, not like him whose Picture the Schollers of Cambridge goe to see at Hogmagog Hills, but rather like him that ought the two Apple Teeth which were digged out of a well in Cambridge, that were little less than a man's head.' When I was a boy, about 1724, I remember my Father or Mother, as it happened I went with one or other of them to Cambridge, the road from Baberham there lying through the Camp (now blocked up by the house and gardens inclosed in it of my Lord Godolphin), always used to stop and show me and my Brother and Sisters the figure of the giant carved on the

Turf; concerning whom there were then many traditions now worn away. What became of the two teeth I never heard."

It is probable that Gogmagog was to be seen in the camp itself, for a tradition, published some years ago by the Master of Jesus in the *Proceedings of the Cambridge Antiquarian Society*, tells us that if we go to the entrance of the camp in the moonlight and cry, "Knight to knight, come forth," a giant will emerge and fight with us. It is possible that the Elizabethan edict which forbade students to attend festivities at Wandlebury is not unconnected with the survival of fertility rites performed at this figure. It is curious that a similar figure also existed at Oxford. I have been unable to trace the slightest sign of our Gogmagog either on the ground or from the air.

Gog looks for the figure of the giant Gogmagog cut on the patch of rough meadow-land between the trees on the slope leading up to Wandlebury Camp, but he can only discern tall grasses moving in the wind. He walks down Wormwood Hill, stumbling over the tufts that conceal hidden ruts, then climbs under the beech trees which shade the rise to the ditch and brick walls round the ancient camp. As he reaches the clearing before the entrance to the hill-fort, he looks down at the grasses as if his vision may penetrate them like some X-ray or the new invisible detection beams. The turf grows over chalk, and from time immemorial, figures were cut and scoured out from that covering mass. Gog closes his eyes to see an inner vision. Skewers of light suggest electric signals as he screws up his lids to conjure shapes from prophecy and hindsight, from fantasy and memory. On the two dark screens of his shut eyelids, Gog sees the symbols of a gigantic half-man brandishing a sword, then a moon-eyed giantess riding a beaked charger which drags a chariot, then white curves swirling to suggest a god coming from a sunspot. What are these symbols? Wayland the Smith, the ancient British vast artificer? The warrior Moon-goddess, that some call Ma-Gog and others Astarte, the mother of the night and of the earth? And the Sun-god Gog, that is Ezekiel's devil in the Bible under the name of Og, King of Bashan, and is the Ogmios of the Gauls, and is the Lug of the Irish, and is the

Ludd with the silver hand of the Welsh, and is the Hog of the Scots who still welcome him as the black stranger on Hogmanay? Old researches with their variant signs crowd the blank spaces behind Gog's shut eyes, and as he opens his sight to day, an explosion of light dazzles him. He speaks to himself the lines that he has long rehearsed from the catalogue in couplets of England's legends and rivers, *Poly-olbion*:

> Old Gogmagog, a hill of long and great renown,
> Which near to Cambridge set, o'er-looks that learn'd
>   town,
> A giant was become; for man he cared not,
> And so the fearful name of Gogmagog had got:
> Who long had borne good-will to most delicious Granta,
> But doubting lest some god his greatness might supplant.
> For as that dainty flood by Cambridge keeps her course,
> He found the Muses left their old Boetian source.
> Wherefore this hill with love, being foully overgone,
> He leaves one day to find the lovely nymph alone,
> Thus woos her; "Sweeting mine, if thou mine own wilt
>   be,
> "I've many a pretty gaud I keep in store for thee.
> "I'll smouch thee every morn, before the sun can rise,
> "And look my manly face, in thy sweet glaring eyes."
> Thus said, he smudged his beard, and stroked up his
>   hair,
> As one that for her love he thought had offered fair:
> Which to the Muses, Granta did presently report,
> Wherewith they many a year shall make them wondrous
>   sport,
> While she shall say, "How shall I marry then
> Rude hills and ditches, digged by discontented men?"

As he declaims to himself, Gog can see the silver snail's trail of the Granta stream behind the hill, but now he walks across the causeway over the ditch past brick garden walls into Wandlebury Camp. It is noon, not midnight. There is a pale sun loitering in the high sky, but no moon. He should not call out like Sir Osbert Fitzhugh, "Knight to knight, come forth!" and strike down a huge ghost on a giant horse that he may ride until cock-crow before it shall vanish. Yet Gog in daylight does shout the ancient challenge: "Knight to knight, come forth!" And to his surprise, from Lord Godolphin's long low house arrived alien within the archaic deep ditches, a hobgoblin does sally forth, his face a seamed crab-apple, both wizened and glossy in its sour appeal.

"Griffin, you idiot! I can hardly believe it."

"Well met, Doctor Miniver," Gog says. "May I express an equal surprise."

"Knight to knight, come forth! You cannot still be shouting that old gibberish like any yokel from Stapleford. All of a goggle, are you? Cumpuffled as usual? In a confloption?"

Miniver likes to show off his knowledge of local dialect as a peacock displays its tail. He claims to know more village speech than a universal cottager, and if Cambridge ever endows a Seat of Folklore, Miniver will be sitting on it in his best britches.

"I'm walking along the straight and narrow path, Doctor Miniver. The old ley line from the Gogmagog Hills through Wandlebury Camp and the crossroads at Wort's Causeway to Christ's College and the Round Church of the Holy Sepulchre."

As the dwarfish Miniver peers up at the looming Gog, he pushes up his mouth in such a sneer of disbelief that he makes Gog sneeze too late to block the down-blast with a hand. The expelled air ruffles the few remaining rat's-tails that plaster Miniver's pate.

"Sneeze on a Sunday," Miniver intones, "your safety seek. The devil will have you the whole of the week."

"It's Monday, I think," Gog says.

"Sneeze on a Monday, you sneeze for danger. Sneeze on a Tuesday, you kiss a stranger."

"Lucky it's not Tuesday, Miniver, I might have to kiss you."

From the Godolphin house, a slim figure appears. Man or woman, Gog cannot tell. He or she wears a white suit with black stripes, long turn-ups at the end of the creased trousers, wide padded shoulders above the blades of the jacket lapels. A cream silk shirt is held at the neck by a black bow tie in the shape of the butterfly rune in Gog's pocket. Ebony hair is cut and slicked to the skull above white smooth cheeks and lips more vermilion than those of Putney Bowles. The figure walks as if a puppet hung on strings from a hidden bar across the back of its neck.

"Who it is?" The soft French accent transposes the words. "A big fellow."

"George Griffin." Miniver introduces him to the mannish young woman. "This is Maire. A friend of your brother Magnus, come down to Cambridge to see the sights."

Gog recognises the eyes of Maire, pale blue under the sooted M of her plucked and meeting brows. They are the sea haze when the ocean meets sky without horizon. They are the lingering of evening when day will not yield to night. They are the blue mountains of Pembroke that confuse peak and distance in the long sight over the range. They are the faint azure of wave rim on sandbeach, the bleached cerulean of rain-washed pebblebanks, the faded denim of workshirts on factory wash-lines, the streak of kingfisher through marsh mist. In that recognition, Gog knows he will never be free again. He damns his romantic word-play.

"*Elle est retrouvée*," he says in his heavy French. "*Quoi?*"

"*L'éternité*," Maire says, still blinding his eyes with the blue infinities of her own. "*C'est la mer allée avec le soleil.*"

"That is your eyes," Gog says. "Eternity. The sea gone away with the sun."

Maire laughs, her mouth splitting open in a cleft plum.

"Magnus he never tell me this. His brother, his rich brother – he call him Gog – Mad Gog like Noël he sing, Mad Gog and Englishmen go out in the midday sun. Magnus he not tell me Gog he is *romantique*, he know Rimbaud, he tell me how much my eyes."

"How much your eyes?" Miniver is abuzz, a black hornet trapped in a jamjar. "Your eyes, Maire, are two saucers of absolute *rien*, meaning nothing. You do not see through them, you show them off to the gullible. Your eyes are in your fingertips, counting money, feeling furs, massaging egos."

Maire ignores Miniver and does touch the back of Gog's hand with fingertips that feel as if four silver coins from a buried hoard had been put on his skin. Gog shivers.

"Minnee, minnee, Miniver," Maire mocks. "He speak like childs in France. They not do Eeny meeny miny mo. They do Am stram gram. Picqué picqué calligram. Bourré bourré ratatam. Am stram gram."

Gog is excited.

"That's a magic language. Very old. The calligram is in the kabbala. It could date all the way back to the Druids. You know how traditional children are. Their language lasts over thousands of years. They pass it on to each other in centuries of playgrounds. Your children still count like that in France?"

"*Vraiment.*"

"Really," Miniver says, "we do not welcome your intrusion, Griffin. Why don't you toddle along the ley line or lie line you are pursuing?"

"It goes right through that house."

"Then deviate. Maire and I are going for a stroll round the earthworks. In case you believe those gaps in it are something to do with Celtic astronomy, I must point out that they were actually made for Lord Godolphin's muckcarts."

"It's Tuesday after all," Gog says. "I know it is. So before we go, I must fulfil your wise old folklore." He gives a snort that could be a sneeze. "Sneeze on a Tuesday, kiss a stranger." He bends forward and kisses Maire on her full white cheek that is rose-petal smooth. "I live in Trinity. My name is Gog Griffin."

"Gog," Maire says. "Your brother he tell of you. And he tell wrong."

"He always does," Gog says. "Au revoir. Doctor Miniver wants to give you a supervision and keep you under his." He walks off past the clock tower of the old house, leaving Maire smiling and Miniver hopping behind him. As he goes, he hears Miniver say, "I must apologise for that lout Griffin. He thinks savoir-faire is fish and chips wrapped in *The Times*." And he hears the brittle laughter of Maire, the sound of mirror-glass breaking in derision at his clodhopper's approach.

Gog's way ahead leads him over the far rings of Wandlebury Camp and downslope past Caius Farm to where the old Roman road across the marshes, Wort's Causeway, traverses the lane that leads to Addenbrooke's Hospital. To stick to his straight ley line that runs north-west to the spires of the university town, he must shove through a hedge, scratch himself with bramble and briar, mortify his flesh for his social sins. He squelches through a ditch and trudges past a disused chalkpit towards the suburban gardens of Cambridge. There is no way through the privet and the wicker, the posts and the wire, the rough stone and the red brick that the English use to defend the personal patches that they call their gardens, as if their pansy-proud borders and marigold beds were miniscule Edens. Gog skirts the barriers that defend the tidy homes of Britain and reaches the roads that separate the rows of villas in their series on a grille of tarmacadam. It is called town-planning, as if towns can be planned when they neglect the ancient lines of the underearth.

A meadow is flung down between the ranks of houses. Gog traverses Parker's Piece and passes by the slumbering fronts of Christ's College and Sidney Sussex College. As he steps off the pavement to stick to his ley line, young men on bicycles swoop on him in a charge of cavaliers on wheels. They whizz and wobble past the great lumbering figure marching direct along his invisible path towards the Church of the Holy Sepulchre. That round keep of God is locked as if the Knights Templar who built it eight hundred years before were still conducting their secret magic ceremonies within. Gog does not pause to break down the church door and search out the mysteries, but plunges ahead along the road over the River Cam that follows the ley line to its terminus on Castle Hill.

Signs and symbols are scrawled in red paint and white chalk on the walls of the colleges and houses beyond Magdalen Bridge. For every ten signs of ⚔ which has no meaning in the runes, but only for these red times, there is one ☀ that is found on Celtic crosses in Welsh Carew, the ancient mystical symbol for the sun and well-being. Gog looks at the friezes round the tattoos on the backs of his own hands, the sickles with the wheatsheaves round GOG, the joined wheels and chained crowns round MAGOG. He knows the significance of those signs, the eternal fight of the people on the left hand against those in power on the right hand, but the modern emblems do not mean much to Gog. He pushes on past the beached hulk of St Giles's Church up the hill, behind a horde of baggy-trousered and flop-haired undergraduates, who are tailing a hundred men in cloth caps and ragged jackets shiny with labour and long marching.

A dozen choirboys, diminutive under black top hats, appear suddenly in the churchyard of redundant St Peter's, only displaying the sign of the cross in the iron stays that hold its tower together. The children shrill higher than larks and fall in behind Gog in the procession uphill. They pass a red-brick Methodist chapel and the Castle pub, where fat men raise flagons of ale to the good health of the hunger marchers and down the brew in sympathy for their own stomachs. The throng veers right behind the pub and climbs the grassy mound that was the base of William the Conqueror's fortress and now is a knoll looking back over the spires of Cambridge to Wandlebury Camp and the Gogmagog Hills nine miles away over the university city.

Hoisted on to shoulders, the golden curls of Rupert Fox rise above the milling heads and caps and gowns. The watchwords of the time, the slogans of the hour, reach Gog's ears in snatches. "Franco's Fascists . . . Bastard democracy . . . Real hunger . . . March on Westminster . . . Student and miner's solidarity . . . We are all workers now . . ." Then from the threshing mob and muddle soars a tenor voice. The words are old words of William Blake, beyond class and time.

> And did those feet in ancient time
> Walk upon England's mountains green . . .

There are cries about Gog. "Reet! Oor bluidy feet!" But more mouths are joining in the hymn of people's protest.

> And was the holy lamb of God
> On England's pleasant pastures seen . . .

Confused shouting against the song is capped by the dozen treble voices of the choirboys uplifting the words into the skies over Cambridge, the tiny agents provocateurs of Christ.

> And did the countenance divine
> Shine forth upon our clouded hills?
> And was Jerusalem . . .

There is a slap and a scream and a wail. Gog turns to see
Putney Bowles, his arm raised to give a second choirboy a
cuff on the ear. Already one infant is snivelling and choking,
his top-hat knocked off his head. Gog catches Putney's wrist
and crushes it between his broad fingers and thumb. The two
young men stare at each other, locked in a conflict of the
eyes.

> . . . builded here
> Among these dark satanic mills.

"Was it, Putney?" Gog asks. "Perhaps Jerusalem was. I've
been walking to it all day."
    Putney's lips are drawn back over his white teeth. His
mouth seems a gash to the bone. Gog forces him to listen to
the swelling lines.

> Bring me my bow of burning gold.
> Bring me my arrows of desire.
> Bring me my spear. O clouds unfold!
> Bring me my chariot of fire . . .

Putney breaks Gog's lock on his wrist and massages his
crushed flesh with his other hand. The choirboys shrill about
him, their top-hats making manholes below his shoulders.
    "You fool, Gog," Putney says. "You utter fool. Will you
never learn?"
    The old words reach their final statement, telling the air.

> I will not cease from mental fight
> Nor shall my sword sleep in my hand
> Till we have built Jerusalem
> In England's green and pleasant land.

"We will too, Putney," Gog says. "I know we will build it."
    "How? Outside your head?"

PART TWO

Gog's Journey, July 1937

5

Tolpuddle.

It should be called Tolpiddle, Gog only knows. The little river is called the Piddle and runs down the Piddle Valley through Piddletrenthide and Piddlehinton. Only when it flows near Dorchester does it become respectable at Puddletown and Turner's Puddle and Affpuddle and Tolpuddle. It would not do for the first six trade-union martyrs to come from Tolpiddle. They were not piss-artists writing their names in snow, but worker-saints. They need even more support than the sycamore tree, which shaded their meetings on the village green a hundred years ago, and now is set about with props and crutches in case it may fall down.

Gog starts his pilgrimage at Tolpuddle. Not because he wants to change his mind about the Luddites, but because, in this great depression, young thinkers need to stress that they also use the inky hands of toil. The brain shall lie down with the brawn, the pen strike the paper as the hammer, the word cut sharper than the sickle. The clerks need not betray, but be brothers to the workers. In the long ago, Gog knows there was no division between bard and tribe, nor should there be any now. From Tolpuddle to Maiden Castle, from Cerne to Milton Abbas, from Camelot to Stonehenge, Gog has mapped on the Ordnance Survey grid the way of the people as one British people, as they were and are not and shall be despite history and money, class and machine. Sponsoring his own walk, Gog will tread the people's way. For the places abide and connect, as the people pass on and are reborn the people.

The Tolpuddle victims were mainly Methodists, Celts and Dissenters. More than enough for condemnation. That is still plain. By the yellow-jacketed bed-and-breakfast house – NO VACANCIES – the squat dun chapel has inscriptions written on one side of its low memorial arch:

ERECTED IN HONOUR
OF THE
FAITHFUL AND BRAVE MEN
OF THIS VILLAGE
WHO IN 1834 SO NOBLY
SUFFERED TRANSPORTATION
IN THE CAUSE OF
LIBERTY, JUSTICE
AND RIGHTEOUSNESS
AND AS A STIMULUS
TO OUR OWN
AND FUTURE GENERATIONS

GEORGE LOVELESS
JAMES LOVELESS
JAMES HAMMETT
THOMAS STANDFIELD
JOHN STANDFIELD
JAMES BRINE

George Loveless speaks on the other side of the arch, black words in his own and his brothers' defence:

We have injured no man's reputation, character, person or property; we were uniting together to preserve ourselves, our wives and our children from utter degradation and starvation.

And so they were, and still are uniting together, in this great depression, one hundred years later. No doubt of that. There had been wage cuts in Dorset down from ten shillings to six shillings a week, and no man could feed his family on those pennies from heaven. No more than the Welsh miners can now, their wages docked, wandering the land offering to dig swimming-pools for the last of the rich, new pits for the affluent, turning coal into water. Back then at Tolpuddle, George Loveless had founded his Friendly Society of Agricultural Labourers to push up wages, and he had bound its members to secrecy by dues and oaths. These had bound him and his brothers to leg-irons and chains. They were not convicted for forming a union, for what is the sin of brotherhood? They were convicted for a conspiracy against their rulers. In the labyrinths of the law, the six Dorset labourers were caught and sentenced on the evidence of a turncoat named Legg. They were gaoled in the hulks and sent as convicts to New South Wales and Van Diemen's Land, serving three hard years before full pardon and passage home. They returned as little heroes, but to no good life. Five of them ended in Canada with its cold opportunity and certain graves.

A bald story, but a beginning. Every movement needs its oaths and martyrs. Gog plods down the road beyond a pub called the Martyr's Inn. Come in, come in, traveller, and buy a pint for George Loveless, now he's loved more for the trade he brings in. Have a pale ale for the brothers, best bitter for the victims. Gog does not enter the inn, but passes James Hammett's grave in the churchyard and reaches the outskirts of Tolpuddle. There builders are working, local men earning fair wages, putting up memorial cottages for the Trades Union Congress, three connected high triangles, as tight and trim and trivet as the 'thirties can create them, tiled tea-cosies to crown the heads of the martyrs, silly brick *memento mori*s to stifle all rebels. Give the money to the people to march, to protest, to pull down. Don't build a petty structure to laud and magnify trades unions far gone from their origins. A memorial to a radical, that is betrayal. Treason, it's a treason to pen the Dorset Labourers in linked cottages, each branded name set over each snug door.

Treason is on Gog's mind as he takes the Dorchester road, lolloping by the gentle hills with the hedgerows holding their lines and the trees not daring to break out of the occasional spinneys and copses. Naturally, or unnaturally, the neat net of hedges drove the Tolpuddle men to greater despair, when it was flung over the commons and the free grazing and through the felled woodlands, enclosing a villager's right to grass and ground and fuel. Now the hedges are friends, the kind skein that defines the beloved map of southern England in its oblongs and infinite variety of geometry, patchworks of greens and yellows and browns from valley bottoms to ridges. But that quick quilt is not two centuries old. Once there were heaths and open downs, commons for the people before the hedges came to enclose and exclude and degrade the villager to the labourer at the mercy of the gentleman, private in his new property behind picket fence, gatehouse and green wall.

Time hallows treason, if it becomes an institution. And it is time again for treason. Those tickling points from Maximilian Mann become a cap of nails within Gog's skull. Where is his country, his people? On Albion or on earth? Do the white cliffs limit the masses that are his concern? Or do the oppressed of the whole globe call out for his allegiance? As Gog lumbers through Puddletown and sees the down-at-heel hovels, he knows that commitment, like charity, begins at home. And in the green arches of the wood beyond, he seems to find a sort of solution in his own suffering. His soft graduate student feet in their new hard army boots are his private pair of martyrs, blistered and swollen in a mere five miles of walking. He sinks back on a grassy bank and undoes the laces and slips off the boots. The pain ebbs. Then fatigue envelops him in its shroud, and sleep in its winding-sheet . . .

Gog hears the man in a smock kick away the box from under his feet and finds him dancing on a rope's end. He shins into the fork of the tree and clasps his hands over the gibbet branch and breaks it with his dropping weight, cracking down with the hanging man onto the dead leaves on the ground. The knot round the man's throat has not been set breakneck. So Gog can loosen the rope and work at the man's chest with stroking thumbs, pressing air back through gullet into lungs. The man gags and grunts and begins to breathe with a regular rasp. Gog slips the rope over the man's head and stands up and coils the length of the hemp around the noose and stows it in the pocket of his jacket. Waste not, want not. A man can always be at the end of his rope.

The lying man sits up, feeling his throat with the halter of his hands. A flush comes into his cheeks, words trip and tumble on his tongue. Gog watches him and listens. He knows a man who has to speak.

"Ker – Ker – Clegg's the name. Ker – Clegg." The man stutters as if he were not sure. "And I'll thank you for letting me down, sir. Man has mercy when God has none. Should I say that, sir? Do I speak to the believing?"

Gog does not nod or shake his head. The man in a smock has to speak. Gog may not want to hear.

"Believing, unbelieving, it's all the same," the man says. "But death, that's something to believe in." The man looks beyond Gog at a distance far away from the wood. "What would you say, sir, if you were blindfolded and taken to a room and the blindfold was taken off your eyes and the first sight you saw was Death himself? Yes, Death a-standing with scythe, ready to reap your legs away? And Time, skeleton Time with his sickle, too. Six foot high, the pair of them, as big as we. Your first sight after a blindfold! And a voice a-saying, 'Remember thine end!' As if you could forget your end with a sight like that. You'd take an oath then, sir, would you not? With your knees a-jelly and your marrow melting, you'd swear blind and quaking not to tell a living soul what you had seen. I'm no philosopher, sir, just a countryman who has had the time to study for the good of his soul. But a sight like that, the Grim Reaper! Remember thine end!"

The man in the smock feels his neck and stares past Gog. What he sees does not show on his face. He has to confess. It does not matter who is there. Gog is.

"Legg's the name," the man says. "Not Clegg. You have given me life back. So how shall I lie in the presence of my saviour, so to speak? I do not mean to blaspheme, sir, but godliness, where does it get you? To Van Diemen's Land, that's where."

The man laughs with a rattle of sticks in his throat. The red choker round his neck is darkening into a chain of bruises, linked by welts.

"You've heard of the Dorset Labourers, sir, the six transported for swearing an oath not to tell of the oath we took. Oh, that's tricky, sir. The law's a great trickster. They were sent away for making me swear an oath not to tell of the oath I had sworn. The law's tricky with words, and swearing an oath to combine is no crime, but swearing not to tell of an oath sworn, why, it's a conspiracy. Study the law, sir, and

57

keep your legs out of irons and your neck out of a noose –
except of your own free will."

The man in the smock laughs again drily. His throat sounds
clickety-clack. Gog hears the warning and does not speak.

"I come from Tolpuddle too, sir. So I knew George
Loveless. Loveless by name and loveless by nature, as those
who love God can be. As if loving God was the just excuse
for not loving your neighbour! Oh, Loveless called it love,
his union, his combination. But it was not love to bind us
with an oath before his paintings of Death and Time, to scare
us into swearing to his book of rules and payments. Yes, his
union was not free. A shilling down and a penny a week into
his pocket. If that is love, sir, what profits love but profit?
Tithe for the parson, that Loveless could not abide. But tithe
for the Friendly Society led by himself, that Loveless called
love of his fellow working men. A tithe's still a tithe, for God
or our own good. When you pay your dues, your pocket's
still empty."

The man laughs for the third and last time, the rattle
shaking his loose lips. Gog finds that he is fingering the noose
as a rosary in his pocket.

"What's there to tell you now, sir? Legg's the name, I'll
not hide it. Oliver Legg. When the magistrates took me, I
spoke under oath on the Good Book of the oath I had taken
to George Loveless not to speak of his oath or his union.
But, sir, my oath to Loveless was sworn on Death and Time,
but every oath at the Assizes was sworn on God and eternity.
I had to speak the truth, sir. So I gave the evidence that sent
the six Dorset men to the hulks and the Antipodes. In
Tolpuddle, well – they do not know what love is. Love, sir
– God's love is mercy. To love thy neighbour is to let him
be. Do not make him swear a false oath, do not make him
enter a conspiracy, let him be, let him be. That is God's love.
Let him be."

Gog takes the coiled rope out of his pocket and hands it
back to the man in the smock, who does not take it.

"Let him be?" Gog says. "On that tree, did I let you be?"

"On the Cross," Legg says, "did not God leave Jesus on
the Cross? Let him be."

Gog drops the rope in the man's lap. God made Judas
betray Jesus to bring about the Crucifixion. Judas should be

a saint like the other apostles. Legg should be the seventh Dorset Martyr because without his betrayal there would have been no martyrdom and no saints for the trades unions.

Yet Judas had to hang himself on a tree for it.

"You'll need the rope again," Gog says. "You'll not let yourself be."

Gog wakes in the wood. His head is as heavy as if it has just burst out of a sack of coal. He lurches to his feet, puts on his boots, and blunders through the trees. If he were a butterfly watcher, he would see Brimstones and Gatekeepers, Orange Tips and Painted Ladies, Ringlets and Green-veined Whites, feeding on sorrell and dogwood, cuckoo flowers and bird's-foot trefoil. But he is not. Nor does he stop to admire the goose-grass and herb robert, woundwort and prickly sowthistle, common speedwell and bugle. All that he notices is that there is a gamey smell from the ground as if the branches have hung too long until their bark is carrion and their leaves are compost on their stems. All is ghast and grim.

To modern travellers under the greenwood tree almost every species of tree has its dance as well as its feature. At the passing of the breeze the fir trees waltz and tango no less distinctly than they rock; the ash shimmies amid its quiverings; the beech boogies while its flat boughs bump and grind. On this warm and steamy June afternoon within living memory Gog is passing through Thorncombe Wood towards Thomas Hardy's birthplace in the darkness of a plantation that plays big bands thus distinctively to his intelligence. He comes from the trees to see a long, low cottage with a hipped roof of new thatch, having dormer-windows breaking up into the eaves, a chimney standing in the middle of the ridge and another at each end. Also standing in the middle of the ridge on the top of a ladder is a thatcher with black hair and a red jacket. He is driving in broken pointed withies with the flat of his hammer to hold the dry cut grasses in place under a plaited net of reeds. The thatcher turns on the ladder, shaking his knee-pads in provocation at the man below. Then he smacks his rubicund lips and seems to say, "And when the thatch is on fire, whenever you look up, there I shall be – and whenever I look down, there will you be."

Or words to that effect. But his Dorset accent is so thick that he might be asking Gog for a packet of Woodbines or singing a Higher Beckhampton version of the latest Fred Astaire.

"I'm hearing things," Gog mutters to himself and flees far from the madding crowd towards Stinsford. He knows that his head is stuffed with goose-feathers of literature and history, and that he cannot see the wood for the associations. He cannot hear the words for the books. It's hard enough to hear what an Englishman is mumbling in the shires without having some dead writer put his marbles in his mouth.

In Stinsford churchyard a couple of miles on, Hardy's heart is buried under a yew, the melancholy tree of blood and war, ceremoniously planted to feed its red roots and hard boughs from the bodies and bones of dead men, then to be stripped of its branches for the longbows of Old England, whittled and stretched to arch their arrows high and piercing through sur-coat and corselet, horse and knight, the fallen fruit of Crécy and Poitiers and Agincourt skewered from the graveyard tree, nourished by the corpses within its shade and range.

Hardy is not alone, but lying with his family. Under the stone ridge of the tomb, his heart is equally divided between his two wives, Emma Lavinia and Florence Emily, recumbent on either side. Two other ridged lids keep down more of the Hardy brood, while four flanking thin stones also stand on guard to prove that the Old Man, Order of Merit, had kith and kin when he wrote of earth and place and doom. He knew that country people were buried where they lived. They breathed their mortal clay. Only in the city streets did people forget among strangers that they were born in howling and woe to die too soon and anon.

Behind Gog, evil in curls and thick glasses, a witch-woman speaks to her fat daughter.

"Don't you believe it," she says, pointing to Hardy's grave. "A cat ate his heart. It isn't there."

Ten Morris dancers caper and kickshaw in front of the old Dorchester pump. Beneath the twin horns on top of the stone pillar, the dancing men cavort in their white britches and grey toppers with red bands and red-white-and-blue rosettes twirling their ribbons while the silver bells jingle on their calves. From each wrist, handkerchiefs flaunt and tease and wave to the beat of squeeze-box and drum. The tune is "The Duke of Marlborough", and elbows jerk up together, this one for Blenheim, that for Malplaquet. Like human ensigns, they fly the flag for a lionheart and Merrie England. And who shall say them nay?

A tiny hand is put into Gog's hand, and a woman's voice booms in his ear:

"It's yer father, Arthur. Ole Goggie. 'Appen this time 'e woant scarper from a simple coontry maiden what all world takes in."

Gog sees far below him the scowling face of a boy in a sailor suit, standing on tiptoe to hold Gog's hand. The small boy takes his feet off the ground and begins to swing off Gog's fingers, while Gog looks up to view a gypsy tent covered with mauve geraniums, sporting a huge heavy head garlanded with sausage rolls of hair. There is a body under the big top. Rosie, now a Fat Girl.

"Doant yer tell me yer doant know yer Rosie. Or did yer put yer tongue on toast an' swallow 'im fer tea."

"Rosie," Gog says, trying to encompass the sight of her with only two eyes. "You're looking wonderfully well."

"Bloan oop a bit I 'ave," Rosie says. "Worry. Worry meks yer scoff yer trough. Yer've got ter fill in t'oles like. Big 'oles like when Daddy scarpers an' leaves bun in t'oven an' nowt ter raise brat."

"I never knew," Gog says. "How did you know me?"

"Doant yer ever 'ave a dekko at yer maulers? Doant yer know where yer got them tattoos?"

And Gog does remember the fairground where he first meets Rosie, the hissing flare of the gas-jet and the dare, the drunken frenzy that makes him yield the backs of his hands to the tattoo man, who injects indelibly the patterns in blue and red that move each time Gog clenches his fists, prick-prick-prick like Kafka's punishment machine until G O G is lettered on his left hand and surrounded by a frieze of wheatsheaves and sickles, and M A G O G is lettered on his right hand between a square of wheels joined with a lever and crowns linked with a chain. Now the small boy is swinging off the hand marked G O G that reminds him for ever of the madness of that evening three years ago, and its afterthought.

Arthur suddenly lets go in mid-swing and lands plump on the pavement. He bawls, backed by the jingle-bells of the Morris men. The Fat Girl scoops him on to her voluminous bosom and stares accusingly at Gog.

"Drop 'im, will yer? Like yer dropped me. In shit. 'Ad yer foon, all t' foon of t' fair."

"As I remember," Gog says, "half the fun of the fair was having you – and half the fair did. How do I know Arthur's mine?"

A swinging blow from an arm bigger than a bullock's haunch makes Gog's ears ring louder than the silver bells. He staggers back, as the little crowd turns away from the dancers to their favourite attraction, a disturbance of the peace.

"'E's yers because 'e's yers." Rosie turns her menace on the nipper cradled on her bosom. "'Oo's the big lug, Arthur? Daddy. That's 'oo!" And she pinches Arthur to make her point.

"Daddy," the little boy screams, sobbing, but he is looking at a policeman shouldering his way towards them.

"He doesn't seem too sure about it," Gog says.

"'Ow can 'e be, when yer've never seen t' little booger?"

"Madam," says the policeman, small mustachios making an accent over his thin lips, "would you kindly moderate your language? There are children here."

"An' one of 'em's mine!" Rosie shouts. "An' t' big bastid's! An' 'e woant say so. Poor little booger –"

She bursts into a howling and a wailing with Arthur in full cry. Together, they sound like a Force Nine gale off Cromarty and Forth. The policeman looks at Gog. The crowd looks at Gog. Gog does not know where to look. He does know that embarrassing others, even more than attempting suicide, gets you what you want.

"All right," Gog says, patting the wailing brat on its cropped head. "Arthur, my son –"

A great smile bursts through Rosie's storm of tears like Wookey Hole after the Flood.

"I know my Goggie. 'E'll do yer right in t'end. An' if 'e doant, 'e'll get sooch a thoompin' 'e'll wish 'is 'ead were dumplin's."

Gog puts an arm round the soft Table Mountain of Rosie's shoulders.

"*Quo vadis*, Rosie?"

"Quo whattis?"

"Whither away?"

"Oh, ter t'Antelope. I weer maid theer, but I woant be maid theer termorrow."

Maid she was not there tomorrow, if maid she had ever been anywhere. As Gog clambers upon her, spread more amply across the double-bed in the Antelope Hotel than a goose-down quilt, her thighs and arms sloping over the edges of the mattress, he remembers a plump Rosie at the fairground four years ago. Then it was not like diving into a vat of stuffing – more like landing on a trampoline, a certain vast resilience in the flesh that kept Gog bouncing back for more. And there had been the thrill of imminent discovery. On the other side of the flap, a huge sign:

QUEEN KANGA

She's Naked! Furry! Thirteen
Feet Tall and Dances!
Seeing is Believing!
Touching is Instant Death!!
YOU HAVE BEEN WARNED

Only 3d

Rosie had been the nether end of Queen Kanga. Pieces of coconut-matting still adhered to her thighs which made entering her abrasive and stimulating. Outside, the clash of the Dodgems, the clangour of the Whip and the sting of the Scorpion, the barkers' voices prophesying the gain on the swings and the loss on the roundabouts. Inside the flap, Gog heaving up and down on the pneumatic scratchiness of a girl of the people he claimed to love so well.

"Two quid," Rosie had said. "Yer a gent 'oo can pay an'

yer took yer time an' time's money when yer can get it from Rose what all world takes in."

She took in all the world. Gog could see that, buttoning his trousers as he came through the flap and passed the queue of soldiers and navvies, salesmen and laddies waiting under Queen Kanga's painted crotch for their turn at her hairy delights. Ashamed and proud at his first proletarian peccadillo, Gog had gone away boosted and bow-legged. To be in with the folk is having a bang with the gang.

And now, in the room in the Antelope with little Arthur asleep on the corner cot, Arthur sprung from the spurting seed of every man in the whereabouts of Wessex, Gog is again mounting the yielding immensities of the Fat Girl, who would give Mother Earth a mile around the girdle. Gog slips into fathomless deeps, rounds pulpy Cape Horns, skids over lubricious longitudes, skirts insatiable latitudes, views oleaginous horizons, passes flabby meridians, and falls plumbline and sextant into the Atlantic Trench, where he finally swings his lead.

"Okey-pokey, penny a loomp," the Fat Girl says smugly. "More yer 'ave, more yer boomp."

Gog will remember that. But now, engulfed in a Biscay Bay of smothering arms, Gog sleeps, a drowned man floating on the steady swell of Rosie, breathing regularly.

Gog wakes at dawn. Panic slops its salt chuck deep in his gorge. The soft seas of Rosie still billow on his flank, heaving in the ebb tide of her sleeping. Gog slides out of the side of the bed, gathers together his clothes and his boots, removes all the bank-notes from his pockets except for three pounds, and leaves the money on the dressing-table. Naked, he steps across to Arthur's cot and looks for a minute at the hot small boy, lost in sweet oblivion, anybody's child but his, anybody's child and his.

The door is Gog's conspirator. It does not squeak when it is opened and it closes with hardly a click. Gog dresses in the corridor and steals down the stairs of the Antelope. There is no night porter, so Gog can undo the bolts on the main door and let himself out alone into Cornhill and High West Street. He passes Judge Jeffreys's Lodging where, as solid as gibbets, six square oak posts hold up the bay windows on the first floor. King James's Judge of the bastard Duke of Monmouth's dirty rebels at the Bloody Assizes, he didn't hang about, but he condemned three hundred men for high treason in only five court days in Dorchester, men despatched like pigs for the wanton slaughter, *drawn upon a hurdle to the place of execution, where you shall be hanged up by the neck, but cut down alive, your entrails and privy members cut off your body, and burnt in your sight, your head to be severed from your body, and your body divided into four parts, and disposed at the King's pleasure. And the Lord have mercy upon your soul.*

Oh, high treason then had a summary judgment with the careful sheriffs having faggots prepared for burning the bowels of the traitors, cauldrons for boiling their heads and quarters, bushels of salt for pickling their several pieces, and tar for preserving the remnants stuck up on spears and poles to encourage their neighbours to love their King and England and not His enemies.

High treason now is in whispers at the High Table, in dishes of tea shared on the Fellows' Lawn or boyfriends shared discreetly on the Cambridge Backs, in arguments that the masses mean more than the nation, in hopes that a comrade is worth more than a country. There's no Judge Jeffreys now to condemn such civilisation in support of brotherhood and the *Internationale*. It's patriotism for the pillory, Albion for the place of execution. Your brains and your meaningful statements are mocked and burnt in your sight, your weak head is severed from logic and history, your arguments divided into non-sequiturs and disposed of at the King's dons' pleasure. And no Lenin has mercy upon your soul. Even he will condemn Gog for deserting his only son and stealing away into the dawn.

As Gog sucks in the sharp morning air on the steep slope up to Maiden Castle, he finds his head clearing of treason and conspiracy. The acts of the Cognoscenti may be as innocent as Arthur, mere verbal naughtiness deserving a spanking. They exclude him rightly for his slow wits and lack of sympathy. It is in Maiden Castle, not in the Cambridge colleges, that his perceptions are, or most of them. And crossing the four great ditches, each dug above the circumference of the others, Gog finds himself on the huge flat green placenta of the ancient fortress with only sheep to keep him company. As he walks the long round of the highest ridge, he sees a giant baby curled up in the earth womb, the baby Gogmagog, who time and ago burst out bawling from his earth mother, the thirty-third daughter of King Diocletian, before the Durotriges constructed their Iron Age capital. At that monstrous appearance, the red deluge of the afterbirth must have swept away the Celts' huts below, flooding and clearing the ground for the Romans to build their Durnovaria on the spilt blood of the Druids and their faith. For if Gogmagog were not born here, the leader of the ancient giants of Albion, how explain such a monumental scratching at the earth's surface, such a shaping of hilltop contours to sculpt a whole landscape? It was not done to defend man, but to please God or give birth to a giant. Such is the matter of Gog's secret thesis, *The True History of Gog and Magog and King Ludd from the Beginning of Albion to the End of England*. But with Maximilian Mann for a supervisor at Cambridge and Marxism in fashion, Gog knows that he cannot submit it. He will end in a madhouse in Madingley, not in the new bardic chair at the Eisteddfod.

The low sun gilds Dorchester below Maiden Castle. Gog walks downhill over the turf towards the north. There is a true earth giant thousands of years old and only eight miles away at Cerne Abbas. Fee-fi-fo-fum, he can smell the blood of an Englishman, he can hear the heart of a Gog Griffin in quest of his homeland.

6

Trudge along the Poundbury Road, straight and Roman,
past the asbestos warehouses built beneath another neolithic
earthwork, where small boys play cricket on its grassy rings.
Turn north under the brick bridge supporting the straightest
Roman road of them all, the Victorian railroad that ruled
out Albion in iron lines more absolute than the Great North
Road or Watling Street or the Fosse Way. Now drop and sit,
legs dangling towards the river daisies, on the little footbridge
over the River Frome, watching the midges dance over the
weedy waters, hustling between the narrow banks, stiff with
reeds, gaudy with buttercups. Then up the bridle path to
Charminster Down, Hog Hill, and along to Nutcombe
Bottom. A sudden wild orchid springs and glares in the high
hedgerow. Gog leaves it to grow and turns towards two
clipped bay hunters coming towards him, ready for sugar,
with heads so small that Stubbs might have made them. The
midday sun is milky-soft in the curdled cloud, and all is green
and wildflower-cool at this cow-parsley noon.

Gog now walks along the yellowing edge of the fields
ploughed into the downland. The corn is springing, but his
boots tread on the cracked flint-stones shrugged aside by the
ploughshares. The sharp shards are no weapons now, but
they will be again when the wind blows away the thin topsoil
and the chalk brings back the grass and the down once more.

There are sudden brick blockhouses on the hill. They are
little prisons without windows. A humming sound that is not
bees. As Gog approaches the first blockhouse, he sees the
door is slightly open. A red light shines in the crack. Without
thinking, Gog pushes his way within.

Small mesh cells are stacked tier on tier on either side of
the prison. In each of them, a few hens, a waterbowl, an
artificial plaited nest, and a trough full of pellets that drop
from a pipe. Gog has read of the new factory farming of
battery hens, but the words have not reached his imagination.
The sight turns him to rage.

67

Nails and a claw-hammer have been left on a table by the door. Gog seizes the hammer and begins ripping the mesh off the cages. The hens jerk back and flutter their wings, naked skin showing through their draggled feathers. Their squawking is a frenzy of fright and protest.

Gog reaches with his free hand into the cages, scooping the hens out on to the floor. Their beaks peck, bloodying his knuckles.

"Go free," he shouts. "In the grass. Peck dirt. Eat worms. Go free."

He shoos a few hens into the open doorway. Their legs are feeble. They stagger and huddle. The shock of the daylight blinds them as they emerge. They pause on the threshold, then flutter back towards their cages and the fond red light, which is their safety.

"Go free," Gog yells. "Shoo."

Again he tries to drive the hens outside, but they scatter and return. The thousands of birds behind the mesh are killing themselves in their fear, dashing themselves against the back wall and wire, chipping their beaks, shredding their feathers. Gog is the invader, the enemy, the destroyer. They do not want a free range. They want where they know.

Gog throws down the hammer and runs away down the hill towards the road, until he comes to the smallest inn in the world in Godmanstone. So the sign boasts, and titchy it is, an old smithy where Charles the Second stopped to have his horse shod. He asked for an ale, but the blacksmith said that he had no licence to serve one. "You have now," the King said, using his prerogative to get his beer. Gog toasts the King as he lowers his pint of bitter.

Three miles along the road past the burgeoning hedges, twelve-foot high in the riot of madsummer, and then on the flank of the hill above Cerne Abbas, the Giant appears, abandoned on his back, ignoring the square spire and pepper-pot hat of the Jacobean church below. The rain begins as Gog reaches the outskirts of the old village, prettier than the limits of a postcard in its sprawling charm. He is hungry and goes into the Red Lion for supper and hard cider. The Morris dancers have mysteriously arrived before him and are singing, "It's a long, long way to Tipperary", to the sweet scrape of an Irish fiddle. Gog enjoys the music, scoffs at his Scotch eggs and cheese, and joins in the chorus for a line or two. It is a long, long way to go.

Gog is nudged by a squat man in a brown suit with lips that slither and slide, with dark hair so slick that his skull could be potted at snooker. He is holding out an upturned brown bowler.

"A bob for my Maurice dancers what's givin' their all and 'andsome for the starvin' millions. What starvin' millions you may well ask? The starvin' millions what can eat 'igh on the 'og for a tanner a thousand. They don't look a gift 'orse in the mouth, they eats the 'orse an' the saddle. They even eats dirt in Abyssinia where the starvin' millions is an' a bob's the difference between plenty an' the poor'ouse."

"Your dancers aren't dancing," Gog says. "They're drinking. So why should I give anything?"

"Oo'd be watchin' my Maurice dancers if they was doin' the kickaroo and skippin' in the rain? They're singin', ain't they? An' 'ow does that 'elp the starvin' millions? Give a bob, guvnor, an' save an 'ole tribe from the knackers' yard."

Gog fishes in his pocket and puts a florin in the hat. No sooner does the silver drop down than the squat man with the glib lips is off and away quicker than a scalded eel, squirming between two large Morris dancers coming up with empty mugs to be filled with beer. They try to grab him, but he's gone, slipping the coin into his hand and sliding the bowler back on to his head.

"He didn't touch you, did he?" the first Morris dancer asks, jingling his knee-bells involuntarily as he comes up to the bar. "Saying it was for the starving millions in Abyssinia."

"Yes," Gog says. "He did."

"Maurice Mowler," the second dancer says. "He says we're his dancers, M-a-u-r-i-c-e dancers. But he's nothing to do with us. Suddenly pops up out of nowhere and starts collecting for charity. It sticks in his pocket. He's starving for millions to put in the bank."

"Thanks for telling me," Gog says. "You make me feel a fool."

He pays and leaves the pub and walks out into the rain. He has seen huge oaks and sycamores growing on the hill halfway high to the Giant. The trees will keep the raindrops off him. Lying on their roots will return him to the earth,

which can only be known by sleeping on the ground like a
fox or a lamb, hearing the whispering of the night wind in
the leaves, the moles snuffling from their secret places, the
cry of the coney caught by the ferret, the far bark of the dog
proving a good sentinel, the owl on the bough hooting death
to the fieldmouse, the myriad complaints of the creatures of
darkness in search of food and cover. No silence in the
woodland, only the many voices of the night, alive, alive O.

Gog cannot sleep. The noises among the trees are different. The pattering of rain is the hesitance of feet. The
susurrus of the leaves is the muttering of lovers in their
persuasions. The twisting of the roots below and the branches
overhead is the writhing of limbs. The sudden moan of the
wind is the pleasure that is pain. The plaint of the nightjar
is the protest of the maiden, her hymen torn for ever. What
did Stubbs say in his *Anatomy of Abuses*, telling of the black
time spent in Cerne Abbas wood, after the women and girls
had danced round the maypole, set on the Giant's hill and
draped with St John's wort, vervein and rue? *Of an hundred
maids going to the wood, there have scarcely the third part of
them returned home again as they went.* Gog hears the lovers
now, entwining and sighing, lusting and longing, straining
and sudden lax. His closed eyes are peeping at breasts
springing to the hand, buttocks turning to the touch, legs
limber over thighs, cocks hard to brushed lips, then lost in
the dark open wounds of the women. There's no sleep at all
for Gog, each raindrop on his face a slap of guilt or grace to
deny the sexual stirring of his body. His cold cock pushes
useless against the crotch of his corduroys.

Dawn comes greyly and welcome, so that he can move his
stiff limbs and stagger uphill from the dark wood. The steep
makes hard going to the Giant's bed, beset with stupid wire
said to stop erosion. Yet white and black sheep are stomping
his outline with their hoofs and chewing his grass frame with
their incessant jaws. Over the fence to the Trendle on top of
the hill, a twice-dyked turf shield, then downhill now over
the turf on to the body, limned in chalk outline fifty yards
long. There's been one decency done. The Giant's eyes and
nose – once two balls and cock downdropping – are picked
out newly to give him the appearance of a dunderhead, not
a prick-face. Down, down, down over the white strips of his

ribs to the vast organ, pointing up to the Trendle and the sun in its rising. Life to life, what else? The seed salutes the sun.

Self-consciously symbolic, Gog lies down along the great grass cock, and hardly covers one-third of it. So he crawls to the tussock of the Giant's left ball, where many a wife has sat, spreading out her skirt and setting ample buttocks on the turf testicle, to be impregnated by force of earth and later instrument of man. There Gog is impregnated by lassitude, and the grass is his swooning sheet.

Great fingers of loam come from the sky as the Giant moves the upturned palm of his left hand to lift Gog and hold him on high, suspended over earth above the chalk trench of the Giant's mouth and the thrice-knobbled club brandished in his right hand.

The chalk trench opens. Like as the tail of the serpent of the North which girdles the world nine times and holds it together, a black tongue moves in a white mouth.

"I am Cerne, I am Ogmios, the God of the Druids. My antlers are gone to grass as the loins of the Celts have lost their seed, the wombs of their women barren or bearing foreign bastards. How shall the Celts rut as the stag when they lay down their arms to Saxon and Dane? How shall they lift their horns when the Norman rapes their maidens and makes serfs of their freemen? The hare in my left hand that holds you now is fled to the moon, giver of gladness and big bellies to women. The great snake whose tail is my tongue is buried deep in the tumulus, waiting for two thousand years to waken and hold the sick earth in place by the belt of his scales.

"My club you still see, for it was iron. The Druids knew that the Age of Iron was but begun and would last three thousand years until its club had broken men upon the iron wheel and the iron rail, the iron hammer and the iron spike. And only the great phallus that is the second club of mine will still batter at the closed doors of the wives and break down the lock into their bellies and burst forth in seed for generation after generation to work in the mines and the sheds of the long Age of Iron.

"I am Lug, I am Ludd, the god of the Celts. You do not see my wings, which spread their span to master the sun, to be lost in his fire and his light and his life. You do not see my torque, the twisted gold collar of my magic and my majesty, for it has moved on its motion deep into the cave of the dragon. And gone to grass is my great dog, who excelled in the hunt of the wild boar, whose flesh is sweeter than the flesh of ox or deer or lamb. And I am the Celtic Giant, the brother by my mother of Gogmagog and the score and four giants who fought King Brutus and Corineus and the Trojans at Totnes and fell back to earth there, their bones dried to fossil stones, their metal run to ore.

"Yet my true name is not Cerne, not Ogmios, but Lug also called Ludd. I am the child of the sun and the guard of the gate to hell. For man is born blind until the rays of the light shall open his eyes, and man dies blind until the gatekeeper shall guide his soul to the nether world. He is brought from nothing by the power of brightness, he goes into nothing in the maw of darkness. I am Ludd who intercedes between the life to come and the life that must end. My dominion is between birthing and dying, between being and not being, between living and unliving. I am Ludd. You may forget me, yet I will meet you at the cradle and the grave. You may ignore me, yet I shall swaddle you in bands and shroud in bandages. I am the mediator between the brightness of heaven and the bowels of the earth.

"Know me, Ludd."

Gog feels two fingertips of loam press on each of his eyelids until they seem stakes of soil driving his vision into the depths of the inner earth to see the truth and insignificance of his existence. And lo, beneath the hill, there lies a great plate set on the back of the immense tortoise-shell of the world, and that plate grinds against another plate, and from their grinding the mountain ranges are pushed high, the Alps and the Andes, the Urals and the Himalayas, the Rockies and the Mountains of the Moon. The peaks are but infinitesimal flakes from the scraping of the plates that shift beneath the surface of the whole earth and the seven seas.

Down, down, down, Gog's eyes are driven to the fiery regions where the lava is ichor in the veins of the belly of the tortoise planet, where the rocks are molten as lead in the cauldron, where red granite is boiling blood and quartz is as bubbling quicksilver. And at the heart of the tortoise that is the earth the very flame is blacker than sun-blindness striking hotter than the heat of the noon of noons. In the fathoms of hell, illumination. At the core of darkness, the black brightness of the light.

The Giant's fingertips are taken from Gog's eyes, and he speaks.

"Know me, Ludd. I sleep on this hill, the last of the giants still cherished in this country other than the Long Man at Wilmington with his twin measuring rods that cannot mark out the immeasurable or map the unknowable. I guard the downs from the fire below and the fire above. The volcano shall not burn here or the meteorite fall, for I am Ludd who stands between hell and heaven. As long as I lie here, there shall be no Vulcan's fire, no comet's tail, no blast from underearth or brimstone from the clouds.

"There were many of us, and now there are two. The dragons sleep in their caves, the giants are gone to grass and ground, only the names of places still honour them, and the memories of the folk. Forget them at your peril, for they were the guardians of the green peace of the earth, they stood against the desolation below and the devastation from on high.

"Because man has forgotten them, he plots his own destruction. While he cared for them, he cared for the green peace and the mystery of the ground. Now he pollutes the ploughed land with powder that destroys, with acid in the rain and alkali in the rivers. Even now, he seeks to split the grain that is at the centre of all grains, the speck of God that is the being of all that moves and breathes and lives. In that unholy fission, he will unleash an ultimate destruction that will be nothing after nothing after nothing. And then there will be no green peace kept by the giants, for there shall be no green. And there will be no children sprung from the giants, for there shall be no children. And there will be no scouring of the chalk in memory of me, for there shall be no servants to scour me. And all the earth shall be the abomination of desolation, yea, for generation after generation, for there will be no generation until the lichen shall grow legs and the algae shall grow fins and bring again the ages of the giants and the dragons and the holy places that guard the green peace of the world."

So the Giant speaks to Gog. And the black serpent's tail of his tongue sinks back into the chalk trench which closes in a single white lip. And he brings Gog down on the earthen palm of his left hand. Fingers of loam knead Gog and palp him and expel him, so that he is born again of earth and prophecy, of the old wisdom of the gods and in the new ways of man that will lead to no men and no earth and nothing at all.

Gog wakes, shaking the slumber and the dream from his head. Blearily he looks down at Cerne Abbas below. He feels silly sitting on the turf testicle, a symbol only of his own folly and fantasy about the chalk cock of a grass giant that nobody credits now except himself. Yet the words still sound in Gog's ears in the buzz of after-sleep. Ludd will not be forgotten, the keeper of the place and the peace, the holder of the balance between the sun and the inferno, the begetter of the men children who will betray him at their peril.

Moving up the dark slope of the chalk hill, Gog sees ahead a fox, stock-still and watching the skyline rabbits. Gog stops. The fox moves forward, two paces, as cautious as if playing grandmother's footsteps. The rabbits duck to nibble, then pause, upright and ears high. The fox crouches, then moves slowly up the slope, following a scent.

When Gog toils up to the ridge, rabbits are bucketing bobbity all about him. The fox is pelting at him, scut of young rabbit just in front of his jaws. The victim jinks past Gog's left foot, and the fox halts, surprised. Its sharp red face is so like half-brother Magnus in a rage that Gog laughs, and the fox veers away without its breakfast. The warren settles as Gog takes the turf track along the Great Ridgeway, curving in a vast arm flung towards the sun, holding in its crook the pattern of fields below.

Crossing a stile to take the eastern paths to the Dorsetshire Gap, Gog surprises a deer, which considers him before bolting into a thicket, leaving Gog to kick through long wet grass that soaks his boots. The miles of cracked chalk track that amble up and down make a pleasant stroll in the silksoft morning. Yet as Gog skirts the long serpent wood on Church Hill and reaches the rise, he can see fifteen miles away on Bulbarrow Hill twin iron masts like the horns of the new devil at the crossways of the ancient ridge roads.

Gog thinks that these twin rods of modern power are mirages. For he soon loses sight of them, dropping down to the Folly, the old inn this side of the Dorsetshire Gap. But the carts don't pass now, rutting the ridgeways, nor do the migrant labourers in search of the next harvest. The cars whizz by on other roads, and the grunting lorries have taken the loads from the horse-drivers on their wains. So the Folly is weatherbeaten now. No lamp shines above its black door. There is no welcome there.

Trying to reach the last ridge before Bulbarrow Hill, Gog falls into a conspiracy of farmers. Paths are ploughed up, barbed wire lies in tangles across rights of way, passage is denied by ditches and nettlebeds. Scratched, stung and sprained, Gog takes two hours to cover half a mile to the snaggle of the Dorsetshire Gap, and there he pronounces an anathema on the near villages, howling in the teeth of the wind like a zany Zephaniah.

Woe unto you, farmers of Albion,
Respect ye the way of the walker,
Before the day pass as the chaff,
Before the day of Gog's anger come upon you –
Surely Alton Pancras shall be as Sodom,
And the children of Anstey as Gomorrah,
Even the breeding of nettles,
And saltpits,
And a perpetual desolation.
This shall they have for their pride
Because they have planted wheat on the sacred ways,
Because they have barbed wire in the paths of the
*   righteous.*
Gog will be terrible unto them.
He will stretch out his hand against the north
And destroy Mappowder.
And will make Melcombe Bingham a desolation
And dry like a wilderness.
And flocks shall lie down in the midst of her,

All the beasts of the nations;
Both the cormorant and the bittern
Shall lodge in the upper lintels of it;
Their voice shall sing in the windows;
Desolation shall be in the threshold.
For Gog shall uncover the dry rot.
Every walker that passeth by her
Shall hiss, and wag his hand.

Shouting his vain curses into the indifferent air, Gog breaks through this persecution of farmers, and descends from the Dorsetshire Gap down cart-ruts, leading him across the Devil's Brook at the Lydden, Ludd's own stream flowing north to the Blackmoor Vale. He passes through meadows that lie along the green flank of the land. He can see Bulbarrow Hill ahead, but first the climb past Breach Wood and Hatherly Farm up, up the steep slope where the ancient men have carved out their earth lines, changing the face of the hill. Gorse is the only defence now, and wet cowpats more sticky-dangerous than anti-personnel mines, brambles to boobytrap, briars to prick like shrapnel, nettles to sting like mustard gas, and black horseflies diving like Stukas to blitz and pierce. Over the first ridge ditch and drop down, then cross again the doubleditch and circle the grassy ring on top where a solitary cow chews cud.

The sight is worth the climb. Below, the patched hide of Dorset flung flat for fifty miles, stitched by hedge and lane, as far as the Celtic mist of the horizon where hillocks confuse with cloud. The western ridgeways seem furrows now, half a stride to step over, not half a day. To the north, the Vale of the White Hart in Blackmoor, a level trudge on to Somerset. To the east, the ridgeway rearing its hump up Woolland Hill and Bell Hill and down to Okeford Fitzpaine. But behind to the south, contradictions. A large cross of old trees roughly nailed together, Christ in this pagan castle, Jesus come lately. And beyond, where the chalk track meanders up to the peak, the nightmare that is truth, the twin iron masts, girdered and rearing, the antlers of Magog.

Sick at heart, Gog turns to the double threat at his back, the shape of things to come. He reaches the road and follows it to a steel-bright enclosure, so spanking new that it might have been built for tomorrow and a day, but covered with warnings:

Yet there is no one to guard the place, no sign of soldiers. So Gog bellies over the top bar of the iron gate and drops inside the enclosure. As he comes to a hut with asbestos sides, a strange figure emerges and assaults him with a voice of deadly intent.

"Hands up! And in them, anything you have to contribute to the cause of Israel."

Facing Gog is a thin, stooping man in an old khaki great-coat. Grey-white hair sprouts from his brow and deluges past his sharp nose to foam on his chin in a flowing beard. An outstretched hand menaces Gog with a rusty iron cross attached by a chain to the neck of the apparition.

Gog laughs.

"I know we have nothing to spend on defence, but if you're the sentry . . ."

"I work not for the misgovernment, brother, but for Israel in Albion. It is from here that the new air waves will be sent to enlighten the Philistines and preach repentance to the ungodly of Sarum and Gomorrah. And I shall be master of those transmitters and proclaim the coming of the New Jerusalem. Here in Albion, gelded into England. But for that, funds in the hand . . ."

Gog reaches into his pocket and feels out a pound note. As it emerges into the light of day, it is whisked away from between his finger and thumb by a legerdemain that lies betwixt filching and magic.

"You're a gentleman, sir, and a prayer. What might be the name God gave you – and other men?"

"Griffin," Gog says. "George Griffin. I am usually called Gog."

The man in the greatcoat stares at Gog, then shakes his locks and whiskers in a hairy spray.

"So be it," he says. "Gog. As the Lord saith to Ezekiel, 'Son of Man, set thy face against Gog, the land of Magog. Thou shalt come from thy place out of the north parts . . .'"

"Just out of Bulbarrow Hill," Gog interrupts, but cannot staunch the flow of the voice prophesying the ruin to come.

"Thou shalt come up against my people of Israel, as a cloud to cover the land. Surely in that day there shall be a great shaking in the land of Israel: so that the fishes of the sea, and the fowls of the heaven, and the beasts of the field, and all creeping things that creep upon the earth, shall shake at my presence, and the mountains shall be thrown down, and the steep places shall fall, and every wall shall fall to the ground."

Here the man in the greatcoat looks up at the twin patterned towers of Magog in the Ministry of Defence enclosure and addresses the high girders. "That is the reason for these two monitors of Magog. They are the warning towers against the war to come. They shall tell of the aeroplanes bearing the fire from heaven in their bomb-doors, of the brimstone that will consume utterly Bristol and Coventry, Portsmouth and Plymouth. They are radar, Gog. Mark the word. Radar. Rays of ether and particles like the warning rays of a bat that shall tell us of the invisible steel worms that fly in the night and the iron pestilence that will fall from the stars and destroy the unrighteous that heed not the word of the Lord. If they will not grant me the power of the radar and the air waves so that I may create Israel in Albion's ancient Druid rocky shore, then surely the Lord will inflict on unregenerate England what He inflicted upon Gog and his host in the past Israel – great hailstones, fire and brimstone."

"That's all very well," Gog says, "but I'm not an invader of your new Israel. The land may be Magog's, but I'm for the people. Gog is for the people."

"What people?" the man in the greatcoat asks. "People like me? I am Wayland Merlin Blake Smith, otherwise known as the Bagman. Are you for giving me the power of the ether, so that my voice may tell the nations of the peace that must be on earth, not this ill-will among men? Or are you Magog's brother, as saith the Book of Revelations? The end of the world is at hand, and you will bring it about by your final struggle with your brother. The first coming of Gog and Magog drove the first Israel from Albion to Palestine, and the last battle between Gog and Magog shall bring back the third and last Israel with the fourth coming of *Me*."

"Wayland," Gog says, "the ancient smith and north god. Merlin the wizard and King Arthur's sorcerer. William Blake the poet and visionary extraordinary. Now Smith, the man of the people's name who shall lead us by radio out of the slough of despond. What is your real name?"

"Those. Those four names. They are my true names as revealed to me in a blinding light from heaven on the road to Doncaster. Since then, I have had the gift of tongues, but not the gift of the transmitters. Another quid from your overflowing pocket, and I will be able to place a protest against the denial of my rights at the centre of iniquity and his satanic majesty, Portland Place, from where the Broadcasting Corporation advocates its lies, folly and filth."

"It's my last quid," Gog says. "I need it for the road."

"How can you speak of your need, your greed, when it is a matter of the enlightenment of the multitudes, the illumination of the masses, the salvation of the misbegotten . . ."

A wire twangs. Some man, some animal is at the barbed fence. The Bagman puts black crooked fingers on Gog's arm.

"We are observed. By stealth, we shall outwit them."

The Bagman sets off at an unsteady crouching scuttle, like a crab without one claw, under the lee of the asbestos hut. Gog follows afterwards, ducking his head in courtesy, as visible as a bullock in a haystack. Ahead of him, the Bagman is already halfway to the perimeter, where a hole has been cut under the wire that is big enough for a sheep to pass through. The Bagman scrabbles beneath the top barbed wires on hands and knees, leaving only a tuft of whisker on a raking point, while Gog has to throw himself on to his belly and pull himself forward on elbows and kneecaps to undergo the barrier.

On the far side of the wire, the Bagman is waiting for Gog under the shadow of a clump of old elm trees. Above their heads, a rookery is a cacophony of croaking and cawing with nests perched on the branches in decomposing parasols.

"They nearly clobbered us, Brother Gog. The spies of Magog are set all about us to deny me the air waves and keep the secrets that oppress us." Cunning suddenly flashes in the Bagman's glance. "Or are you a spy of Magog, your brother, sent to seek me out and denounce me?"

"No," Gog says, "I am not. Magog and his men . . . are they everywhere?"

"Everywhere. Spying. Sneaking. Telling on us."

"I am here," Gog says, "to walk and discover why the people in their millions are out of work, what went wrong in the land of Magog so that Gog and his brothers are not able to ply their trades and earn their bread in plenty and peace."

"So you say, so you say. Yet I tell you, Gog, if the millions are now out of work, there shall be tens of millions. As the coming of Gog and Magog is the sign and forerunner of the end of the world, so the coming of this radar is the sign and forerunner of the end of full employment. Once there were steam engines and stocking looms, and the hundreds of thousands were in want for the coming of them. Now there is gold and its false standard, and the millions are in want for the dross of it. But after the coming of the radar, there will be more particles and other particles, more machines that are lesser machines, whole factories in circuits as large as the palm of your hand, whole buildings of clerks in chips smaller than the peelings from the potato fingers you fry with your fish. There is a revolution to come of the new particles, the new ether, that will make the old industrial revolution look like a tiny tot in a tantrum. Woe to you, workers, if you give me not the air waves and let me build Israel in Albion before it is too late."

"I'm writing about Ludd," Gog says. "The Luddites wrecked the machines then. Can't they smash your circuits and crush your chips to come?"

"No," the Bagman says. "You can see a loom and wreck it with a hammer. How can you find a circuit as big as a biscuit, how can you fight a foe smaller than a splinter? Inexorable, the particles. Inevitable, the future. Where there are millions without work now, there shall be tens of millions idle. Where there is want, there shall be despair."

"Shall they never find work again," Gog asks, "in your electronic Armageddon? Are they doomed to wring useless hands and weep by the amusements of Babylon?"

"Aye," the Bagman says, "there will be tens of millions too many within the chalk cliffs of Albion as there already are. This was a green and pleasant land, and now is a foul and filthy one. Where there was sward, there are streets.

Where there was flint, there are bricks. Where there was water, there are sewers. If the fire and the brimstone that shall fall from heaven in the next world war shall not destroy the British people in its millions and its tens of millions, then there will be a retribution from the work that shall be taken away from them. Write not of Ludd and Luddism, Gog. Write not of the people who must rise against Magog to defend the work that is not there. Write of people and too many people. Write of tens of millions who must go to the far and the barren places of the earth to make the wilderness blossom as the rose. Write of tens of millions sinking into sloth and desolation if they leave not Albion's ancient Druid rocky shore. Tell not the people to break the machines and the circuits, the factories and the particles. For they shall not conquer. Tell the people to banish babies, cut off children, welcome disease, oppress the aged, and rejoice at death. If the people are to be well, they must know the truth. The end of Albion lies not in the many, but in too many. Not in the masses, but in men amassed.''

"Malthus is Magog's true brother," Gog says. "He says too many people will starve themselves back to too few until there are too many again. Are you wanting that?"

"I speak for Israel in England," the Bagman says. "I speak for Albion, groaning under the yoke of smoke-stacks and the burden of slums and the cries of fifty million mouths screaming for sustenance from a land that can feed one in three of them. We shall not build the new Jerusalem here until I may make the unhearing hear the truth of ancient times, until I may speak to the deaf of the new times that must be . . ."

With the skitter of shrapnel, a rook's nest falls from an elm fork and bounces off a branch beneath. It detonates on Gog's head, exploding in twigs and dry moss, feathers and eggshell. A stench of old yolk as stinking as the smell of an unhatched plot scrapes the nostrils of the blinded and scrabbling Gog, while he tears the debris out of his hair. Brushing and scratching the muck off his face, he drives the dirt further into his eyes so that it is a matter of minutes before he can blink open his rheumy lids to see that the Bagman is vanished away as if he had never been, leaving no trace behind him.

"Talking to yourself," Gog says, talking to himself. And so saying, he begins to believe he has been talking to himself. Yet as he fingers inside his pocket, he finds only one pound note there, not two. Surely he has made his contribution to the New Jerusalem. And as he moves back towards the road beyond the elm trees, he is certain that he hears the wire twang once more. Glancing back between the tree-trunks at the Ministry of Defence enclosure, he seems to see through his red eyes a dark figure in a trilby set against the wire as a scarecrow, arms akimbo, making with elbows and chest the dark initial of M his master.

Gog hurries on, passing a single dead elm on the edge of the copse. It is blasted and blighted, eaten to a skeleton by beetles breeding on a fungus that is their manna from hell. The one extinct tree in its neglect and solitude has not spread its contagion over the green strength of its fellows, but stands ignored except by a magpie, sitting on a broken branch, a black-and-white messenger of what Gog does not know. The bird flies north and Gog follows its direction. He looks back for Magog's spy, who must be following him invisibly, the fox round the corner, the harrier the far side of the hedge.

Downhill all the way to Anstey Cross, and stop at the inn for beer, bread and cheese, only to jib away from staring eyes until the reason why is plain as Worzel Gummidge in the mirror of the piss-place, a thatch of brown hair full of moss and twigs, a two days' growth of stubble fit to be burned off, and a wild man's eyes that see inner things unseen. So flee south to Melcombe Bingham past Nordon Hill, its flank rowelled by gargantuan spurs into welts of grasses. Ahead at the Cross Lanes by the bus shelter, the familiar oblong telephone box, picked out in red square outlines between its grimy panes, taller than a standing coffin, and this one has a body wearing a trilby in it.

Magog's man has gone ahead to report. He's speaking into the black receiver, so hush-hush that his hat brim hides his mouth. Now Gog's at the door, lugging the iron and glass weight open, confronting the spy on his scent, the monkey on his back, the movie dick on his tail.

"Ya following me," Gog hisses.

The man in the trilby slams the black receiver on to its

hook. It pings like a shot from a silenced revolver, which misses.

"Never saw ya before, mister," the man snarls.

"Ya seeing me now," Gog sneers.

"So what?" the man ripostes.

"So this, kiddo," Gog cracks back, curling his lip and his elbow round the man's throat. "Ya gotta new necktie." Gog tightens his forearm on the man's windpipe, choking him. "Ya betta squeal." The man gurgles. He cannot squeal.

The iron door of the telephone box closes tight. The two men are locked in a mortal embrace. Gog cannot move. The man in the trilby cannot move. His face goes red, then orange, then yellow, then green, then blue, then indigo, then violet. A rainbow asphyxiation.

"You'll talk," Gog announces, uncurling his arm and sticking it straight up in the air. There is no other room for it.

The man's many-hued face goes violet, then indigo, then blue, then green, then yellow, then orange, then red. The spectrum of recovery. Then he talks, or rather croaks.

"I'll spill all the beans."

"So start with Magog . . ."

The man starts with Magog by starting violently. He starts so violently his trilby falls off his head on to the telephone box.

"How did ya know his name?" the man utters aghast.

"I know what I know," Gog gnashes grimly. "I wanna know what ya know."

"Magog . . . I gotta tell Magog any guy who spies with his little eye something beginning with R."

"Radar," Gog sneers triumphantly. "You betcha know I know."

"You won't live to tell Moscow."

"So it's you or me?"

"After you, Gog."

"After you, Trilby."

It's a fight to the death in the telephone box, only they're squeezed so tight there's no room to swing a cosh or knee a groin or gouge an eye or chew the fat. It's a hokey-chokey of deadly disaster. Gog puts his left foot in, he puts his left foot out, he does the hokey-chokey and he shakes it all about, only he's so squashed that he can only manage a shimmy like his sister Kate, shimmy like a jelly on a plate. He gasps for air in the iron box, but there's no quarter in that terminal hug. The two men are so close that they might be one man, the secret sharer shared, the doppelganger in one man, the shadow in the flesh. Only suddenly Gog finds his arms pummelling his own ribs as he jigs about in the iron box all alone, while a young man is rapping on the glass pane of the door and pointing to a trilby hat, forgotten, by the telephone.

Feeling foolish, Gog picks up the trilby and opens the door of the red box and gives the hat to the young man.

"I say," the young man says, "thanks awfully. I forgot the old titfer."

He saunters off, his wide flannel trousers billowing with his motion, as harmless as a Red Admiral in a field of buttercups.

There can be no more delusions of cinematic conspiracy on that June evening, as Gog takes the easy road that skirts Henning Hill.

And as night slowly shadows the sky with grey-black wings, Gog slogs into Cheselbourne past symbolic thatched cottages cheek by jowl with newly-developed bungalows, then over the rise until he can coast down towards the ridged oystershell of Bramblecombe valley. White posts exorcise the little bridge over Devil's Brook, fringed with bracken and nettle and thorn. Gog pisses a yellow libation into the stream to give his opinion, then heads west over shaggy fields towards Gallow's Corner, where the roads once crossed before they shunned the place. He knows he'll sleep quiet there, but first over the furrows to the wet chalk track that runs straight beneath low overhanging trees that splay out their warped branches to catch the dropping moon. There is no gallows at the corner now, only a brick sump to mark where the old ways crossed and a rebel was hanged, highwayman or traitor or thief, till his tarred parts rotted and fell to carrion and oblivion.

Gog lies between two thorn trees. Each of them has had its low branches lopped to stop them blocking the chalk way. Gog counts six stumps on either tree trunk above his head. He closes his eyes and sees the Tarot vision of the Hanged

Man, dangling easily upside down on a rope tied to his left ankle and knotted round a branch slung between the two thorn trees, his right leg making a cross as it sticks sideways behind the left knee, his arms akimbo in twin triangles, his golden hair falling down into a radiant sun set in a halo behind his smiling face. The Hanged Man has hanged himself by his left ankle and exults in his hanging. He appears and speaks to Gog in his mind's eye and ear, hearing the secrets of the runes.

"Chance is the noose. Fate is the knot. And a man has only one neck. Yet he must choose his fate and hang gladly.

"There are judgments. But the first judgment is before a man is born, what is in that man to be. And the last judgment is after he is dead, when he will rise again to be judged for what he has not done, although it was not in him to do it. Yet he must choose his judgment and hang gladly.

"A man is born to one country. If he loves another country and works for it against his own country, he will hang gladly. The judgment of him will justify him. His treason will be his triumph. He will have chosen to deny his birthright, and he will exalt his deathwrong for the sake of his other country. A traitor for the sake of his second country hangs gladly.

"Jesus Christ himself was crucified as a traitor and was hanged sadly. His sadness lay in his betrayal by a beloved apostle and his error lay in thinking God had forsaken him, when God had chosen him. The Hanged Man is Odinn, who offered himself to be sacrificed to himself on the gallows-tree, Havamel. A willing hanging for the sake of one's own image is to hang gladly. For the wounded Odinn stayed on the gallows-tree for nine days and nine nights to learn the secrets of the eighteen runes, which were revealed to him. They gave him no bread, they gave him no mead: he looked down: with a loud cry, he fell from the tree and took up the runes.

"And the runes were made before man was made, and Odinn gave himself to himself to learn their secret, how to cut them and to read them, how to stain them and to prove them, how to call them and make them holy, how to send them that they shall be true.

"And the first rune is help, and it did not help me off this gallows-tree. And the second rune is healing, and it did not cure my broken neck. And the runes to eleven concern me not.

"And the twelfth rune makes the hanged man speak, as I am speaking now. Lo, look, for Gog has called me up, and the rune is at his feet."

And in his sleep Gog looks down and sees that his legs are crossed as an ⅄ , making the sign of the twelfth rune. And the voice of the Hanged Man speaks above him.

"And the thirteenth rune is a cup of water that makes a soaked man invulnerable, and the fourteenth rune is the names of the Gods and the High Ones, and the fifteenth rune tells tomorrow as it were today and yesterday, and the sixteenth rune is pleasing to women, so that they cannot deny their white thighs.

"And the seventeenth rune keeps a woman that is fickle for ever faithful, and the eighteenth rune is a secret rune, never to be told except to my only love as she lies in my arms, for it binds us together for ever and ever.

"These are the runes that the wounded Odinn discovered when he hanged himself for nine days and nine nights on the gallows-tree. Hear you, Gog, the teaching of Odinn, the Rune-Master. Do not suffer the world to make a martyr out of you. Elect your suffering, for to suffering you are elected. Deny your heritage, do more than you may do, be greater than you are. Then you too will end as the Hanged Man; hanging gladly."

The rope round the left ankle of the Hanged Man snaps. His body falls on Gog. The golden halo behind his hair blinds Gog's insight and makes a sunburst in Gog's skull. The Man's blue jerkin fills Gog with the space and the joy of the sky, the Man's red britches infuse Gog's blood to hammer and race in his veins. Gog wakes exultant to drizzle at dawn. But the vision of liberation from his cares and obsessions is lost in his stiff limbs and dull weight. As he trudges away along the chalk track between the thorn trees, he sets up a woodpigeon that flutters like a disturbed soul among the spiked branches, and the Hanged Man is lost, shuffled in the Tarot cards of the day.

7

Outside Capability Brown's model cottages, Gog sees people he knows.

"Doctor Miniver," Gog cries. "Fancy meeting you again."

Gog can see what brings to Milton Abbas the learned pixie with his seamed pippin of a face and Tom Thumb tweed suit. He is showing his fancy a pretty part of England. Maire stands, black trouser-legs astride the air, arms akimbo with white silk shirt tight at the armpits to lift her round breasts high, white slouch hat with a dark band stuck over her raven fringe of hair, shaped downwards to a point level with her eyes. Her ripe lips swell from beneath her sharp thin nose, her bleached blue eyes stare insolently at Gog.

"You seem inevitable, Griffin," Miniver says, peering up at Gog, his head hardly reaching the woman's shoulder. "It must be the long arm of coincidence."

"I thought only the law had long arms," Gog says.

"So do you," Maire says, "you big lug." She uses American slang like all Parisians do, loving the chic and despising the source. "Your arm show it."

Gog holds out his arm sideways, six feet off the ground. Maire comes up to him and catches hold of his arm with both her hands and swings off it, her high heels tucked off the grass. Gog takes the strain, then has to ease her down.

"Not bad," she says. "That Louise Brooks do that in *Lulu*. I always want do that."

"Napoleon," Miniver says, "was just about my height. I can't see the advantage of being a walking elm. Rooks might nest in your hair."

Maire laughs, and Gog stands, clumsy and knotted. Miniver is his superior, a lecturer in the history department. Position is more than height.

"It is a coincidence," Gog manages to say at last, "meeting you here."

"Even the random," Miniver says, "can be taken into account. There is an uncertainty *principle*, as you know.

Hazard can be followed." He smiles. At the top of the sloping street by the door of the last far thatched cottage, a man in a trilby hat is waiting. "Maire and I are staying at Spitpoole. Your mother Merry's there with friends. And I hear your half-brother's coming down. It might be quite a reunion, if you could come and join us."

"Really a coincidence," Gog says.

"Really a coincidence," Miniver agrees. "Let's make the most of it." He pauses delicately. "You didn't tramp here by Bulbarrow Hill?"

"I did," Gog says. "And a desecration it is. There's two vast iron towers spoiling the ridgeway."

"Some old wireless, I suppose."

"Radar," Gog says. "It tracks aeroplanes."

Miniver's eyes are lost in the petty paunches beneath his dark brows.

"Radar. Where did you hear that?"

"From a tramp called Wayland. Wayland Merlin Blake Smith, if you can believe any of his four names. Though, goodness knows, we all live under aliases. We don't even select the names our parents choose to christen us with. So we're certainly entitled to choose our own to suit our history or our personality."

"No one knows of radar," Miniver says, "outside a few scientists. And that isn't your line."

"Or yours," Gog says. "But walk and learn." He smiles at Maire, who smiles back at him in a kind of appraisal.

"Walk and learn if you choose the route," Miniver says. "How's Cambridge? What was that society you mentioned to me? The Disciples?"

"Let's call it that," Gog says. "It's secret. And I don't remember saying anything about it to you."

"You did, you did," Miniver says. "Your memory was always excellent at blocking out your indiscretions. Except in your history papers, of course, where you remember to set out all your indiscretions and call them an analysis of the facts."

"I don't remember telling you anything," Gog says. "And if I did, let's forget it and have some tea."

The three of them take tea outside on the grass. They sit at a table opposite the stone almshouses for six poor widows, moved lock, stock and charity from the old community under

Milton Abbey, when Lord Milton destroyed the houses and the monastic buildings to construct a mansion and a park and even a designed ruin, yet commanded his landscaper to set up a model high street for the dispossessed, the first of the new town planning, all at Lord Milton's bidding and whim. He would have his man-made Eden round his new Abbey House, where monks would never be. Those who would not go were deluged by a Flood, sluiced from the gates of the Lord's new lake. No ark saved the leases of these stubborn householders, so they went uphill to live above the waters in the new High Street, prettier than any picture with dozens of white walls crowned by old straw bonnets and set apart on careful lawns. This is the story of Lord Milton and his dictate, which Miniver tells, his black eyes bright as pips of pleasure at the moral.

"Lord Milton did everything wrong, flouted everybody's wishes, imposed himself totally, yet got away with it and became Earl of Dorchester. An eighteenth-century Mussolini of the Age of Reason. But he was right. Look now. The prettiest village in Dorset where everyone is contented and the old families still live on. A miracle of town-planning to set an example to us all. And the park down in the valley a natural monument to our greatest landscape artist, Capability Brown, surrounding a huge building that must become a useful institution or school, built at costs that we could not match now. Selfishness, my dear Maire, is the secret of posterity. One generation may suffer, that future generations may enjoy and applaud the man of iron."

"I don't agree," Gog says. "He evicted the people. Lord Milton. He might as well be Satan."

"We'll see you at Spitpoole," Miniver says, rising. "Now there's a park for you. Would you settle the necessary?"

With only a pound in his pocket, Gog still feels too polite to plead poverty. Miniver is a master at forgetting that situation in others. As Maire rises, Gog rises with her. She puts out a finger and scores his palm with a red talon, speaking over his ouch with a fervent wish.

"I hope we meet again, big lug."

Gog watches her walk away with the pixie Miniver, her buttocks tight in black trousers swaying below the narrow stem of her waist. Lust grabs him in the loins, so that he must bend forward over the tea-table to disguise the battle of the bulge. The embarrassment makes him sit down until the bill comes, fingering his stigmata from Maire's scratch and relishing the pain. By Miniver's Mercedes, Maire turns and waves, her breasts moving with her upraised hand. Gog groans with desire.

"I hope you enjoyed the cakes," the waitress says with reproach. "They're home-made. Five and thruppence." She is as plain in her gingham as only sixteen can be, all puppy fat and primness.

Gog gives her ninepence for her tip and to forget the groan.

High on the hill under the lee of St Catherine's Chapel, Gog looks down the steep-cut grass steps between the trees to the Abbey Church below, squat tower shaking its spears to the indifferent sky and ignoring the near-by flintstone barracks, Lord Milton's house of pride, still without a fall. Low, wooded hills sleep in soft haunches beyond, a soothing landscape denying by its presence and permanence any past massage by Capability Brown. Trying to rearrange the earth is so trivial that Gog shrugs to see such immense labour for so little notice. What did Horace Walpole say of Brown? So closely did he copy Nature that his works will be mistaken for it.

Gog rests his head against the crumbling stonework of the Chapel wall and closes his eyes. Stupor drugs him with the laudanum of the long day. A Satan casts his vast shadow over the land, his two spread wings bound to his body making the monogram of the devil of the cleared estate, M, Milton the Lord. And Gog hears a mighty voice from high, proclaiming the manifold beauties of the mismaking of the Abbey park:

LORD MILTON: Look back on the hideous ruin of Saint Catherine's Chapel, which has stood there unadorned for a thousand years since King Athelstan built it in bloody memory of butchering five kings at Brunanburh. The Wood behind was never yet touched by the finger of taste: thick, intricate, and gloomy with impervious shades. How can the cultivated eye endure th' horrid sight?

GOG GRIFFIN: It is ancient, it is natural, it is magical, it is human.

LORD MILTON: Now here is the Valley corrected – trimmed – polished – decorated – adorned. It is a Garden made from a

Desart in the Classick and the Rustick and the Gothick mode. Here sweeps a plantation in a regular curve: there winds a gravel walk: here are parts of the old Wood disposed to delight the eye where Nature failed to cheer. From a rude, neglected bottom, overrun with bush and fern, the Rhododendron and the Arbutus grow. And the green steps have quite reformed th' uneven slope, although nobody should walk upon them in order not to disturb the grass.

GOG GRIFFIN: It is correction by the cat o' nine tails, it is clipping to a fingernail's parings, it is cutting the head off Nature. It is deformity, not embellishment; a Desart, not an Art.

LORD MILTON: Your unhewn Wilderness is base, common and popular. Such a thing you may see anywhere, but not here. Consider the lake, where the banks are perfectly smooth and green, sloping without rush or mud to the water's edge. And beyond, the Gothick tower, moss-grown and ivy-twined, half-bosomed in the trees, so designed by Wyatt himself to be ruined instanter, but exactly in that aweful spot where location inspires wonder in the savage cultured scene. Not every man can execute a Ruin. To give the stone its mouldering appearance – to make the crack run naturally through the joints – to mantle the battlements with mosses – to scatter fragments round with negligence and ease – these are great efforts of Genius and Culture.

GOG GRIFFIN: Genius and Culture have nothing to do with artificial wildness, or else Apes would play Mozart in tails.

LORD MILTON: Apes already have tails, and as for Wolfgang Amadeus Mozart, the Musick was far superior to the Man, just as a discipline of Nature is far above the unkempt sprawl of the seasons. Who would have toads in a vile ditch or wolves on a common heath, when he might view cows safely grazing in a meadow beyond an invisible ha-ha?

GOG GRIFFIN (*visibly*): Ha-ha.

Gog wakens now, his limbs stiff from the first chill of the evening air. He pulls his legs up with his hands, feeling Maire's scratch smarting on his palm, then he staggers to his feet and lurches down the hill towards the road, awkward as any gargoyle gone to ground. Temptation passes and stops, a green bus bound to Blandford Forum and to Sherborne, only a long stroll away from Spitpoole, where Gog means to go tomorrow, if only to lust for Maire at a closer distance.

The strident vehicle jounces Gog along the country roads, past the flint walls of Winterborne Stickland, between the red-brick new poorhouses invading Saxon Rise, and beside fat Guernseys cropping daisies under telegraph-poles. The bus stops at Blandford for fifteen minutes, giving Gog time to stretch the cramps from his legs in the Brothers Bastard's Italian town, where cupola and Paladian town hall and terraced market make a Borromini of a Dorset Forum. In the church of St Peter and St Paul, the Bastard builders have left a legacy, six hundred pounds to teach thirty-five boys and girls to read, while William Williams, Welsh ragtrader gone to gentry, has left three thousand pounds for the benefit of poor clothiers, serge and stuff makers, linen and felt weavers. Charity shall banish the barricades. Elegance shall hold out the tip of its glove to the sons of toil and cry pity to find a finger bitten off.

Gog's reverie makes him late to catch the bus, which is only done by run, jump, pant and scrabble, and the loss of half of the ten bob left in his pocket, just to pay the fare. Late evening tars the trees, limns the hedgerows with soot, makes the meadows into black tarns. Piddles Wood on the horizon of high Sturminster Common crooks pitchy fingers to hold the dying of the light. By Bishop's Caundle, only one furnace glows from the last smithy in Blackmore Vale, ting-ting-ting-ting the hammer of the smith, faint as a bicycle bell through the bus windows. Darkling on through North Wootton to the night stop on Dancing Hill, where Gog clambers off with his pack, to walk down to Sherborne Castle, the River Yeo moonbright on his sinister side, shiny as the sinuous track of a snail dragon just gone.

The lake shore is easily reached. There Gog unrolls his bed for the night. The ruins of the old castle, undone in uncivil war, cast their shadows heavily at the ebony mirror of the waters, shattering the glass surface in broken ripples and burying themselves in the greater darkness of the depths. The lake grows blacker from the shadows, swallowing the dark presence of the stones into its nothingness.

So Gog is swallowed into his slumbers by the lake where Sir Walter Raleigh once built his lodge, no slug he, but a damnable proud bold man, high-browed and long-faced with pig's eyes and a natural curl to the end of his beard. He might know how to puddle his cloak for a queen, but his fickle obedience put any monarch in dread of being upended by him, especially if she were woman. Upended are the raven mysteries of Maire, come again as Sir Walter's maid of honour in the dark Wood, as he boards her up against a tree, forcing the black moss and splitting the white oak, until Aubrey's wayward words cry in Gog's dreamy lucubrations, "Sweet Sir Gog, what doe you me ask? Will you undoe me? Nay, sweet Sir Gog! Sweet Sir Gog! Sir Gog." At last, as the danger and the pleasure at the same time grow higher, Maire cries in the ecstasy, "Sweggie Swiggie Swog Sweggie Swiggie Swog."

Gog wakes to a wet crotch and a waterbird faintly mocking Maire's cries, "Swiggie Swog Swog." The echo haunts him through the chill dawn, as he retreats up the hill from the great H of the new castle, built by the Digbys to enclose Raleigh's brick lodge. He finds a workers' caff in the town near the Abbey, fat bacon and lardy eggs, bread and marge and sweet tea for one-and-three. A newsboy comes in. For a threepenny bit, Gog wearily returns to modern times. Another lot of unemployed marchers were reaching Westminster, and the Mother of Parliaments was doing nothing for them. Chain-letters were linking Depression America: everyone would be rich if the chains were not broken, but everyone was breaking their chains to save a dime, and none was still free of debt. The civil war in Spain was getting worse, the Moroccans were at the gates of Madrid, but what could you expect of the Spanish, who couldn't even police the Mediterranean and had to have the British at Gibraltar to do it for them?

The news is no news to Gog, lost in time past, margarine no *petite madeleine*, seeking a way back from his turmoil to an Age of Reason in this time of treason. And he finds his exemplar in the south transept of Sherborne Abbey at the marble memorial of John, Lord Digby. Under the fan vaults that web the holy roof, ready to catch any snitch of conspiracy before it offends the eardrums of the Almighty, the polished sculpture of the nobleman stands upright in britches and sword and wig, flanked on either side by a wife and weeping cherub, a skull and crossbones set on a laurel wreath below.

Its inscription spells the virtues of watchful withdrawal and the good life, if you be rich, if you be rich:

HERE LYES JOHN LORD DIGBY BARON DIGBY OF SHERBORNE
    and EARL OF BRISTOL
Titles to which ye merit of his Grandfather first gave
    lustre
And which he himself laid down unsullied.
He was naturally enclined to avoid the Hurry of a publick
    Life,
Yet carefull to keep up the post of his Quality.
Was willing to be at ease, but scorned obscurity;
And therefore never made his Retirement a pretence to
    draw
Himself within a narrower compass, or to shun such
    expense
As Charity, Hospitality, and his Honour called for.
His Religion was that which by LAW is Established;
And the Conduct of his life shew'd the power of it in his
    Heart.
His distinction from others never made him forget himself
    or them:
He was kind and obliging to his Neighbours, generous
    and condescending
to his Inferiours, and just to all Mankind.
Nor had the temptations of honour & pleasure in this
    world
Strength enough to withdraw his Eyes from that great
Object of hope, which we reasonably assure ourselves he
    now enjoys.
Dyed Sept: xii: Ann: Dom: MDCCCVIII

Gog has only three shillings to jingle, and it's a long long way to Spitpoole, and in the eastern bay of the Abbey, a man is standing in a trilby hat below the boss of a mermaid with a comb and mirror, vainglorious of her golden scaly tail. A man who wears a hat in a Christian church is up to no good, so Gog hurries away, glancing back to see the man in the trilby studying the mermaid's stone breasts, in no hurry at all.

8

Gog stalks out of Sherborne past a tin chapel flaking with
yellow paint up the Coombe and Sandford Orcas road past
furrowed hillocks of grass so frequent that ancient men or
giants seem to have kneaded and rowelled every turf slope
in Wessex. Sprouting hedgerows funnel Gog past a fir wood,
where ivy climbs fifty feet up the trunks to the parasols of
the high branches. Over the rise to the view of the vale
beyond, clipt into enclosures, and on past the stone walls of
village houses, where each Englishman's home is his castle,
every man a king round his cottage breakfast-table. There's
a garage with leaded Gothic windows, built as a chapel
for some sacred Morris, beside a modern bungalow called
Agincourt on the gate. The inn carries a sign of a bishop's
mitre, and white doves fly on celestial missions above the
crumbling yellow gatehouse to the manor. Among the old
iron Celtic crosses in the graveyard of Sandford Orcas,
Gog finds a monument crusted with winged cherubs in
memory of the Leggs, Henry and David and John and
James and Elias, but never a mention of Oliver, the traitor
of Tolpuddle.

Strike along Corton Ridge now, that long whaleback of a
ride to Camelot for the knights passing through fields of
barley and of rye to the hump of Cadbury Castle ahead. Two
great earthworks protect King Arthur's retreat, and Gog
must clamber above another high haunch of grass to reach
the approach to Camelot. Sheep bleat and scuttle away from
him. Then sudden, the baa-baa of terror, and the Blood of
the Lamb.

Six crows are pecking at a ewe, struggling on her side.
Two beaks pluck at the jelly of her eyes, while the other
crows rend and tear at the newborn lamb, bloody between
her legs. Gog runs in, flailing and booting at the black birds
of prey which flap, graceless and lethargic, into the torn sky.

With gory hands, Gog squeezes out the lamb, then turns
to the ewe, which fights upright on her spindled legs and

shows one eye bright, the other eyeball hanging down her cheek. Gog seizes her head and presses the eyeball back into its socket, the ewe squirming and kicking, then breaking free. She does not run, but licks at the lying lamb. Gog wipes his red hands on the grass and walks towards Camelot. A flintstone stubs his boot. He bends to pick it up and hurl it at a solitary crow, still squatting on the turf in hope of raw flesh.

Four great turf steps lead up to the low wall that confines the fir, oak, ash and thorn beneath Camelot. A straddle of the stone puts Gog among the bushes under the trees, and he must push through flicking branches and slog up broken turf to reach the final three ditches and ridges before the vast round table that is the top of Cadbury Castle. Black and brindled bullocks graze there, beef to be. Ten thousand ladies' belts could not girdle this great mound. And it would take a score of belts and more to girdle the great waist and waste of Rosie, spread out ampler than a hamper on the grass, giving the spoilt brat Arthur his picnic snack and herself her tenth stuffing of the day.

"Look 'oo's 'ere, Arthur. Yer booger of a dad. 'As 'is okey-pokey, 'e do, then 'e's creepy-crawly off in the night without an 'ow's yer father. An' 'ow *is* Arthur's father?"

"How did you get here?" Gog asks.

"No thanks ter you. We knew as you weer comin'. All that daft stoof in yer noggin aboot knights an' ladies fair. I call 'im Arthur, doant I? 'E's got to be heer."

She stretches out a rock bun in Arthur's direction. It has a penknife stuck in a crack in the rock.

"Arthur may be a little sod," his mother says, "but 'e knows 'oo 'e is. *Yer* boy."

HOW ARTHUR PULLED OUT THE PENKNIFE DIVERS TIMES.

Now essay, said Fair Rosie unto Sir Gog. And anon he pulled at the penknife with all his might, but it would not be. Now shall ye essay, said Fair Rosie to Arthur. I will well, said Arthur, and pulled it out easily. And therewithal Sir Gog knelt down to the earth. Alas, said Arthur, my own dear father, why kneel ye to me? Nay, nay, my lord Arthur, it is not so, I was never your father nor of your blood, but I wot well ye are of a higher blood than I weened ye were, all the

divers people that lay with your fair mother. Then Arthur
made great doole when he understood that Sir Gog was not
his father.

Such great doole does Arthur make when Gog declares that
he is not the boy's father that Gog would stop up his ears, only
they are boxed and coxed by two thunderclaps from Rosie's
hands. Gog's head rings, and things would go from bad to
worse, if Merlin did not come to his deliverance in wondrous
guise, as he did in the olden days of Camelot.

Behind Gog, a small gaudy tent on a wheeled cart is being
pushed by hidden hands across the grass plateau of Cadbury
Castle. As it approaches, Gog sees that it is a little theatre. It
stops, and, as if by spell and incantation, Arthur stops dooling.
There is a wriggle within the tent on wheels, then a familiar
mannikin appears on one side of the little stage in his floppy
cockscomb hat and stripey doublet, his truncheon on his
shoulder, old Punch himself. And on the other side, in white
frilly mobcap and gown, his Judy. The traditional words sound
from beneath the stage, as Punch smiles and holds his club
hidden behind his back.

> Here is funny Mister Gog,
>> So fond of giving blows.
> We may know he hates Magog,
>> And by his large red nose.

Gog finds himself fingering his own big conk, and he scowls
at Rosie, who is laughing at him, while Arthur watches,
entranced at the ancient puppet play. Punch Gog's growl
now changes to a shrill harridan's cry.

> Gog, mind what you're about,
>> You will make the baby cry;
> Your stick is very stout,
>> And may black poor Rosie's eye.
> Oh! yes, we hear you sing
>> Populi, people, poo.
> Pray, Gog, is that the only thing
>> That you were taught to do?

Now Judy Rosie brings up a baby in her cloth arms and Punch Gog tries to pet it, while a wail sounds from the depths of the tent, followed by the growling voice.

> Populi, Rosie! pretty, pretty dear!
> I am so glad to see you here!
> Oh what a pretty baby – rather!
> The very image of his father.

Gog receives a dig in the ribs that might stove in the armour-plate on the *Ark Royal*.

"Now theer yer see!" Rosie shouts. "Arthur's like 'is father. 'E's yers!"

On the puppet stage, Punch Gog gives his plump wife a clout with his club.

> What! Rosie, do you mean to cry?
> Why, yes – you hit me in the eye.

The little boy laughs to see the wife puppet tumble on to the stage and the baby flung away widdershins into the wings. Punch Gog goes on thumping cruelly the fallen lady, who wails:

> I'll just lie down, and kick, and die!
> Oh dear! You've hit me on the head.
> I'll tell old Magog – I am dead.

Punch Gog does not care a hoot, but hoots even louder.

> *Populi*, people, people, pie
> Rosie's happy – so am I.

Rosie in the flesh and girth is not happy. She fetches Gog a wallop on the back which drives his spine into the back of his mouth.

"Murderer," she cries. "Doant yer want ter croak me? I tell yer, yer woant. The coppers'll 'ave yer an' 'ang yer an' good riddance ter bad roobish. If yer weern't Arthur's father . . ."

On stage, a stick-thin puppet, snotty and sneaky, appears in his cocked commanding hat. Punch Gog spots him.

But here is old Magog,
And he is all agog.

Now Magog speaks, sneering through his sharp nose.

You bad man, Gog, naughtee,
You must now go with me.

Go with you? Go where?

Why, to prison, down there,
For beating your wife,
And taking her life.

Is that all, you old clown?
I'll soon knock you down.

Punch Gog knocks old Magog with his club, thwackety
whackety crack, and Magog's beat right off the stage with
Punch Gog hooting his triumph.

I'll soon settle you,
With people, people, poo.

Arthur has a shrieking fit of glee to see Mother get her
clubadubdub, and old Magog, too. A sudden wind begins to
flutter the tent and ruffle the grasses, as a white ghostly figure
wafts up beside Punch Gog, so fearsome that he drops the
club from his hand.

Populi, people – Oh! what's that?
Why, He's a She without a hat.

The apparition spookily speaks,

I'm Rosie's Ghost,
So come with me.

Punch Gog is not fooled.

No! I'll stay here,
We can't agree.

The wind whistles, shaking the stage, as Rosie's Ghost plucks
at Punch Gog's arm.

You must come now,
So just be quick.

Punch Gog recovers his weapon and raises it high.

If you don't go,
I'll use my stick.

He bashes at the Ghost, and, as she flies away, the wind catches the gaudy tent and blows it clear, whirling up to the storm-clouds. Now Arthur's gone, rolling across the grass and down Cadbury slope with Rosie bellying after, the wind in her skirts, a galleon in full sail in pursuit of her son. Gog can hardly keep to his feet from the air buffeting and slapping him, but Merlin is revealed, his grey-white locks blowing above his cadaverous countenance, standing on his bare wheeled cart, come to Camelot to deliver Sir Gog. His voice booms in the wild wind.

"My second coming was as Merlin, prophesying woe. As the voice of the raven, I sang of blood and sword.

"And Magog ruled in London, and his machines ate men. And their wives were harlots in the city, and their sons and daughters stricken.

"And when Gog and the people rose up as wheat in the fields, Magog scattered them as chaff beneath the flail."

Gog shouts into the gale, interrupting Wayland Merlin Blake Smith.

"Why did you come here with a Punch and Judy show? Why was it about me?"

The prophet yells back into the teeth of the storm.

"When Adam and Eve were cast from the Garden of Eden, they took the name of Punch and Judy. It was man's lot to have his heel bruised and be beaten down by toil and to beat his wife. It was woman's lot to bear a child and be beaten. And though Punch's son was no better than Cain and Adam's son no worse than Abel, yet you shall not cast your son aside as Punch cast away his baby in our play. For your son, Gog, is Arthur, who was killed by the evil Mordred, and now shall rise again after fifteen hundred years to fight against Magog and all of his machines. And his name shall not be Arthur the Second, but King Ludd, gone again to

London to overthrow Moloch and build once more the New Jerusalem in England's green and pleasant land."

"My son Arthur," Gog says. "He shall be King Ludd?"

"So it is written in the deeds and the words to come. Recognise your son Arthur, teach him of King Ludd and of Ned Ludd, your ancestor, and send him forth against Magog and Moloch and Mammon. For he shall break brass and rend iron and crack steel. He shall tell the masters of the machines, Ye are cast down into abomination and the pit of desolation. Where the wheel turned, the chaffinch shall build her nest. Where the men toiled, the marmalade cats shall lie asleep. Where the piston moved, the Red Admirals will flutter by. Where the effluent flowed, the salmon shall leap to the fly. Close your factories and your mines, shut down your offices and your towers. Each to his and her craft, each to his and her home. King Ludd commands you. In my name, all shall come to pass. So it is written, Gog. You shall recognise your son Arthur and teach him the ways of Ludd."

"But he's not *my* son Arthur!" Gog howls to the tempest.

"He is chosen to be your only son," Merlin decrees. "We do not choose a child. The child may choose us. It's a wise father who knows his own son. Gog, take Arthur. Make him King Ludd."

A twister catches Wayland Merlin Blake Smith and whisks him skywards, whirling faster than a dervish, flying over Camelot towards the west. Gog is hurtled by eddies of air, spinning full circle round the Cadbury rings. The landscape below is a moving ocean. To the south, the green cornfields are patterned into whirlpools by harrow and rake before they rise to the great billow of Corton Ridge. To the east, a horseshoe breaker as high as Compton Castle. To the west, the Blackmoor gulf of the White Horses, a thirty-mile sea to the far ridgeways, the Dorset Gap the only dip in the crest of the earth comber. Sou'-west, a ship as a church in distress, its spire flying mast-high a red banner of danger. Nor'-nor'-west, a vast undulation of verdigris marshland, once drained into fields, now windswept into marine motion. Glastonbury Tor a far rock on the horizon, and St Gog's tower on its tip as a mark to hindsight and inner sight and the foresight of what will be and must be. Holy as a dove from the Ark flies the eye from Camelot to Glastonbury, the old straight track, the sacred way from Arthur's castle to Arthur's grave.

Gog is blown to the north of the rings where he may overview the ridges and hillocks marking the hardway to Stonehenge. And a hardway is beginning for Gog as he stumbles and falls, cartwheel and rolypoly, down the track to the bottom of the hill past St Thomas à Becket's church with its pepperpot spire to come to rest in front of Mr Miles's emporium, CARPENTER & DECORATOR & FUNERAL DIRECTOR. Gog feels that he needs some glue and joinery to put him together, all Chippendale and dandy. If not, he'll settle for a coffin. Looking back at the steep of Cadbury Hill, he cannot imagine he ever climbed to the top, or encountered Rosie and Arthur and Merlin up there. The wind is no lion, but a lambkin breeze. Memory seems conjecture and mazy imagination. Yet the stricture sounds in Gog's skull – Arthur is your son. Make him King Ludd.

9

A stone cannonball falls off the castle walls and rolls behind the fleeing Gog down the hill to Compton Pauncefoot. Louder than the hounds of hell, insatiable Alsatians bark at the intruder. KEEP OUT – NO ADMITTANCE – DANGER – GUARD DOGS LOOSE – the signs do signify at Compton Castle. And when there are men in trilby hats in Gog's wake for no known purpose, then objects will fall on him as they tend to do on innocent Celts minding other people's business. Did not the Celts tell Alexander the Great that they had one greater fear than the fear of Alexander, that the clear sky would break apart and brain them with blue bricks?

Gog maunders for many miles of meandering lanes past cottages with stone toadstools outside their doors, where wandering warlocks may take their rest. The hedges are set so close that twigs and thorns pluck and scratch at either shoulder of a passing man. The Hardway proper begins at the inn at Shepton Montague, where Gog spends his last shilling on a pint of cider, bread and Cheddar, before slogging along the tarmac to the ridge. Ahead, he cannot believe his eyes. Beside the roadway, twin towers stand free and joined, making a gigantic gateway in the shape of an M, battlements as a lower jawbone gnashing at the sky. On the left, the Gog tower, scarred by a lone rose window, indissolubly bound over the high arch leading nowhere to the Magog tower on the right, the simulacrum of false democracy, the structure of might and majesty *in nomine populi*.

On the Magog tower, an elongated figure with a slicked skull stands in a golden robe, carrying a red book big as a lectern Bible. The voice is the voice of the Cognoscenti. The voice is the voice of Maximilian Mann.

"I am Marx and the Masses, and I command you, rise up and be recruited. Who is not for me is against me, even if he is not seen."

The ground crumbles at Gog's feet. He has to stagger back to stop himself falling down a hole, from which emerges a quivering black snout surmounted by spectacles, a face and body covered with smooth fur as dark as an academic gown. Mole, it is a human Mole, burrowed up from under the Magog tower to answer the Cognoscenti.

"Dear Master," the Mole says, "I leave the underground at your command."

Maximilian giggles from on high.

"I spy with my little eye," he says, "something beginning with M."

"Mole," says the Mole.

"And how many little Moles do you meet underground?" Maximilian asks.

In front of Gog's eyes, the Mole's face seems to slither into metamorphosis, a transfiguration of aliases, now Rupert glimmers and is gone for John, now James glances darkly giving way to Putney, now Anthony and Maximilian, but all snout and enquiry with soft nostrils quivering to the air.

"No Mole encounters the other Moles underground," the Mole says. "But in the light of day . . ."

"Where there are Cognoscenti, a Mole may be."

"Yes, Master."

"Burrow upwards," Maximilian instructs. "Do not burrow in the pit and the dark. Leave that to the coal-miners, who interest us not at all. Burrow tall. Dig inside my tower, the tower of Magog, that you may appear at the high table and the palace balcony and the battlements of the establishment, yet none shall know you are a Mole. You shall be an elevated Mole, a knighted Mole, a Mole honoured for his services to his country and another country. Oh Mole, esteemed Mole, dig upwards."

"I hear and obey, Master."

The Mole emerges in his full sleek form and measures Gog for size. He is displeased.

"Moles are not observed. We bury witnesses."

With a sweep of his powerful digging foot, the Mole upends Gog and stuffs him head first down the hole. Gog is engulfed in loam, choked on marl and clay, mouth in a tomb of earth, legs kicking above the ground. He struggles and scrabbles and humps his haunches to achieve salvation, then sits by the hole to wipe the mud from his eyes. The twin towers are empty. The apparition has disappeared as airily as he appeared, while the Mole must be elevated inside the bricks of Magog's edifice.

As Gog turns back to the Hardway, a great gleaming car bonnet hoves down the road and draws up beside him. A voice rich with port and promise hails Gog as her son. Gauzes and chiffons float about Merry's body as if fritillaries were bearing a queen bee away. A cartwheel straw hat secured by a silk scarf under her chin completes Merry's motoring costume.

"I came to look for you, Gog. Miniver told us you'd be toddling this way. Just in time. Have you fallen in a muck-heap?"

"Just fallen, Mother."

"Poor Goggie head-in-air," Merry says. "You never watch your feet. Losing your grip as well. Jump in. Otto's waiting with the picnic, and Otto doesn't like waiting. In his country, everything runs on time."

Gog clambers into the luxurious rear end of the Lagonda. The red leather seats sigh in protest at his earthy weight. The chauffeur's back is rigid with disdain.

"Who's Otto?"

"He's the Hun of the moment. He's my latest conquest, and I am his."

"Is he a Nazi?"

"No, he went to Christ Church. That makes him only Far Right and all right. He's more British than the Brits. Life to Otto is shootin', shootin' and shootin'. He thinks Herr Hitler is common, though a man to watch."

The Lagonda chunters up the slope towards a huge folly in a forest, a triangular brick memorial to King Alfred as tall as Big Ben. Merry's bright eyes are anxious above her pink smooth cheeks. Her plumpness has pushed out all wrinkles, so that she seems girlish for her age.

"You're not going to insult him, Gog, just because he's half a kraut. There's a whole nation who can't help being krauts. He's asked to come especially to meet Magnus. Some private diplomacy, all very hush-hush. And Miniver's here, too. And you know his interest in all those dialects. I dare say he's in intelligence like everyone. It must be the money. Dons are worse paid than dustmen. Shouldn't go into it without a large income, which you haven't got yet, Gog.

Lucky you don't have to support your old mother . . ."

"Who supports herself very well," Gog says. "You were saying about my brother? Why's he coming?"

"They're setting up a sort of friendship society, Anglo-German. Peace and cultural exchanges. We send them Noël Coward, they send us Wagner. Anyway, you're to be good."

"I'll try, Mother."

"No, don't try. It's when you try you're worst."

A chaise-longue with griffon's heads and gilt legs has been set under the tall memorial. On the damson silk seat is a toad of a man with lids so heavy on his bulbous stare that they seem to be holding his eyes from popping out. The man does not rise to greet Gog.

"This is my eldest son George," Merry says. "He needs a bath, but we didn't see one en route."

"Otto von Tattersall," the toad croaks. Merry bends over him and gives him a kiss on his bald patch, but no kiss will change him into a prince. Perhaps into a toadstool.

"Where is the picnic?" Otto asks. "I could eat a hippopotamus. The tongue and the ear are passable. Which do you prefer?"

"I've never tried hippo," Gog says.

"They're a bore to shoot," Otto says. "They just wallow in the water, showing you their eyes so that one can shoot between them. Big game isn't necessarily the best game. In fact, hitting a duiker deer is more challenging, though it's hardly bigger than one's hand. It does jig about a bit."

Otto claps his palms together. From behind the tower, two young footmen appear, wearing dun liveries, spick and span with silver buttons shining. Between them they carry a hamper. A third young footman follows behind, bearing a Chippendale table, while a sumptuous butler brings up the tail of the procession, solemn in tail-coat and white wing collar, bearing a damask tablecloth as grandly as if it covered a sceptre.

"Aren't the servants like a youth camp," Otto says. "It's wonderful how mass unemployment gives one the right to choose again, only the first class."

The table is laid with the cloth and a feast is set out in

front of Otto and Merry and Gog. There are the luxuries that are beyond price and stocked at Fortnum's. Partridge and grouse, hare and venison; quail's eggs and asparagus, pâté de foie gras from a Dijon tin, burgundy from the year of the Armistice, hock from the vintage of the General Strike, port only as old as the Great Crash. Gog eats and drinks himself sick and silly, while his mother apologises. "I'm so sorry. You shouldn't have been passing by on the one day the head cook is off."

"*Déjeuner sur l'herbe,*" Otto yawns over his brandy, which dates from the Kaiser if not Napoleon. "Take all your clothes off, Merry my dear, and the illusion would be complete."

"I would with pleasure," Merry says. "But really, a son can see too much of his own mother. At least, Gog thinks so. He hardly ever comes to see me."

"I'm right here," Gog says, "by some sort of planned accident. It's like a dream. To be gorged when I thought I was starving. There's one thing certain. It's a feast I'll always remember to my dying day. And meeting you in this improbable place."

He peers up at the triangular height of the Alfred Memorial, then down at his mother and her lover. He is committing the scene to his recollection, but imperfectly. Later, he knows, hindsight will have its due of fitful clarity.

"Tell me what Cambridge is thinking," Otto says. "About Germany. I was an Oxford man."

"Nobody thinks about Germany," Gog says. "Germany is something that happens to other people outside it. Thinking can't change what happens in it. Hitler will go his own sweet way."

"He does like cream and chocolate," Otto says. "Cream cakes, the vice of the Viennese. He's a vegetarian. So how can people see him as a man of blood and iron?"

"Eating vegetables has nothing to do with being peaceful," Merry says. "Look at that George Bernard Shaw, he's always quarrelling with everyone. Somebody who's yellow with carrot juice can still pull a trigger or drop a bomb. I bet Hitler will."

"He wants peace with England," Otto says. "It's the old dream and the right policy. The Anglo-German alliance to stop Russia and keep the peace of the world."

"Queen Victoria wanted that," Gog says. "But since then and a world war, it's been suspect."

"Time to revive it," Otto says. "With the Red Army waiting to strike, and Communism and subversion, I hear, even at Cambridge . . ."

Gog prefers to ignore the last remark.

"The Red Army will have to strike the Poles first," he says. "They're in the way."

"The Poles will have to be taken over," Otto says. "I should say, taken back into the fold. They were presented with so much German land at the end of the last war. And without us, they wouldn't last a day against the Kremlin hordes."

"Politics," Merry says, "or hunting or history. All are bunk. Otto would be happiest, my dear Gog, if there were a Bolshevik drive. You know, beaters flushing up the reds from under the beds and driving them into the guns. Six hundred brace of Bolsheviks in a day. What a bag."

"Shooting them would be fun, but inefficient," Otto says. "We were thinking of reviving that wonderful invention of yours in the Boer War. Camps."

"Boy Scout camps?"

"Concentration camps," Otto says. "Where they concentrate undesirable people."

"Concentrates the mind wonderfully, too," Gog says.

"What? The camps?"

"Death. The prospect of it concentrates the mind."

"Death has nothing to do with the camps."

"Nothing," Gog says. "Just talking about the word concentration."

"The camps I advocate would rehabilitate Communists and deviants and Slavs."

"And Jews."

"Send them back to Palestine," Otto says. "We should all concentrate on that. I don't want any disagreements in our Anglo-German Folk Society. We want our homelands, let them have theirs. We'll be the best friends the Zionists ever had. Hitler will create an Israel in Palestine."

"By persecuting the Jews? Forcing them to flee? A pogrom is not an assisted passage elsewhere."

"By encouraging the Jews to go home," Otto says. "So should you."

"Oh, I don't know," Gog says. "We never encouraged the Germans to come here. Yet come they did, all those tribes who took over the Midlands, Angles and Saxons and Jutes and the other Teuton tribes."

"I always liked the Jews," Merry says. "They're not stingy. And they like living abroad like the British. There's no place like away."

"You have to be careful of people who are attached to two countries," Otto says. "Is a Jew for England or for Palestine?"

"And you," Gog says, "for England or Germany, your mother's country?"

"They shall be friends," Otto says. "Then I shall not have to choose between them. Only in a conflict of interest is there a hard choice."

"Treason," Gog says.

"Don't exaggerate," Otto says. "What a word for a picnic – or a disagreement about what's going on at Oxford or Cambridge. Let's all be friends."

"I wouldn't have Otto taking pot shots at you, Gog," Merry says. "He'll pot you all right."

"I bet," Gog says. "I feel dead."

He lies back tipsily with his head on the grass. A wave of drunkenness surges up from his belly into his brain. In his wobbly vision, the high tower seems to waver and descend in an avalanche of rubble, a topple greater than Babel, a thunder louder than Thor dropping his worst clanger. How just, Gog thinks, if King Alfred's Monument were to fall down and bury Otto utterly.

10

"*Procul, o procul este profani,*" Magog murmurs to his half-brother, as Gog sits uneasily on a marble throne in a classical rotunda, surrounded by urns and Roman busts, each uncanny in its likeness to Mussolini. Sharp-nosed Magog, translating the Latin inscription engraved on the stone wall, is vulpine and unctuous. "'Get out, get out of here, uninitiate.' I prefer the word 'uninitiate' to 'profane'. You're not profane, George, you just haven't been initiated into the right clubs and circles."

"By choice," Gog says. "Not by blackmail, Magog."

"Magnus, please. How many times do I have to say that?" The invisible vice that seems to squeeze Magog's face into an expression of permanent pain and surprise now arches his eyebrows in mock despair. "Only you call me that. Nobody else would know who you were talking about. And though most of your conversation with others does seem to be a matter of you talking to yourself in company . . . Rupert's staying at Spitpoole, by the way. Did you know?"

Magog's interjection makes his question seem trivial. His art is to appear artless.

"I saw him just before I left to come on this walk," Gog says. "He looks more like a fallen angel than ever. He sent you his love. We had a chat about treason."

"How boring," Magog says, as grand people tend to say when they are interested. "I'll go up to Cambridge myself soon."

"Saturday night," Gog says. "For the conversazione."

"What conversation? And with whom?"

"The Cognoscenti," Gog says. "Who else?"

"You don't know about them."

"It's an open secret."

"But you're not an initiate, as I said," Magog says. "*Procul, profani.* You will never be let inside." He looks out with Gog through the pillars at the entrance to the rotunda. Across the little lake other classical temples rise in pediments and domes, set on grassy knolls among the elms, while grottoes and Gothic cottages lurk among glades on eyelines that follow the cunning contours of the landscape. One turf and one iron bridge respect the traverse between nature and design. If there is harmony in a pleasure park, it has been made at Stourhead, the Xanadu of the Age of Reason adjacent to the stately home of Spitpoole. But such harmony is apostasy to Gog.

"I'm sick of it," he says. "Where every prospect pleases, and only working men are vile. They don't want this. They want window-boxes, allotments, somewhere to grow things. Geraniums, pansies, potatoes, leeks, not these bloody azaleas."

"Nonsense," Magog says. "This is something to aspire to. It will be a proletarian park in the end. What begins in privilege ends in popularity. I do agree with you, George, the future is to the masses. The thing is, to guide them so that they do not become a mob. Ah, Rupert . . ."

Rupert's bronze curls proclaim a divinity dropping to earth in a shower of golden coins. He hangs languidly on to a cornice, tired after his etherial journey.

"Well met by sunlight, proud Magnolia," he declaims.

Gog sees his half-brother blush, if that were possible, and rise to meet the challenge with a kiss on Rupert's cheek. But Rupert turns his face to brush his mouth on Magog's.

"How could you tear yourself away from the Ministry just to meet me?" he says. "Our country is temporarily undefended. Our skies are open to blitzkrieg from the Luftwaffe. Remember Guernica. Next time, Gravesend."

"Don't be silly," Magog says. "Hitler wants peace with us. He can't afford a war and wouldn't want it if he knew what we had."

"And for what we are about to have, may the Lord make us truly thankful."

"That too." Magog smiles at Rupert. "You shouldn't know about that. Do I tell you too much?"

"My lips are sealed," Rupert said, "particularly with a kiss."

He pecks at Magog's surprised mouth, then moves out of the rotunda. "We must go back to our hosts. The elegant toad is arriving. Herr von Ribbentrop. And too much de trop, too."

"Be nice to him, Rupert. He is the ambassador. And you know, Otto takes the Anglo-German Fellowship very seriously, as most of us do."

"I wish our mother," Gog interrupts Magog, "had nothing to do with that bounder. I feel violated."

"Don't we wish we were," Rupert says, and runs away down the slope towards the lake with Magog pursuing his white-flanneled legs and cotton shirt billowing from his flight. The chase round the lake ends in the Grotto, where Gog finally lumbers beneath the pitted black rocks to reach the central dome and see a chaste nymph baring one breast in eternal rest beside a spring that falls into a small pool. Rupert has one arm round Magog's neck and is declaiming Pope's salute to the guardian engraved on the rock:

> Nymph of the grot, these sacred springs I keep
> And to the murmur of these waters sleep.
> Ah, spare my slumbers, gently tread the cave
> And drink in silence or in silence, lave.

A jagged porthole in the wild stone roof throws down a speckled beam of light and crowns Rupert with a golden aureole, while Magog's sharp silhouette is the dark reverse of his beloved friend. Gog leaves them in their intimate contradiction and moves from the Grotto to where Neptune stands stock and statue still, caught in the act of pouring out another trickle of fresh water from a great jug. Beyond the sea god, Gog looks across the lake to a cascade and a temple to the wise Apollo. There a small figure dressed in floating turquoise and cerise creates a tiny disturbance to the eye. It is Merry waving her arms, no bigger than a midge of many colours, but a minimal offence to the absolute cultivation of the scene.

"We must go back," Gog calls out. "Mother is always right."

The Baptist's neck looks fresh from the abattoir. A trick of light makes the varnish on the ridges of red paint glitter in fresh blood. The platter that the naked Salome carries discreetly in front of her pudenda is pewter, while the nude dancer seems to wear a seventh veil of dust. Except for the severed head, the erotic charge of the baroque painting is muted by the dull shawl of the centuries. It now looks more crude than violent.

"Herod was quite right," Otto says. "I cannot bear babies, much as I admire the right kind of young men. There are no innocents to massacre, only those guilty of being snivelling brats. I really think the Hitler *Jugend* should leap fully formed from the Führer's thigh like the children of Zeus."

"I will suggest that to the Führer," Ribbentrop says. "He will find a way to do it. He always does."

"And Salome," Maire says, "she is *sympathique*. You chop me head of old bore, *Monsieur l'Ambassadeur*? If he" – pointing at Gog – "or he" – pointing at Miniver – "bore me at dinner, you chop chop with your little guillotine."

"That is a French invention, madame," Ribbentrop says. "Although we do have our methods."

"I am sure you do," Gog says. "The truncheon, the jackboot, the –"

"Understanding of how necessary it is to keep in order antisocial and revolutionary elements in all societies," Magog continues. His eyes are hot knife-points at Gog's impertinence. "Particularly in these times when the right sort of understanding can be so wrongly understood."

Ribbentrop nods and clicks his heels. The small noise reverberates round the grand salon of Spitpoole where he seems out of place, a magpie in his dinner-jacket among egrets in their evening wear. Only Miniver appears more diminutive and dowdy, his black jacket bottle-green from ancient use. Rupert wears a white canvas coat and red silk choker in magnificent disdain of convention, but Gog and his brother Magnus, Otto and the French-American financier Bedaux all wear the white tie and tails of ultimate propriety and Fred Astaire's best musical numbers. Maire's austerity, a black crepe sheath cut into two upflung and wired V's over her breasts, making a rim shaped like an M below her alabaster shoulders, contrasts with Merry's flamboyant blue ball-gown, spreading out like a peacock's tail beneath her cerulean bodice fringed with azure silk and buttoned with aquamarines. Merry always looks the centre of attention, even if she does not sound so.

"You always say the right thing, Magnus," she says, "in

the right place. But it doesn't mean it's correct. His brother George" – Merry tugs at the crease on Ribbentrop's sleeve – "always says the wrong thing, but he's often righter, if you know what I mean."

Ribbentrop twitches himself free with a flick of the cuff.

"Not exactly," he says, then turns to Otto. "Oh, I have news. Our friends are married."

"That makes a change," Otto says. "Merry and I don't believe in it."

"You don't," Merry says. "Call that an Anglo-German misunderstanding."

"The Mosleys," Ribbentrop says. "You know how dear Diana and Oswald are always denying it. But they were married in my colleague Goebbels's house in Berlin in Hermann Goeringstrasse. And do you know what the Führer gave them? A signed photograph of himself in a silver frame."

"I lent the Windsors my château at Candé for their wedding," Bedaux says. "They liked it."

"I heard that," Ribbentrop says. "It was very understanding of you."

"They're going to stay at another place of mine. A castle in Hungary. Poor things, they do not have so many places to go after their abdication."

"It was a mistake," Ribbentrop says. "The influence of your Church, your Jewish press, and your Boy Scouts."

"The people who run our country," Rupert says without a smile.

"Exactly. King Edward, he was for the German-English understanding. We hope he will come to Germany soon."

"I will arrange it for next year," Bedaux says. "The King, he listens to me. As you know, Mister Ambassador, I believe profoundly in an understanding with the Germans."

"We took over your factories, Mister Bedaux. But it was all a bureaucratic mistake. You know what these damn bureaucrats are. I hear your factories in France are models of efficiency. The workers actually work. You make them work. You could teach us."

"I can only learn from the new Germany," Bedaux says. "As can we all."

He looks round the circle of guests as if to challenge them.

There is a silence. No one chooses to deny the statement. Then Gog speaks.

"We've done a thing or two lately at Cambridge. Splitting the atom. Inventing cloud chambers to track down the electrons. Radio research. Radar."

The silence is utter now.

"What is that?" Ribbentrop asks, as if he did not know.

"A new application of radio waves to astronomy," Magog says. "Radio stellar, abbreviated to radar. My brother doesn't know the first thing about science. In fact, if he thinks he's announcing something new like John the Baptist did, he should have his head cut off to shut him up."

"We can stop you," Gog says, "if you ever want to attack us."

"Why should we?" Ribbentrop says. "We wish to be friends. Together, perhaps, we will take on the Russians. We will never be friends with them. And as for you splitting the atom, that does not worry us. We can do it also. Our Professor Hahn at Heidelberg, he knows it."

"Mainly from us," Gog says. "We told everyone how to split the atom."

"Too many," Ribbentrop says. "The Russians are trying, too."

"Too many cooks spoil the hotpot," Miniver says. "It's an old Lancashire saying, Mister Ambassador. I hear Herr Hitler is a vegetarian. I suppose he likes salads and *crudités*."

"Sauerkraut and cream cakes," Ribbentrop says. "But not together."

The laughter is ended by the sound of a gong. Merry takes Ribbentrop's arm to lead him to dinner, while Otto commandeers Maire. "The *droit de seigneur*," he tells her, "still runs at Spitpoole."

"Pity," she says, "I wish I was still *vierge*."

But Magog wrenches at Gog's wrist to pull him to one side and hiss in his ear.

"How dare you mention radar? It's top secret."

"What's in a word? He doesn't know what it is. I'll tell him it is a death ray to planes. That will deter him."

"You will say nothing anymore to him."

"If not, you will. The Anglo-German Fellowship. Isn't that what this week-end is all about?"

"You're impossible, George. God knows how you're any relative of mine."

"God does. And so does Mother."

As they leave the salon to follow the rest of the house-party into dinner, they can hear the mellifluous chuckles of Rupert ahead.

"You don't say. Goebbels admires Eisenstein. What's your next epic, Mister Ambassador? The Battleship Wankin'? Or Ivan the 'Orrible?"

11

Ahead, the Rufus Stone that is no stone, but a mutilated rock enclosed in an iron triangle to keep it from defacement. It is set in a glade of the Stricknage Woods. By the short metal pillar stands a red-faced man in a brown doublet, which is no camouflage, for the setting sun makes a mark of him, picking out his ruddy skin and russet breast in clean target against the backing trees. On Gog's left, *"Tiens* – Ho Ho!" hunting cries and the bugle of hounds in the north wood. A deer breaks cover and leaps down the alley of grass. The red-faced man draws his longbow and aims into the evening glare an arrow that flies high and useless, seeking to put out the sun's eye as the Norman arrow put out the sight of the Saxon King Harold at dusk on the battlefield near Hastings, that feathered shaft the future sceptre of William the Conqueror.

Down the glade, a stag now buckets from the thicket, taking Gog's glance to a second dun figure raising his bow and launching his arrow at the quarry – Walter of Poix, known as Tyrrel the Murderer. A dark streak deflects off the stag's back towards the metal stump of the Rufus Stone. It falls vain to the ground. By the iron marker, the red-faced man shields his eyes with his hand. Sudden, a shaft sticks in his breast. He drops his hand to break the wood that skewers him. He falls. From the shade of the elder tree that gave the wood to peg out Christ's body steps a fellow in green jerkin with silver horn, his bow the true executioner. Rufus is dead, King Rufus, by the arm of his head huntsman. "Trahison, trahison, treason, treason," the light wind murmurs as it catches the thousand clappers of the tinfoil leaves, metal bright in the evening sun. "Henry, Henry, brother, kill brother," the reeds of the marsh murmur at Gog's back. "Blood, blood, king's blood," cry goldcrest and firecrest. "All fall down, all for a Crown," shrieks a distant crossbill. The head huntsman lifts his royal master, royal mark, on to the iron triangle as if an offering on an altar, then points his bow accusing the innocent Walter on the west side of the clearing. Walter stands still, incredulous, uncertain that his arrow is the king-killer. The head huntsman raises his horn to summon vengeance, and Walter breaks like a roebuck in fear, plunging past Gog to escape from the New Forest. "King Henry, Henry King," cry goldcrest and firecrest as the light and the wind die in the dusk and the shining leaves dull to dark tongues without speech.

Gog walks back to the Mercedes-Benz, the hearse waiting under the oak trees. In his head, the reverberations of the words of the *Chronicle* of the Anglo-Saxons, "On the morrow of Lammas, King William was killed with an arrow while hunting by one of his men." But the mind behind the hand that sent the arrow was the mind of a brother. Magog, Magog, do not think you are safe in high places. Beware the greed of your kin, the direction of a servant, the verdict of the people. It is no treason to kill a tyrant. It is no treason to deliver the throne from the seat of a man who betrays his subjects and calls it the divine right of conquest. Bloody is the head that wears the crown, uneasy the aim of those who serve it.

"You took your time," Magog says as Gog climbs into the back seat of the limousine.

"Time is what it takes," Gog says. "Centuries to clear up the least thing."

The chauffeur, with the sleek slender shoulders sloping to his neck and the rim of his black cap, swings the car up the gravel path under the arching branches. Oak and beech, the ancient trees of the New Forest, etched against sky by headlights, hemlock growing in their shade.

"You and your mad theories of history," Magog says. "There is no continuity now. All change from the past. All our religions are nineteenth century at the best. Two of them materialist, of which one has faith. Our religion is capitalism, a dying belief based on an unsuccessful industrial revolution and an overextensive empire. Then there is dialectical materialism, that primitive Bolshevik creed that will end with the revolution eating up itself into a reaction like the snake swallowing its own tail. Stalin is doing it right now with his purges, killing millions of his best people and losing the next war against the last of the Crusaders."

"Crusaders," Gog says. "Do you mean Nazis?"

"The Crusaders were fanatics. They were illogical, unreasonable, feudal and utterly ruthless. When they took Jerusalem, they exterminated the whole population."

"Isn't that what Hitler is trying to do now to the Jews?"

"Much exaggerated those reports," Magog says. "I know. The Anglo-German Fellows make it quite clear that these new villages at Buchenwald and Auschwitz are health camps for rest, recreation and re-education. The three R's of the new Fascism."

"I thought the fasces on Mussolini's flags were the rods used to whip Roman criminals. The axe that the rods were wrapped round then beheaded the bleeding victims. If the scourge and the blade are the symbols of your centres for rest, recreation and re-education, I don't think I'll book my holidays there."

Magog pats Gog's knee in reassurance.

"As I told you, Gog, past history is no longer relevant. Fascism is new, powerful, credible. Our only faith now can lie in the will of a leader who knows what is best for the folk, the people. Only he can unite the nation in a form of socialism and wipe out those moribund materialist twins, communism and capitalism."

"So we go with Sir Oswald Mosley and his pathetic Blackshirts . . ."

"I never said that." Magog is certain. "He is only the figurehead here. The puppet, the man of puff and posture. Behind him –" He falls silent. The black trees lining the Hampshire road rush past, giant sentries on an inspection at the gallop.

"Behind him," Gog says. "Who?"

"The man we need," Magog says.

"Magog."

"Oh you and your fantasies of antiquity," Magog says. "You don't mean me."

"I mean what you stand for," Gog says. "It never changes. You always throw up the leader you need to keep yourself in power. Then you persuade the people they need him too. Where are you going?"

"A castle on the Solent. The sort of stuff your dreams are made of. We'll check on those rays that your friends in the

Cavendish are working on. Radar. You must tell me anything you hear from them."

"I think they're spotter rays. A step up from wireless. Marconi had his laboratory in a tower opposite the Isle of Wight. He flew his aerials up on kites to transmit over the sea. He had to fix up a whole radio system for Queen Victoria at Osborne so she could find out daily how the Prince of Wales's gammy knee was doing on the royal yacht off-shore."

"You never cease to amaze me, Gog. You are like Ripley in 'Believe It Or Not'. An unending store of useless information."

"It connects," Gog says. "All connects. Millions and millions of pieces of intelligence. They seem at random. By happenstance. No point or plot in getting them together. Then, later, you see the connections, the links between past and present and future. The mind sifts and winnows, forgetting the useless, recording the line of thought you only perceive later from all the circumstances, experiences, facts, trivia of your existence to date, of your prophecies to be. There is no haphazard. Only the laziness of hindsight. And foresight."

"You're quite incorrigible, Gog. And you never forget anything, even the irrelevant."

"It comes in handy," Gog says. "From time to time."

Off Calshot Castle, the seaplanes float, frozen as gulls in landing on great web feet with splayed wings and fish-full bellies. There are the biplanes, the Stranaer with its two Pelican engines, and the Walrus with its one pusher that catapults it off the boat-deck as well as the sea-waves. Then the Supermarine fighters that win the Schneider Trophy, and the old Gloucester Napier that set a record across the Atlantic eight years back, only to sink on landing in the *Mauretania*'s wake. And one Empire Flying-Boat, the link of the Dominions, lake-hopping and river-roosting down Africa from Nile White and Blue to Lake Uganda and the Zambezi River. Gog watches the aircraft bobbing on the sea, then paces the circle of the battlements to view the squat hangars of the Royal Air Force striped in crazy patterns like the coats

120

of badgers. On the marshland towards Southampton, on the gravel beach towards Lymington, rotted palings thrust up their weedy teeth towards the moon.

So Gog surveys the scene from Henry the Eighth's bailiwick against the attack of the armada of the King of Spain that did not arrive until his daughter reached the throne. Magog is below in conference with the air-commodore. Gog has been detailed to circumnavigate the castle. His security clearance is insufficient. It is the story of his life. Somehow his papers are never in order.

A liner is streaming down the Solent. One of the Queens, *Elizabeth* or *Mary*. Gog cannot count the number of funnels, three or four, because of the blaze of the ship's lights, hundreds of tiny circles and oblongs and squares of yellow perforations in the hulk, a Hallowe'en mask for a leviathan. The lifeboats on the side are illuminated as if ready to drop and row away. This will be no *Titanic*, steaming out to cross the Atlantic, Marconi missing the boat and his small son watching it sail by to its rendezvous with the iceberg, his father's electrical waves tapped out useless by the operator sinking aboard, the dots and dashes of vain salvation, C Q D, Come Quick Danger, $- . - / - - . - / - . .$, then S O S, Save Our Souls, $. . . / - - - / . . .$, like the points and lines of the Gogam Script, but only some are saved because deaf ears are turned to the messages on the aerial waves that are heard too late.

"You must be chilly," Magog's voice speaks behind Gog. "They'll put us up overnight and send us on our way in the morning. By seaplane. There are some installations I should like to see."

"What are they?"

"Radar, indeed."

"I've seen them on Bulbarrow Hill."

"I have not. And if you have already seen them it will be no breach of security to take you to see them again."

"How can I breach security when I want to defend Albion? But I'm sure your foreign friends will be happy to hear of our new device for our common security."

Magog's voice was chilly with integrity.

"I would never dream of mentioning anything relevant to our national defences to anyone who was not a national.

Unlike some of your Cambridge friends, I would certainly betray my friend before my country. That is why I am trusted, Gog, and you are not."

"Yet the company you keep –"

"Is for the peace of Europe. Hitler will win, you know. I would rather be on his side. And he on ours. Heil."

The forward cabin of the Empire Flying-Boat would suit a ketch. It even sports a bar with stools bolted to the floor. The big-bellied aircraft is a yacht on wings. After a short night at the Calshot RAF mess, once the Owl and Crescent pub, Gog has been roused at dawn to fly with Magog above the west coast to see the secret listening towers of the airwaves. One is hidden at Calshot itself, but others are set on the cliffs of Hampshire and Dorset, waiting for the invader planes to come from the south and France. So the Romans came in their ships and the Angles and the Saxons and the Jutes and the Normans, and so the aircraft and the flying-boats will come, whoever the enemy is, be prepared.

The four great engines roar on high, the boat lurches forward on its keel and pontoons, spray obscures the cabin windows in a whitewash of spume, the sea drags back as the boat lurches up, shaking off the brine and shuddering towards the horizon. The pilot banks right to keep close to the coastline, and a tower pricks the long line of the land, aerials and dishes on its high tip narrow as a smokestack, but rounding down to a Regency turret set on green lawns and in formal gardens.

"Marconi's tower," Gog says. "He sent out his aerial waves from there. The survivors of the *Titanic* wanted to call them Marconi waves, not Hertzian."

"All I know about Marconi," Magog says, "is the scandals. Didn't he bribe some cabinet ministers by selling them insider shares? He bought Lord Reading, the Attorney-General, and Lloyd George, the Chancellor of the Exchequer. And he got the contract to wire up the whole Empire."

"He didn't do that," Gog says. "Anyway, a public inquiry cleared everybody."

"Public inquiries always do," Magog says. "They are not public and they inquire about nothing important. Do you really think a cabinet minister would ever be convicted of anything?"

"No." The tower has receded so far behind them that only the new metal discs glint in first light. "What's that kitchen-ware they've got on the roof?"

"That radar of yours," Magog says. "The new early-warning system against foreign bombers."

"Temple Luttrell built that folly," Gog says, "only it wasn't a folly for him. He used mirrors and lamps to signal to smugglers coming in from France. There are tunnels under the tower leading to the beach. They were full of brandy and tobacco. The English never caught Temple Luttrell, because his brother was in the Customs and Excise, as well as being a magistrate. But the French Revolution caught Temple. He died in a Paris prison. All those signals to France. He must have sent the wrong message."

"It is difficult," Magog says, "deciphering precisely what *you* mean."

"It's just communications," Gog answers. "Only the techniques change. Never what you mean."

The coastline flattens to salt-marsh and estuary, as the Empire flies past the coastguard houses at Lepe and the parallel twin rows of brick cottages at Buckler's Hard that once built Nelson's *Agamemnon* on the gravel to launch down the Beaulieu River. Fly, fly oversea to Hurst Castle with its hearsay tunnel across to the Isle of Wight, then leave the Needles to starboard and cut the arc of the English shore to Hengistbury Head. Steer sou'sou' west, ignoring the jerry-built chines of Bournemouth, to round Swanage and come at cliff again off St Adhelm's Head. There on the brow of the crest of that sainted protuberance of Albion, a wrinkle is cut, plastered with concrete, pincushioned with aerials.

"I want to see that," Magog says. "We land here."

The Empire banks to port and glides down. Ahead the hidden bay of Chapman's Pool. The flying-boat bounces on the swell and settles down. A motor-boat comes out from the slipway beside the tar-paper shacks that fringe the shore of the cleft in the high head, its cliffs bright with lichen and samphire. In the stern of the craft, a seated sailor in white: in the bows, a bleached petty officer, ramrod straight as the dragon prow of a Viking ship. Magog and Gog climb down a rope-ladder from the cabin of the Empire into the rocking boat. Gog slips and half-falls into the scuppers, nearly sending Magog pitching over the rails. But his clumsiness leads to no accident. The men settle themselves and the motor-boat heads towards the shore of Chapman's Pool.

The Mercedes-Benz is waiting to meet them with its chauffeur looking even more ambiguous in his black uniform with his wide hips and narrow shoulders and smooth cheeks. The car must go inland to Worth Matravers, then double south on tracks across the strip lynchets which the oxen ploughed six hundred years ago between the quarries and the tumuli, then on to St Adhelm's Head and the radar station, set on the cliffs beneath the Norman chapel dedicated to the ancient holy missionary. A cliff path straggles straight there, and this Gog elects to take. The stink of aerofuel lines his nostrils, his head is abuzz with faint conspiracies. Keeping the milk-maid sea on his right, he breasts the first hill to look down on the manoeuvres of the cormorants on their flight paths only feet above the swell, bleak and greedy as night bombers while they scan the surface for their targets at swim, their wings swept back from the long fuselage of their necks.

Now it is plunge and slip and scrabble feet and bump bottom down the muddy slide to the base of the slash hewn from the head before the cottages of the coastguard station and the chapel, then it is toil and trouble, thigh lock and sinew sore up the track to the level five hundred feet above the English Channel. Panting and pierced by cramps, Gog rests and looks over sea-grass to the girdle of water that encircles Albion. A peregrine falcon drops against a raven, forcing it down to the ground fifty feet from Gog. The black wounded messenger of woe flaps and cowers on the turf, while the smaller bird of prey wafts on wind current up to its high patrol. England is defended. The omens wing fair.

The chapel on the headland is a small cube of stone, bulwarked by buttresses. Within, a central pillar upholds four domed roofs over the quartered sacred place. Little wooden pens in the south and north sections face towards the table that is the altar in the east, lit by a slit window so narrow that a head might stick in it. A round font stands by the western entrance door, and Gog dips his finger in the water and makes the sign of the cross on his forehead before he kneels to pray and conjure up pictures of the saint and his works, as only Gog can do with his memory stacks and mind's eye and inner vision transcending time, when and if the stones are eight hundred years old and the missionary saint has gone a thousand years and more, and the reverberations of antiquity let slip the noose of reason.

Adhelm, Adhelm, you brought back the rule of Rome to Albion, who had thrown aside the yoke of Caesar and broken the straight roads that bound her down and trod again the curves of Celtic tracks. And Arthur reigned in Camelot until Augustine and Adhelm came with the keys of St Peter that unlock no door to truth, but close the gates on the liberties of Albion by fiat of legate and cardinal's cap and papal bull. Adhelm, Adhelm, you were the master of monasteries, you spread the skein and the privilege of the cloistered privateers of heaven from St Catherine's at Abbotsbury down the pebble beach of Chesil all the way north to Fountains and Rievaulx. And in the mystic heart of Albion, that Avalon where Arthur lies, you set the Abbots to wax fat at Glastonbury. Call the roll, Adhelm, call the roll, the litany of five hundred years of English names playing at Roman rule till the Normans put in their own tyrants for the next four hundred years, from WORGRET, LADEMUND, BREGORET and BEOWARD, ALDBEORTH, ATFRITH, KEMGISEL and GUBA, to BRICHTWIN, AEGELWARD, AEGELNOTH and THURSTIN, HERLEWIN, SIEGFRIED, then vile HENRY of BLOIS . . . Never such names at the roll calls in Gog's school, cold ranks of bare-kneed brats in the playground, gym-master wheezing out gutturals from mustard-gassed lungs: SMITH, BROWN MINOR, WILLIAMS and GRIFFIN. Yes, GRIFFIN, GOG GRIFFIN, come to uncover the old gods and the lost ways of Albion at the price of mockery and persecution, even if he shall end as the last Abbot of Glastonbury, RICHARD WHYTHING, dragged on hurdles past the jeering people to be executed on the Tor one gold cup from the King's Visitors at the dissolution of the monasteries.

A cough soft as a falling silk cushion disturbs Gog's prayers and reverie. The chauffeur stands at the chapel door. It is time to leave with Magog on the drive back to Spitpoole. He has seen the new radar station and gleaned his intelligence from it.

"You did not come and see it," Magog tells his half-brother in the back of the Mercedes. "I would have valued your comments. To see if your friends at the Cavendish have invented more than they are now installing. I would like to know."

"Radar is only an electronic system for detecting aeroplanes," Gog says. "Not a way in to the electronics of the mind, of memory, of the particles that flash between past and present and future. Will the Battle of Hastings show on your radar screen? Or the Battle of Britain that is to come *before* it is fought in air? My internal radar, my inner vision makes me see what was and is and may be. That is true radar, Magog."

"That is rubbish, George, and you know it. Sometimes I think you should be committed."

"I am," Gog says, "to what I know."

The Mercedes winds round the darkling mass of Corfe Castle, its mighty ruins set athwart the road to the south. Ahead lies Wareham Forest and the army camp at Bovington. The car hits a bump, wobbles, swerves and straightens.

"What was that?" Magog asks to the chauffeur's neck.

"Body on the road," the chauffeur says. "Sheep or dog, one or the other. Security, you see, I couldn't stop."

"It was the ghost of T. E. Lawrence," Gog says. "He fell off his motor-bike near here."

"Shut up," Magog says. "Your fantasies are not funny. He was a great man, T.E., and coming round to support the Anglo-German Alliance just before he died. He is a great loss to us."

"He should have died in Arabia," Gog says. "The rest of his life was a postscript. So many are."

12

Plunge deeper than grottoes, further than caverns where Alph runs, beyond the Omegas of the abysses, into the very bowels of the earth. This terrible swift sword that the Black Prince drew, this shaft shot from longbow piercing armour at Agincourt, this lance thrust gutward at Field of Cloth of Gold, drive desperate into fond foe, harrow harlot and prick princess, rake jade and spur slut, impel her moan in pain and passion, as she scores her ravisher's back with bloody nails, stripping off the flesh in parallels of lust. Gog is mounting Maire at Stourhead, and the Hundred Years War is fought again in ten minutes. Jeanne d'Arc burns on England's vengeful stake, and cries out in the fire of her fulfilment.

"*Mon* Gog," Maire whispers in release and slackness. "*Que tu es fort.*"

His weight pins down her body with her knees raised in an M flying two white banners of surrender. Her neck is bleeding from bite and kiss. Her pale cheeks are red-rough with bristle and nuzzle. Her lips are swollen into crushed damsons, her blue eyes crimson with desire spent. She is engorged.

Gog rolls to lie at her side and look at the porthole of the grotto above. The evening star that is the planet Venus is framed within the jagged circle of the rock in the night sky that shimmers with the light of lingering day. Gog cups his left hand over Maire's near breast, exploring the beat of her heart through that raised and swollen mound of curds and concupiscence. His palm strokes down the slopes of rib and swell of belly to where her legs meet in their bush and stream of spent force and sweet impalement. Gog is lost in the hyperbole of love.

"Big lug," Maire says. "*Mon doux* big lug. *Mon* Gog."

"I love you, Maire," Gog says. "Never, never, never, never, never like this. I am lost in you. All of me is in you."

"So I know." Maire sits up and moves her weight from

127

hip to hip. "*Mon cul* it is all stones and *merde*. I never sit down now. Next time we go to bed, Gog. Or I lose my ass."

"Come here. Lie on me."

Gog pulls Maire down to lie on his chest and flank. Her head nestles on his shoulder, her breasts divide on his ribcage, her thighs part on his hipbone, while his right hand strokes her from neck to waist to buttock to back of knee, brushing off the grit and dirt that have stamped their imprints in her pale skin.

"I didn't know you wanted me, Maire."

"Liar. You always know."

"No man ever knows. He thinks he knows. But when he tries, he can get a slap in the face. A knee in the groin."

"No. I keep him. I need him other time."

Maire's hand feels at Gog's sex, sticky and soft after its spurt of spendthrift rage. A spasm tightens the loose flesh, his lower belly quivers. He sighs.

"You don't want me. I'm not your sort. Not brilliant like my brother. Not mean like Miniver. My mind's like a bull in a Sèvres shop. My thoughts go flip-flop. My memory's like a magpie's nest, full of bright trifles, glittering odds and sods from antiquity and mythology. I'm an awkward, blundering, overgrown booby – a bit of a joke. And you're so beautiful, sophisticated, *French* –"

"So what, big lug. *Vive la différence.* What our friend Magnus say what Karl Marx he say – all is *thèse, antithèse,* then *synthèse.*"

"Thesis, antithesis, then synthesis."

"You thesis, Gog. I antithesis, Maire –"

"No, I'll be the thesis, the man of the people. And Magnus, Magog, the antithesis, the man of power, the government. That makes you, Maire, the *synthèse*, the woman between us, who puts us together. Somehow."

"I make you kill him," Maire says. "Or perhaps he kill you. I am not chic, Gog. Not sophisticate. Artist's model. *Maîtresse de Montparnasse.* I know them all – Utrillo, Picasso, Van Dongen – and they know me and Kiki. Magnus, he find me in café. He dress me, take me England. Low life, he call me. *Adorable Bohemia.*"

Jealousy puts a sudden salt plug in Gog's throat. He swallows, gags, splutters, then blurts out:

"I didn't know you were so close."

Maire's fingers squeeze into his sex. Gog yelps. Then the fingers feel and stroke. Gog stiffens.

"Don't be jealous. He jealous of you. He bastard, no?"

"He's a bastard," Gog says, "in every meaning of the word. My mother had him a year after my father died. His father's an English major, now dead and gone. He was adopted by a rich family, the Ponsonbys."

"He jealous because you will be rich. Your *tante* Grace. You true mother's son. He bastard."

There is no sun in the night, but Gog feels a shadow cold as a corpse stand between his flesh and Venus. He shudders and looks up to see a black shape obscuring the high porthole of the grotto. A verdict looms over them.

"Get off George," Magog says.

Maire gives a laugh, musical and sharp, like a wine-glass breaking on marble.

"Go away, Magnus. I see you after."

"Get off."

Magnus is pulling at Maire's arm, lifting her upright. Her naked body rises above Gog in its white swells and arcs of desire. He sits up and is knocked flat on his shoulder-blades by Magog's shoe kicking his chest.

"You swine. She's mine."

"I am me," Maire says. She picks up her chequered dress of black-and-cream squares and shrugs it over her head. Muffled, her voice sounds.

"Maire. I go where I go. I want who I want. *Va t'en*, Magog."

"Don't call me that. He calls me that. My bloody brother."

Gog is sitting up again and pulling on his pants. He is cold and foolish. No one can fight with his trousers down. Abel would have lived if Cain had been debagged. Obscurely, Gog feels that he has wronged Magog, who brought Maire across from Paris, paid for her betrayal of him. But she denounces Gog's odd proprieties, savaging the hand that fed her, Magog.

"You have your Rupert," Maire says. "You suck your *ange rouge*. Gog, he know how put his thing. In me. Not in a Kremlin *emmerdeur*. A beauty parlour *communiste*." Broken glass tinkles in her derision. "And you, a *fasciste* fairy. *Le rouge et le noir.* The red and the black. *Quelle mésalliance.*"

Barefoot Gog straightens to buckle his belt and threaten the dark hat-stand of his brother, who holds Maire by the shoulders and shakes her.

"I'll throw you back to the sewer you came from. And as for you, George, you'll be slung out of Spitpoole. You can spend the rest of the night in your usual ditch."

"That's for Mother to say," Gog answers. "And Otto. I don't think they bother too much about morality. Or immorality."

"You will not speak like that. Merry is our mother, alas. One must defend her."

"Must one?"

"Poof," Maire says. "I go back. You take me, Magnus, and stop your *crise nerveuse.* You play with Rupert, I play with Gog. *Coûte que coûte.* Fair play, what you say?" She stands on tiptoe, tilts up her face and kisses Gog with her spread lips. "See you, big lug."

"I will never forgive you for this," Magog declares, pulling Maire away out of the grotto.

"For the first time in my life," Gog says, "I can truly thank my brother. For bringing you to me, Maire."

"*Au revoir.*" And Maire is gone with Magog, and the chill air is a damp shirt on Gog's bare back and he knows that he will walk on tomorrow towards the end of his journey – Avebury, where the marred stone circles may venture some conciliations for the warring visions that torment him.

At Jack's Castle, the tumulus above Alfred's Tower in King's Wood Warren, the Leadway from the Mendip mines meets the Hardway over the ridges. There Gog stands, imagining the oxen dragging the carts of ore, the drovers with their long whips and longer curses, the ponies with the panniers and the porters with their sacks on their backs. This sad molten stuff was poured into moulds to make pellets and birdshot, musket balls and pistol slugs, bullets and dum-dums, soft metal spreading on impact to shatter sinew and squash flesh, gouge body and splatter blood in civil war and strife abroad, in volley and sniping and sharpshooting and ambuscade, in felling sentries and regiments and squadrons and thin red lines, in filling cripples' homes and mortuaries and bandoliers and souvenir cases, and also in coating church and cathedral with its dull cloak to keep God's rain off the houses built by men to praise Him.

At Witham Friary where the monks long ago chanted their final Angelus, the Leadway meets the Ironway, which runs even straighter on its twin parallel lines than the old Roman road across Bruton Forest that was once hacked through the wayward trees to correct the meandering paths of the Britons and Caractacus. The Serene and Delightful – or Slow and Dirty as travellers call the Somerset and Dorset Railway – set its iron routes on bridges and through cuttings from Bath over the Mendip Hills down the Stour Valley to the sea, defining the frontier of the West Country by wooden sleepers and metal rims. Where the Romans bound down giant Albion more securely than Lemuel Gulliver by road and rule stretching from the Fosse to the Icknield Way, the Victorians stamped an iron grid on the living earth, imprisoning by mesh and manacle, clamp and chain, the rude, rough stirrings of the green and vibrant land. And now Gog stands at the halt at the old Friary, waiting for a Puffing Billy to steam by piston and cylinder along the Ironway to Marlborough, and take him where he wishes to be.

As he waits, he studies the last invisible grille that patterns the vagaries and mysteries of Britain in a folly of squares. The faint blue lines of the grid on Gog's Ordnance Survey map seem coy in their pretensions, hardly daring to suggest confines for the jerk and switch of the yellow country roads, the slant corners and zigzags of the green copses and woods, the pools and detours of the actual blue rivers, the mazes and meanders of the brown hill contours, the specks and dashes of quarries and knolls, the sinews and ganglions of red main routes, the whole hopscotch and patchwork of the surface of Albion that no logic can construct, no set-square can put to right angles, no pattern can mark down.

Now the black engine grinds slow to halt at the platform blowing a cloud of grime and smoke over Gog so that his face suddenly sweats in muck. He lumbers up the steps of a railway carriage into an empty compartment, where particles of dust float as midges in the sunlight, and the seats smell of

ancient pews and decomposing hassocks. A lethargy over-
whelms Gog and drugs him into a doze. As his eyes close,
he seems to see a shape pass in the corridor, wearing a trilby.
But how can that be, when he was alone at the Friary halt,
and no one could have followed him on his recent elaborate
peregrinations? Bishop Berkeley was right. Men only exist
in the eye of God. And in that celestial surveillance, who
shall wonder that His agents may have a taste for trilbies?

"Tickets, please."

The collector, that menial of Mammon, leans over Gog,
lying back in the corner of the compartment. His peaked cap
shadows his eyes. Below the rim, his cheeks are full and
inscrutable, his lips purple and sunk against his protruding
teeth. On the shoulders of his dark uniform, Gog reads the
letters S & D R in braid, and the same are stamped on the
small steel machine hanging from the man's neck, probably
containing handcuffs. Gog fiddles in his top pocket to find
the ticket to Frome and on to Marlborough, but the collector
is not interested in it.

"Where were you between three-three and three-thirteen
this afternoon precisely, sir?"

"Are you working out timetables?" Gog asks. A question
is the softest answer.

"Did you see a lady in tweeds with the face of a Pekinese
and a Pekinese with the face of a lady?"

"Is this an investigation? The transmigration of visages.
Do we send for a vet or a Brahmin or Hercule Poirot?"

"It is advisable to answer my questions, sir," the collector
says. "The neck of the headless woman's torso discovered in
the lavatory of the ten-eighteen from Weston-super-Mare
fits the head of the Roman gladiator's bust discovered in the
hatrack on the milk train from Blandford Forum. The trains
only switched points at Evercreek Junction. About where
were your whereabouts wherever you were?"

"There is a man in a trilby hat who has been following me
for weeks," Gog says. "He knows the answer to all your
questions. Ask the lady in the crêpe veil eating scones in the
dining-car. She wears the veil to hide her sorrow and disguise
the fact that the butter sticks to her moustache."

"Very interesting," the collector says. "But why is the
bald Sikh wearing a turban in Compartment Q?"

"He must not give away his lobotomy."

"And when the Maharanee took off her wooden leg in the Golden Sleeper, what was concealed in her false kneecap?"

"Her nightcap. A fifth of *grappa*."

"The oily Levantine playing backgammon with the hirsute Armenian on the Vuitton trunk in the baggage van has only three fingers on his right hand. Where is his missing finger?"

"In a dyke in Amsterdam. She bit it off."

"The passenger list bears the following names: Marple, Holmes, Brown, Lupin, Watson, Wimsey. Who is the suspect?"

"The damned foreigner."

"You know the score," the collector says. "But what have you to say about the fact that you were seen in the company of a French lady of pleasure answering to the name of Maire, a relation of Mata Hari and an agent of several foreign powers?"

"I am proud to have been in her company and intend to renew her acquaintance deeply as soon as possible."

"At Castle Cary, a man with a false hump boarded the train. Inside that hump were the plans for the latest radar technology. He was found stabbed to death in the guard's compartment and the intelligence was gone."

"Where was the guard?"

"He was the guard. As you know, sir, in our line of writing, the murderer is usually the victim. In this clear case of suicide, the coroner will bring in the verdict: murder by person or persons unknown until the last page."

Gog now starts awake from his dream of Murder on the Slow and Dirty Express as a real ticket collector pulls open the carriage door and says: "Tickets, please." Or is he real? His peaked cap is too big for him: it sits upon his ears. Gog starts up and snatches off the cap. Beneath it, a red line crosses the collector's forehead, the watermark of a trilby hat.

"Unmasked," Gog cries, "at last."

"Uncapped." The collector seizes back his hat. "Will you please respect railway property and give me your ticket?"

"Who are you working for?" Gog demands. "MI Two, Three, Four, Five, Six, Eleven, Eighteen, Ninety-two? Russia, France, America, Monaco, the Triobrand Islands?

Or are you a private investigator? Has Magog put you on my trail? What's his motive? The secrets of the Cavendish, jealousy over Maire, sibling rivalry? Who pays you? The Treasury, the Comintern, Fort Knox or used five-pound notes? Confess, or we will grapple to the death in the tunnel hard by Black Dog Woods."

"Grapple then," says the collector and leaps for Gog's throat as they enter the darkness of the tunnel. He puts his hands on Gog's windpipe. Gog puts his hands on the man's windpipe. He presses Gog's Adam's apple till the pips squeak. Gog presses the man's apple till the pips squeak. The man butts Gog on the nose with his head. "Ouch." Gog butts the man on the nose with his head. "Double ouch." The man bangs Gog's skull against the compartment window. Gog sees stars. Gog bangs the man's head against the compartment windows. He sees nebulae. "Copycat," the man croaks as Gog chokes him. "Dirty rat," Gog croaks as the man chokes him. Then the train is out of the tunnel and both men release their grips on each other's necks and fall into an embrace, singing simultaneously,

"Stick his bum in bacon fat."

And as Gog dreams the second part of his schoolboy Great Games and Greenmantle, he hears "Tickets, please" for the third time and awakens to find the genuine article, a little man with eyes behind pebble glasses big as an owl's who tells him that the next stop is Marlborough and he had better look pretty nippy because the train doesn't stop more than a minute and many a passenger's gone on to London without the option. Gog thanks him and tells him he has never had such a thriller as having a snooze on the Serene and Delightful Railway.

There is room at the Robin Hood Inn on the fringe of Savernake Forest, where the original Robin was said to hang out when the Sheriff of Nottingham was making matters too hot for him and his Merry Men in Sherwood. Over the old oak bar, a sign has been set:

> *Traveller, if you think it good*
> *Stay and drink with Robin Hood.*

Should Robin from his house be gone
Then stay and drink with Little John.

Gog stays and drinks too much scrumpy hard cider with all the large youths in the bar, the incredible thanes of Wessex, bearded and gentle and tattooed with crowns and anchors and swastikas: they look like the house-carls who died at King Harold's side at Hastings. They show him the well in the bar floor where they say that they drop unwanted guests and folk who don't like the Social Credit back-to-the-land boys. With the cover off, the well-shaft is seventy-feet down to the black pool of memory and oblivion. And as there's nothing to do but drink, Gog agrees to lurch with them to the hall near-by, where the thanes are rehearsing their next pantomime, *Robin Hood*, what else? Gog's childhood sparkles in his skull, Jack climbing the beanstalk to put fireworks in the Giant's Boot . . . Fee-fi-fo-fum, I smell the blood of an Englishman . . . Turn again, Whittington, Lord Mayor of London, and the Cat catches the mice big as children in whiskers, and why can't I be one? . . . Mother Goose, Mother Goose, is your Widow Twankey a man in skirts? And as for Dandini and Prince Charming, anyone can see they are girls in thigh-boots, but their strut and swagger put Beau Brummell to shame . . . and the Ugly Sisters, knock knockabout just as bad as Gog and Magog, brother bash brother . . . only Cinderella and Snow White are pretty awful with their dimity dresses and golden coaches and glass slippers, with Gog yelling in his treble as Cindy gets her royal kiss, "Pathetic! Disgusting!" And he brings the pantomime roof down and escapes a smacking because his mother Merry is creased with laughter too.

Now in the church hall, the Savernake thanes are changed to Lincoln green with chairs set out for trees and billiard cues for bows, while Maid Mairion (so Gog reads it in his borrowed script) wears black boots and stockings, white britches and jacket, offering her ripe all as the Principal Boy to the Merry Men. Fat Tuck is a Black Friar, his robe ballooning over his girth in swart solemnity. The script starts with Robin himself complaining about the inconsistencies of his forest foraging:

ROBIN HOOD:

> I robs the rich, give to the
> poor,
> But the people says: More,
> more, more.
> I robs the middlin' of their
> store,
> But the people says: More,
> Robin, more
> If Robin's robbin' more for
> you,
> Robbin' you's all I can do.
> The middlin' and the rich are
> skint,
> I'll rob the poor and make a
> mint.
> But then you'll swear and say
> I am
> The same as Sheriff of
> Nottingham.
> Robin Hood is fair and free
> When he robs them and don't
> rob me.

FRIAR TUCK
(laughing):

> Your argument is heaven-
> sent.
> You talk just like the govern-
> ment.
> Give to them who have, and
> take
> From them who have not.

LITTLE JOHN:

>   I will break
> Your bald numbskull.

LITTLE JOHN, who is very large, advances on FRIAR TUCK, swinging his quarter-staff.

FRIAR TUCK:

> Pooh for you.
> Ha-ha. Hee-hee.
> *As LITTLE JOHN swings his staff, TUCK ducks and the*

136

> *staff strikes MAID MAIRION*
> *a blow on her bum.*

MAID MAIRION: Ow-ow. Ooh-ooh.
Robin and his Merry Men.
How shall I have you all again?
How shall I favour all of you
When my bum is black and
blue?

Gog cannot quite believe his ears. There were blue jokes in the pantos of long ago . . . "Where can I put it, Widow Twankey?" "Up me chimney, darling" . . . but even if all the audience wanted the Principal Boy to bend over so they could give him/her one up his/her delectable rump, the Boy always spoke prettier than picture postcards, leaving the saucy seaside jests for the Ugly Sisters. But Maid Mairion is so scripted. Gog can read the lines on his knee, except the words are heaving up and down like his bellyful of rough cider, and he no longer sees what he seems to see or hears what he thinks he hears. The pantomime goes on with the Black Friar Tuck whipping Maid Mairion's backside with the rope that holds in his cassock.

FRIAR TUCK: I often find that a good whack
Stimulates the sexual act.

ROBIN HOOD: Marry enough, my merries
now!
Hark! 'Tis an enemy, I trow.

*Enter the SHERIFF OF
NOTTINGHAM, dressed in
black knee-britches and Fascist
blackshirt. He raises his arm.*

SHERIFF: Sieg Hood! Sieg Hood! You
are the Folk.
You free us from the Norman
yoke.
I Sheriff am, but follow you
Who is the Will of England
too.

LITTLE JOHN, who is very large, swings his quarter-staff round his head.

LITTLE JOHN: I do not give a good goddam.
I break the head of
    Nottingham.

ROBIN HOOD: Stay, Little John. For our old
    foe
Is right. I am the Folk Hero,
The Man in Green. I leave the
    trees,
Now get you all upon your
    knees.
And say with me, "Hail Hood!
    Hail Hood!
He leads his people from the
    wood
To rule in this unruly land,
Their will be at his command."

LITTLE JOHN: I'll break thy head, bad Robin
    Good,
You shall not lead us from the
    wood.
Here is a man both strong and
    free,
As is a deer, his liberty.
God's teeth! King Robin you
    would be,
So death to Hood and slavery.

FRIAR TUCK and the SHERIFF OF NOTTING-HAM come behind LITTLE JOHN, who is very large, and catch his arms and break his quarter-staff.

ROBIN HOOD: Take that traitor. He is dead.
I bid thee, Sheriff, lop his
    head.
Use his blood to print decrees:

138

WORK IS FREEDOM.
BRICKS ARE TREES.
I am your good, your life, your
    King,
Robbin' you of everything.
Those foreigners we fight in
    wars
Have Caesars, Führers,
    Duces, Czars.
King Robin now the people
    crown –
Make Britain Great! Rise
    Albion!

*A gold crown as tall as Charing
Cross descends from the gods
on wires and covers up ROBIN
HOOD.*

MAID MAIRION: To celebrate th' occasion,
                 I'll have you boyos one by one.

And Gog sees Maid Mairion turn backside to the empty rows
of chairs in the church hall and pull down her britches and
bare her twin moons to him and the Merry Men onstage.
And he is rushing forward in lust and despair, hurling his
chest on to the boards, pulling himself up among the male
legs jerking and kicking to get first inside the naked cheeks
of Mairion. Now he hurls aside the Merry Men, striking them
with fist and forearm, clobbering their slaver and slobber,
cracking down their rampant pricks, releasing his own rearing
member to ram home in the cleft of black hair and split of
round flesh and . . . thrash and thresh of sweaty sheet as
Gog wakes in his night bed in the Robin Hood Inn, blear-
mouthed and head-heavy from the scrumpy, to a wet dream
of Maire, whose body is now the succubus of his soul, the
itch of his obsessions, the salt on the wound of his need.

13

In Robin's wood of Savernake, grand avenues of beech and silver birch are planted, great guardsmen to stand sentry over the wild woodland. Gog follows the tree-lines beneath a morning sun that limns the black clouds scudding by in the west wind. It is sudden dappled-bright, then dark beneath the branches, alternate dazzle and grim. Then Gog turns aside into a glade where each mushroom or stump conjures up fairy names, Peaseblossom and Cobweb to serve this new blundering Bottom, his head asinine enough to believe his rural rambles will solve the mayhem of his mad historical visions. Brown leaves already matt the grass and loam underfoot, oak and ash and thorn signify the ancient forests of Albion. But then Savernake breaks open into a grass ride leading to a tall column, set up in triumph at the tamed great wood, where the dead Druids no longer search for mistletoe and Robin Hood is the name of a children's game or a pub sign.

Over the Kennet River down to its canal. As Gog passes a farm, he sees pigs rooting in a spinney. A sow has a large worm writhing in its jaws, a viper. It breaks the serpent's back, drops it, tramples it to death and bolts it down. Its pork will be as tangy as the ham from Estremadura that is piquant with snake venom. Gog cannot read the omen: he leaves it for the Romans. He remembers the famous game pig Slut from the New Forest that used to point its trotter at roe-deer or partridge, no dog better, none with such a snout for the quarry. Pigs deserve a better name, but Gog cannot find one on his trail to the canal.

The noonday is still milksoft and clear. On the shady bank, anglers are spaced along the towpath, baiting their hooks with live roach to catch the fearsome pike. Off the far bank, the moorhens fuss among the rushes, their heads tick-tocking as regular as upright pendulums. A silent railway runs alongside the canal beyond a hedge, usurping its course and function. No horses pulling barges plod the path, only anglers and walkers. Trade has left the waterway to the fish and their pursuers. The locks themselves are breaking down, the great timbers rotten in water, the winches and chains rusting into immobility. The brick warehouse at Burbage Wharf has broken windows, and no load swings from the huge wooden crane without. At Cudley Lock, the keeper's cottage sports drawn blinds, at Heathey Close Lock, turf has grown over the crumbling redbrick bridge. Two swans glide down the weedy canal, that once seamed England with neighbour waterways before all went up in steam, and engines pumped where men had floated. But the white royal birds are messengers of time past. Behind them, a shire stallion clops its hairy fetlocks along the canal path, dragging a black barge behind. Gog steps back into the brambles to avoid a trampling by its hoofs. He cannot but notice the pole between its hind legs that is its sex, seeking mares where none may graze. And on the dark bows of the craft pulled by the towrope, a name is pricked in red Gothic capitals, SINOPTICON.

On the stern beside the tiller, a man sits in a rainbow of light. A fuzz of golden hair covers his ruddy skin and burning tufts lie on the brown nipples upon his bare chest. As the barge draws so near to Gog that he may jump on board, he sees the yellow eyes of a ram staring at his own, and in the left eye a split pupil so that a black smear drains into the iris and disconcerts the gaze.

"'Op on," the man says. "Call me Crook. Yer'll see what yer'll see. Booger if yer don't on the good ship *Sinopticon*."

As Gog hesitates, Crook reaches out an arm stronger than a hawser and jerks Gog off the bank by his wrist, feet scrabbling in the canal water until he thumps on the deck with a never ask why, and Crook is bending over him with the stare of the gammy yellow eye compelling nightmare obedience.

"You got owt in your trews, then pull it out, and 'ave it 'ow yer fancy in cabin." His hand grabs at Gog's hip, nipping his pocket and pulling out two pound notes and a scatter of silver. "'Ave to do, don't it? Get on wi' it. Yer's willin'. Men is."

Crook leaves the tiller to push Gog down into the cabin of the good ship *Sinopticon*. The gloom blinds Gog after the glare outside, and a smell of rotten musk wrinkles his nostrils and tightens his groin. As his eyes adjust to the dim light, he sees walls screened with silver and couches with gilt legs and off-purple upholstery, lamps each made from a single false baroque pearl, and twin Corinthian pillars supporting a frieze of nymphs and satyrs. In frozen couplings, the shaggy godlings bash, bollock, clinch, crunch, grind, gut, jam, jerk, pierce, pound, rack, ram, score, sluice, tear, thrust, wallop, work into every crack, cranny, crevice, cup, fissure, fold, gap, gash, hole, hollow, mouth, mound, nest, nook, organ, orifice, pit, pock, seam, split of the sylvan beauts, bints cuddles, cherries, dolls, doxies, fairies, foxes, gals, geishas, harpies, houris, jades, janes, et cetera. These are the commas of desire, the syllabus of sex.

Now a small cupola begins to revolve in the cabin roof. An outside light projects magic lantern slides on to the silver screens of the walls. They make the murals at Pompeii look like a nursery primer, they turn the Karmasutra into a kindergarten game. Priapic hordes pleasure themselves in gangs on single concubines, each pleat of breast or fold of knee or stroke of toe making the men gush in geysers on lubricious skin. Naked dancers kick high as phalli impale them fore and aft or else do the splits on male loins recumbent, their faces leant back to push their lips on groins plunging from above. Bound on the rails of pirate ships, spread out on Mongol saddles, pegged between four stakes by bandit ropes, chained wrist to ankle for the convenience of gaolers, the bodies of women lie open and defenceless to the assault of lust. Gog groans as slides show bare acrobats on bar and trapeze contrive their many intricate penetrations by exquisite contortions of the flesh. All the ingenuities of imagination and all the sinuosities of limbs akimbo are depicted to stimulate Gog's perception of one simple act. He has to have Maire. He has to have her now. The might of desire possesses him. He must have her.

Now on a couch standing on its gilt legs, a white shape begins to inflate on the off-purple upholstery. Bemused, Gog sees a sloughed human skin grow into a woman stricken with anorexia, then puff up more and more until her legs are two peeled hazel branches, her belly the swell of a milky wave, her breasts pop firm in two pink peaks, her lips part full and ripe between her pouting cheeks, and Maire lies there, nude and still, awaiting Gog's advance.

He is on her in the fury of his desperate want, but he is grasping at rubber nothings, Maire as a gasbag, a downed dirigible, his fingers digging into barrage balloons of buttocks, his lips sucking a nipple as satisfactory as a baby's pacifier, his cock plunging into the inner tube of a bicycle, coated with a gelid grease that belies the warm secretions of a willing woman. Yet such is his need and his obsession that Gog pumps willy-nilly his seed into this cold contraption that has answered to the fevers of his libido, the rabies of his desire.

"'Oo did yer think 'er is? The Bargee's Bint." Crook's hand passes Gog's ear and pulls out a stopper from the ear of the false creature beneath him. There is a whoosh of stale air stinking with marsh gas that makes Gog retch and cough. The body under him collapses and leaves him lying on a white synthetic clammy couch cover that has shrivelled like his cock into a chilly squash. "Yer can 'ave her 'ow yer want and 'oo yer want. Mae West. Jean 'Arlow. Queen Mum. Miss X fer ecstasy. 'Ooever, 'owever, whenever. The Bargee's Bint."

Crook's palm slaps Gog's rump, then his fingers goose Gog and spur him in a scramble to his feet. Crook drives him up the steps from the cabin on to deck, as he tries frantically to button up his flies while hanging his head down to stop bumping it on the hatch. The barge is moored at Cuckoo's Knob by Milkhouse Water under a road-bridge. The shire stallion is eating cow-parsley and burdocks growing by a hedge. Gog is hefted on to the bank, half-thrown and half-heaved ashore across the towpath. He stumbles and falls, hitting his head on the lower step of a stile that leads into a meadow by the road. He lies, dazed in a dream of afternoon, unknowing where he is.

Time passes. The rumble of a lorry brings him to his feet, and he sees the arches of the bridge crossing the canal. There is no Shire stallion, no Crook, no good ship *Sinopticon*. But on the towpath, the prints of large horseshoes, good luck stamped on the earth, proof positive only of Gog's lonely lucubrations in pursuit of Maire that have left him with a moist crotch. He wanders on towards Pewsey Wharf, where a few river-boats are moored in painted oblongs and garish crates afloat. He crosses the bridge there to the sunny side of the canal, passes the firs and thorns adroop in water, the artificial woodland contradicting the Georgian blockhouse that reigns over Stowell Park, then on he ambles to Wilcot and the sign of the Golden Sun, where the pub is still open and Gog can fill the void in his belly with cheese and potatoes in their jackets and warm bitter beer that tastes like fond defeat and spent sensuality.

The road strikes north to reach the track up to the Wansdyke. Between bramble hedges, Gog leaves the flat Vale of Pewsey and slogs up Tor Hill, flailing his hands at the torment of flies that make a whizzing cloud about the sweat on his face. The slopes of the chalk hills are gouged and furrowed, shaped into ditch and hump and mound by some gargantuan digger who wished to escape oblivion by scratching at the contours of the land. On the peak of Tor Hill, Gog turns back to look across the valley to where the Great Ridgeway drops down past Puck Shipton over the River Avon to reach the old Lydeway or Luddway that is metalled and numbered now on Gog's Ordnance Survey map and called the Andover-Devizes Road. Around and ahead lie the vast earth circles and arcs of neolithic camps before Knap Hill, also the wrinkles and bumps of turf on Adam's Grave.

Gog moves on the verges of ploughed fields rough with flintstones towards a horizon that signals the Wansdyke. A great bird floats up over the ridge ahead and swoops down on Gog. It is no bird. Beneath black batswings, a grid is fastened. Spreadeagled on the metal bars, a man's shape flies, his helmet a dark round hat festooned with cockleshells, his face a skull pushing points of bone against his drawn skin, his flying suit and boots a black robe and sandals. The wingtip knocks Gog's scalp as the aerial machine glides to ground. Gog eats a tuft of grass and spits it out, before swivelling and sitting up to see the sky-pilot in the cockleshell hat bending over him and saying, "Pardon me."

"Bloody well pardon you," Gog says. "Bonking me with your infernal contraption."

"You were brushed by the wings of angels," the pilot says. "And you cannot pardon me. For I am the Pardoner. I can shrive your sins at a price. For this gift of pardoning, I wear the cockleshells on my hat. In them your vices may be washed clean."

"I've heard of flying doctors on mercy missions in the bush of Africa. But flying Pardoners in search of sinners, never."

"I am not the first, pardon me." The man's face beneath the wide brim of his hat is a kite of points of bone, nose and cheekbones and chin, pushing through his thin skin. His voice is both solemn and prissy. "Know you not of Brother Elmer of the Abbey of Malmesbury? Eight hundred years ago he flew on wings from the top of the Abbey tower. For a furlong he glided in the air, then crashed to the ground, breaking both his legs. He wanted to fly again with a tail, but the Abbot forbade him, saying only the Devil had a tail. And, of course, Brother Elmer was not the first."

"There was Daedalus and his son Icarus," Gog says. "They flew and Icarus crashed. Sun melted the wax on his wings."

"Pish to the Greeks," the Pardoner says. "And where do you think they got it from? The Magi? Never. Their alchemy was underearth. They sought the secrets of the mines and the deep currents and the philosopher's stone. The Brahmins never flew except in their spirits which could leave their bodies under meditation and gravitate a thousand leagues away. It was the Druids who flew corporeally, the real *corpus* in the ether, to give them the overview of their vast creations. Pardon me, but how else could they see the sculpture of the earth which their slaves patted into place handful by million million handfuls from Hod Hill to the White Horse of Uffington, from Maes Knoll where the Wansdyke ends to the Seven Barrows of its lost beginnings? Along the seven ley lines that were the invisible flight paths of the Druids, you must swoop and soar with the hawk by day, you must flit with the bat by night, if you would be as the Druids were and know the language writ on English hill and dale."

The Pardoner takes Gog by the hand and leads him from the flying machine to the brink of Knap Hill. Below the scarp, the long serpent of the Wansdyke, moat and turf wall squirming fifty miles over Wessex, and beyond in valley bottom, the pimple of Silbury Hill, the largest mound made

by man in all the world, the hub, the radial, the focus of all
the scape in the ancient holy bowl below.

"No one knows why men laboured for centuries to build
Silbury Hill. But pardon me, I know. It was the base for the
oak mast set on its top by the Druids and crowned by a bush
of mistletoe as a beacon. And on those white berries and the
ley lines the flying Druids threw their visions by night and
listened to the returning echoes, and so they came safe to
ground as the bats do on their nocturnal flights."

"Radar," Gog says. "We have discovered it again."

"And what is new, pardon me? If there is one thing
needing pardon, and at great price, it is the pride of inventors.
We invent nothing, we discover again the lost wisdom. There
shall be men flying here hanging on gliders and in their
ignorance they shall believe they are the first. But you, Gog,
you seek to travel through time and beyond reason."

"How do you know my name?"

"You are foretold in the Book of Revelation. I was
directed here to meet you by the makers of this vast earth
sanctuary. Come fly with me and all shall be revealed to you.
That is, pardon me, if you may read the message inscribed
on the land."

"I know the runes," Gog says, "and I know the lines
incised on Celtic stones that are older than the runes, old
as the Druids. The Ogam or the Gogam Script, that I
know."

"Then you may read the land."

The Pardoner takes Gog back to the flying machine with
the batswings. Both of them seize the grid beneath the
aircraft and hoist the contraption high. It is curiously light.
The thin cloth or skin that covers the bent willow withies of
the wings seems to catch the wind and impel Gog and the
Pardoner forward to the edge of Knap Hill, so their trudge
becomes a trot then a charge over the brink, and lo, they are
hanging by their hands from the metal bars as they plunge
over the cliff above the moat and bank of the Wansdyke,
where they veer left on the waft of the eastern breeze that
carries them above the Cotswolds along the course of the
serpentine dyke, an interminable runnel and ridge upon the
earth that peters out on the approach to the River Avon
below the kempt stone crescents on the hills of Bath City,

then is dug deep again before the circles of Stantonbury Camp until it runs into the terminal buffer of Maes Knoll.

Gog is still hanging by his hands from the grid below the batswings, but the Pardoner has swung up his legs to perch like a crow on the metal struts. "Leg up and over," he calls, "or you'll fall." And Gog swings his big body forward and back until he can catch the heel of a boot over a bar and bring up the other boot to straddle the rear of the grid. Jolted by his swinging movement and a mysterious shift of the wind that now blows from the north, the aircraft veers south over Stanton Drew and the Mendip Hills. Far below, traced on the turf, Gog can see the tiny Priddy Circles before the batswings whirl them past the great gap-mouth of Wookey Hole.

"Prepare for the Druid one ley line over Glastonbury," the Pardoner shouts to Gog. "For there, pardon me, was the beginning and will be the end of the mysteries of the discovery of Albion."

They swoop over the spire of St Nicholas Church at Brockley, then along an invisible ruler in air above Cleeve Hill to Holy Trinity Church in Burrington, where they slide past the tower and rise to the ancient henge of Gorsey Bigbury. Then on to the entrance to the wishbone traced in soil at Westbury Beacon Camp before the batswings plunge down from the Mendip heights. Seen from above, the drained marshes about Glastonbury Tor show the patchwork and embroidery of stone walls and hedgerows, that stitching which the farmers use to hem the outskirts of their fields. A greater force than gravity pulls Gog's weight down and directs the aircraft along a direction straighter than arrow-flight. They fly over the Yarley crossroads and Callow Hill towards the maze on Glastonbury Tor, crowned by the tower of St Michael's Chapel, where Gog has willed his grave, if he is to achieve a Christian burial at all. In seven descending irregular ellipses, the maze on Glastonbury winds down the green slopes of the Tor, furrowed in bank and terrace, scalloped and entrenched in the meanings of the meanderings round the holy hill.

"Merlin made that maze," the Pardoner calls through the wind, "when King Arthur ruled here. You may walk it and walk it and never reach St Michael's on the top. Pardon me, this is no place for a Christian, but a Druid to understand. We'll end on a third spire for luck and the Trinity."

The batswings pass the belfry of St Leonard's at Butleigh. The force of the ley lines dies, and the wind veers south-east, taking them over the plain to the great rings of Cadbury Castle, then on to the ancient gouges on the Dorset hills, Hambledon and Hod Hill, before the west wind blows them over Pimperne to the weird geometry of the Dorset Cursus. Looking down, Gog can perceive six miles of neolithic cup-and-ring markings, bent parallels and curves and angles and corners, a scrabble of runes carved gigantic on the surface of the planet, mile-long suggestions of his own name, $\times$ $\diamondsuit$ $\times$, but nowhere the terrible crossed hurdle of the Rune of might and majesty and M, $\bowtie$.

"This earth language is later than the Druids," he calls to the Pardoner.

"How do you know?"

"I have studied the runes."

"You have studied well."

The batswings fly north-west over Ackling and Bockerly Dykes, where the land is scored again for many miles, then above the great house of Wilton in its chunk of magnificence. The skein and the warp of the fields is haphazard now with wriggling rivers and scattered spinneys disturbing the cautious partitions of property and the exact division of high-road and railway.

"Druid Two ley line," the Pardoner calls. "Hold your hats for Stonehenge."

The pull of the ground-force nearly plucks Gog loose as it slings the batswings in a missile over Stonehenge. Below him, Gog perceives the indented giant horseshoe of an old camp, then a dew-pond, then the great turf garter of Groveley Castle, then a bell-barrow, and now swoop low towards the standing stones of the vast henge and the pits for the bluestones from far Pembrokeshire. Pass over the outer circle of the great trilithons which form the Π and the letter L in the Gogam script, and look upside down from a head lying backwards over the iron grid, and see the trilithons form the $\amalg$ $\amalg$ that show the D D in the Gogam script, leaving only the $\#$ or U to find. This groundmark Gog can discern clearly as his eyes draw two upright lines between the four

Station Stones set to signal moonrise and sunrise, moonset and sunset, and the crossline made by the ley line that hurls him over the Druid observatory. Gog can read the name of the Celtic god writ clearly in sarsen stone and earth current.

"LUDD!" Gog shouts to the Pardoner. "I have read the name of Ludd on Stonehenge. The god of the sun and the silver hand!"

"Pardon me," shrieks the Pardoner, "only ye shall read who can read."

So strong is the earth force that the wings bucket through the air, shaking their passengers violently as they screech over Sidbury Camp and two more tumuli in their flight path. Then the force shrugs them off, and they catapult sideways to the west where another tumulus stands big as a pimple on Durrington Down, the marker for the third Druid ley line.

"Return ticket," shouts the Pardoner, "for Old Sarum and Salisbury."

The velocity of the aircraft makes the wooden withies in the wings sing a plainsong and the wind whistle madrigals in Gog's ears. Again his inverted gaze sees the name of LUDD imprinted on Stonehenge, but as he rises straight over the rubbled mound of Old Sarum, he sees his own name and the name of the giant god of the Celts rearing from the landscape. The ruin of the old keep makes a broken ⊥ or G in alignment with the rearing ⊥ of Salisbury Cathedral spire, a marker 404 feet high for the parallel gashes of the ditches that surround Old Sarum, crossed by the line of the entrance causeway and forming the pattern of ⫟ that signifies the O and middle letter of GOG in the Gogam script.

"GOG!" shouts Gog. "I have read my name."

The aircraft seems to be directed straight at the spire, but passes a gossamer away from the east of the monument. A flock of great white birds scatter from the path of the infernal projectile which flies faster than Lucifer across the cathedral city.

"The birds by the spire mean the bishop is dying," the Pardoner yells. "Mercy on him, O Lord."

"And us," Gog intones.

They whirl on to the wooded clump of Clearbury Ring, then straight to the Iron Age camp at Frankenbury, where trees hide the outworks, and the ley force dies in the blanket of the woods. The wings shudder and begin to glide to the south-west, where the evening lamplights of Southampton are reflected on its channel running out to the Solent and the Isle of Wight. The landscape is ordered now in old Euclid's vision of a classical world, a regularity of square and crescent and terrace and close, of avenue and High Street and road and lane, of brick box and tile roof and garage and garden shed, the cautious geometry of suburb and resort and retirement homes that imposes on the south of England its measure and negation of the shape of forest and down.

The spire of Winchester Cathedral is a foresight ahead, and the batswings bank northwards as the force of the fourth Druid ley line catches them in its invisible grip above the ragged earth circle of Tilbury Ring to fling them over a long barrow towards the little spire of St Bartholomew's Church in Winchester in the middle of King Alfred's Palace, then over the Hyde Gate where the bones of the lawgiver king cry up to Gog, "Misrule, misrule, why are Magog and Mammon the lords of modern misrule?" Over the Lady Chapel of the great cathedral which sits as a stone *Titanic* lodged on its log raft over the hidden springs below. Sink, cathedral, sink down on rotten wood to bog and oblivion, but seek salvation in the deep diver now working in the bowels of the marsh, putting in handfuls of concrete year after year to sustain such a fantastic folly to the glory of God. The aircraft hurtles over the hills on the ley line until it is caught in the etherial whirlpool above St Catherine's Hill or Wheel. Gog and the Pardoner are spun seven times widdershins round the Mizmaze of the turf labyrinth in the middle of the earthworks, so Gog cannot decipher the cryptic lines drawn upon the old ground before he is flung off over the remains of a bowl barrow north towards the Thames Valley.

A south wind sustains the batswings, sweeping the aircraft up in its currents three thousand feet above the countryside. Necklets of streetlights make chains of bright dots on the darkling land . . . seeming to infinity, man's answer to the Milky Way. But these are as specks of stars in the space of the grey and ebon and nigger of the skerried ground, blocked and patched with copse and field, curved with knoll and whorled with gulley, only the satin-black sheen of rivers trailing their serpentine ribbons across the shades of the geography.

"Seven Barrows," shouts the Pardoner, "where the Wansdyke used to end. Beacon Hill Camp and Combe Gibbet. Then over the Thames to Dragon Hill, where you shall understand, if you have the understanding."

The fifth of the Druid ley lines locks the wings into its directional charge above a standing tumulus crowned by a post making a $\perp$ in the evening, then impels the craft over the lines of the triple earthworks on Farncombe Down that imprint a black $+\!+\!+$ on the surface of the earth, then again the flying machine swoops over the $\perp$ of an impaled tumulus so that Gog can read his name for the second time conjured in Druid script upon the ground. The giant horseshoe of the ditches round Uffington Castle suggest good fortune for the airflight, but over the flat top of Dragon's Hill, a paralysing beam, a numbing ray strikes up from the barren soil where no grass grows. The aerial craft hovers motionless above the dim plateau of the hilltop.

"St George killed the dragon here," the Pardoner says. "Where the dragon's blood was spilt, nothing has ever grown. You can see the beast's shape sketched on the chalk slope. They call him a white horse, the fools, but he is a dragon, and we are held in the dragon's current of his death."

Racked on his high grid, Gog can barely discern the arcs and jigsaw pieces of the White Horse of Uffington, cut into the turf of its hill. Horse or dragon it may be, beast of mythology it is. And as he closes his eyes on the hilltop below, Gog sees a firework exploding in spirals and trails of light as if the night were breathing out the fiery breath of dragons to light the lines of their flight on their scaly wings across the landscape. In the Chinese geomancy of *feng shiu*, Gog knows that no tomb or house is built along a dragon path, only where the natural shape of the land favours the site. And the current of the White Dragon that holds their craft in air begins to sap Gog's grip on the metal grid, to drain his blood, until his mind reels inside his skull. His fingers slip as he faints, but while he loosens his hold on safety and sense, he hears the Pardoner intone:

"By Saint George and Saint Michael, the slayers of dragons, by Saint Christopher, the traveller's friend, and by the holy Bladud, who flew above Ludgate, get thee gone, foul serpent, thy blood shall have power no more. Amen."

At the end of this prayer, the flying machine is suddenly thrown away as a flat stone, skimming above the hills and bouncing in ducks-and-drakes over the cross on the spire of St Mary's Church in Uffington. Then the ley force releases the aerial navigators, and they coast southwards on a balmy breeze towards the end of their journey.

"The last two of the Druid leys cross over Avebury," the Pardoner instructs Gog. "As you may know, it is the largest and most ancient of all the megalithic circles – with Silbury Hill, the twin hub and radial centre of the whole Druid earth sculpture. You may see the serpent's paths of the old dragon avenues that once snaked from the stone enclosure. The antiquary Stukeley drew them –"

"I have seen his drawing," Gog says, "the curving avenues leading to the circles dedicated to the sun and the moon."

"You may not oversee them now, pardon me, but you will see them truly because you have the hindsight of the seer Stukeley who saw truly and has passed his truth on to the hidden eye of those that may still read the land. For what was seen truly is visible now and will be seen even if it is no longer there."

The force of the sixth Druid ley line grips the sky travellers above the rough double diamond of the coal-black earthworks of Martinsell Hill Camp, and launches them over a crossroads and a long barrow and the Wansdyke and the Ridgeway to the north-east arc of the circle of great Sarsen stones, so many of them shattered by the Herostratus of Avebury, Tom Robinson the builder of the village within the sanctuary, who used burning-pits to shatter the megaliths and turn them into building-blocks for cottage walls. Yet even now, Gog can perceive the size of the black blobs marking the sacred circle below and follow the pits and stone projections in the fields around that suggest the serpent avenues. In the gloaming, his eyes see what his mind imagines, the inner vision of memory more accurate than the evidence of corneas, the wish fulfilment truer than the fact.

Over the carbuncles of tumuli on the dark slopes, the craft is directed to Windmill Hill, crowned by three earth circles with three more arcs of moats stretching down the apron of its flank. For the last time, the ley force sloughs the airmen off to float easy through the night air. Real bats whizz by, faster than the tracer bullets of the Devil. An owl hoots to see such an intruder in its dark realm. But the skymen reach the heights above the double ditches of Bincknoll Castle, and the radial beam of the seventh and last Druid ley line draws them over a well and the churchyard of St Peter's at Broad Hinton back to the edge of the Avebury ring of stones and on to Silbury Hill, where an updraught pushes them high over the vast cupcake where the Druid oak beacon pole once signalled their celestial ways with its bush of mistletoe, then down by the Kennet long barrow where seven black stones guard the inner burial chamber, and on to the pitch-blende channel and back of the Wansdyke where the flight began.

"Down, down!" the Pardoner commands, but the Druid force hears him not and hurtles the craft towards the end of the seventh ley line, the huge ellipse of Mardon Henge, overgrown with gorse and stunted trees. In sudden dive down, the aerial contrivance plunges as the earth-power fails.

"'Ware, 'ware," the Pardoner howls. "Pardon me."

The craft crashes into a fence of metal hurdles, which break through the wooden withies on its wings and shred their skin-cover to tatters. The grid under the flying machine crushes the Pardoner's legs, trapping him beneath its weight. Gog is flung clear into a bed of nettles that sting him into fury and self-pity so that he rises, crying and yelling at his fate. But he hears the Pardoner whimpering under the carriage of the crashed machine.

"Pardon me, help me. My legs, they are broken. Help me."

As Gog wrestles with the wreckage of the aircraft, he finds that he cannot move it. Four linked and rooted metal hurdles, shaped as ⋈ in the sign of Magog, have cut into the batswings and engaged the lower grid in an immovable mantrap. Sweat and strain as Gog may, he cannot budge the obstruction of the hurdles. So he returns to the imprisoned Pardoner, who is whimpering in the night.

"I will go for help," Gog says. "What is this place?"

"Mardon Henge," the Pardoner says. "Pardon me, I will wait. I must. But next time, I will not fly with the batswings and the Devil. I will take a donkey with Jesus Christ and reach the New Jerusalem."

Gog struggles away over the ditch from Mardon Henge back towards the Wansdyke where a batswing first brushed his skull and the Pardoner came to fly him on the Druid flight paths over their ancient places in Wessex. He can hardly discover his way in the dark, he stumbles and falls more often than he can tell until he reaches the top of Knap Hill where his aerial journey began. And there he takes a last toss that bangs his head into a slight concussion. And in his dream he sees the soft and springing south land overprinted with the many lines set to mark out its given meanderings, the ley lines stamped by barrow and turf and butt, by cairn and cromlech and dolmen, by garn and how and knapp, by mary and moat and mound and mount, by toot and tump and tumulus, by bury and castle and fort and knoll, in order to define the straight tracks of the currents of the underearth; then the Roman roads that the legions trod in their wars against the men of the forest; then the canals that conjoined the evasive rivers by their grid of locks and waterways; then the iron routes of the railways that divided the subtle harmonies of meadow and down; then the macadam and the tarmac of the motorways already now abuilding for the petrol-driven chariots of modern times; then the gaspipes taking over the dragon paths with their fiery breaths, while below and above ground the electric wires in hidden ducts and on poles and pylons cut the lower air into segments of space as they carry the streams of particles in counterstance to the buried charges of the inner earth-lines; then the network of sewers to flush away the dung of the middens and the slurry of the cattle, polluting the underground wells and streams while water-pipes wash diluted chemicals into the mouths of the drinkers; and, more frequent on their flight paths than the Druids, are the high aeroplanes that leave white tracings and residues in the unsullied heaven. That is the vision that Gog remembers when he wakes in the morning in an agony of nettlerash and takes the bus back to Cambridge. He only thinks of the Pardoner when he is halfway back to the university, and then dismisses the thought as a figment of his imagination, which has too many fragments and fantasies already within its constructions. "Pardon me," Gog murmurs to nobody in particular, and pardons himself for abandoning the Pardoner, if such he be, to his fate.

The True History of King Ludd

(as submitted to Professor Maximilian Mann,
King's College, Cambridge, on September 20th, 1937)

Nottinghamshire, 1817

The London delegate was a peeled raw shrimp of a fellow, dressed in his black suit, his face both pasty and wrinkled, his hair slicked to his skull when he took his wig off and hung it on the knob of his chair. He joked to the white false hair with its big empty mouth hanging open beside him.

"Oh, you are a witness and a rogue, Sir Wig. You're listening to all we say. Perhaps you'll off to the Home Secretary and betray us all. Run with the *hair* . . ." the London delegate winked. "And hunt with the hounds, O treacherous Whig!"

The Nottingham delegates did not laugh. What were puns to stocking-knitters? Joking about the rising was putting the evil eye on it. And Brandreth was hot to start.

"There's no treachery here," Brandreth said. "Devil a word did the magistrates hear of Ned Ludd and his captains in Nottingham. Yet there were informers thick as midges in May." He looked round the other local delegates, the old reformer Tom Bacon, Turner, large Ludlam, fat Weightman and the rest, empty faces looking back at him, solid as walls. "We know each other, you see. Villagers. Nobody talks to foreigners, and that means over the hill."

The London delegate winked again and stroked his wig, arranging the curls.

"Yet, my radical friends," he said, "what use is a rising in Nottingham, if there is not one in London? There are seventy thousand men ready to take the Tower. Birmingham is ripe, Derby on the boil. Unless all rise together, we'll all be buried together. Look at your Ned Ludd. You smashed a few factories, you had your wages rise for a year, and now you're back in the gutter, worse off than ever. If Ludd had got to London, why then, he would be King Ludd and all England was yours, the machines were all broken for ever. Live and learn. Union or confusion."

Large Ludlam broke the silence that usually followed the London delegate's speeches. He had the gift of words, the

Londoner, but glib words that seemed to trap rather than reassure.

"What proof?" Ludlam said. "How do we know all's set for the ninth of June?"

"You've my word on it," the London delegate said. "As my name's Oliver."

"How do we know?" Ludlam said.

"I don't carry papers," Oliver said. "You Luddites here, you weren't ever found out because nothing was written and nobody spoke. My credentials are my neck, stuck straight in the noose." Like a cat, Oliver pounced and pointed at Ludlam. "You, sir. Perhaps you're a spy. My life is in your hands. I am instigating a national rising. I don't deny it. I am sent to you by Hunt and the London radicals, as you know. How should I hope to escape if the rising does not happen? I'll hang for it. And I shall not speak. Lord, could the rising have got this far, four days to go before all England is aflame for liberty, if I could not hold my tongue?"

The web of words settled on their doubts again, netted them, held them in the hope and snare of national conspiracy. Fat Weightman spoke.

"Yorkshire you've been?"

"Yes. Ten thousand men will rise there and take Huddersfield. Even the military are on our side. They'll hand over the barracks."

"You've not heard of Thornhill Lees, then?"

"Where's that?" Oliver asked. His face was bland.

"General Byng took all the delegates there with his troops yesterday. He was told of it. You were there, too. You got away. Treachery, they say."

"Where did you hear of this?" Oliver said.

"From t'other delegate who slipped the troops," Fat Weightman said. "Spy, he said you were."

Oliver hardly paused before answering. As always, he seemed in command, especially of himself, even of others.

"Yes, I was at Thornhill Lees. And that is the first lesson of insurrection. Never tell where you have been. Feign ignorance. Is that right, Brandreth?"

"Aye," Brandreth said. His nose had begun to cock at the sniff of treachery.

"I got away," Oliver said, "and I came back here. There's work to do, and I must back to London tonight to see all is done, and done right for the rising."

"Someone told," Weightman said. "General Byng and the troops was there. Someone told."

"Yes, someone did," Oliver said. "I was lucky to get away."

"Aye," Brandreth said. "Luck's a fine friend, but a general's a finer friend. You got away. There'll be no rising in Yorkshire then?"

"There will be," Oliver said. "The Thornhill Lees delegates were only *part* of it. A decoy, you may say. I tell you more than I should."

"Perhaps you'd better tell," Brandreth said. He looked across the room to Large Ludlam, who could break a head with his fist as easy as he could break a machine with his Enoch. King Ludd's cousin, they said, in the great days, but who could prove it? Perhaps it was just the name.

"I knew there was treachery in Yorkshire," Oliver said. "So the true section, the good Yorkshire delegates, they're still free. Not a soul knows of them, but I. Huddersfield will still fall, I tell you, on the ninth. I never let the good ones near the rotten ones at Thornhill Lees – not all of them rotten, but where the traitors were, and they fell to treachery. But like you, citizen Brandreth . . ." Here Oliver lifted his pale nose in a little parody of Brandreth's cocking of his beak. "I can sniff treason in the wind. And I take precautions. The way out of the trap, the splitting of the radicals, not telling one of the other. I am old at this work, citizens. Trust me."

Large Ludlam spoke again.

"Old at what work?" he said. "The work of Judas?"

Oliver laughed.

"You're a biblical man," he said. "Old at Ruth's work. I toil amid the alien corn."

"We're all Methodists and Baptists here," Fat Weightman said. "You'll swear on the Book it's the truth you say?"

"Lord's word on it," Oliver said. "My hand on the Book."

"We're not fond of being hanged for nowt in Nottingham," Brandreth said. "That's Yorkshire for you. You'd swear by your nose that there are no spies here?"

Oliver looked each of the delegates in the eye, turning his slick head.

"None that I can see," he said.

"And I can see," Brandreth said, looking at Oliver.

"None that you can see," Oliver said, then turned to look at his wig. "Except this pernicious Whig!"

Nobody laughed. The Nottingham men looked at each other. Then Brandreth rose. There was an impatience in him. Even at his stocking-frame, he never left a job half-finished. His wife would have to feed him standing at the knitting. Sixteen hours while the light lasted he would labour without a break. Well begun was not half-done for him. The thing was to get it over with, to be done.

"Words," he said, "words! We've been planning for this six years since King Ludd went back to Sherwood Forest. We'll take Nottingham Castle on the ninth, wipe out all debt, have all our delegates in a free parliament in a week. The Midlands will rise and rule themselves, London or no."

"I'll be in command of the Tower and the City in three days," Oliver said. "Count on me."

"Hurry then," Brandreth said. "It's a long road to London." He sat again, his sudden strength sapped.

"And your men will meet at Ripley?"

"Pentridge," Brandreth said. "Under the Peak. We'll march in and give the people time to rise in Nottingham when they hear of our coming."

"Pentridge," Oliver said. "You should not have told me that. The first rule of insurrection, remember. Do not talk. But as there are no spies here . . ."

He rose from his chair and put on his wig. It did not add much to his little height, but somehow the action of putting it on above the black suit made him seem to the sitting men as if he were the judge above them all. "No matter. Enough is said. I will go now. We rise on the ninth. Act, and liberty is ours. Fail and we are all dead men. Citizens, I count on you."

Oliver left abruptly. No one stirred from his seat. They looked at each other in a long silence. Brandreth rose again.

"There's a job to be done," he said.

The men nodded and rose too.

"Aye," they said.

Now Tom Bacon, the thinking one, the old reformer who still had his life to show for it, spoke for the first time.

"I'll be there," he said.

Bacon was not there on June 9th. Perhaps the rain kept him at home or sent him fishing after pike in the Trent. But Large Ludlam was there, and his larger cousin, the smith Ned Griffin who fought at fourteen at Trafalgar, and the Turners and the Weightmans and most of the men from the villages under the Peak, Ripley and South Wingfield and Pentridge, where Brandreth sat in the inn, ticking off the men's names, picking out the few who had a weapon to take, scythe or fowling-piece or mattock. There was no cease in the rain, a drizzling and drenching pour from the grey clouds which the Peak seemed to tear apart so that the heavens spilled their watery guts on to the rising below.

Fourteen miles in the rain was a long march to Nottingham for the three hundred men, and their courage was doused with their hats, their hope was as sopping as their boots. Only Brandreth seemed to get more determined on the long trudge. The raindrops were ale to him, a soaking was his drinking.

"Roast beef!" he shouted. "Free beef and a trip down the Trent. Nottingham will feast us tomorrow! We'll have the keys of the city and the taverns! Praise the clouds! They are we! Northern clouds to sweep up all England! All others shall be shot!"

Now they are at the farm where they know Farmer Platt has a gun, and the door is locked and the windows blockaded, and none's to answer the shouted summons, none's to give up the gun and beer for the thirst of the marchers, none shows himself as Brandreth lifts his fowling-piece in anger, but suddenly there's a foolish fearful face at the window, then the blast of Brandreth's piece and the glass is broken and the foolish man is faceless, and it's first blood to the rising, only it's all Brandreth's work, and the villagers begin to slip away, muttering, "Murder, murder." Shall England not fall into their arms without a shot? Blood is blood and should not stain their cause which is justice and fair wages.

Through the night they trudge, and through the rain, fewer

and fewer of them, and the villagers in their way bolt the doors, though they blow their horns and fire their guns, making the noise of an army, not a couple of hundred. By morning, the smoke of Nottingham's near, and the marchers look out to the city gates, waiting for the women to flock out with flowers and hymns, and the bells to peal their welcome, *Work is Rising, Wages Rising, Men are Rising to Set Us Free!* But there is nobody to meet them, only the silence of the stubborn walls. Then the sound of troops, clink of metal, rattle of stirrups, shouts of command, and forty Hussars swing out of the city and ride towards them, armoured and plumed, sabres at the ready. Is this the key of the city, Brandreth? Or the bloody way to the keys of heaven? The horses trot up quick as nightmares, they toss their heads and strike fear from the stones, the Hussars high and gleaming, ready to hack and maim.

So the marchers begin to fall aside, run away, hide in the ditches, throwing their fowling-pieces and scythes into thickets and nettle-patches. "We were not there, Your Honour, never, Your Worship, just come out for the mowing, Your Reverend, have mercy, Your Grace." But nobody's asking for explanations now, just prisoners, and the Hussars ride down the running men and tie their hands with leather straps and lead them back to Nottingham Castle, Brandreth and Large Ludlam and Turner and Fat Weightman and thirty more, even Tom Bacon who has gone fishing, all in for treason. But Ned Griffin is gone, as if he never were.

The trial is a showpiece with Oliver hiding in Derby, passing himself off as a Doctor Miniver, quack and apothecary, now claiming to heal distempers of the body politic, not to cause them. But he's not called as a witness, the Crown's too scared that its spy will be shown as the ringleader, not the informer. And Brandreth is doomed anyway, for the killing of a man. But Turner and Ludlam and Weightman must be executed too, though Tom Bacon and the rest are let live on a plea of guilty. There's no mercy to be had for the four in Oliver's web, no mercy on earth, though in heaven, God will surely forgive, for His Son knew his Oliver too.

As for the informer, he vanishes and comes again, for he is always with us, instigator and betrayer, the traitor at the hearth. And as for Brandreth, Turner, Fat Weightman and Large Ludlam, they go to the scaffold, silent and unrepentant; though by the gibbet, some say Ludlam looks up in hope to a huge shadow that looms on the prison wall and hangs over the executioner and the soldiers.

"He is come again from the forest!" he exclaims.

"Ludd?" the chaplain cries in terror. "King Ludd?"

There is a moment of fear and the soldiers look to their muskets, but the shadow passes as a cloud over the sun, and the chaplain becomes holy again.

"Call to God, my son. Not Ludd."

No hand stops their execution, but their bodies are not found again. Some say the government does not want the relics of martyrs; some say it is the work of the Resurrectionists; and others say that Brandreth and Turner and Fat Weightman and Large Ludlam have gone to Sherwood or Savernake Forest to join their king and General Ludd, and they will live for ever in the trees until the time comes for the final rising when misrule shall be no more and each man's hand shall work his own loom for a day's pay and brother shall deal with brother according to the promise that even the lion shall lie down with the lamb. But that is the last men talk of Ludd for eight years until he throws his hat in the ring for gold.

Gogmagog Hills, 1825

The magistrates of Lincoln were stroppy and threatened to send in the constables, so the purse-holders moved the ring over the county border on to the chalk grassland of the Gogmagog Hills, where the twin giants of ancient time were buried under the turf. The coach-drivers and the cabmen and the hacks were doubling their guineas and trebling their tipple as they lurched with the thousands of the fancy in carriages and chaises seven miles along the lane to where the new ring was being hammered home, four stakes struck deep at the corner of the twenty-four foot square of ropes that would set George Edward Griffin that the fancy gave the monicker of King Ludd in bare-knuckle battle with the Gas-lit Man till one of them could rise no more from his second's knee. A hundred guineas a side, winner take all, pocket full of gold and your enemy's favour knotted round your neck above your own. A match, of sorts.

When King Ludd's billycock hat was pitched into the ring by his second, Belcher, the London swells set up such a chattering and a hissing that even the starlings flew for their lives. A hick like Ludd to beat the Gas-lit Man! Why, the cockney pug was quick as the flare of a flaming jet. You'd cough up your gullet with one whiff of his fist near your throat or breadbasket! Three to one on the Gas-lit Man against the yokel! No takers, until Ludd himself followed Spring, his other second, into the ring and unknotted his red kerchief from his neck and tied it to a corner stake and stripped off jerkin and shirt to leave himself green britches bare. Then the city mob was mousehole hushed as the cockneys saw the hairy arms of Ludd, knotted and sinewed and runnelled as the bark of twin oak branches, fists as scarred as old lopped sapling stumps, head hunched into wide shoulders as wise and downy as an owl on a tree top, massive trunk rooted into loins and heavy thighs without weakening of waist, large feet on the grass of the ring flat and planted

164

as market stones, saying *This Man Is Of This Place And Shall Not Budge Nor Fall.*

The Norfolk fancy huzza'd to see their man and took the bets, driving the odds down to 5–2 and even 9–4. Six thousand guineas were wagered before Oliver and Dutch Sam chucked the high hat of the Gas-lit Man into the ring and brought in their noble bruiser, while the city mob yelled and bellowed like a Smithfield Market to see its bloke knot his black favour above Ludd's red kerchief on the stake, then strip himself to the waist above his black silk breeches and black soft shoes. What a sight to make Phidias fumble and slip his chisel! Growing from loins slender as a column, a chest spread out in a Corinthean capital firm with muscle and moulding into two long arms fit for Achilles to reach out and wreak revenge on all sundry and handy. The Gas-lit Man had a head that seemed helmeted by nature, bald without crest and bronzed by sun and wind, its metal cheeks making the eyes sunken and the nose flattened, so that he peered out of his eyes through a visor of bone and flesh. No hope for Ludd of putting those ogles into mourning, no chance of bruising those backward peepers black and blue! Stone-bodied and armoured by the bony flanges of his skull, the Gas-lit Man breathed fire. "I'll gut and giblet 'im! I'll crack 'is bones for marrow! I'll crush 'is head and fib 'is face to rashers."

The battle immemorial of the giants of the Gogmagog hills is fought again.

Round One. At the bell, the Gas-lit Man dances out like an Angelo, dukes forward in the gentleman's way, and he's in with a bodier and facer at Ludd with his left, a one and a two so quick that the hick giant can't even stop them. Ludd hardly moves from the centre of the ring, but he pivots on his right heel round and round, left foot planted to face his foe, fists low and ready, no more wary of his daring enemy than of a gnat or a flea. But the Gas-lit Man's close in again, his left planting a doubler on Ludd's ivories, and the claret begins to trickle out of the corner of the giant's mouth. Ludd hasn't swung a mauley yet, he's circling slow and watchful, seeking a slip.

"Five to one, Gas-lit, give him a right in the chops." But the Gas-lit Man flashes in with his left for the third time and thrice, one-two-three on the bony bristle over Ludd's left eye. The giant's brow takes the first blow, the skin slices open on the knife-edge of the Gas-lit Man's thumbnail, and a flap of flesh is a sudden second bloody lid to Ludd's eye.

"Blinkered, by God!" Dutch Sam yells from his corner, as the red sheets down over Ludd's face and shoulder.

Five minutes the round has gone and still Ludd hasn't planted a blow, swivelling round slow and steady, facing the Gas-lit Man with his good eye and mauleys low. Then as the Gas-lit Man swoops in for another brace of facers, Ludd catches him round the ribs and hugs him dreadfully. There is a thin scream of whistle and breath as Ludd crushes, then a crack of rib sharp as a dry breaking branch, then a cross-buttock by Ludd that pitches the Gas-lit Man arse over tip like hay on a fork, and he's down and flat out with Ludd falling like a tree on his body to pound him to clay.

At this end of Round One, Oliver and Dutch Sam have to carry their hero back to his corner and slip a drop of water-of-life between his ivories. But even the brandy doesn't make the Gas-lit Man sit up until Oliver damn near severs his left ear with his teeth, making his boy wake with the pain and get off Dutch Sam's knee to meet the bell.

Over in Ludd's corner, Belcher sets to work with the sponge dipped in gin and Spring tries the beeswax at the corner of Ludd's bloody eye to keep the peeper open. But it don't suit. "You'll have to fight like a pirate, cove," Belcher says. "Eye-patch and all. But give him the blunderbuss, Ludd. Show him who's King."

Round Two. Ludd goes to the corner where the favours flutter in the wind, black and red, and he leans back on the stake, his arms on the ropes, waiting for the Gas-lit Man to come back and mill blow to blow and chest to chest. But the Gas-lit Man is slower now, puffling and pained, and he hangs back till fat Sir Sam, the referee, tells Ludd to come out and fight. "Not game, the yokel! No bottom! A tenner to a turnip on the cockney cove!"

Backed by hissing and booing, Ludd comes out and puts in a facer with his right at the Gas-lit Man, which would quite stove in his helmet, only the Gas-lit Man shows his science and ducks the blow and peppers Ludd with four bodiers, right and left, right and left, before he's out and away, more shuffle than dance now, but Ludd's panting like an old bellows at the anvil, and he's mad enough to plod forward in cold pursuit of his tormentor.

Now the Gas-lit Man's backing and Ludd's flicking his head to take the blows on forehead or blunt nose, and the gore from his gashed eyebrow is spraying the fancy in the front row like the plague of bloody rain in Egypt. But Ludd's still coming on, trying to trap the slippery cockney cove in a corner, but it's rat-tat-tap in his bread-basket for the sixth time, and Ludd's winded and stopped, and as he shakes his mop, the blood gets into his good eye, and he's blinded. He should go down, but he don't. He flails about him to disguise he's done, but the Gas-lit Man waits out of range, then he plants a right like a pole-axe on Ludd's right ear and fells him on the grass, dead as a bull in the butcher's.

So it is Eclipse to a lame donkey on the Gas-lit Man, as Belcher and Spring try to get Ludd ready for the next round in their corner. His ear's like a purple cabbage on his skull and his face is a raw side of beef, but he's sponged and pinched and pummelled upright when the bell goes, ding-ding-ding, for the funeral.

Round Three. As the heroes come up to the bell, the Almighty opens his sluices on the fancy and the rain comes down, tom-cats and bulldogs, howling and shrieking with wind and woe. Never so bad a storm since Cribb beat the black Molyneaux for the first time, peerless Champion of England, while the mob got a soaking that was worse than the Ark before Ararat. Still, the fresh sky water washes the blood off Ludd's eyes quick as it appears and the cold raindrops staunch the flow, while the shivers are smelling salts to the Gas-lit Man, as he wonderfully revives with the drenching and the drowning. So it's all slip and slide now on the slick grass, as the heroes lunge and parry and thrust at each other, with the heavens open above and the blackhorse clouds riding through the lightning and the thunder fit to split your eardrums. Four facers from the Gas-lit Man nobble Ludd till he gets his foe in a clincher, then hugs the cockney's bald helmet head under his arm as strong as a yoke, then fibs him dreadfully about mouth and chops and eyes till the Gas-lit Man hooks him with a cross-leg on to the grass.

Round Four to Sixteen. The fancy did not view the contest overmuch during these rounds, because it was black as midnight between the thunder-flashes and every one of the swells was trying to bury himself under a coat or a tree and keep the water out of his peepers and the wagers in his pocket. In the ring, Ludd and the Gas-lit Man fought on, with the rallies going in favour of the hugging giant, who would catch the cockney as he slipped on the wet grass, and give him a cracking in a clinch or a fibbing and a fall. Three to one on the yokel, and no takers.

Round Seventeen. The sun flashes through the dark like a Congreve rocket and the clouds course away to hell and under, and the fancy come out to see Ludd pinning the Gas-lit Man in the corner where the black and red favours are knotted to the stake. It's a sovereign to a herring that Ludd will pound in the cockney's head for barley bread, but as the right mauley of the giant strikes down the final hammer-blow from heaven, the Gas-lit Man wriggles and weaves halfway between the ropes, so that Ludd's fist smashes on to the stake and chops it in twain, and the sound of his finger-bones breaking and knuckles crunching is caught up in the splintering of the timber and the splitting of the stake. The Gas-lit Man then butts Ludd in the belly with his skull, and both slip down and walk back to their seconds, with the ring broken at one corner now and the contest fifty-five minutes long.

Belcher feels Ludd's right hand and Ludd does not say a word, but a tear of blood runs out his closed left eye and he bites more claret from the edge of his lip. "I'll throw in the towel," Belcher says. "You'll not box with a broken hand." But Ludd takes the towel in his good left hand and puts it between his ivories and tears the coward rag in two. "Let him maul on," Spring says, "till he's done."

Rounds Eighteen to Thirty-two. Even when Carter beat Spring or the Game Chicken fought thirty rounds with one hand, never did the fancy see a man take so much execution as Ludd that storm-bright day. Round after round the Gas-lit Man came out to pound and pulp the giant into quitting, until there wasn't a patch on his body not red or black like the favours on the broken stake. His arms were mottled like a blood-pudding from the milling, his face was a mummer's mask of scarlet from the rallies. Yet he would not go down, round after round, till his legs were chopped from under him by a blow from the Gas-lit Man, or he slipped from weakness on to his knees. He was game through and through, all the fancy declared. Like the fire that attacks the old log, blackening it and burning it, making charcoal of its life, ashes its veins, so the Gas-lit Man won fourteen rounds in a row off Ludd, who only raised his left hand to defend himself and would not go down.

Round Thirty-three. Belcher did not want to let his man rise for the bell, but Ludd rose and swept out his good arm to knock his second out of the ring, and went forward. It was five minutes short of two hours since the first round.

Stay up, Ned. Stay up.
Blind, blind, blind! See like a mole. Hear! Feel! Listen!
Ah, pain. One – two. One – two. Four in the ribs. Dull
    mind.
Stay up, Ludd. Stay up.
Ah, the bad ear! Split skull, crack sense! Nail the brain!
Flail fists. Swing, swing!
Where are you? Where?
Circle now. Crook left arm. Set the trap. Blind bait.
A doubler in the ribs. Wait. Not done, never done.
    Ludd's not down.
Ah, clout and close, fool! Crook him by the neck! Ludd's
    not down!
Stay up, stay up. If he slips, the bell to save him. Stay
    up!
Strangle him. Lock him in the left arm, choke him, throat
    on bone!
Pulp away, masher! Break nose, break eyes, break ears,
    break, break! But don't break the hold.
Blind, blind, choke, choke! Stay up, Ludd! Let him hang
    on the gibbet of a crooked arm.
What's that? Fat Sir Sam. "Break, break!" Damn you,
    break, sir?
Break?
Fall then, lockfast, neck tight, noose bone. Fall!

When the bell sounded for the end of the Thirty-third Round, the seconds came out to get their men. It took Belcher and Spring a full minute to break the lock that Ludd had put on the Gas-lit Man's neck, and they led him back blind to his corner, his whole face and body and feet crimson as a clown, and his green britches soaked black with sweat and blood.

When Oliver and Dutch Sam got the Gas-lit Man back to his corner, his head lay on his shoulder as on a shelf. When the bell went, it was still laying there. They reckoned he had his neck broken, but on the roaring of the fancy for the blinded Ludd, led to the centre of the ring to have his smashed head held high and the red and black favours knotted round his bloody neck, then the neck of the Gas-lit Man lifted with a click, and he came up on his feet and moved forwards his dukes held high, ready for another round although it was all over. "Just like a bloody steam-engine," Oliver said, admiring, though he himself was a pug who had to have his boiler blown before he would stop.

So the Gas-lit Man held up the ropes for the blind Ludd to be led out of the ring, and though he was offered a purse of two hundred guineas to fight King Ludd again, he said he would keep to his pub, the Crown and Anchor in Eastcheap. Something was broken inside him, he said, like a jemmy in the works.

PART THREE

Cambridge, late September 1937
France, October 1937 – September 1938
Prague, September 1938

14

"Boxing," Maximilian Mann sneers. "Fisticuffs, and written in the style of a Victorian hack sports reporter. What relevance has pugilism to the workers' revolution? Do you really believe Joe Louis has anything to do with the Luddites, or indeed with Lenin?"

"Paul Robeson has, sir," Gog says.

"Singers are no more capable of conducting revolutionary change than boxers. You are not writing history, Griffin, you are writing fiction. There is not a shred of scientific evidence behind your assertions about the early origins of the Luddites, which you put in the form of historical romance and parody."

As Gog looks down at his two new chapters of *The True History of King Ludd*, now covered with red ink, he can see that his supervisor is also guilty of parody. "SUBLIME PUGILISM AND NONSENSE" is scrawled across the account of the prize-fight in the Gogmagog Hills. Gog wonders how to justify himself to the quiz of the supercilious Mann.

"George Edward Griffin, or Ned Ludd, really was my great-grandfather, sir. My grandmother Maria, his daughter, swears he was. And so, I see my thesis on the Luddites more in the nature of a family history – and told in the form of a family saga rather than in a series of biographies. I believe, particularly in the case of kin, that the author has the right – and the power – to be present where his relations were. A sort of audition on his ancestors. It's in the blood."

"Kinship, you assert, gives you the ability to travel through time and be a fly on the wall during the repression in England after Waterloo?"

"Something like that," Gog says. "An affinity, at least, for time past because my family were there. That's why I write *The True History of King Ludd* in the form of historical fiction so I don't have to confuse technical historians who expect all the apparatus of facts and footnotes. But it is still

173

true history, sir, if you see what I mean, presented in the form of fiction.'

"I do not see what you mean," Mann says, rising to turn his back on Gog and look over the quadrangle of King's at the indifferent pinnacles of the college chapel. "I am a scientific historian. If you want to study English here, you should go to Richards or that inconsiderable Leavis. Though I beg leave to doubt that either of them teaches historical romantic fiction." He turns, stooping forward from the bright window, his head bent judiciously from his thin body like an archbishop's crook. "I do not think I can act as your supervisor any longer, Griffin. Nor can I recommend that you complete your thesis within the requirements and disciplines of the History faculty at Cambridge. You may be more suited to be a purveyor of novelettes to shopgirls than a researcher into the history of the workers' revolt."

"I have a piece coming out which may interest you more," Gog says. "It is a new Modest Proposal taken from Jonathan Swift's original one. But instead of proposing that we eat Irish babies to solve the famine there, I propose that we eat British workers to solve mass unemployment."

"You are too large, Griffin, to be an enfant terrible. While you may wish to *épater les bourgeois*, do remember that you may cause offence to the workers and those who truly support their interests. You say this piece is coming out?"

"Putney Bowles is printing it in a special issue on unemployment in *Granta*," Gog says. "Isn't it funny? Because Granta – the stream not the magazine – was what the giant Gogmagog Hill fell in love with in the *Poly-olbion*, except she spurned him."

"I never cease to marvel at the wealth of irrelevance inside your head, Griffin." Mann sounds more annoyed than usual. "Putney never told me about this special issue of *Granta*. I hope his formulations on unemployment are correct."

"Marxist? I am sure they are." Gog smiles. "He has such good supervisors on that."

Maximilian Mann's liquid eyes are brilliant in their scrutiny of his erstwhile graduate student Gog.

"If I have been unable to teach you anything, Griffin," he says in a voice fit to scratch silk, "I am sure that you would agree that the fault is not mine. One cannot raise

174

consciousness if the subject has no consciousness whatever to raise. On another matter, your brother Magnus is coming up this week-end. He asked me to tell you he would like to drop in and see you on Saturday evening in spite of some contretemps you may have had over some French *woman*. And if you might ask one or two of your friends to be there – the one or two friends you may have – like that uncouth mathematician Graveling. And Putney, of course, now he has become your printer and editor."

"That's what Ned Ludd did with the prize-money he won in his fight with the Gas-lit Man," Gog says. "He bought old lead type so he could print pamphlets. In the beginning of the revolution is the word, and you'd agree you have to have the means of production to spread the word. So that's what Ludd earned with his fists – the power of print. In the next episode of his *True History*, he prints a pamphlet for Captain Swing in Norfolk in the Bread and Blood riots –"

Maximilian Mann's interruption is as peremptory as the volley of a firing squad.

"I am so sorry that I shall not have the pleasure of reading your future effusions. Why don't you try Victor Gollancz or the Left Book Club? With the Trotskyite and Anarchist rubbish they are printing about the war in Spain, they would adore your populist inventions. Their fictions, after all, they swear are the facts."

Graveling says that he will come to meet Magog on that Saturday evening, but he does not appear in Gog's rooms in Trinity. The conversation between Gog and his half-brother and Putney Bowles is cryptic and uneasy, as if snipers from Seville or Madrid have infiltrated Nevile's Court and are firing through Gog's dormer windows. Julian Bell from Bloomsbury and King's and the Cognoscenti has been killed, following the death in action of James Cornford, the revolutionary poet from Trinity. These two undergraduate martyrs in Spain cause fusillades between Magog and Putney, with Magog seeming to support the Fascist intervention on Franco's side in the Civil War and Putney excoriating it, while Gog tries to keep the truce. Yet he has no need to try. There is a curious understanding between Magog and Putney

while they fight their ideological battles between right and
left, as if they are engaged on a formal dispute without
meaning for Gog's sole benefit, and between them a higher
logic comprehends their contradictions in a perfect meeting
of rare minds. Putney does praise Gog for his Swiftian piece
on the solution to mass unemployment – "That should shock
the litmus-test liberals who prefer pink to blue and won't see
red" – but he leaves arm-in-arm with his intellectual enemy
Magog for the secret meeting of the Cognoscenti in King's,
where all differences are mental games in which the beauty
of word play means that all is forgiven among friends.

Only two minutes after they have left, Colin Graveling
comes past Gog's oak door. He may have been waiting and
watching for the others to leave. Or so Gog thinks after
Graveling has begun to speak.

"I'm sorry, Griffin, I should have told you I wasn't coming.
Friends of mine – *particular* friends of mine – told me your
brother Magnus may be in the Ministry of Defence, but he's
hardly impartial. Pro-German, isn't he?"

Gog looks at the hirsute Graveling with the blackbird
wings of his moustache and decides that honesty is better
than loyalty to a brother that is no brother to him.

"Yes, Magog is pro-German, though he says he's impartial. We were at Spitpoole in July. A lot to do with the
Anglo-German Fellowship. Our mother's all tied up with a
horrible Hun. Von Ribbentrop himself was there."

"I thought so." Graveling is pleased. "Why do you tell me
this?"

"I hate it," Gog says.

"You hate your brother?"

"My half-brother. He hates me. It's got to do with him
being younger and cleverer and with inheritance, of course.
Sibling rivalry is usually only about property, as you know."

"But he's been trying to pump you, hasn't he? About what
we talk about, the new ciphers."

"Chiefly about radar," Gog says. "He's very interested in
that. I don't know what he knows about codes and your new
computers."

"Quite a lot," Graveling says. "And that's why he wanted
you to introduce me to him. Or so my friends say."

"Are your friends in the Ministry of Defence, too?"

176

Graveling does not answer Gog's question.

"That ancient script of yours, the Gogam one you discovered or invented –"

"That can be the same process," Gog says.

"It has been conceptually useful to me. And to some other people." Graveling looks at Gog with the eye of an assessor examining ersatz gold quartz. "Have you any good reason to go to France? Or to Eastern Europe?"

"The best," Gog says. "I'm in love with a French woman. . I took her off my half-brother. And that little squirt, Miniver."

"Interesting." Graveling sucks the ends of his moustache with his bottom lip. "Wheels within wheels. Can you trust her?"

"Not at all. She's totally faithless. An artist's model, I think."

"Good. So your brother Magnus and Miniver and the German faction would think she would be their contact as far as you are concerned. And she would pass on to them anything you tell her."

"If I tell her anything."

"That's the point. They would presume you would tell her everything. Secrets of the bedchamber. Isn't that it?"

"I would never tell Maire anything secret," Gog says. "Anything to do with security or the safety of my country. Unless I wanted the whole world to know about it."

"Deliberate deception," Graveling says, "false leaks, they are part of the apparatus of government. And certainly of intelligence systems. I disapprove, of course. But then I am now engaged, as you may have guessed, on secret and vital work for our country. And I have put your name forward – because of your knowledge of symbols – and because nobody would ever suspect *you* of intelligence –"

Graveling suddenly realises what he has said and bursts out laughing. Gog joins in.

"Intelligence is not my forte," he says.

"I mean," Graveling says, "no one would ever suspect you of *working* for Intelligence. You don't give that sort of impression . . ."

"What could I do? Is it really vital?"

"You will be asked to meet some people. In Paris – and

perhaps in Warsaw or Prague. It is essential for our security against Hitler, that is all I can tell you."

"But I will be briefed."

"No, that is the point. You will not be briefed." Graveling seems to be smiling at Gog in understanding, not in mockery. "You must not know what you are doing. You are interested in Druid writing, the Gogam script, the dots and dashes of ancient communication, not so much in their modern use, like the Morse code or computer language." Graveling reaches into the bulging pocket of his bristling tweed jacket and takes out some perforated cards. He ruffles them, but they seem to be joined together as if he were demonstrating a card trick with a magician's pack. "What do these remind you of?"

"The rolls you put in mechanical pianos," Gog says. "The perforations play the pianola music."

"Excellent." Graveling stuffs the joined cards back in his pocket. "That is all you want to know. What a brilliant cover story! You are intelligence incarnate, Griffin."

"Call me Gog."

"Call me Colin. But not a word to anyone. Not to Magnus or your Maire or even Putney Bowles."

"Of course not. Mum's the word." It is Gog's turn to assess Graveling. "And you. What do you tell the red angel, Rupert Fox? My brother's great friend – and yours."

A sudden blush spreads fire over Graveling's face. Rupert's name is sunburn on his cheeks. He stutters, makes no sense, starts again, choosing his statement with care.

"My companions . . . my close friends . . . are my private affair. They have nothing to do with what I feel for my country."

"I hope so," Gog says. "Passion often confuses with patriotism."

"Not in my case." Graveling's emphasis is strong enough to convince him that he means what he says. "Rupert knows no more than you what those perforated cards mean. He will never know."

"They're only to make music," Gog says. "Shall we try them on my gramophone?"

*   *   *

The last time that Gog sees Putney Bowles at Cambridge is in the middle of the night. He is working late, trying to collate all the reams of cards of his Celtic and mythological studies, which he did in the early 'thirties before he discovered that he could not work an index. Anything he filed in one, he lost. He spent all his time writing things on cards to put in the wrong place instead of just writing things. So now he is making a vain effort to arrange thousands of pieces of stiff paper when Putney drifts into the room, his forelock flopping over the extreme pallor of his prominent forehead, all his blood drained into his full lips, which are more than usually vermilion. His baggy trousers are ripped at one turn-up, caught on a spoke while Putney was climbing into college over the Trinity walls.

"I hope I am not interrupting you, Gog."

"You're saving my life." Gog throws his handful of filing cards into the air to fall where they may. "I give up. I shall never have an index system. What I can't remember can go blow."

"Organisation was never for you – nor was an organisation." Putney looks at Gog. "You won't be seeing me again. I came to say good-bye."

"But it's the beginning of the academic year. You're not going down, or being sent down?"

"Going across. Being sent up, which, in Eton terminology, also means I am being made a fool of. An organisation, which shall be nameless –"

"The one without a name."

"Exactly, the nameless one which is extremely active internationally, has told me to vanish, do the disappearing trick. I don't know why. It may even have something to do with you."

"Improbable," Gog says. "We don't know what each other knows. We only know each other."

"That is sufficient to condemn me among certain of my friends," Putney says. "Knowing you is proof of being in a conspiracy, when the actual conspiracy I am in is knowing certain of my friends. Anyway, enough of semantics. The fact is, nothing is straight any more. Have you seen Rupert Fox since he suddenly declared last week that Goering and his Stukas were angels of mercy and Hitler was a bit of all right?"

"Impossible. It can't be."

"Only the impossible exists for the organisation. You put on the face it wishes you to wear. So we're all pro-German now, rah rah for Franco's Moors, may they bugger another million workers' backsides, the Republic in Spain is a conspiracy of the bourgeois-democratic-reactionary classes, the Kremlin's going to make a deal with the Third Reich over the next couple of years, you will swear red is black despite the evidence of your own eyes, because that is the evidence of your own eyes the organisation wishes you to see."

"So you're saying, some of your friends – you yourself – you're pretending to love Berlin because you're hiding the fact that you love Moscow – but also the fact is, Berlin is going to do a deal with Moscow, and sod the democracies."

"Exactly. That is my analysis." Putney languidly brushes back his forelock above his brow. His soft hair seems almost too heavy for his hand to lift. "So I came to say good-bye. And to tell only you the truth, because you're the only person I don't want to believe what they're going to say about my disappearance."

"Where are you going, Putney? Tell me."

"I can't."

"I must know."

"You must not. You're in too much trouble as it is. More than you know. It's partially because I'm printing your modern parody of Jonathan Swift's modest proposal to eat Irish babies. It really does shock the organisation, and it proves I spend my time with the politically unreliable – and perhaps infiltrators and agents – like you."

Gog finds it hard to laugh, but he does. "An infiltrator like me? An agent? Come on, Putney, you know I never could be."

"I know, or I wouldn't be telling you all this. They don't know, so they suspect me because I like your work and your mad mind. It proves I am unreliable, too. Anyway, Gog, here it is – an advance copy of *Granta*. I've featured your piece. You'll like it."

He hands Gog a folded copy of *Granta*. Gog opens the flimsy pages of the undergraduate magazine. He finds his article, headed A NEW MODEST PROPOSAL by *Gog Griffin*.

"Thank you for calling me Gog, not George," he says. "I appreciate that."

"Get ready for some brickbats when that comes out," Putney says. "I may be disappearing, but there's talk of sending you down for this."

"It's not blasphemous, so I can't be sent down. The only heresy at Cambridge is still religious, not political."

"Max Mann's made the first step. He's ploughed your Luddite thesis, recommended you are struck off the graduate student list. And the college housing committee in Trinity, which is naturally run by other friends of mine as it gets them all the best rooms, are going to take your rooms back, as you won't have any reason to be here."

"Really? How do you know so much?"

"They tell me, hoping I will tell you, so that it will prove I am in a conspiracy with you against them." Putney's voice breaks in a possibility of self-pity. "I am *so* tired of plots. There aren't any plots, only friendships. And Stalin's putting all his friends and top brass on trial to prove there are plots everywhere, and he has no need of friends or top brass. Everyone will be purged or disappear. Like me."

"Don't," Gog says. "Stay with me. I'll help you. My Aunt Grace is dying. She's going to leave me a fortune."

"You filthy rich capitalist you," Putney says, smiling. "Good luck. I'm glad the system is doing something for someone. Anyway, my friend Gog, I only have one word of advice about all these factional wars of words between Communists, Trotskyites, Fascists and Liberals. Discount all ideology. Most of those people you know are on every side at once so that they will have to be on the side of the winner."

Gog stretches out a large hand to clamp it on Putney's shoulder and keep him where he is.

"You're a cynic, Putney. So you keep out. You don't have to disappear."

"I am afraid I have to, Gog. And I have to because I am afraid."

Putney gives a wriggle with his shoulder and escapes Gog's clasp. He ducks forward and kisses the amazed Gog on the cheek. "Not used to that, are you?" Then he is gone before Gog can protest. "Abyssinia," he calls from beyond the door, "only Mussolini got there first."

Gog is left holding the last issue of the Cambridge magazine which Putney has edited. He turns to his article to read it.

A NEW MODEST PROPOSAL
for
*Preventing the surplus people in Britain from being
a burden to their government or country, and for
making them beneficial to the public*

It is a melancholy sight to those who walk through our great cities, when they see the streets, the post offices and the social services crowded with the unemployed of both sexes and of all ages, asking for jobs or for the dole. These people, instead of being able to work for an honest living, are forced to employ their time in queuing to receive benefits for themselves and for their helpless infants, who, as they grow up, turn thieves for want of work, emigrate or sell their bodies for a pittance. I propose, however, to provide for the unemployed in such a manner that, instead of being a charge on the nation, they shall contribute to the feeding, and partly to the clothing, of many millions.

The number of workers in Britain is usually reckoned at thirty million. Of these, I calculate there may be about ten million who carry out work actually beneficial to this country, in agriculture or those occupations which make living more tolerable in our great cities. The other twenty million either make things or provide services which foreigners do better and cheaper. The purpose of our governments is to employ these workers in unnecessary factories or behind superfluous desks in order to keep them off the streets.

While one person does the needful work rather than three, two people share the work of one in order to protect their jobs. Although such care for one another is the better part of comradeship, it is the worse part of trade. And willy-nilly, once machines replace the minds and the hands of men, the jobs of the many shall be eaten away even more swiftly than in the time of the enclosures, when sheep ate men.

I have been assured by a very knowing American in London, that, in ancient times, the Aztecs ate their prisoners in order to remedy a deficiency of protein. He asserts that a healthy human body is a most delicious, nourishing and wholesome food, whether stewed, roasted, baked or boiled. I do not doubt that it will equally serve for a fricassee or ragout.

I do therefore humbly offer it to public consideration, that of the thirty million workers already computed, one-third of the essential workers may be preserved, men and women in equal numbers, to avoid any discrimination. The remaining twenty million may be offered by stages for sale to restaurants and foreign countries of quality and sound economies, after a last month of plentiful nutrition to render them plump and fat for a good table. Served hot or cold, a worker will make a noble entertainment for friends at dinner; and when the family dines alone, the leg or backside will make a reasonable meal. If flavoured with a little pepper or salt, the meal will be very good boiled on the fourth day, especially in winter.

Human flesh will be in season throughout the year; but more plentiful in March, and a little before or after. The cost of fattening the meat supply for market will rise in winter, therefore increasing the advantage to the economy if slaughtering takes place during the cold season.

I believe that no gentleman would object to giving fifty pounds for the carcass of a good fat worker, which will make ten dishes of excellent nutritious meat. Those who are more thrifty (as I must confess the times require) may flay the carcass. Its skin, artificially dressed, will make admirable gloves for ladies and summer boots for fine gentlemen.

Butchers will find good employment, although I rather recommend buying the workers alive, and dressing them hot from the knife, as we do roasting pigs.

I think the advantages of the proposal which I have made are obvious and many, as well as of the highest importance. For, first, it would greatly lessen the number of immigrants from the Commonwealth and from Ireland, by whom we are yearly overrun. They are the principal breeders in the nation, as well as our most dangerous enemies. They come here on purpose with a design to deliver the kingdom to alien influences. They hope to gain their advantage by the absence of so many good Englishmen, who have chosen to leave their country rather than stay at home and pay taxes against their conscience to an inhuman Inland Revenue. The principle of choosing who shall be eaten the sooner shall be simple: last into the country, first on the table.

Second, the poorer families will have an income by the sale of their useless members, and will so learn to stand on their own feet and not depend on the dole.

Third, while the maintenance of two million unemployed at the present time can be calculated to lose the nation as much as £1 billion per annum, the number of the jobless will diminish monthly by consumption instead of increasing. There will be an end to strikes, because there will be more jobs than people to fill them. Wages will be higher as there will be fewer to pay. And men and women will work harder, because they will have to do so much for themselves. Besides, there will be profits for all in the new meat business. The money will circulate among ourselves, the goods being entirely of our own growth and manufacture.

Fourth, the constant breeders, besides gaining £50 per annum for the sale of each child, will be rid of the charge of feeding it. So a hungry mouth will become another's food. ˝

Fifth, this United Kingdom is reckoned to be able to feed only half of its present population, which puts it at a disadvantage to its European neighbours, particularly France and Germany. The eating of twenty million workers and the regular sale for consumption of children and the neglect of the aged will reduce the population here to thirty million people, something which all governments must highly desire.

Sixth, this would be a great inducement to marriage, which all wise nations have encouraged by rewards or enforced by laws and penalties. It would increase the care and tenderness of mothers towards their children, when they were sure of a quick profit from them instead of a long expense. We should soon see an honest rivalry among married women, which of them could bring the fattest child to market. Men would become as fond of their wives during the time of their pregnancy as they are now of their mares in foal, their cows in calf, or sows when they are ready to farrow. And there would be an end to battered wives and babies for fear of a miscarriage or damaged goods.

Yet the chief advantage would be the prevention of the waste of our human material in the exercise of our strong and just foreign policy. In their wisdom, every one of our governments since the last world war has developed our Air Force while failing to provide shelters for the British people against a blitzkrieg. In the probable event of another world war, losses of millions of our people are confidently expected. I submit that it is more desirable to eat these superfluous people now, thus adding to the nation's food supply, and to use the money saved by eating them to build shelters for the rest. Otherwise, the next world war will incinerate half our population without discrimination or benefit to our larders. Naturally, the governments, which have rightly built shelters for themselves and other civil servants, will survive the blitzkrieg to defend our honour and dignity. But how much wiser to select the future survivors now instead of allowing the blind choice of bombs to destroy the fit along with the unfit. Moreover, the meat of the dead will be unfit to eat.

I profess, in the sincerity of my heart, that I have not the least personal interest in endeavouring to promote this necessary work. I have no other motive than the public good of my country, by advancing our trade, providing for workers and children, relieving the poor, and giving some pleasure to the rich. I have one child, through whom I can propose to earn £50 when he is of weight. His mother is not past childbearing, but in the circumstances, she will not bear another one. Besides, she is very fat and will fetch a good price herself.

GOG GRIFFIN

15

"Cambridge has no place for you," Maximilian Mann says. "It is not only that your New Modest Proposal lacks taste. It is obscene and profoundly contemptuous of the workers, on whom you live. In the Bolshevik Revolution, you would have been shot."

"But not eaten," Gog says. "That is my point. The Russians wouldn't have starved so much under the Bolsheviks if they had eaten useless counter-revolutionaries like me."

"Humour, Griffin, is not one of your accomplishments. It might be better if you were to go down voluntarily rather than undergo the dreary process of being sent down."

"How about a show trial, sir? Purge me. Stalin rules by the Cam. Isn't that what you want?"

Only the narrowed iris in Mann's eye betrays his weary tolerance.

"Facetious, too. The point of coming up to Cambridge is to learn. If you are ineluctably ineducable, and we may teach you nothing because you invent it all, then there is no point in your staying up. Go down, Griffin, go down, and inflict your modern Malthus on the suffering world. If eating people is right and overpopulation is our problem, remove yourself utterly – and serve yourself for dinner."

"What's happened to Putney Bowles?" Gog asks with intended inconsequence. "He's removed himself utterly."

A silence hides Mann's temporary confusion.

"How should I know? And why is this relevant to your departure from here?"

"He told me it was," Gog says.

"I do not believe you. Another of your historical inventions."

"Where is he? You know. You are one of the Cognoscenti."

"Another invention." Mann's tone is deeply languid. "But if you insist – I have heard Putney is in Germany. Something to do with that playboy, the Duke of Windsor. It appears that Putney has suddenly been afflicted like Job. Instead of boils and lost asses, he suffers from a bad case of the royals and lost ideals."

Gog smiles. Putney was right. He too had gone German on the orders of the organisation and would be pilloried as an apparent convert to Fascism.

"Job was restored to favour in the end," Gog says. "He got back even more asses and ideals. Let us pray for Putney." He rises and lifts one large shoe off the Chinese carpet in Maximilian Mann's room and waggles his toecap over the silk waterlilies. "Good-bye. I am going down. I am shaking the dust of Cambridge off my left foot."

"A clown to the last, Griffin." Mann raises a hand flopping at the wrist in a final farewell.

"Better than being a conjuror," Gog says to him, "who makes us disappear with a wave and become other than we are."

Gog can afford the luxury of his wit and his going down. A lawyer's letter lies among the debris and the holes in the carpet on the floor of his Trinity room. Messrs Anstruther & Thring inform him that he is the major beneficiary in the last will and testament of his aunt, the Lady Grace Magnussen, the widow of an immigrant Scandinavian manufacturer, who made a fortune in munitions and picture postcards in the First World War. Gog writes to Maire, telling her of his good fortune and his imminent arrival in Paris. Money – he is sure – will lubricate his pursuit of her and see to his doctorate elsewhere. He arranges for his library of Celtic mythology and ancient literature to be put into store, and he refuses to see his half-brother Magnus before his departure for France. If he is to steal Maire away, he does not want recrimination before abduction. And he is visited once more by the mathematician Graveling, who gives him a portion of the roll of perforated cards. In Paris, Gog is to see Captain Roland in French Intelligence and to deliver the roll of cards. The password is OGAM. Gog will appreciate that.

Gog meets Maire at the Coupole in Montparnasse. The pillars of the huge café are painted by the local artists, and Maire herself must have just been modelling for Picasso, for she is naked under her silk dress, which sticks to her. She smiles at Gog, calls him "*Mon* Gog, *ma* Gog" as if she does not know her grammar or wants to taunt him about his brother. She goes back with him to his hotel and lets him make love to her, but she is too tired to pretend a passion. He begs her to come away with him and escape the heat and see the châteaux of the Loire. She wants to stay in Paris with her friends. He says he will rent a studio where they can live on their return to Paris. He is rich now. He can afford her.

"Give me money," Maire says. "I come with you. But I say good-bye to my friends."

"Which friends? How long?"

"Never ask Maire. I come, I go. Wait here for me."

She leaves him, taking five hundred pounds in cash. He rages, despairs, remembers his duty. He hunts down Captain Roland, a brisk small man, alert and suspicious. He recognises the password OGAM and takes the joined perforated cards holed with dots and dashes. He examines Gog at length and does not believe that the huge Englishman knows nothing. "With the English, it is always the same. They play the big fools to put us off our guard." Gog cannot persuade Captain Roland that, like Socrates, he only knows that he knows nothing. Especially as he mentions that he knows Putney Bowles, who has surfaced in Germany in the entourage of the Windsors and Charles Bedaux, the manufacturer whom Gog has met at Spitpoole. "You know Bedaux," Roland says. "He is dangerous. He take your Duke of Windsor, who was king, and his American *maîtresse* who wants to be queen, to see Hitler who want them to be king and queen again. The Anglo-German *rapprochement*. It is our nightmare. Except for the Russian-German alliance. That is worse. To know of this, to know exactly of this, we need your friend Graveling and his little rolls of paper. That so?"

"That so," Gog agrees because he is meant to agree and knows so little about it all. And he leaves Roland, not much the wiser. And Maire is waiting for him back in the hotel beside the bags he has already packed to take to the Loire alone.

"*Assez de cette merde*," she says. "I come with you, Golly-at." Golly-at turns out to be Goliath, her new term of endearment for Gog. He tells her that she looks like a

188

Renaissance David, a rounded beautiful boy with her bag held like a slingshot in her hand. Gog Goliath will fall to any stone she cares to sling. But he will take her down the Loire. In journeys, not in cities, are lovers made.

The twin towers of Chartres are distant over the plain, two stubby prongs in the golden haze. Closer, they are contradictory, the right spire unadorned and magical under its high conical slate witch's hat, the left one fussy and fritillary with yellowish embroidery, petit point and corn-stitch and lacework in stone, ragged antlers pricking skyward round the barbed unicorn of the main prong. Maire at Gog's side is chattering and excited, her words rushing as sparrows, picking as hens, as she comments on the muggy air, the other women, the price of bread, her hairdresser's boyfriend, Léon Blum, *céleri rémoulade*, Rodin who knew what a woman looked like, and Picasso who does not. Gog looks down at her cropped black hair curled forward into twin licks under her cheekbones, her full breasts hard against her tiger blouse, yellow-and-black cotton stripes against the animal flesh, flared black skirt swinging from her haunch as she pads towards the cathedral in dark sandals, bird-loud and beast after prey and prayer.

For she does kneel inside the darkness of the cathedral, groping to the first row of wooden chairs, asking God for something she wants, the Catholic girl praying pretty-please to her Father for a gift from above, showing the fond Almighty on her knees that she may vote Communist, but her heart still hopes for heaven and a handout from on high; there's dragees and chocolate almonds and rumbabas and *pâtés de nonnes* to be showered from the celestial pâtisserie, and even Gog on a plate, if she asks for him. Gog is standing beside her, looking at the jewel-boxes of the medieval glass windows, rubies and lapis lazuli and sapphire and diamonds spread in arches and lozenges, fans and shining roses, all creation in coloured lights as crystalline as kaleidoscopes. Gog examines the Zodiac window. January with the three heads of Aquarius, seeing past and present and future as the one skein of time, the continuous presence of the heretoward and the here and the hereafter. February before a fire, huddling. March, pruning vines. April in flowers, May hawking, June mowing, July with a reaping-hook. August is Leo and Maire, threshed as the corn. Virgo is September, grapes trodden in the tub. Gog sits astride a wine cask in Scorpio October, then slaughters the November pig as the archer Sagittarius. Christ alone rules over Christmas and Capricorn, sitting between Alpha and Omega, the beginning and the end of timeless time.

"If you look," Gog says, "all the windows, they're in sacred fours, like the gospels. Or multiples of four by the mystic three, the Trinity, like the twelve apostles or the months or the signs of the Zodiac. There's a significance in numbers. A meaning."

"You can count your bank balance, *hein*?"

"Don't be coarse, Maire. You just pretend to be."

"Scratch a Parisian, Gog – there is peasant. We count sou by sou."

"To hell with money. This is sacred."

"What builds it? Money. The people, they give. They get sous to build it. And what will you give, *Golly-at*?"

Gog puts his hand in his pocket and drops a franc into the slit of the collection box. It is gone. A thank-offering. It is counted.

At Chambord, they discover the mystery of Leonardo's staircase. The great keep is laid out in the shape of the cross with the four chambers of the guardroom corresponding to the points of the compass and the humours of the body of the fortress. In the centre grows a stone staircase, Leonardo's concept of the secret of ascension, of communication, of moving towards desire, of the meaning of life. Gog and Maire in her verdigris smock climb on opposite spirals of the stairs, looking at each other through the pillars, smiling and divided, walking towards each other and never meeting, lovers that pass in the day in the labyrinth within the cruciform, then they descend to the base of the steps and there, turning inwards, they meet in the circle of space that has divided them in the double helix of the stairs.

"I thought I'd never meet you again," Gog says. "We were together and apart. I don't know how it works."

"Siamese twins," Maire says. "Two stairs together, but two people not. There were famous Siameses in Paris. Rosa-

Josepha. Joined at the hip." She laughs. "Like us some nights."

"It's so clever," Gog says. "Leonardo must have invented it. Witty and profound. When in France, do as the Italians do."

They have seen Leonardo's tomb at Amboise in a flamboyant chapel on the battlements, curlicues and fretwork all over the walls and buttresses, and on the spire, the stag's horns of St Hubert, the hunter saint who adored the stag with the Christ cross between the twelve points of its antlers.

"This is hunting country," Gog says. "And treachery. All these castles changing hands. Death and adultery. Catherine de' Medici with her three sons all kings and all murdered, seizing back the castles from their mistresses. Ruggieri, her astrologer, another Italian, foretelling their deaths. What do you prophesy for me, Maire, my darling Maire?"

"Horns," Maire says. "And twins. I can see twins. Sisters. We call them Rosa-Josepha."

At the château of Villandry on the high terrace, Gog looks down at the four gardens of love, which meet as the four corners of the earth meet round a little fountain of eternal desire, its single jet spraying and falling. Here is the garden of tender love, the garden of passionate love, the garden of winged love, the garden of tragic love. Clipped box trees and hedgerows and sentry yews at the corners define their intimate geometries. In between the cropped green leaves, flowers fly their banners, red and orange and yellow. Here is the pattern of tender love, which Gog sees from above.

"Look," Gog says, "at those hedges making four hearts separated by those masks in the centre. The masks we put on to hide our soft feelings. Or we would eat each other alive. Put on the masks."

Maire in her saffron gypsy blouse, looks at the orange flowers flaming between the outlines of the green hearts.

"Englishmen never grow up," she says. "*Enfants. Les enfants toujours.*"

Here is the design of passionate love.

"Those are not shields," Gog says. "Not defences thrown away. They are pieces of broken hearts. All dancing and trying to join together again. In one ring of love. You will marry me?"

Maire laughs.

"The flowers in the hedges," she says, "they are not all red. They are yellow like my blouse."

"Yellow," Gog says. "The yellow streak. That means a coward in England. I'll always be brave if I'm with you."

"Yellow," Maire says. "In France is to deceive."

She looks at Gog with blue eyes candid with the truth of the moment, the lie of next time.

"You'll never deceive me, Maire."
"*Emmerdeur.*"
"Deceive me then. Just a little bit. Not too much of it."
"Just a little bit, *mon* Gog."

Here are the signals of winged love. Instant love. Adulterous love.

"Round the edge of the design," Gog says, "I see horns and fans. Horns for the husbands' heads, fans to hide the wives' mouths, whispering infidelities. And in the middle, letters like paper darts, thrown by women's hands to flutter to their lovers. You'll betray me, won't you, Maire?"
"*Tu le dis, mon* Gog."
"With the man who'll hurt me most. Magog."
"*Tu le dis,* Gog. You like to suffer." She says it without raising her voice at the end of the sentence. It is a statement, not a question. Gog does not disagree, so Maire continues, "Perhaps I like to hurt you. Then you know you love me."
"Your blouse is yellow," Gog says.
"Coincidence."

Here is the text of the fourth and last garden of love. Red blooms inside the hedgerows. Tragic love.

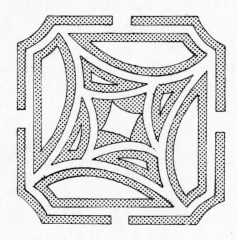

"All blood," Gog says. "All bloody blossoms between the four green swords and the four green daggers and the four green axe-blades at the centre. We must fight and bleed, hack and hew, for love of you."

"And Marianne," Maire says. "France is a woman. There is war soon."

"Hitler," Gog says. "Over the border. The Rhineland. But not a war in our lifetime."

"It is now," Maire says. "Spain today. The world tomorrow."

"You think I should go and fight in Spain to stop it?"

"You stay here, Gog. Call me France." She takes his hand and puts it on one saffron breast, then on the other. "*C'est ton* Verdun. *Et ta* Somme." Now she puts his hand in the channel between her breasts. "*Et ta Manche.*"

Gog knows that he will walk with and without Maire through all the paths between all the aisles and turns of the four gardens of love. He will not be spared the pain and the blood, the breach and the wound. He will not escape from the patterns and designs and signals and texts of the gardens of Villandry. He cannot read them as runes or as the Gogam script. They have their own messages and he must suffer them in France.

They go riding on twin white mares over the flat fields to Loches, the hill city on its pimple beyond the poplars. Maire wears a white sailor suit, her black short hair scalloping her pale face as a magpie's wing. A red sash is tied round her waist and slashes the horse's rump. Gog remembers a tale of the Great Mutiny, when an English general decides to use terror to break the sepoys before the battles. Living prisoners are bound to the bare mouths of twelve cannon. At each dawn, the salute of blood is fired, the salute to the Raj that will never end. An unknown lady, dressed in white on a white horse, rides past beyond the guns. She has suffered a wrong for the sake of India, a husband or son hacked by the rebels, a sister used as a naked filly by the Delhi mob. The gunners light the fuses, the charges explode. The veins of the bound men dissolve into rain. The white lady and the white horse are glossy with sudden vermilion. They wear again the wet, red coats of Empire.

Now Maire canters ahead, her red sash making a second horsetail as she rides towards Loches, where Joan of Arc met the dauphin after she had bloodied the noses of the English at Orléans and had made the Loire run scarlet, where Joan begged the dauphin to be anointed king at Reims and end the invasion of the Goddams. Maire can read Gog's mind, or perhaps it is still coincidence. She reins in, and he canters up to her side.

"You burn her," she says, "the English. You burn Jeanne d'Arc. Why you burn her? She says true. Will you burn me, Gog? Bloody limeys."

"Not for speaking the truth, Maire. Not for that."

"But I tell lies. You know. It pass the time of day in Venezuela. You burn me for a little lie?"

In Loches, Gog sees the cages that represent his future torture with Maire. They are cages a man cannot stand in, cannot sit in, cannot lie in. Their inventor was put in them for eight years to test them. Will it be that long with Maire? Longer?

"Look at Agnes Sorel," Maire says. "Her tomb. The king's *maîtresse*. Old Long-Nose the king he has childs with Agnes Sorel." Maire smiles. "How long your nose, Gog, is how long your thing." Maire laughs. "You have a long nose, Gog, like old Capet. He give Agnes childs, four daughters. Then the dauphin poison Agnes, so the king not marry her. So she is dead, and they bury her here. She is carved on the top. You see those *agneaux* at her feet – the lambs of God. Then the Revolution, they are brave, they dig up her bones *pour les violer – violer* her hip-bones. But she is French – *maîtresse-en-titre* – she is woman of France – she get her own back – *regarde!*''

Maire shows Gog the two pictures of Agnes Sorel. There is the Fouquet, with Agnes as the Virgin Mother, holding her milky breast to the naked Christ child, fat and rosy and winking, while scarlet cherubs and blue bright angels wave a tricolour in the frame. Then a hundred years on, an unknown painter clothes the dark Agnes in black and grey, making her sly and quiet, her narrow eyes and fingers creeping over a holy book, but deceiving no one with her bodice undone to bare the same fine full breast, not to give life to Him that shall give life, but to allow each passing stranger to view her undress and offering.

Gog and Maire buy a tapestry cushion on the walk down from the castle, the unicorn laying his white horn in the Virgin's lap, and her binding him with a gold chain, for how else can he be caught for ever? Then the ride back to the château-hotel in silence, and the long dinner, all the terrines and the pâtés, the quenelles and the brochets, and ragouts and the cassoulets, the millefeuilles and the confits, the sorbets and the gourmandises, the dictionary of the stomach, the vocabulary of the belly. They drink Sancerre, the wine blessed by Hemingway, it is a good wine and makes the earth move – after three bottles of it. And they talk of the Four Horsemen of the Apocalypse that are riding from Tokyo and Moscow, Berlin and Rome.

''They are dying in Nanking, Gog. The Japanese, they kill more than they count. And Chiang fight Mao, he burn them alive in train engines.''

''What can we do, Maire? Do you want a *framboise*? Or a *fine*?''

''In Abyssinia, mustard gas on the blacks. In Ukraine, death to the *kulaks*. Hitler, they say he has the Jews and the Reds in camps – the one you make against the Boers, what you call it?''

''Concentration camps. I don't know why.''

"In Spain those Stukas and Mussolini's bombers and Moors carving up women for priests and Franco. Who for we fight, Gog? Yet we must fight. The world is mad."

"Come to bed."

"You not listen. You not care. You burn Jeanne d'Arc. You men kill us all. What we have? This?"

Into her low yellow blouse, Maire puts her right hand and takes out her breast, round and white, the breast of Agnes Sorel. She shows it to Gog, to the waiter, to the other couples in the château restaurant. A table of Americans stop in a hush of awe. There is the silence of shock, of reverence.

"What we have?" Maire says. "Women. This? You kill this?"

"Put it away."

"*C'est ça.* Why hide it? Feed your babies. You suck it, too."

"Maire."

The maître d'hôtel fusses up, and Maire sheaths her breast in her blouse. They leave their table and go to their room. Gog fumes, but fumes gladly, guilty at the scandal and the pleasure of the scandal, his woman exposing her beauty and herself for her belief. In bed he settles all and settles nothing, he buries his eyes in her breasts, he plunges between her buttocks finding no limit, he is lost in the vertigos of the spaces in her packed body that is all fall and dear delight and darling liberation.

"All I know, you deny," Gog says. "All I believe shouldn't be done, you do. All I was taught, you call ignorance. All I am, you change. Blast you, Maire, you possess me."

"You never possess me," Maire says. "*Mon* Gog. No, I call you *Ma* Gog, like you call Brother Magnus. *Ma* Gog." Then she caresses his thing, as an old woman in Périgord may caress the throat of a goose, inducing an appetite so that its liver will become fatter and it will die of its greed and lust for more. "Other men," she says, "they desire me. Cold English. You burn French woman to keep your cold thing warm."

So Gog hardens himself and has her again in her moaning and her complaining, he hears the cries of the victim that she has provoked from him, the voice of the sufferer asking the torturer for her own sweet torment, then turning from him to blame him for his experiments.

"Pig," she says. "Animal. You only want me in bed. You never hear me. Men."

She sleeps deeply, leaving him awake, glutted and tormented, knowing that she has condemned him to the *peine forte et dure* without ending, *mon* Gog, *ma* Gog.

The heat wave continues throughout October. There is no autumn mist that year, no season of mellow fruitfulness. The haze is a torrid torpor that lies upon the land and the streets of Paris. Gog has found a splendid studio to rent in Montparnasse, but he cannot escape from the itch of his lust. Each day of sweat and languor puts Gog more and more at Maire's mercy.

"I have to have you."

"Do," Maire says.

She sounds as if she were offering him a helping of blancmange. She is lying on the sofa with dark sweat sticking her raw silk kimono to her breasts. Her hair is greased to her scalp in a beret above her bleached face and moist black lips. On that late October day in the studio, the flies are so fat and slow that two of them are squashed on the page of the book Gog is closing. Balzac, *Splendeurs et Misères des Courtesanes*.

Gog rises through air as warm-wet as a barber's towel. He unbuttons his trousers as he moves to the Mae West sofa made by Maire's friend Blanquet. It represents Mae's hips, two plump curves of white leather joined by a strip of blonde fur. There Maire lies, peeling her kimono from her damp flesh, whiter than the luxurious hide of the screen star's mighty ass.

Gog kneels and kisses Maire's breasts, trying to make them hard round the nipple rising. But they slump soft, too slack to move at finger or tongue. So Gog licks the length of her body, supping at her navel, kissing and mouthing the slight swell of her lower belly down to the jet thicket on her mount of Venus. He parts torpid thighs, heavy as gravity, and searches with his lips for the sick rose. His dark secret love discovers her bed of crimson joy. His hands scurry from

bosom to bottom, quick as a pair of five-legged mice in quest
of Camembert. All is useless. Nothing stirs. Looking with
one half-buried eye along the snow slopes of Maire's torso,
Gog sees a bland bored mask set above two breasts, plateaux
of inertia.

"Have me," Maire says, "if you have to."

So Gog lies on her, pushing her deep between Mae West's
hips, pulling himself into her by grasping her spread buttocks
that have no more life in them than two sacks of fine flour.
The thrust and hurt of him will not let him roll away, so he
pumps up and down, his face squashed sadly into the smooth
leather by Maire's cheek. So he comes, uselessly ridding
himself of what he calls desire. And so he sits up, the sweat
cold upon him.

"*Fini*," Maire says.

Gog does not know whether she is saying the whole affair
is over or just his act of sex.

"I've come," he says.

He begins tracing the geography of Maire's body with his
hand, the rounded M of her shoulders meeting in the division
of her breasts, the lovely hollow of her middle with its end
in the rough knot tying the long grace of her legs. His hands
seek to learn her white skin as if he were blind and her flesh
were braille. On and on, his fingertips read her lines. He
must record her for ever. This may be the last time. It is the
first time he has failed with her.

"You have your fun, Gog?"

"Not too much of it."

"Then why?"

"I had to."

"And me? You care?"

"I do. I love you."

"And if always it is this?"

"I love you. It won't be."

"And if it is?"

"It can't be."

Gog looks down at Maire's blue eyes, lidded and contem-
plating him. They are opaque. The little glint in them is
calculation, not desire.

"You want me pretend? Like a *putain*."

"No. No pretence. Love."

Maire laughs.

"And if I have no feel for you? Only feel for other men, not you. Because you love me de trop. Because you pay for me. And they don't care for me. *Ça me plait*."

Gog feels the rage swell in his hands. They grip Maire's thighs, trying to hurt her into feeling, but the flesh is too loose, undone.

"You want to torture me, Maire?"

"You torture me." At Maire's smile, Gog slackens his fingers until they slide down her skin. "Hear me, *ma* Gog. Don't love me de trop. You lose me that way. I have to hurt you. If I stay, it is not for your *beau sexe*."

"I cannot let you go. I want you. I have to have you."

Maire laughs again, the high tinkle of breaking glass. She has learnt the pitch from Arletty. She takes one of Gog's hands and puts it over her left breast.

"Why tell me that? Idiot. You make me torturer. You make you victim. Feel –"

She shuts his fingers on her breast. He can only sense a handful of soft flesh that will not answer to his touch.

"*Rien, ma* Gog. *Nada.* Feel my heart. Is that what you want, my heart? And why you can not feel it? Because my breast is there. You want that, you want it much. But it is skin – fat – milk. It hide my heart, which I do not have. *Mon pauvre* Gog, *ma* Gog . . .*"

Gog starts up in his shirt and bare trembling legs.

"I won't have your pity. I won't be called your poor Gog. Love or nothing."

Outside in the street, a Citroën engine coughs a requiem. A motor-bike drums staccato taps. Inside the studio, Maire shakes her head.

"You love me," she says. "You have to have me." She closes her kimono, sticking the silk to her moist body that drives Gog mad. "So you have me, *mon pauvre* Gog. If I am here. And I have you."

And Gog knows that the years to come with Maire will be torment after torment, the want of what cannot be had, the desire in pursuit of the unholy, the waiting for the key that does not turn in the door, the light burning for the knock that will not come in the night, the yelling at her to stay away, the sick fear that she may, the carapace of not seeming to care, the wound because the mask of indifference is not seen to be a mask, the grovelling after her caprice, the howling storm at her casualness, and the need, oh, the need that must lead to all the pain, and his life destroy.

Gog marries Maire in the *mairie* of the *arrondissement* in the spring next year. He asks his mother Merry to come to the ceremony, or lack of it, but she is travelling with Otto in Germany. A postcard of the Nazi Rally in Nuremberg comes from her with this message:

> Be happy, my son, although Otto says to be happy with a Frenchwoman is a contradiction in terms. We met two charming friends of yours at a Hitler Youth festivity, Rupert Fox and Putney Bowles. They know Magnus, too. Isn't it a small world, thank God?
> all my love
> MERRY x x x

Gog does not show this postcard to Maire, but tells her that he wants his wedding to be totally private. There is no question, naturally, of asking Magog, who has shown no sign of renewing his relationship with Maire.

Until the end of the summer, life is quiet in Montparnasse, if any life with Maire can be said to be quiet. Gog works at his *The True History of King Ludd*, while Maire leaves him for days at a time without explanation. At first, Gog demands to know what she has been doing, where she has been going, but as she only laughs or lies or rations her sexual favours as a punishment, Gog soon gives up the questioning and nurses in silence his jealousy without a cause.

The income from Aunt Grace's legacy is considerable. It is almost embarrassing in a decade of world depression. But Maire finds no embarrassment in disposing of the money. She has never had so much to spend before, and Gog can deny her nothing. He sends for his books in store and his childhood possessions and has them shipped to Paris. They are all he needs. Maire can have the rest.

Curiosity rather than guilt leads Maire to ask about Aunt Grace one day. She has no interest in Gog's writings, as these bring in no money. "You will have to read *The True History of King Ludd*," Gog says. "What there is of it as far as I've got, which is up to Aunt Grace and the munitions maker, who made picture postcards too. After that, it's really my autobiography, and I don't know if that is interesting. Or at least, not yet."

"No, but I read your *King Ludd*. What is there. I am your wife. I like to know your family, where money come from."

"It's written in an odd style," Gog warns. "I had better try and explain to you why. Please have a look at this."

He takes from the pile of his childhood books a large volume with embossed frayed covers. He gives it to Maire, knowing it will baffle her. She reads its title, *Highlights of History*. Then she flicks through the pages with their large print and coloured illustrations in the mock-heroic style. "Alfred burn the cakes! Queen Elizabeth burn the Armada! Why I see don't you burn Jeanne d'Arc! Childs *merde*! Is your joke."

"It's no joke," Gog says. "That's how history is to me. Highlights. It's my theory of perception."

How to explain the dim pool of his memory, where correspondences rise like goldfish to illumine the surface, but sink before he can describe the meticulous overlapping of their scales. How to explain the quality of his own mind, which he seems to find in most other minds – the exclusion of the trivial, the repetition of the significant experience into the well-worn story, the embroidery of the truth in the telling until the words themselves change the recollection of events. If Tom Eliot is right and time past is time future, then history is a seeking for prophecy in research, a quest for a way forward in the backways now lost, an invention of what has happened to fit the sense of immediacy and the need for direction, an interpretation of facts no more and no less true than the study of the entrails of the sacrificial goat.

"Liver and lights," Gog says. "The Romans thought all was explained if you looked at the liver and lights of a victim. Well, for me, it's lives and highlights. The things worth remembering. Myth, not fact, and family before all."

"You and the *famille* Griffin," Maire says. "Why your family is so important? Are you so small you not see bigger?"

202

"My family," Gog says, "back to Ned Griffin is as far as it goes, genealogically that is. But then, we are all descended from Adam – and Gog, of course."

Maire rises in her black silk pyjamas, wide in the leg and ending on her breasts in twin triangles held up by a halter-strap, making a black M below her white bare shoulders. She walks over to where the piles of typescript lie on the oak table and she riffles the pages sideways across the wood, spreading out her contempt.

"Tell me," she says, "you have spent a year here while the Nazis take over Europe and Mussolini think castor oil better than the *commedia dell'arte* – a year you writing about the *famille* Griffin – a year you do nothing . . ."

"I do a lot," Gog says. "There was a George Edward Griffin and a George Albert Griffin and another George Griffin. They're in the parish registers."

"You write them in," Maire says. "You make them up."

Gog looks at the smooth pale face of his wife and hates to love her.

"I write them down," he says, "but I do not make them up. I may be a Celt and a mystic, but you're a rationalist and a liar."

Maire laughs.

"*Naturellement, chéri*," she says. "A woman has to lie. But you prefer your highlights to real history. It is dull. Your highlights are not true."

"I am interested in the truth," Gog says, "not in the facts. A family is history, is all history. In Ned Griffin, living at that time, King Ludd lived and the machine-breakers and the pugs and the radicals. And if he was not there, he was of the time and place. It is for me – wanting to know why I feel as I do and where I am going – to search for my dark and obscure roots – to dive into that underground stream where my blood meets those sources of history that obsess me – to seek for *myself* there, not for anything more. I feel – it's ridiculous, but I feel – somehow, if one man could know all the myths and reasons and lies that from the time of his island's beginning had made him what he uncertainly is, then he would be liberated, able to act . . ."

"You want to be God," Maire says coldly. "Everyone say that of you. Not Gog. God."

"No," Gog says. "I just want to be a free man."

"Then why you are writing lies as history?" Maire asks. "You are Doctor Goebbels or a *romancier*?"

"I only want the history of one small family," Gog says, "but with all its associations and circumstances, nuances and clouds and powers, madnesses and excuses. I . . ."

"*Tu le dis*. I." Maire walks over to the door. "Well, I go have a bath, then I go and sleep with your brother, who *do* something in his Ministry."

This is actually what Maire is going to do. She knows the best lie is the absurd truth. Gog simply will not believe her. And so he does not, until later.

"Magog's not in Paris," Gog says. "He hasn't been in touch with us since our marriage." A doubt nags at Gog. "Or has he?"

"Don't ask me," Maire says. "Don't believe me."

"I don't," Gog says.

"Do," Maire says. "Don't believe me."

"I never do."

"Nor do I," Maire says, and leaves the room.

Gog does not even bother to switch on the news that night, so misses the announcer telling of Germany's ultimatum to Czechoslovakia. He is writing a chapter in *The True History of King Ludd* about his childhood in Holyhead. He does not want to remember it. Instead he will bring his diary up to date.

After Maire has left the studio, he cannot write at all. Perhaps she really is going to commit incest with his brother Magog. Perhaps something important was on the news and will be in the newspapers next day. The trouble with writing about oneself in the third person as Gog, in history or a diary, is that one is only wise after the event, as always. Even recording something at the time does not make it important. Diaries have few highlights. And so early to bed, Gog's own, not hers.

The True History of King Ludd

(as shown to Maire Griffin in Montparnasse, Paris, in September 1938, and accepted as a thesis for a Doctorate of History at the Universitas Extra Muribus, Iowa, 1940)

1829

(In which Ned Ludd leaves the trades of Smith and Pugilist to use his Prize-money to acquire the Means of Production and become a Caster of Letters and Knocker-up of Balls and a Press-man so as to manufacture such Pamphlets as may restore Albion to the People thereof, according to Moxon's 'Mechanick Exercises on the Whole Art of Printing'.)

Now he comes to *Casting*. Wherefore placing the under-half of the *Mold* in his left hand, with the *Hook* or *Hag* forward, he clutches the ends of its *Wood* between the lower part of the *Ball* of his Thumb and his three hind-Fingers. Then he lays the upper half of the *Mold* upon the under half, so as the *Male-Gages* may fall into the *Female-Gages*, and at the same time the *Foot* of the *Matrice* place it self upon the *Stool*. And clasping his left-hand Thumb strong over the upper half of the *Mold*, he nimbly catches hold of the *Bow* or *Spring* with his right-hand Fingers at the top of it, and his Thumb under it, and places the point of it against the middle of the *Notch* in the backside of the *Matrice*, pressing it as well forwards towards the *Mold*, as downwards by the *Sholder* of the *Notch* close upon the *Stool*, while at the same time with his hinder-Fingers as aforesaid, he draws the under-half of the *Mold* towards the *Ball* of his Thumb, and thrusts by the *Ball* of his Thumb the upper part towards his Fingers, that both the *Registers* of the *Mold* may press against both sides of the *Matrice*, and his Thumb and Fingers press both Halves of the *Mold* close together.

Then he takes the Handle of his *Ladle* in his right Hand, and with the *Boll* of it gives a stroak two or three outwards upon the *Surface* of the *Melted Mettal* to scum or cleer it from the Film or Dust that may swim upon it. Then takes up the *Ladle* full of *Mettal*, and having his *Mold* as aforesaid in his left hand, he a little twists the left-side of his *Body* from the *Furnance*, and brings the *Geat* of his *Ladle* (full of *Mettal*) to the *Mouth* of the *Mold*, and twists the upper part of his right-hand towards him to turn the *Mettal* into it, while at the same moment of Time he Jilts the *Mold* in his left hand forwards to receive the *Mettal* with a strong *Shake* (as it is call'd) not only into the *Bodies* of the *Mold*, but while the *Mettal* is yet hot, running swift and strongly into the very *Face* of the *Matrice* to receive its perfect Form there, as well as in the *Shanck*.

Then he takes the upper half of the *Mold* off the under half, by placing his right-Hand Thumb on the end of the *Wood* next his left-Hand Thumb, and his two middle Fingers at the other end of the *Wood*, and finding the Letter and *Break* lie in the under-Half of the *Mold* (as most commonly by reason of its weight it does) he throws or tosses the Letter, *Break* and all, upon a Sheet of Waste Paper laid for that purpose on the *Bench* just a little beyond his left-hand, and is then ready to *Cast* another Letter as before, and also the whole number that is to be *Cast* with that *Matrice*.

And when the casting is done, there is the breaking, rubbing, kerning, and setting up of letters. Breaking off and rubbing of the letters is commonly boys' work, but Ned Ludd has no boys to help him, but he must put on fingerstalls of old ball-leather to fit the lead type to be composed in the stick, and dressed. He must cut for himself six dozen composing-sticks of beechwood, which wood in the Anglo-Saxon is rendered as *boc* or book, for all ancient English books were carved upon beechwood or tally-sticks of beech. And when Ludd has set up his letters on his sticks and racks ready to receive them, he shall be the dresser with his dressing-sticks and bench and blocks, both male and female, and wedges and hook and knife and plough and mallet and buff. And when he has dressed the letters, he shall prepare to compose them by papering the boxes in his case, both upper and lower, and by opening and unlocking the form and the quoins, and by rinsing and stripping the quarters, and by pressing his riglet or distributing-stick upon the face of the letter of the farthest line, and by spreading and squabbling the shanks of the letters between his fingers askew, till his taking-off be quite distributed, and so continues his takings-off till his case is full. Then he shall address himself to composing by looking over his copy, and by sliding up his composing-stick to pinch the fullest line between the cheeks and the head till it stands as stiff or hard in the stick as he intends to justify all the rest of his lines, and by placing his galley on his upper case on the right hand. And so Ludd may fall to composing the copy of his pamphlet line by line until his stick be full, which he then may empty into the case and find all his lines be justified and his page be out and ready for its typing up. Then shall the letters be prepared for the imposing of the sheet, when the inks shall also be mixed. Old Gutenberg, who printed the first Bible with movable type, used metal in his ink, lead and copper, but Ludd uses lead type and vegetable dye in his ink. And he must be his own press-man to knock up the balls for the inking and the pressing and the pulling of the sheets according to the *Mechanick Exercises* of the text of his new trade.

Having *Knockt up* one *Ball* well, he *Knocks up* the other, as the first.

The *Balls* are well *Knockt up*, when the Wooll is equally dispersed about all the Sides, and the middle smoothly covered with the *Leather*, viz. not rising in Hillocks, or falling into Dales, not having too much Wooll in them, for that will subject them to soon hardning and quickly be uneasie for the *Press-man* to Work with; or too little, for that will make the *Leathers*, as the Wooll settles with Working, soon flap, and wrap over itself into Wrinkles. So that he cannot so well destribute his *Balls*: But the *Balls* ought to be indifferently plump, to feel like an Hard stuft Bed-pillow, or a strong Spunge a little moistned with Water.

Having now *Taken Inck*, and gotten the *Balls* in his Hands, in that posture, he Works them side-ways upon one another to and from him, and with a craft (acquired by use) in the Handling of the *Balls*, all the while keeps the Handles, and consequently the whole *Ball-stocks* (both) turning round in his Hands and in a motion contrary to each other.

To *Come down the Form*, he skips his *Balls* both at once from the first and third Row to the second and fourth Row, and brings them down as he carried them up; only, as before, he bended the *Handles* of the *Ball-stocks* a little towards him, so now he bends them a little from him: That the *Ball-leathers* (now *Coming down*) drag not, as aforesaid. Then in like manner he again skips the *Balls* from the second and fourth Row to the first and third Row, and again *Goes up the Form* with the *Balls*, as he did before. And then again skips, as before, and *Comes down the Form* again with the *Balls*.

Having thus gone twice upwards and twice downwards with the *Balls*, the *Form* is sufficiently *Beaten* in a train of Work, when the *Face* of the *Letter Takes* well.

Having used his balls to see that the face of the letters takes well, Ludd must make register, order the points, and otherwise make ready the form. Then he must lay on the sheet, lay down the tympans and the frisket, run the carriage in and out, take up the tympans and the frisket, pick up the form, take off the sheet and place it on the heap. So he shall pull the first pull, and having the rounce still in his left hand, he shall turn it about again and repeat all he has done until the last pull be pulled. Then Ned Ludd shall fold his sheets against a brass rule and take them to the people and distribute the work of his brain and his hands and his balls, and say unto them, "In the beginning of the change that will be is the word, and lo, I bring it among you."

Norfolk, 1830 – Kent, 1836

The moping men stand by the wall in Diss market. They are for hiring. They stand for one day, two days, three days. If they are clutching at straws because they know the farmers are not hiring, what can a labourer do except offer his labour? And if they are sucking at straws like true yokels, what can a mouth do which has no food in it? There are so many men standing in the market that the magistrates are troubled and think of calling up the yeomanry, but no look of riot sharpens the men's faces, just the apathy of waiting that is not yet despair.

Then the green gig comes or does not come. Some swear it has black wheels and some say its spokes are red, but all agree the carriage is green. As for the horse, some say roan and some say nigger, but horse there has to be for those that swear to the gig. And as for the man inside, the witnesses vouch for his top-boots, shiny as wet coal with strange split blunt toes. Then some say he has scarlet britches with a dark swallow-tail coat, and some say his britches are pitch-blende, but his swallow-tail is crimson velvet. His face, though, nobody will describe except that the man has a fiery or a coaly beard and a high hat that seems fixed above his ears by two inner prongs so that even a gale cannot blow it off. His expression, too, seems both jovial and evil, amiable and execrable, persuasive and suspicious. In all, the man in the gig is a mountebank who may have been in the market or not – but devil take the argument!

What is certain is that copies of a handbill fall out of the green gig or from the sky and pass among the men waiting to be hired. The handbill is printed on crude lead type and it reads:

O YE PARSONS AND SQUIRES, WHO STRAIN AT A GNAT AND SWALLOW A CAMEL, WOE WOE WOE UNTO YOU – GOD ALMIGHTY HAVE BROUGHT OUR BLOOD TO A PROPER CIRCULATION, THAT HAVE BEEN IN A VERY BAD STATE A LONG TIME, AND NOW

211

WITHOUT AN ALTERATION OF THE FORESAID, WE MEAN TO
CIRCULATE YOUR BLOOD WITH THE LEAVE OF GOD —
WE HAVE COUNTED UP THAT WE HAVE GOTTEN ABOUT 60 OF
US TO ONE OF YOU —
THEREFORE SHOULD YOU GOVERN, SO MANY TO ONE?

CAPTAIN SWING

As the few men who can read spell out the bill to the many
who are waiting, the silence grows to a murmur, then to
speech, then to shouting. More people see the man in the
green gig now, the bold Captain Swing, who has set the
workhouses burning from Kent to Dorset, so the poor in
the south are set free again to do the work of the thrashing
machine, that has been sent by the devil to take the harvest
work away.

Swing, Swing, they say, Captain Swing has taken the
parson by his nose and pinched it till he has given up his
tithes and taxes. Swing has taken the new machines driven
by the teams of horses or steam-engines, and he has broken
them flail by flail and put the pieces back into the hands of
the labourers to beat out the grain as they have always done.
He has torn down hedges and let the village sheep graze in
the commons once more. He has thrown magistrates in the
duck-pond and sobered constables under the pump. Now
Swing is the man by the green gig, who passes through so
quick and so curious, leaving no certain trace behind him,
only the sharp smell of rage and fear, the burned-out taste
in the mouth and nostrils of risk to come, a line of abject
men turned on the sudden to a mob.

Away then, Ned Griffin, the knowing one, not hiring his
labour, but testing his luck. Seeing the mob, he does not
head it, but backs it up, hedging in the likely lads, thrusting
back the stragglers towards the door of The Lamb Inn, where
the magistrates are taking pot luck, if that name serves for
two pheasants apiece, hare pie, claret and cheese and a bottle
of Madeira. The magistrates called to the bow windows of
The Lamb are met with mud and pitchforks and a sign
stating, BREAD OR BLOOD, which gives them the wind in
their britches as well as in their bellies. The military is an
afternoon's ride away and the mob a stone's throw near, so
they promise everyone a shilling a day more and work for

all. And aren't they all gentlemen, so it must be true? For if one of them is reading the Riot Act ready for the charge of the troops to come, turning murder into law by a mumble of clauses, why, he's whispering the small print down the hole in the earth-closet so that only the cesspit can hear him with God deaf on high . . .

EXTRACT FROM THE REPORT OF THE MAGISTRATES OF DISS IN THE COUNTY OF NORFOLK TO LORD MELBOURNE, OCTOBER 19TH, 1831

Despite the Act being read thoroughly and loudly in the market-place to the aforesaid Riotous Poor, demanding the false and seditious Reduction of Tithes and laying aside of Thrashing Machines, the Rioters did later most maliciously misuse the Person and Property of the Reverend Ponsonby of North Walsham as well as committing divers other Breaches of the Peace, and in consequence, the Queen's Dragoons were summoned from their encampment and did most expeditiously put to flight the Rioters outside The Cock and Bull, whence they had repaired with their Fowling-pieces, Muck Chromes, Bludgeons, Pitchforks, and other offensive Weapons, to the great peril of the County and confusion of the Country . . . Of the nine Rioters sent to the Assizes for Hanging or Transportation, none will answer to the name or description of Captain Swing, although he was reported severally in the market in black and red attire in company with a certain seditious fellow from Nottingham, a Ned Ludd or King Ludd, a printer of seditious handbills, yet no trace may be found of either of these Miscreants, who have left others to suffer in their place in the name of the law . . .

Ned Ludd does not escape this time, but the constables track him to the old Gordy woodyard at Bury St Edmunds, where twelve arms of the law are needed to apprehend him, the seasoning timber flying in the mighty battle, rafters of oak and joists of beech and fir planks crashing and falling as a forest in a storm when the smith is handcuffed and led away to gaol before the sentencing at the sessions court. His lead letters are discovered, his composing-sticks and his cases, all the matter of a jobbing printer of seditious pamphlets. It is impounded as the evidence against George Edward Griffin alias Ned Ludd, that will send him to the gallows to swing alongside his captain or to Botany Bay to work out his treason in the Antipodes.

In Norwich gaol, it is bread and hard commons for the fettered giant, for the leg-irons are left on him in fear of his rage. But the prison walls cannot keep out the news of riots and the reform that is setting sparks to the people and the stubble of the land. On the stones and the bricks that separate the cells, the messages are struck out, one tap for an A, two taps for an E, up to five taps for a U to complete the vowels, then one single blow for a B up to nine single blows for an M for the first nine consonants, then one double blow for an N, thump-thump, up to twelve double blows for the latter twelve consonants ending in a Z. These taps and single blows and double thumps, these aural dots and dashes and repetitions of sounds, they are the code of the prisoners, the communication of incarceration. There is no barrier that may stop the words of men to men.

So Ludd hears of the shoemaker Zion Ward, the breaker of images, spreading the word of the prophetess Joanna, come again as Shiloh and as Judah, yea even as Satan turned to Jesus Christ, to set his people free. He has the power of the printed word that Ludd once had and now is tapped by fingers and fists through prison walls. "Alarm! Alarm! Priestcraft detected! Its overthrow projected! How effected! Down with His Grease of Canterbury! Down with the canting bishops that will not suffer Joanna's Box of Prophecies to be opened! Woe unto the mummery of the church!" So Ludd translates the teaching of Zion Ward from hearing the taps and blows on the walls, and then he receives in a hollow within his daily half-loaf a pamphlet entitled *The Return of Joanna*, in which Ward claims to be the son of the prophetess, also Shiloh and the devil himself returned as the Son of God. And Ludd believes that a prophet is come again, and he pledges himself to the cause of reform and the overthrow of the Church of England, the bishops and their misgovernance, for he has always been of that persuasion. And lo, as if by a miracle, there is a trembling of the bowels of the earth, a great yawning of the mouth of hell, and the walls of Norwich gaol do part as did the Red Sea for Moses and the Israelites. So Ludd walks free, unshackling his leg-irons from the rubble, and he has them struck off on the anvil hard by the gaol, for what smith can refuse the need of the great Ludd, "As you shoe a mare, so shall you unshoe me now!"

And the reform is no reform as no reform ever is, but only another betrayal of the people. Sure, and there is a Bill that is called the Great Reform Bill, but it is a Bill that only reforms the Great more firmly in their powers over the people. If you have property and you are a man, why, you shall vote, but what of the poor and the many and the women and the distressed? There is no way except to have a Charter for all the people, for are we not millions when they are but thousands, are we not bees when they are but maggots, are we not givers when they do but partake? So Ludd lends his craft and his strong arms to William Cobbett and to Carlile, to Bronterre O'Brien and to Feargus O'Connor, for the pamphlets, *The Register* and *The Gauntlet* and *The Destructive and Poor Man's Conservative*. The signing of the People's Charter by the millions is slow work, and there is quicker work to do, in Wales where the miners shall kill the military at Newport and set Vincent free, and in Kent, where the king of the New Jerusalem is come again according to the prophecies of Joanna, and Ludd is now gone to aid that last good hope that the folk shall rise again.

Sir William Courtenay, whom the powers of Mammon and Magog call a lunatic and a perjurer named Tom, has set up his standard under an oak tree. Beneath a rampant lion on the blue and white banner, the king of the New Jerusalem preaches in his eastern robes to the men that work the forests and fields of Kent. "Go to now, ye rich men," King Courtenay declares in the words of the apostle, "weep and howl for your miseries that shall come upon you. Behold, the hire of the labourers who have reaped down your fields, is of you kept back by fraud, and the Lord God crieth: 'My wrath be upon you, the fire everlasting and the day of reckoning.'" And then a fat black pig is hanged squealing over the faggots, Satan and Mammon to be cleansed by the flames, and the brands are lit and the logs are burned and the flesh of unrighteousness is consumed utterly. And as the stink of charred hide offends the nostrils, so the redcoats come to Blean Wood to arrest King Courtenay for the murder of a constable. He sounds a trumpet, rah-rah: "They shall hear me at Jerusalem!" he cries. "Ten thousand men of Gilead shall aid us!" It is muskets and bayonets for the military against cudgels and bludgeons for the people. Courtenay is killed as he kills a redcoat officer. A dozen of the Kentish men are shot or skewered to bloody deaths. Ludd embraces a redcoat and squeezes his ribs until they crackle as the burnt pigskin, but the butt of a musket clubs him down for his second taking on charges of riot, affray and sedition.

There is no escape now from the sweating rot of the hulks and the transporting to Botany Bay beside the martyrs of Tolpuddle and of the Newport rising and of the many unions and brotherhoods of the people that the Whigs and the Tories denounce as conspiracies and treasons. And so ends the first part of the history of Ned Ludd in England, sent away for ten years' hard labour to the wilderness of Australia, there to work out his rebellion with an axe on eucalyptus and gum trees and the alien forests of the aborigines in their far continent. The Luddites can do no more in the new age of the mechanics and the machines, the weary revolution by piston and cylinder, by crankshaft and pump, by boiler and steam press, that must break yoke and crack milkbowl and blunt scythe. Oh, Ludd, thy glory is departed as Ichabod. The lilies of the field are the looms of the factories, where now they toil and they spin, as God pleaseth in the catechism of the age.

London, 1848–51

As he writes *The True History of King Ludd*, Gog can look through a spyhole into the Crystal Palace. He closes his left eye and approaches with his right eye the paper picture of the Palace entrance that celebrates in French and Italian, English and German, *Das Innere des Glaspalastes in London*. At the round hole that replaces the real entrance, Gog's eye stops to see the extension of the central aisle under the curve of the paper transept roof simulating glass and ironwork: bee-large ladies in bright jackets and crinolines promenade beside gentlemen in beavers and billycock hats under the enclosed elm trees where the Duke of Wellington set his sparrowhawks to clear the crystal prison of small birds. An ornate fountain stands at the centre of the transept, and infinite exhibits fringe the main hall and the galleries. This is a paper peep-show of the miracle of iron and glass of its age, a souvenir given to Gog by his grandmother Maria Griffin, who was conceived in the structure upon the printing and envelope-folding machine of Thos. de la Rue and Company by her father George Edward Griffin, alias Ned Ludd, and proved none the worse for it.

Ned Ludd has been released from the Antipodes after ten years' hard labour to find the revolution spluttering out all over Europe. Mazzini is beaten in Rome, Manin in Venice, a Bonaparte rules again in Paris. In England, the Great Charter has only two million signers and the leaders of the luminaries are arrested and transported as Ludd was. Printing is no more as Ludd knows it. The inked cylinder, which steamrolls over a flat bed of type, prints five thousand copies of *The Times* in the hour, and this is the truth of the new times when machines eat men. The ironways have forced their tracks into London, where brick palaces with glass roofs are constructed as stations to accommodate them: London Bridge is now a rail terminus, also Euston and Paddington, Waterloo and Bishopsgate with King's Cross a-building. Where tens of thousands travelled on the Roman roads

217

radiating from the island capital, tens of millions roll proud and smutty along the eastern counties, the London and Birmingham, the Great Western, the South Western, and the London and Brighton lines, while the Houses of Parliament debate a Metropolitan circle between the great stations to link them in a metal hoop as the hub of all the chains that bind down Albion.

Ned Ludd has lost. He knows not what he may do. He goes to grief and ground, working for an antiquarian bookseller and occasional printer in Clerkenwell, Norman Pickens and Daughter. He immerses himself in faded ink and vellumbound dictionaries of ancient languages and curious hypotheses. Did the Phoenicians invent the runes, or the Magi or the Druids, or the Greeks? Certain it is that there are strange similarities in all the scripts, from the Syriac Olaph and Arabic Elif, the single upward stroke that is the Ogam line and the Runic Is and the Thracian Iota; yet the dissimilarities are more than the correspondences, and all is obscure in the vagaries of the ancient scripts, where very meanings are lost as are the scripts themselves. For what has preserved the letters that survive? Hesiod was the first to be inscribed on tablets of lead and deposited in the Temple of the Muses in Boeotia, and Greek women were used as intelligencers to carry messages scratched on wafers of rolled lead and made into earrings. Of Job, it is written that his words were graven with an iron pen into rock and filled with lead. So the Romans inscribed the Laws of the Twelve Tables on brass as well as on ivory and oak and papyrus. But the other ancient scripts were set upon clay, not upon rock, and thus is the wisdom of the Magi broken and crumbled to the winds. The prophets wrote their Hebrew upon scrolls of parchment that are shredded by time. The Romans also carved upon wooden tables, painted with wax, and these are consumed in the decay of oblivion. So it is with the letters consigned to word and to paper made from pulp or bark or reed or leaf or linen or hide. Where are the laws of the Swedes, written on their *balkars* or beams? Where are the gouged planks the Greeks called their schedules? Where are the graven gateposts of Deuteronomy or the nicked splinters of the Scythians or the four-sided beech elucidators of the ancient Britons, of which one alone survives and these four lines, as Ludd translates them:

The weapon of the wise is reason:
The swineherd is proud of his swine:
A gale is but ice in a narrow place:
The enemy of an enemy is a friend.

Only the tally-sticks still notched at the Exchequer signify the wooden writings of time immemorial and those scripts buried in the vaults of the centuries.

Ned Ludd also studies the pictures of the early languages, the characters of the hieroglyphs, the eye that is the symbol of knowledge, the circle which has no end and means eternity, the feather that is honour and the viper that is ingratitude, the fly of impudence and the ant of wisdom, the hawk of victory and the eel of the evil man, the spotted robe of indignity and the cup of misery that is never full. But the pictures are only pictures in Ned Ludd's mind as the old letters are only letters. Their mysteries and meanings appear to him in most occasional significance.

His master's daughter Margaret appears more and more beside the carved lectern that Ludd has taken as his own temple of thought, where he stoops his huge shoulders over the manuscripts and the parchments. Margaret has the skin of a foxed page; freckles sprinkle the pallor of her face framed by ornate patterns of red hair. Her green eyes are moist and bulge slightly with curiosity. Her thin body is bound by bodice and corset, but her lips are loose as she considers the size of Ned Ludd and the huge hands that fondle the yellow vellum with a gentle hesitation. Ned Ludd is slow and halting, she is fervid and impatient. And finally, she breaks with convention and proposes that he escort her to the Great Exhibition in the Crystal Palace that Mr Joseph Paxton has designed for Prince Albert as the showcase for the works of industry of all nations, though inspired by the ribbed and floating leaves of the lilies in the Duke of Devonshire's lily house at Chatsworth, where Mr Paxton is severally head gardener and designer and best friend.

So George Edward Griffin, otherwise Ned Ludd, takes Margaret Pickens on a knife-board horse bus that runs from Clerkenwell to the Great Exhibition in Hyde Park. Ned buys a copy of *The Times*, printed by the new Augustus Applegarth rotary printing machine that has its type fixed to a vertical cylinder the height of a man, and is surrounded by eight impression cylinders feeding sheets to the central machine, and eight men as minders of the modern Moloch capable of producing ten thousand copies of the newspaper every hour. Where have all the hand printers gone? For gone they are and hardly lamented. From *The Times*, Margaret reads to Ned Ludd a verse from Mr Thackeray's Ode to the new Iron Empire of Britain housed in its Crystal Palace:

> Look yonder where the engines toil:
> These England's arms of conquest are,
> The trophies of her bloodless war:
> Brave weapons these.
> Victorious over wave and soil,
> With these she sails, she weaves, she toils,
> Pierces the everlasting hills
> And spans the seas.

"Aye," Ned Ludd says, "happen that be so. If the poets are saying it, happen that be true. Once it were only said by monsters like the Steam Intellect Society."

"It is not called that, Mister Griffin," Margaret says.

"It is, by all who know them. Officially, it is called the Society for the Diffusion of Useful Knowledge, but it only talks of steam and hot air. And now the poets talk so too . . ."

Ned falls into silence as the horse bus halts a mile from the Crystal Palace. Beside him on the knife-board sits a jaunty journalist, the mellifluous Mayhew, and they see the pandemonium and confusion of getting to the Glass Hive of Industry. From the Prince of Wales's Gate to the Duke of Wellington's Apsley House there stretches one long line of cabs, omnibuses, carriages, broughams, flies, now moving for a few minutes, and now stopping for double the time, while the impatient visitors within let down the blinds and thrust out their heads to see how far the line extends. At every intersecting thoroughfare stand clusters of busy bobbies, seizing horses by the reins, and detaining the vehicles till the cross-current has in a measure ceased. And here may be seen persons threading between the blocked carriages, and bobbing beneath the horses' heads, in order to pass from one side of the road to the other. To seek to pass through the park gates is about as dangerous an experiment as shooting the race in the centre arch of old London Bridge.

But pass they do and reach the entrance of the Great Exhibition. There Ned Ludd purchases Margaret Pickens the cardboard and paper panopticon of the Crystal Palace that will descend to Gog from his grandmother Maria after she has been conceived upon the printing and envelope folding machine of Thos. de la Rue and Company. But as yet, her crinoline is not hiked over her head, the orange silk hiding her red eyes and hair from Ned Ludd's flushed face above, but the hem of her skirts is brushing the gravel on the ground while the hoops that hide her freckled thighs are crushed by the concourse. Ahead of them, the journalist Mayhew is their Virgil leading them through this industrial inferno of the steam intellect, the innumerable machines driven by subterranean pipes radiating from the gigantic boiler in the north-west corner of the vast glass Avernus.

Here you see – and Ned and Margaret do see – a railway guard, with the silver lettering on his collar, and his japan pouch by his side hurrying towards the locomotive department, while among the agricultural instruments saunter clusters of country-men in smock-frocks. The machinery, which has been from the first the grand focus of attention, is the most peculiar sight of the whole. Here every other man you rub against is habited in a corduroy jacket, or a blouse, or leathern gaiters. You see the farmers, their dusty hats telling of the distance they have come, with their mouths agape, leaning on the bars to see the self-acting Mills and the McCormick mechanical reapers at work. But the chief centres of curiosity are the power-looms, the parents of which were once broken by the lubberly Luddites, but now hum securely in old King Ludd's City of London, and in front of these are gathered small groups of artisans and labourers and young men, whose red coarse hands tell you they do something for their living, all eagerly listening to the attendant in search of their future employment, as he explains the operations, after stopping the looms. At the steam brewery, crowds of men are continually ascending and descending the stairs, while on the steps of the crimson-covered pedestals are seated small groups of women and children, some munching thick slices of bread and meat, the edges of which are yellow from oozing mustard. Youths are watching the model carriages moving along the new pneumatic railway; indeed, whether it be the noisy flax-crushing machine, or the splashing centrifugal pump, or the clatter of the Jacquard lace manufacturer, or the bewildering whirling of the cylindrical steam press – round each and all of these are anxious, intelligent and simple-minded artisans, and farmers and servants and youths and children, clustered, endeavouring to solve the mystery of the mammoth mechanisms.

Enough of Mayhew and his lofty condescensions as a guide to the Great Exhibition. Margaret leads Ned Ludd to a more intriguing machine, which may suggest some caprice or naughtiness to alleviate the melancholy that has settled on his broad brow. A small brass machine no bigger than a quart bottle is turning out ladies' undergarments that still have no title because the parts they enclose are unmentionable. In front of this metal marvel, a mustachioed Italian dances with glee as if to an automatic organ-grinder. "Ha! Ha!" he shouts, "you fancy it is a meat-roaster. It is not. It is a tailor. Yes, a veritable stitcher. Present a piece of cloth to it. Suddenly it agitates. It twists about. It screams audibly." And Margaret does hear a small scream escape her own lips as a pair of scissors projects from the brass machine and cuts the cloth, a needle sets to work, and lo and behold, the process of sewing goes on with feverish activity, and before she can take three steps, a pair of *inexpressibles* is spat at her feet. She covers her face with her hands, but the mustachioed Italian sweeps them up from the floor and presents them to her with a bow. "These are for ladies," he cries, "and God and man know where to put them." Ludd looms over him and takes him by the lapels of his jacket and thrusts him back against the impatient brass machine, fretting and fuming at its inactivity. It seizes the tails of the Italian and appropriates them. Its scissors are whipped out, snip-snip, and with its accustomed intelligence, the machine sets to work. The tailless Italian is sent flying down the gallery, while in a twinkling another broadcloth pair is produced of that article of attire, for which the English under Queen Victoria have been able to discover no name in their most comprehensive vocabulary.

Ned Ludd laughs at last and pockets the tailcoat unmentionables. "These'll take some wearing out," he says. And Margaret does not blush, but turns her freckled pale face towards him. "Take me," she says, "to where you will take me. And I will do what you will do. Try me, Mister Griffin. You will not find me wanting." Ned Ludd nods. "I have heard say that women want though they say they do not want." "They do," Margaret says. "They want."

As the evening drops her dust upon the great panes of glass between the iron pillars, and as the twilight scatters her soot over the vast canopy of the palace, Ned Ludd takes his Margaret to the exit from the passage to machinery to where a stand enclosed by brass rails is set. Two wings of red-plush counters demonstrate bank-notes and printed bills and folded envelopes below large lettering in gold: THOS. DE LA RUE AND COMPANY 10 BUNHILL ROW. Another smaller sign asks: *Visitors Are Particularly Requested Not To Touch Any Article*, though it is hard to keep hands off such bright promise of paper money. Fans of impressed and coloured cards spray out behind the young man in a brown frock coat and black peaked cap closing down his iron press that stands on four black legs pointing two great bald eyeballs of counterweights towards Ned Ludd and Margaret. The flywheels fall dumb, the cogs cease turning, the clamps are released. "No more," the operator says, "no more. Tomorrow is another today." He leaves the stand by the side, where he unhitches the loop of a red rope that hangs between the brass rail and the plush counter. "Good night."

Around Ned Ludd and his Margaret, there is nobody at all. The passages and galleries are empty, the aisles and transepts are clear. Margaret takes Ned's hand and leads him through the dropped red rope towards the patent printing machine on its four legs of black iron. She turns towards him and clutches his great girth. Within her the want of a child, the desperate imperative of procreation. He quickens at her need, throws her backwards between the levers of the press, and pulls up the hoops of her bee-hive skirts, throwing them back over her face. She is wearing none of the inexpressibles made by the small brass machine and presented to her by the mustachioed Italian. Red hair burns about the wound of her sex and hems the open arch of her freckled thighs. Ludd plunges deep into her and withdraws and drives home again and again and again, as the piston-head thrusts through the tight cylinder, as the steam-power forces its pressure through the tube, as the crankshaft turns inside the crankcase, as the key penetrates the oiled lock, as the hot rivet fills the socket and the male metal tongue fills the female groove and the bolt seals the bolthole and the hard nail pierces the soft lead. As steam cries from the kettle and is muffled by the cosy, so Margaret's small shrieks are strangled by the silk stuff of her skirts flung over her head. And then as the blast shakes the furnace, so the molten ore pours from Ned Ludd into the crucible of Margaret, and Maria Griffin is engendered, the grandmother of Gog Griffin, as yet an embryo without a Christian name.

Here ends *The True History of Ned Ludd*, for he has performed the one act that will ensure his memory in posterity, the act called the act of love which is the act of procreation. That he manned the cannon at the Battle of Trafalgar which gave Britain the command of the seven seas, that he broke the machines at Nottingham with his English hammer, that he fought the Gas-lit Man and employed his prize-money to buy a hand-press, that he printed pamphlets for Captain Swing and served the movement for the Great Charter, that he was sent to Norwich gaol from whence he was delivered only to be transported to Australia, these acts are as nothing compared to the act of impressing Maria Griffin upon the willing body of Margaret Pickens during the Great Exhibition for the Works of Industry of All Nations, for so he secured his only progeny, to whom he bequeathed a paper panopticon of the Crystal Palace and an iron box, said to contain the prophecies of Joanna Southcott, the messenger of the divine revelation. From this time forth, George Edward Griffin, otherwise Ned Ludd, passes into the mists of oblivion and the miasma of forgetfulness, and this history of him that his great-grandson George Gog Griffin writes as true, shall be the only memorial to that particular man in that past time.

Benin, 1897

Fighting through the forest is a speciality and there is no better treatise extant on bush-fighting than that by Lord Wolseley in his *Soldiers' Pocket-Book*. In his defeat of the Ashantee, however, Lord Wolseley was not assisted by the rocket-tube, the 7-pounder and the Maxim gun, which give us no small advantage. The chief peculiarity of such fighting is the small front exhibited, and the overwhelming advantages that the enemy has from being able to form ambuscades in the dense bush, also from hidden platforms in the trees. The only way of advancing along the forest paths, which serve as the only practicable way to advance, is by firing precautionary volleys into the trees on either flank, matching the bullet against the cover of Nature. The prodigious consumption of ammunition caused the supply system, e.g. myself as organiser and 2,000 head-carriers, a corresponding excess of labour, but it preserved the lives of our gallant soldiers, Marine and Houssa, white and black. The most weird feature of the whole fighting is the rarity with which the enemy is seen. Shots and volleys are fired, yells and whoops are heard, men fall wounded or killed, yet not a sign of the bushman himself, except the shiver of a moving branch and the doubtful view of a dusky figure. It makes one long for the good open battleground of Europe and a sight of the colour of their eyes in order to take aim and fire with exactitude. There is no sporting instinct in bush warfare, as is evidenced by the use of the African pitfall, where a deep pit is covered and filled with sharp and poisoned stakes, inflicting ghastly and incurable wounds on the unwary. Also the practice of leaving mutilated human victims sans eyes sans legs sans every protuberance on the pathways as a deterrent excites a comment from one of our bluejackets, "High time someone did visit here." It is an example of the usual British phlegm.

The Beni sharpshooters give us a warm time at a stockade erected before their City of Blood, but they are soon shown off by the 7-pounders and the Maxims while the rockets make a jolly blaze in the juju compound beyond the wooden barrier. We debouch into the clearing in front of the king's compound and are met by volleys of old metal scraps. We suffer casualties, viz: one officer killed, two wounded; three men killed, twenty-four wounded. But the Beni have no stomach for our bayonets, and they vacate their city pretty damn quickly, even if the juju of the king forbids him ever to leave his capital of grisly sacrifice.

The city of Benin boasts many compounds, high red-clay walls enclosing huts and the Palava House where the elders sit. Juju palaces and crucifixion trees also abound. The palaces are long sheds ending in an altar black with blood on which are placed antique bronze heads and carved ivory tusks (the ivory of no great worth being discoloured and dead with age). In the centre of these juju sheds is an iron erection like a huge candelabra with sharp hooks for hanging portions of human victims as we once hanged the quarters of our traitors and criminals in the Middle Ages. The smells of human remains and human blood are such that no white man's internal economy can withstand. I am sick four times that day in the City of Blood of Benin. For blood is everywhere; smeared over bronzes, ivory, pest pits, crucifixion trees and even the walls; it speaks the history of that awful city in a clearer way than writing ever can. And this unspeakable blood offering has been going on for centuries! Not the lust of one king, not the climax of a bloody reign, but the religion (save the word!) of the race, given to many regimes of stagnant brutality.

There are trophies to be gathered as the rightful spoils of such an expedition. I will not demean the name of art by comparing the bronze sculptures of these bloodthirsty savages with the dignified marbles of a Phidias or a Michelangelo. The storehouses of the king are filled with the habitual cheap rubbish proper to such a vile nature, such as glass walking-sticks, old uniforms, absurd umbrellas, the cheap finery that traders use to tickle the fancy of the natives. But the bronze heads from the altars are truly cast admirably, although their flattened features betray their native origins. And buried in the dirt of ages are several hundred unique but battered bronze plaques, suggestions of almost Egyptian hieroglyphic design, one of which remains in my possession as a memento of the disaster that was about to befall us.

I believe that the conflagration that consumed the city of

Benin was a cleansing fire, if caused by the hand of Man, yet commanded by the will of God. Most offensive to the good Lord were the crucifixion trees that the king had adapted from the juju which he called Christianity. These trees were not crosses, but hurdles pinned between two cottonwood trunks in the shape of an M. The wretched victims were bound upon the hurdles and mutilated and abandoned to expire of thirst and the attacks of scavengers and insects. At the base of these instruments of death were skulls and bones, literally strewn about; the debris of former sacrifices. Yea, this was a Golgotha and an abomination in the eyes of the Almighty. And He caused the flames to be lit four days later which consumed the city of blood utterly, to the last compound and juju palace, to the final pest pit and crucifixion tree. Sodom and Gomorrah were not more utterly purged by the fire from above. We had to flee with such trophies as we could muster, not forgetting our victuals, our armoury and our stores. For there shall be an accounting on earth as in heaven, and woe unto him who fails to satisfy the audit, to which he is summoned.

GOG NOTE: The above account of the capture of the city of Benin is reconstructed from contemporary writings and the spoken memories of my father, George Griffin. As a young man on the punitive expedition, he represented the values of British imperialism at the zenith of the grab for Africa. In later years, when he became a Celtic nationalist and an Irish rebel within the British ranks, leading to his untimely "execution" in Dublin, he regretted his former role in the destruction of this centre of African art. He did not, however, condone the Beni (now termed Ibo) habit of human sacrifice, although he often referred to the Celtic habit of dedicating all prisoners of war to the goddess Andastra and consigning the victims to fiery wooden cages or to the bottom of peat bogs. "Civilisation or savagery are merely intervals in time," he used to teach. "Judgment on a people depends on the language and the artefacts which it leaves to future ages." By the end of his life, George Griffin had given up the judgment of God for the survival of art and the word. By such a standard, both the art of Benin and the language of the Celts will ensure the just verdict of history.

APPENDIX: This is a representation of the hieroglyphic bronze plaque from Benin bequeathed to me by my father. As yet, I am unable to decipher it.

England and Wales, 1897–1916

The shores of Wessex and the Isle of Wight are serried by protruding dots and dashes. Grey points and lumps make small crenellations on the surface of the sea. Standing at the rail of the boat that brings him home from Africa, George Griffin looks at the far outlines of the bows and profiles of the Home Fleet, drawn up for review by the old Queen Victoria, celebrating her Diamond Jubilee. The destroyers and dreadnoughts are no larger than the signs of the Morse Code writ against the horizon, where white kites fly trailing wires to transmit Count Marconi's mysterious messages by wireless telegraphy. These are the ships that are sovereign over the seven seas, now reduced to distant crumbs and specks set against the long low islands of Britain that have spawned them. Their only significance to George Griffin is that he cannot read any glory in them. He is weary of empire and the blood spilt to maintain it. He is buying his discharge from the Navy.

His father, Albert Smith, and his mother, Maria Griffin, are pleased. They never wanted him to sign on. He ran away to sea, as young men do when they rebel against the patronage of paternal righteousness. His father is a watchmaker, nicknamed the Public Pulse. So unerringly does Albert Smith feel what the voters wish that politicians want to touch him for his insight. He is a counsellor to the Liberals and to the new Labour Party. He claims that David Lloyd-George and Keir Hardie are friends, and certainly they are acquaintances who consult the Public Pulse.

Judicious as he is on national affairs, Albert Smith is harsh to his son George and indulgent to his daughter Grace. Perhaps it is a reaction from the tyranny of his wife Maria, imprinted in embryo like a bank-note on a machine in the Great Exhibition and making men pay for possessing her thereafter. As she dominates him and insists that her son take the surname of Griffin after her, so her husband tries to dominate his son to prove he is not subject to his wife.

His daughter Grace, though, is the loving consolation of his life, her long red hair the envy of the pre-Raphaelite painters. She is his love, she compensates for mother and wife and son, she is the pearl beyond price of paternal care, until the Viking called Magnusson comes to drag her away.

The old Queen dies on the withered arm of her grandson, the Kaiser, the empire expands under the weary rule of the stout roué King Edward, and George Griffin becomes a schoolmaster. He is determined to teach his pupils not to serve as imperial mercenaries as he has served in his misguided youth. At his Shropshire school, he meets the daughter of a neighbouring landowner from an old Catholic family, Miss Merivale "Merry" Bellwether. She is also in rebellion against the conventions of the countryside and finds in the craggy George Griffin a Heathcliff come again to rescue her from the boredom of the Welsh borders. Bakunin and Marx and Engels are now yeast in the batter of his brains. The revolutions that seethe in his mind inflame Merry's rebellion from her own kind. They elope to Anglesey, that island off North Wales where the Druids made their final stand before their massacre by the Romans, where the Welsh nation still helps the Irish in their uprisings against the English yoke because of Celtic brotherhood and the long subjection of Cymru to the might and majesty of London.

After three years of marriage by pastor and by priest, another George Griffin is born. He is called Gog, not after the ancient giant of Albion, but because he loves to eat summer gooseberries or goosegogs, and his greedy baby lips cannot pronounce all the word, just "Gog . . . gog . . . gog." The birth of her son reconciles Merry with her family, who have disowned her. Gog is received into the Catholic faith and a place is secured for him in the great Jesuit college of Downforth. But his boyhood is spent in Holy Isle off Anglesey, where his father and the crookback Evans the Latin teach in the local school and instruct the pupils in the gods and the heroes of the Celts, in the wickedness of the Romans and the Normans and the Plantagenets and the Hanoverians, in the virtues of the bards and of the ancient princes of Scotland and Ireland and Wales, before the English took the crown away and called fat King Edward's sailor son the Prince of Wales, who only speaks the German tongue and not the Gaelic, the guttural and not the *hwyl*. Particularly Gog's father teaches of the ancient Irish god of the sun called King Lug and of the Welsh god of the sun called King Ludd. Both gods were wily and had many guises, smith and warrior, harper and bard, hero and historian, sorcerer and seer. Both carried slingshots as well as spears and could put out the eye of the sun by casting their radiant stones. Both were champions of their people and were victorious over the might of their enemies, although King Ludd lost a hand in the final battle against the Minions and had mechanical fingers crafted upon his stump by the divine smith Govannan, giving Ludd the name in the Welsh language of *Llaw Ereint* or Silver Hand.

These are the generations of George Griffin who writes this text, and so he first was told of *The True History of King Ludd*.

Holyhead, 1916–18

Not a child, not a man, Gog Griffin lies on his mother's Turkish carpet, its patterns zigzag as trenches in the Dardanelles on the battleground of his play. He is looking at his war postcards, imagining the front line in coloured comic cards. Mighty legs in army boots and puttees push a gigantic broom against a pile of minuscule Boche soldiers: the caption is, SWEEPING THE GERMANS OFF THE EARTH. A brown figure with bayonet and braces leaps above the point of an Ulhan helmet: the legend is, OVER THE TOP – HURRAH. Six soldiers in the various uniforms of the Allies charge forwards to the written shout of ARE WE DOWN-HEARTED? NO! NO! NO! A sergeant in the Brigade of Guards pushes out his red tunic with a swelling belly: WE'RE WELL TO THE FRONT! A baby boy and a tubby Tommy wear their uniforms marked KHAKI: it is described as THIS COLOUR DOES NOT RUN! and THIS STUFF WILL NEVER SHRINK! An old country-man with stick and Crimean War medals shakes the hand of his upright burly corporal son off to France – A CHIP OFF THE OLD BLOCK. A white-haired angelic lady hovers over a mounted boy cavalry officer with his sword drawn – MOTHER OF MINE. A lion stands on an African rock, roaring in dumbshow to prides of lions from the empire padding towards him – RESPONDING TO THE CALL. These are true images of the Great War. But what of the false ones that are too close to home? The green Irish flag with the yellow harp crossed with the Union Jack – TWO MINDS WITH BUT A SINGLE THOUGHT – NOW! The shell screaming down on the chained and cowering soldier – THAT 16-INCH SEN-SATION! And the worst of all, the white-faced ninny with his brush and apron sweeping up the trench behind the Tommies firing at the enemy: THE CONSCIENTIOUS OBJECTOR AT THE FRONT!

> While The Shot and Shell Are Flying
>   And the Mighty Cannons Boom,
> He Is Tidying Up the Trenches
>   With a Dust-pan and a Broom!

Oh, father, father, why did you refuse to go? Why did the military take you away? How did they make you serve? When will you come back home? I hate them. I hate you. Coward! Conchie that wasn't! Oh father, the flour thrown on me at school, the white goosefeathers in my desk. Even Evans the Latin cannot save me. Father who is no father to me.

Gog picks up the postcards of hate that he still possesses as the record of his memories. The Kaiser casting his shadow as a black skeleton, weeping TEARS OF GREED as his head grows out of the onion of Europe, burning Reims Cathedral with his fiery brands, looking like a naked boar with boot-prints on his rump, extending his griffin claws to seize Alsace-Lorraine, hanging from a lamppost while the crows peck out his eyes, capering as a firing squad peppers his backside to the refrain:

> When the Kaiser Begins to Prance,
> Whoops! Let's Do It Again!
> Let's Make Billy the German Dance,
> Whoops! Let's Do It Again.
> Now We're Here We Mean to Fight,
> Give Him Beans Till He Screams with Fright,
> It Serves the Swine Jolly Well Right,
> Whoops! Let's Do It Again.

But Gog's favourite card is KAISER BILL "THE TWO FACED TWISTER". When it is turned upside down, the face of the German Emperor in his pointed helmet becomes the face of the devil with horns – HIS SATANIC MAJESTY. He is also the mouth of the goal in *Trench Football*, a hand-game that Gog plays by rolling a silver pellet along a meandering trench past holes marked *Little Willie, Outside Right*, and *Von Tirpitz, Centre Forward*, and *Von Kluck, Outside Left* through a whole squad of hazardous German generals till the pellet is juggled past *Count Zeppelin at Right Back* to score a goal in the Kaiser's open mouth below his black handlebar moustache. War games.

Merry comes into the parlour, her eyes red with weeping.

"They're sending him to Ireland, Gog. To kill our own. George, sent to kill our own."

"Mother. Mother."

Gog stands, awkward and tall as Merry, and holds her in his lumpish arms, his body uneasy at the touch of her plump maternal flesh through the wool of her dress. He does not know what to do. He has always gone crying to her. Grownups don't blub.

"They'll kill your father. I know they'll kill him."

"He'll be all right. I know he will."

"He's coming through on a troop train. We can see him go out of the docks."

"I'll take you there, Mother. I'll look after you. If I'm not at school."

"I'll tell them you're sick and I need you."

Merry has never done this before, never lied to the school, never said she had need of her son. Gog is a man at ten years old now, no longer a boy. The war, and the pictures of war, are doing that for him.

"You've got your postcards all over the carpet," Merry says. Tidiness is first in her order of importance. Then she gives another pair of postcards to Gog.

"Your aunt Grace sent you these. They're the latest from the factory."

"The factory that makes the cards, not the shells."

"Don't say that." Merry starts to weep again. "You know what your father thinks of that. His sister married to somebody who is making bullets and bombs."

"Magnus Magnussen, the Munition Maker." Gog chants his happy families. "Grace Griffin, the Munition Maker's Wife. Gog Griffin, the Munition Maker's Son . . ."

"Don't tease me, Gog. And tidy up this room."

Merry leaves the parlour, and Gog looks at the two cards from the postcard factory that Magnus Magnusson runs to keep up morale while he manufactures the munitions of war that blast the enemy. The first postcard is the postcard of the face imprinted on Gog's silver wrist-watch, two drooping moustaches surrounded by dreadnoughts and marching troops and marked KITCHENER. Now Kitchener is depicted as backed by an angel and the white ensign and a broken ship's sail and drowning bluejackets and a foaming sea. Below him a wreath surrounds the legend: OLD ENGLAND FOR EVER! "*I Know That I Shall Die at Sea.*" LORD KITCHENER. Yes, the great man is gone, sunk on HMS *Hampshire*, its lifebelt storm-shattered on the card commemorating his departure. But the second postcard becomes the later security of Gog's life, the message of the future, the communication to the flow of time that always is. The silhouettes of battleships and cruisers and destroyers and submarines and patrol boats no larger than specks make up the broken outline of a bulldog that guards the North Sea in a bristling watch of hieroglyphs and dashes and dots like Count Marconi's code that links the British fleet. The postcard still informs Gog now of the boy he was then. It sits in front of him as he writes, and he can see its code of rune and pictograph and line and blob that tell him the Royal Navy shall never let the Hun cross the Channel, and Albion may sleep safe on its Holy Isle, even if Hitler now builds the Reich.

THE SILENT WATCHER.

THE NORTH SEA BATTLESHIPS
AS SEEN BY THE MAN IN THE MOON.

But Gog is still on his Holy Island off Anglesey off Albion, and his father is being sent away to fight the Papists across the water, only Merry and Gog are Papists too, and praying to the Virgin Mother and hoping the Pope in Rome does not turn them into traitors, just because the Irish believers have risen in Dublin and are dying for the wearing of the green. Yes, they are killing the king's men in khaki too, and father is one of the long dun file tramping sullen up the gangplank into the old paddle-wheel steamer berthed in the docks of Holyhead. See the troops file into her, men hangdog and silent, never a song among them, with rifles shaped like crutches and puttees wound round their ankles careful as brown bandages. Watch them go sullen and slouching into the iron bowels of the ship, as Gog stands with his mother Merry, and she is blubbing and crossing herself, and Gog pulls at her sleeve. Mother, Mother, not here, Mother, as the crowd shrinks back from her sobbing Hail Marys, as the black-garbed Wesleyans recoil until the only clear space on all the cobbled quay is a ring about Gog and his mother. And the Welsh are all mumbling and whispering and pointing to the two Papist spies among them, Gog all of ten years old and his praying mother, with his father suddenly stepping up the gangplank among the line of soldiers, his father with bare neck under brown cap and Kitchener moustaches desperately drooping, his father looking backward in fear and weariness, looking until he sees Gog and his mother, who runs forward screaming, Griffin, George Griffin, you can't kill them, you can't kill them, my own people, you can't kill them, Blessed Virgin, he can't kill them, his brothers. And the two police-men seize her and pull her back and Gog runs forward and bites the policeman's hand on his mother's wrist, sinks his teeth into the knucklebones and hangs on, until a swipe on his ear sends him cowering on to the cobbles, hands over his head. And he peers upwards again through parted elbows to see his father turn away in denial as he is prodded forward by the khaki men advancing behind him, his father's back turn away bowed under big pack and kitbag and rifle, his father turn away on the treadmill of uniform that falls into the belly of the paddleboat. And he sees no more of his father, except the sepia photographs yellowing at the edges, except the telegram that father is dead for his country in

Dublin, except the letter from the adjutant that the dirty Irish papists have shot father in the back off duty for the wearing of the khaki.

There is no other news of the dying George Griffin, the holy fathers off the ferryboat murmuring through the walls, soldiers on leave looking in for confession or consolation, stray informers just for the hell of it. There is no truth in all this tattle of treason. George Griffin going round the barrack-rooms and seeking out the drafted and the disaffected, telling them of mutiny and mayhem, shooting the officers in the back and joining the rebellion. George Griffin preaching a laying-down of arms, a squatting until armistice, the killing has to stop. George Griffin secretly informing the republicans of the wherefore and the whereabouts of all the English military, and so a small arrangement that he is shot by his own side and called a war hero, no hanging for him in the Tower. But traitor he seems to be, turncoat and two-faced, like Janus and the Kaiser, but all for liberty, for the Celts shall be free.

It's short commons now in the shuttered house with the pinched fingers of charity bringing bowls of dripping for the bread, and the plump priest offering consolation when there's none to be had, and the relatives always at their requiem: Well, what did you expect, Merry, if you would marry beneath you? And one day, Mother puts aside her drab weeds and rises in scarlet and feathers and she's off to the town for the pickings from the procession of soldiers. And the uncles begin to stop by on their way to the ferry, hanging their braided caps on the deer's horns in the hall, their Sam Brownes smelling of polish and linseed, the metal tips of their tan shoes digging dents in the Persian patterns on the carpet. And the uncles give way to a steady comer, the garrison major ready for an Irish counter-sortie, the English squireen who treats Wales as a tribal reservation and Holyhead as a feudal village and Merry as a temporary wife, for any woman he is with must be a lady too respectable to be a whore. And the boys call out at Gog in the streets,

> Blimey, blimey,
> Your ma's got a limey . . .

237

till he's so bruised with blind bashing at his tormentors, his
mother forbids him to go out. O, the fights are bloodier and
not so classy as the fights of the fancy and peerless Tom
Cribb in *Boxiana*, conned page by loved page. But the major
keeps on coming, bold, bluff and booming with small spiky
mustachios, brown and rough as an oak, used to striding
across a whole shire and calling it, My Estate. And when
Merry swells at the belly and talk changes to marriage: How
would you like another father, Gog? How would you like to
go to boarding-school? Don't make a face now, say thank
you to Major Meredith, don't you want to make me happy?
Then the major's off to the Somme for ever, transferred by
request, and the relatives descend like cormorants and gulp
down Gog like a codling, ready to disgorge him to the
Jesuit fishers in the cold northern moorland, where Catholic
schoolboys learn to avoid perdition by rod, rigour and re-
straint, the trinity of three R's so good for the soul.

But Aunt Grace has no children, and she takes to the
lumpen Gog, orphaned by war and the new baby Magnus
Griffin, carefully called after her own husband Magnus Magnusson, Merry sucking up to her estranged sister-in-law in
hope of the millions that may come of it from the making of
munitions. But the Magnussons won't deal with the bastard
of war, and the tiny tot Magnus is adopted after birth by
other wealthy relations, the Ponsonbys of Burke-Gotha, who
put an unencumbered male child above property. But Gog
wants his Aunt Grace to take him to the arsenal of the
mortar-bombs and howitzer shells, the grenades and the
whizz-bangs, but Grace will only take him to his ultimate
treasure-house, the long brick shed where the postcards are
made that keep the troops happy, shell-casings turned to
love-beds, an April Fool fish gobbling up a U-boat, sweet-
hearts embracing in tank turrets and on Sopwith Camels,
pretty nurses kissing war-wounded with peg-legs, old ladies
piercing zeppelins with their brollies, girls firing babies out
of Maxim guns, toddlers piddling in upturned spiked helmets.
Gog's collection grows with a hundred new glossy postcards
in an afternoon, and he acquires his first embroidered ones
from the stitching section at the end of the shed, skivvies
stooped over their embroidery, their needles flicking quicker
than bullets through long grasses, turning out gay cannons

covered with flowers, 1918 on the flags of the Allies, and tributes to our gallant airmen of the RFC, here spelt ROYAL FLING CORPS.

"Oh thank you, Aunt Grace," Gog says, "you can give me no more. You have given me all the war."

And it is all the Great War that Gog remembers because it is still in his keeping, the paper scraps of it and one lead-fringed glass remnant, a fleur-de-lis in stained glass salvaged from the ruins of Ypres Cathedral. To Gog, the Great War ends with the ghastly going to Downforth, the Jesuits and the cells and the double logic of the real and the possible, where nothing is true except the God who is not there. As he leaves for Liverpool Street Station and the London Northern and Eastern Railway, Aunt Grace gives him the last three paper games that he has never lost and are much of his present information of the Great War. Two of them can be unfolded, cut-outs of a German tourist and a commercial traveller. When the flaps are open, the first changes into a fat German soldier in green uniform and jackboots, holding a revolver and a fiery torch to a French cathedral: the second reveals a city at night, lit by incendiaries dropped by biplanes with black crosses on their wings. It is all happening again, the spies from across the Rhine, the moles and the rodent burrowers, tourism and trade the guise for treachery, the smilers with the subversion. But best of all is the third present, Charlie Chaplin shouldering arms in the trenches, two hundred pictures that flicker into motion when ruffled by a thumbnail, Charlie swinging round with his rifle butt knocking off an officer's cap and sticking his bayonet into a backing Boche bottom. It is more by grace than by God that Gog remembers the Great War at all, and as he finishes *The True History of King Ludd* with himself writing in his Paris studio, he picks up the flicker-pictures and runs his fingertips over them to watch Charlie once more dash authority and deflate pride, the one man of mankind who is everyman to all men. And Gog records it and puts down his pen with this full stop.

16

"Your *histoire* of King Ludd," Maire says to Gog, "*ce n'est pas vrai.* It is not true. But it is about your family. That is true. In France, *la famille* is everything. But I do not have."

She pushes aside her plate of chocolate and cream cake, fit for the sweet tooth of a Habsburg empress. She is sitting under a life-size bronze statue of a naked slave-girl, who has a small shelf to her belly as Maire has and two breasts for ever surging towards the guests in the dining-room of the Alkron Hotel in Prague. They might as well be on a cruise liner, for veneered wood and curving brass enclose them, and a seven-piece gypsy orchestra plays "The Blue Danube", scraping sugar from the strings of its fiddles.

"I don't have much of a family either," Gog says. "Historically, yes. Presently, no. A mother. A half-brother. An aunt, who has just died and left me a fortune."

"That is what *la famille* is. Property. Wills. Leave you money."

"And memories," Gog says. "Centuries of memory." He looks at the naked bronze girl offering herself above Maire, who is wearing a black silk shirt with padded shoulders that accentuates the white moon of her face. Desire plucks at his belly. "We'll be happy here. You'll love Prague."

"Better than that bloody walk in the Landes. I leave you."

"No more long walks," Gog says, "or I walk alone."

"It is funny you want to come here, Gog. And now."

"It is funny you do." Gog has his reasons, but he does not know why Maire is so keen to visit Czechoslovakia for a week, especially during an international crisis. "We may find ourselves at the start of the next world war. Hitler invading the Sudetenland."

"I like danger," Maire says. She drops her lids to veil the tops of her blue eyes. "You like danger? It is *aphrodisiaque*."

"That's what we came here for," Gog says. "Or did you have another reason? Someone else you want to meet?"

"No." Maire answers too quickly, laughs too shrilly. "You,

mon Gog. Maybe the big man you tell me of. I like big men. The big man the rabbi make when danger comes."

"The Golem? He's the local version of Gog, a sort of giant who fights for the people. When the Jews were going to be persecuted in the Prague ghettos, Rabbi Löw made the Golem out of clay."

"Why he live if he is clay?"

"He had the Hebrew characters for truth engraved on his forehead – *aleph, mem* and *soph*. When he went mad and attacked his creators, a little girl turned him back to clay by rubbing out the *aleph*. The last two Hebrew letters mean death."

Maire laughs again like a tympani accompanying the honied strings of the orchestra.

"Sign the bill," she says. "Love before death."

That early afternoon, Maire rides Gog as a sea-nymph rides a dolphin, bucking and plunging on the spine of his sex, her knees gripping his ribs and her calves squeezing against his hips to press her thighs deep into his flesh, her black hair flicking his nipples as she strains forward to give the swell of her breasts to the splay of his two hands. As he feels the firm give of her body that enfolds and masters him, he thrusts upwards and breaks as a waterspout within her and shouts to the frieze of wreaths set about the bedroom walls.

"Maire!"

She falls forward, laying her breasts upon the cage of his ribs, putting her ear against the pumping bellows of his heart.

"*Mon* Gog," she breathes. "*Ma* Gog."

For a moment, Gog knows, or thinks he knows, that his brother is here, and that is why Maire is here. But then the ebb of ease that follows the flow of desire washes away the brief conspiracy in his mind. He has his own plot in Prague, and he must be at the trysting-place.

"I love you, Maire." The hardest words to say in the language, the easiest lie, the only truth. "Simply, I love you."

She does not keep him in the bed, but she seems almost eager that he should go for a walk alone to explore the old city of Prague. She will rest, the aeroplane fatigued her, she must not risk a migraine or a *crise de foie* which might make the Czech crisis appear a tempest in the teacup. So Gog leaves the Alkron in good time for his secret meeting. A local map guides him past the Tyl Theatre, where Mozart put on his *Don Giovanni*, to the Old Town Square. The streets curve and bend and slope aslant, all askew as the subterfuges in Gog's skull. Weird towers protrude and balconies jut like the naggings and doubts in Gog's mind. He stops by the medieval clock as the hour clangs one, two, three, four, and a skeleton death tinkles a bell as light as Maire's laugh, and the saints process above two cosmic circles of time, and the four gospellers tock their heads to the strokes of the hour. Gog is late and hurries on to the old cemetery, where the Jews have been crowded in their burials for five hundred years. Behind its high walls, twelve thousand gravestones are packed in a little land. They seem to scrabble through the soil and weeds, sometimes a stone nail for a child's tomb, or whole stone fingers with pointed tips, stone palms spread open as Gog's were spread over the breasts of Maire, even fists or thumbs of stone, all pushing up from the earth. Among these many memorials rise the stone arks of the great rabbis, Mordecai Maisel and Jehuda Liva ben Bacalel, known as Rabbi Löw. And he is standing there, or rather a thin slight man in a grey suit is standing there, stippled with sunlight and the shadows of the thin trunks of the graveyard trees. He has a rolled newspaper under his arm.

"Og-Am," the slight man says indirectly to Gog. He may well be talking to himself or to the ghost of Rabbi Löw.

"Gog I am," Gog replies in the password that Graveling has told him to give.

A grimace that may be a smile puckers the face of the stranger.

"They see you come here?"

"Nobody. Nobody knows. There is no reason to follow me."

Gog and the slight man look over the stone splinters and shards and spikes of the myriad tombs. They are alone. Jewish places are not popular in Prague in 1938, with Hitler threatening invasion.

"I am not followed," the slight man says. "No one know we read the German code. But the Germans, they change the code all the time. They have five rotors now, not three rotors. We work all the time, keeping to the changes."

"I know," Gog says. "Our friend tells me that we cannot decipher the German Code. Our prime minister is flying to Munich to see Herr Hitler and stop a war. But we cannot read their messages. We do not know what is in the Führer's mind."

"This."

The slight man presents the rolled newspaper to Gog. It is thick and heavy. Gog unrolls the front page of Czech newsprint to reveal a bundle of the perforated sheets of paper that Graveling has already shown to him.

"Ah," Gog says, "the music for the pianola."

Once more, the grimace that is a smile passes the slight man's face.

"Let us call it that," he says. "But this is new. Tell our friends in London and in Paris, I have put in a random factor. In the lines and dots on the paper, there is a factor for speed if the Germans change their rotors and scramble their code. It is a theory of permutations, but quick, quick, now with our cyclometer, our *bomba*, and these sheets I make."

"When do we get your cyclometer and your *bomba*?"

"You come to Warsaw. You start with the sheets because your friend, he work on the same. He call it computer not cyclometer. Does he send something for us?"

"He says you may not have time to set them up before the Germans attack you. Radio waves to track enemy aircraft before they fly in. We call it radar. We already have five stations in the Thames Estuary tracking our prime minister, Neville Chamberlain, as he flies out to see Hitler at Munich."

Gog takes a small book out of his pocket and gives it to the Pole, who opens it. For the third time, he grimaces.

"Ah, the Gogam code. I hear of that."

The writing in the book is indeed in the script discovered or invented by Gog – the lines and dots of the ancient Druid alphabet and numerals.

"You have the Gogam keyboard."

"Yes, I have." The Pole puts the book in the pocket of his jacket. "Your radar, it is very interesting. But I agree. We have not the time before Hitler attack Poland. And Russia, too, we think."

"When do you think?"

"It depend on what your prime minister do at Munich. Hitler need one more year to prepare."

"So do we. At least one more year."

"We need a hundred years," the Pole says. "And then we are not ready. Because we have lost four hundred years occupied by other people. Like these Czechs here. It is the tragedy of Middle Europe, always you are occupied – followed – spied . . ."

The thin trees of the cemetery appear to move. Men as tree trunks are shifting their surveillance. The very grave-stones stir. Figures are changing their observation posts. Perhaps only the sun strikes from the earth and the stones and the leaves a gauze of heat that rises and wavers in the air.

"We go," the Pole says. "You leave before me."

Gog nods and walks away between the tombs towards the Klausen synagogue and the cemetery gate. The roll of newspaper under his arm is as heavy as a truncheon that may smash his skull. He hardly dares to breathe until he passes safely through the broken gate into the street. He walks quickly, turning to look back at every corner, seeing nobody in pursuit. He takes to the secret Prague, the arcades and walkways and tunnels that honeycomb the interiors of the city blocks. Along these frequented caverns, the Czechs live their clandestine lives in the cinemas and theatres, markets and taverns called *vinarnas*, their other selves and rude *doppelgängers* denying the bright faces that they must wear in the streets, where the enemy threatens and where the masks of order and obsequiousness must be observed. By the hazard of fate, Gog passes a night-club decorated with Moorish pilasters and plaster houris that boasts the name of the ALHAMBRA. He books a table for that night with Maire.

Gog is glad and disturbed to find Maire gone from their suite at the Alkron. He finds tissue paper which she has discarded, wraps a pair of his trousers round the roll of newspaper and perforated sheets, then encloses it all in the thick tissue, making it look as tidy and soft as a present from Prague. He places it casually on the luggage-rack as a thing of such little importance that it will seem irrelevant in any search of his room. He changes into a white tie and tails, the necessary formality to prove one can pay the bills in the age of depression. And when Maire arrives back at nine o'clock in the evening with the flush in her pale cheeks that indicates no good, Gog does not voice his jealous suspicions of her casual infidelities, but helps her to dress in his favourite black gown, slit to navel in front and coccyx behind, two V's of white flesh depending from the straps on her shoulders, the white beads on the frills of her skirt clicking on the floor. She is naked under the slashed robe, and everybody will know it.

At the Alhambra, they are seated by the dance-floor in the lower tier beneath the stage. A frieze of suggestive golden cupids surrounds the top tier and the private boxes, while nymphs and satyrs cavort across the lilac curtains that drape the little cabaret theatre. Another seven-man band is trying to play jazz, but the alto-saxophone sounds like the Pan pipes and the trumpet is as mellifluous as a hornful of golden syrup. The caviare and the saddle of carp are magnificent, so are the strawberry *torta* and the two bottles of pink champagne. Gog lusts after the bare breasts of Maire, with only the nipples covered by the black halter round her neck. Then with the intelligence of instinct, Gog knows that other men's eyes are admiring her. He looks past a golden Cupid up to the nearest private box, only to see the oiled yellow hair and beady gaze of Magog peering down – and behind him the golden curls of Rupert and the cherry-red pout of Putney Bowles. As he recognises the three Cognoscenti in the box, its red curtains are drawn, leaving him with no evidence of his sighting, or of his insight.

"He's here," Gog accuses Maire. "Magog. Magnus. My brother. My *doppelgänger*. My worser half."

"Don't be silly. Magnus is in London. He works. In the Ministry. He cannot come here."

"He is here. In that box, behind those curtains. I swear I saw . . ."

There is a roll of drums from the band, the stage drapes are opened, and a dwarf ringmaster bursts out of the paper belly of a huge nude in caricature. He takes off his top hat and announces from pantomime placards in Czech and German, French and English – THE ONCE AND FUTURE SHOW – PRAGUE FROM THE GREAT WAR OF 1914 TO THE NEXT WAR AND

Why Prague is the home of the can-can, Gog does not
know, or of the black-bottom or the shimmy, but certainly
the chorus girls can dance all of them when the ringmaster
isn't ripping off their skirts and brassières. Gog only responds
when a monstrous Golem lurches on in clay boots to stomp
around as an earthern maypole while the nearly-naked girls
festoon him with streamers and kisses, and the dwarf stands
on tiptoe to pull out of the giant's crotch a bologna sausage
a yard long. Crude stuff it is, until blackness engulfs the
set and luminous lights pick out a drunken Mickey Mouse
dancing on a fluorescent rope that becomes his noose and
serpentine nemesis. It is the magic lantern of Prague, and
when the magician asks for the audience to join in the
illusion, and Maire leads the way to the stage wriggling in
her slit black gown, Gog must stumble in her wake in his
evening dress, his white tie and black tails.

On the stage, the strange lighting dismembers them. Their
dark costumes disappear, leaving Maire as an M surmounted
by a moon, her white arms and the V of skin above her
bosom supporting her oval face. Gog is a cup of shirt-front
beneath the clefts and crannies of his visage. And as he
looks, he sees three kites floating beyond his reach in the
darkness – the heads of Magog and Rupert and Putney
Bowles, ghastly-green and ghost-purple in the weird lighting
of the magic lantern.

Now Gog rises like a balloon towards them. He gropes
with a hand like a hawk soaring. His fingers are swaddled in
black velvet. He slides to the ground.

Now the shiny head of Magog flies down. "Traitor," it
hisses. "Where are the papers? Where? Where?"

Now Rupert's head descends, trailing golden fires. "Gog,
Gog, give them to me, and I shall be yours."

And Putney Bowles bobs down, his red mouth opening a
tear in the fabric of his face. "Put your friend before your
country. Love me first."

And Gog's hands grip and claw at strands of light and the
cloying cloth of darkness, and he cries, "Treason, trio of
traitors, treason."

And Maire is rising now on her white arms as wings, her

head as a balloon wafting her away. And Gog clutches at her going and his hands wind round the beads at the bottom of her black gown and the strings break and the white glass drops to tinkle and shatter on the floor. And she is gone to the face and the embrace of Magog, and they fly away in luminous lights and abysmal darkness, and Gog is wrath and pulls at the invisible cloths and cloaks and draperies, and they tumble down and enfold him and choke him in their ebony soft dust. All is conspiracy and illusion, for this is Prague.

Next morning, Gog wakes in his bedroom at the Alkron to find his baggage packed and Maire ready to leave. He has never seen her more angry. "You disgrace me," she says. "You are drunk. You wreck the Alhambra. You must go from Prague. The police say OK if you go. I pay, I pay, I pay."

"My money," Gog says. "It must have been that pink champagne. But Magog was there."

"Your brother is not in Prague," Maire says. "I tell you true."

The roll wrapped in tissue-paper has not been packed and is untouched. Gog carries it under his arm to the airport, and the Customs officials do not examine it. When the aeroplane reaches London airport, Gog goes with Maire to Claridge's and leaves her there and takes a taxi to the safe address given to him by Colin Graveling, who is waiting for him. The mathematician examines the rolls of perforated sheets and smiles to see the random factor programmed into the dashes and the dots.

"Five rotors now in the German coding machine," Graveling says. "And we must get the cyclometer and the *bomba* from Warsaw. You did well, my friend. It must have been your Gogam code which got you through. It is so simple that nobody could crack it."

"Simplicity is always best," Gog says. "I left those perforated rolls wrapped in my trousers and in tissue paper openly in my room. I knew the suite would be searched. My things were packed far too neatly in my bags in the morning. Maire couldn't do that, she couldn't pack a toothbrush. Whatever they put in my drink at the Alhambra, they didn't reckon on one thing. Nobody looks at the obvious. The invisible is what stares you in the eye."

"War stares us in the eye," Graveling says. "Although Neville Chamberlain has come back from Munich with the fatuous words – 'Peace in our time.' I just hope we have peace for long enough a time to crack the German code machine and know what the Nazis plan to do." He looks at Gog, who sees him bristling as always with hair awry and sprouting moustache and spiky tweeds. "Your brother Magnus was in Prague, you know. He led a delegation from the Ministry of Defence. Czechoslovakia was our ally, till we sold her down the river at Munich."

"Does he know about those perforated rolls from Poland? Is that why he put Maire after me and drugged me? Does he know we know about German cryptography?"

"I doubt it," Graveling says, "or he might tell the Germans. But he knows you were doing something for me, and he wanted to know what it was. You've done better than him, Gog. Aren't you pleased?"

And Gog is pleased. It is his first victory against Magog in a lifetime of defeats. But if his wife is in the plots and the pay of his brother, he also knows he will lose all the rest of his days. For he loves her and can deny her nothing, and she does not love him and can deny him herself.

PART FOUR

Gog's War, 1942

17

Agnes was a squat lady over eight feet tall. The first of the English Bombes, she had 676 terminals, which matched the twenty-six times twenty-six dots and dashes in each of the perforated sheets developed by the Poles and Graveling and Gog. These sheets contained the German cipher messages recently picked up by the radio security service. Thirty-two drums spun fast and slow, reproducing all the possible settings of the changeable rotors on the German coding machines, now termed Enigma. Twenty-four Wrens served Agnes in her Hut Eleven at Bletchley Park, tending her in three shifts of eight hours each, night and day. Agnes whirled her drums until her menu programmed them to stop. Then readings were taken, fed into another machine, and checked to see if the code was broken, if the cipher corresponded to words, if the enigma was solved. As Agnes was called a lady, she behaved well and delivered the intelligible and the intelligence.

But Robinson is no gentleman. His incredible loops and spiffing wheezes make Agnes look dowdy and down at heel. He uses paper tape holed with dots and dashes. Two strips of it are sped by wheel and pulley through twin photo-electric readers that can scan two thousand characters a second and can feed the info to electronic machines for checking out. An erupting typewriter with eighty valves shudders and smokes as it prints out the data hot as lava to the solitary Wren on duty. Gog cannot believe his eyes. The Druid lines and holes, the cup and ring marks of ancient times, are translated to cards and tapes, then interpreted by Agnes and Robinson, mere machines that still may reconstruct the movements and intentions of the enemies of Albion.

"The entrails of living prisoners," Gog says to Graveling, "that's what the Druids studied to find out what the Romans were doing. Or so the Romans said. Do you think it was more efficient?"

Graveling laughs.

"Don't tell that to Agnes. Or to Robinson. We're working on the big one. We thought we'd call it Colossus. You'd like that." The lone Wren in flat brown shoes and blue jacket flicks the sausage curls of hair on the nape of her neck so that they unroll like the paper tapes of Robinson.

"You've a lot of classical and ancient historians working for you here," Gog says. "Why? Most of them aren't interested in hieroglyphs and runes like me."

"It's a way of scrutiny. A methodology. A chap like Webster from Manchester, who can work out where the Fifteenth Legion was in AD Forty-four from one splinter of pottery and a Roman dogtag, he finds tracking Panzer Corps Fünf a joke with all the decrypts we get from our Bombes. History may be bunk, as the great Ford said. But historians aren't. The way they think, that we can use."

"Is your history really necessary?" Gog asks himself and answers, "Yes."

"Good to hear that." The familiar voice sounds from Gog's elbow. "Especially from you, Griffin."

Miniver is peering upwards, the black pips of his eyes glittering between the seams of his lids set in his withered apple-skin cheeks. Gog sees Graveling scowl, his hairy face becoming as angry as a berserker's, his voice tremulous with anger.

"You haven't got clearance, Min – ninninnin – niver."

"What's that to you, Graveling? You're not Security."

"Dilly Knox asked me – he *insisted* – and I agree – access to the first FISH Bombe is absolutely restricted."

"You think I'm going to tell Adolf Hitler all about it?"

"I didn't say that. I – I – didn't, but Dilly did –" Graveling's incoherence is caused by manners. It is not cricket to call a senior lecturer from Cambridge a possible traitor. Gog lunges to the rescue, swinging out an arm and pushing the dwarfish Miniver towards the door of the windowless hut.

"You have been transferred from Bletchley Park, Miniver. Aren't you going back to cap and gown? Teaching up at Durham?"

"My papers haven't come through. And while I'm still here, I thought –"

"Don't!" Graveling is smoking and erupting more violently than Robinson's electric keyboard. He looks likely to blow

252

a valve. "Keep out of here! I'll see Dilly and I'll see you do. Stick over in Light Blue! Luftwaffe supplies – that's your game. And supply the Luftwaffe – why not?"

Before Miniver can reply to this charge of treason, he is bundled out of the door of the hut by Gog. All around them are the low oblong bungalows and new Nissen huts surrounding the mock-Tudor pile of the secret Buckinghamshire mansion, its grounds now a park for lumpish outbuildings with flat tar roofs, its perimeter a hedgehog of barbed wire and sentries with bayonets.

"Graveling's right," Gog says. "You can't go in there, Miniver."

"Doctor Miniver, if you please."

"Then call me Doctor Griffin."

"You haven't got a doctorate."

"Oh yes I have. In Iowa, from a university without walls. Its dean wanted to build it and I gave a donation which proved the way he wanted to build it was right. By degrees."

"You charlatan."

"I would call you something else," Gog says, "only there is a war on already."

"Now you tell me." Miniver must have been eavesdropping on the Yanks, who have begun to fill the streets of Bletchley and Oxford since Pearl Harbor and the late entry of the United States into the global conflict. "Your gift for stating the obvious, Griffin, has always been your only consistency." Miniver shakes off Gog's arm, removing the yoke from his neck. "Why you should have clearance to visit Robinson – and I not – is only comprehensible to the infinite stupidity of the British military mind."

"Remember Spitpoole," Gog says. "The Anglo-German alliance, the friends of Ribbentrop. I'm surprised you ever got here in the first place."

"I was never a friend of Nazi Germany," Miniver says, suddenly shrilling. "I was an observer. I wanted peace. I still do. But a greater patriot than I does not exist –"

"Not the scoundrel," Gog says. "Patriotism is the last refuge of the insignificant."

"How dare you, Griffin!"

"Very easily," Gog says. "I'm a historian. I remember what people did before the war."

"You told them, did you? You secured my transfer to Durham."

"You always wanted to be a professor, Miniver. Haven't you got the Chair of Dialect there? A convenient appointment."

"I can tell people here about your follies and muddle-headed incompetence. Just because Graveling has some weird notion that those delusions of yours about Druid characters and hieroglyphs are somehow meaningful –"

The war has destroyed Gog's respect for academic authority. He can interrupt.

"I have to get back to see Graveling. Perhaps I'll get up to Durham sometime, take a few classes in deciphering the runes –"

"You will be most unwelcome," Miniver says, and walks away, diminutive and dim among the black squat boxes of the Bletchley huts.

Gog returns inside to find that Graveling is now less explosive than Robinson, whose valves are sparkling like fairground lights.

"We won't see him again," Graveling mutters.

"Never," Gog says. "I hope never."

"Wasn't he in with your brother Magnus and all that pro-German lot? You remember, Lord Rothermere and those wonderful prewar statements – 'Herr Hitler is proud to call himself a man of the people, but my impression is that of a great gentleman.'"

Gog laughs and caps the quotation.

"And that other time Rothermere wrote, 'Herr Hitler – there is no man living whose promise I would sooner take.' Magnus says he never believed that – but he did. I know he did. But it hasn't done him any harm. He rises and rises – something hush-hush in strategic planning. And guess who's in there with him, Putney Bowles and Rupert Fox."

"They'll be openly red again, now Stalin's our ally. What did they claim to be during the Hitler-Stalin pact, before the Nazis invaded Russia? They had claimed to be on both sides, then suddenly they couldn't be on either."

"They claimed they were true blue," Gog says, "if they couldn't be the red or the black."

"I never understood the Cognoscenti," Graveling says.

"They knew so much that they thought themselves better than other people. They were above patriotism, above morality, until the war came. Then suddenly they didn't love Russia or pretend to love Germany – they loved Britain all the time. And now they rise and they rise in the hierarchy – particularly in Intelligence because they are so intelligent – and because they know the people in it. And though the powers that be know the dodgy connections of the Cognoscenti, they know all of them personally. These are still true-blue Englishmen under the temporary dye."

"They only passed for reds and blacks till the rains came," Gog says. "The war has proved they wear woad like the ancient Britons. I only wonder one thing – before Stalin was our ally, during the two years he cosied up to Hitler to rape Poland – what did Rupert and Putney feel? If they were sending information back to Moscow about our war effort, would it not be passed on? Why not to Berlin, when the Wehrmacht was standing twenty miles across the Channel, looking at the white cliffs of Dover like flags of surrender?"

"I don't know," Graveling says, "I don't know. I only know this –"

Robinson blows up. Valves explode like Oerlikon 20mm cannon. The paper tapes shred and split. The solitary Wren in attendance screams and runs to the door. Graveling smiles at Gog and taps him on the shoulder.

"Teething troubles," he says. "Good old Robinson. We can get him right in a jiffy. Anyway, I want a word alone. Have you got a good reason to go into Oxford?"

"I have a son," Gog says, "or rather, I am said to have a son at school there. And Magnus is coming into town. I hear there's been an accident with Rupert."

"I hope not." Graveling speaks as if he knows and is hiding his emotions.

"I'll try to see him with Magnus."

"Good. We want to know something. You remember your tutor before you were sent down. Maximilian Mann."

"How could I forget?"

Robinson emits a hiss and a puff of black smoke.

"Mann is now stationed at Oxford, something in Intelligence, though whose intelligence is not quite clear. He was snooping round here till Dilly got rid of him. We think he's sending back our best stuff to a Soviet ring in Switzerland, the Rote Kapelle, and they are sending it on to the Kremlin."

"But they're our allies now. In this war."

"In this war only. This is Boniface material, only for Churchill. No one else can use it. No one. We think Max Mann has a mole in here in Hut Six. Can you find out? I'll brief you how to get to him. You're an old pupil visiting. You drop a true hint that he can check out – you have access to Robinson. Then, because Mann thinks you're a fool, you give him some vital classified info that he will get later from his source in Hut Six. He will then know it is true and you are genuine. But meanwhile Radio Security Service will detect him passing on your information, which will nail him. And when he confirms it later from his mole in Hut Six, we will know who it is – because all the suspects will each only be fed part of it." Graveling pauses to stare at Gog. "Well – you never liked that bastard Mann, did you?"

"He sent me down," Gog says. "What a pleasure to send him."

Robinson is silent now. The perforated paper tapes are streamers among the wheels and pulleys. Only a small stink of charcoal suggests an accident.

"You should have stuck to carving your dots and dashes on rocks," Gog says. "Stones don't burn."

Graveling puts the heel of his hand in his eye and screws it from side to side.

"Something in my eye."

"Can I help?"

"No, nothing." Graveling drops his hand and blinks fiercely. He scowls, angry at his tears, then he says savagely, "Flesh burns."

"Rupert?"

"He got what he deserved. You get me that mole."

The Beastlies are up Bardwell Road, and it's a dare to see them, one boy who'd seen them two times swapped a spiral for ten titchies, so it proves it, boys who see the Beastlies twice lose their marbles, go bloody mad. Now it's Arthur's turn, dare you, dare you, and natch he dares, so he sings

"Goebbels has only got one ball" as he strolls away from school up the street, his hands stuck in the pockets of his blue short trousers, trying to keep the chilblains off his fingers and only on his bare knees. But his shoes are lead and his feet are ice and his legs are custard, and when he gets to the Banbury Road and sees the brick walls of the head-and-bad-burns hospital – "Ninety per cent croak, me son, nine in ten for the body-snatchers, they don't have nurses in there, just nuns praying for their souls, them as have one –" the school porter's words are louder in his ears than the lorries chundering up the road to St Giles's where you can sit in the cockpit of a Spitfire for sixpence to buy a new one if you've got some pocket-money, but even the longest convoy's got an ending, and Arthur has to cross the road after the ARP man with the big BTM peddling his bike and wearing his gas-mask and his tin hat. And it's slow, slow round the corner into St Margaret's Road, and softly, softly past the hospital entrance, there's a chance none of the Beastlies will come by, but no luck, none at all, there's one, stop still and play statues, but this time you're nailed to the pavement, there's pepper in your throat and pee in your pants. You can't see the Beastly, it's a mummy in thick white bandages, nothing to see but a hole where the mouth is, it's lying in a wicker wheel-chair with a nurse behind it, and walking beside is a Dracula off his grub in a black stripey suit, Uncle Magnus down from London not to visit his nephew Arthur, but bending over the Beastly and shouting softly as if it was dead, "Rupert, it's a lovely day, you'll soon be better, I know it, I'm never wrong." And fat tears are rolling down Uncle's face and making splodges on his white shirt, and he doesn't mop them up, they fall and fall, and then he looks up and cries, "Arthur, what the hell are you doing –" and his words are like slides on the playground, Arthur's feet skid and slip, and he's turning and running round the corner, he's dodging the rusty bikes on the Banbury Road, he's scampering down-hill sprinting for the goalposts till he's safe in 5B with the chipped desks and the torn books, breathing in chalk dust and sudden sweat, and saying, "I saw a Beastly – I swear, I swear – it was with my uncle." And the other boys surround him and bash him and taunt him. "You uncle's a Beastly, a Beastly, a Beastly!" till he bashes back and butts and bonks

them, but the ring of boys closes and they wallop him and
trip him till he's blubbering blindly and lashing out uselessly.

> Arthur's in a bait,
> Arthur's in a bait,
> Arthur's in a bait!

And he is in a bait, but he yells he isn't, he isn't! but they
won't listen or leave him till he falls on the splinters and the
boards and he lies limp, hearing,

> Arthur's in a bait,
> Arthur's in a bait,
> Arthur's in a bait!

And the bell goes, time for tea for the boarders, old bread
and marge with a dab of Marmite, and they leave him lying,
only the last voice saying, "Your uncle's a Beastly," which
isn't exactly a fib, for Gog tells him so.

When Gog meets his half-brother in Oxford at the Randolph
Hotel, Magog is still weeping. Tears form at the corners of
his red eyes and roll down his long cheeks, collect on his
chin, then drop on his lapels or the carpet in the hall.

"I'm sorry," Magog says, "it's Rupert. If he lives, and he
is critically ill – ninety per cent burns – he will look like
no-man's-land. One of Archie McIndoe's little experiments
in skin surgery. And he was so beautiful."

"Can you communicate with him?"

"In a sort of braille. I tap softly on his skull through his
bandages in the Morse Code. He seems to understand. The
bandages round his mouth tremble more than usual."

"I'm sorry, Magnus. He was beautiful. I thought so, too.
How did it happen?"

"The tea at the Randolph's still tolerable," Magog says.
"No rations, and they haven't requisitioned all the armchairs
in the tea-room. I'll tell you about it there. How's Bletchley?"

"Hush," Gog says. "Very hush."

"Walls may have ears, but these invaders don't." Magog
steps aside to let two American airmen, one black and one

white, lounge past, each with an arm round a giggling girl.

"See the shine on their legs," Gog says. "They're the only girls in Britain wearing nylons."

"They earned it," Magog says, ushering Gog into the dim comfort of the tea-room. "They'll be applying for pensions – wounded in the course of duty. Strained their backs in their war effort." He sits on a sofa behind a table decked with a frilly cloth and pats the cushion beside him. "Please be seated here. It's more private. We'll have the set tea with the scones. I do love scones, they remind me of nursery tea."

Magog has stopped weeping, as if the memory of the security of infancy and luxury has reassured him against the horrors of the war. He gives his order to a waitress, who is all of dumpy fourteen, then leans close and confidential to Gog. "Rupert was on a mission for us. A dangerous rendezvous."

"You said it was an incendiary. He was burned all over."

"We don't know if it was a time-bomb dropped by our Nazi visitors or an explosive device planted by God know's whom. The house exploded, blazing chemicals were everywhere, Rupert was burned and taken to hospital."

"Oxford doesn't get bombed. What was he doing here at all?"

"You know I can't tell you, George. What are you doing? Ah, scones –" The waitress dumps a silver tray on the table-cloth. Hardly has the clangour diminished when Magog is reaching for his hot treat. "I love scones," he says again. "I'll butter my own."

"Marge," the waitress says. "And no raspberry jam, it's turnip. Raspberry's off. And seven shillings."

"That's robbery," Magog says, but pays. "What did you say you were doing?"

"I can't say," Gog says, "like you can't say."

"Oh, I get to see some of your work," Magog says. "That interesting research you're doing on that St Boniface, isn't it?" He enjoys seeing Gog start. "I know it's only meant for Winston and the very few, but I'll let you into a little secret. I'm one of those planning the invasion."

"You always were," Gog says.

"What do you mean?"

"The invasion of England. You and your German friends."

Magog bites through his scone as if it were a breadstick.

"The war hasn't improved your sense of humour."

"Should it, Magog?"

"Don't call me that."

"What happened to your friends in the Anglo-German alliance?"

"Oh that! Just a charade. I was gleaning information for the Ministry of Defence."

"Or giving it."

"George!"

"I am told that when Hitler's deputy Hess flew over to Scotland, he had a list of pro-Nazi sympathisers in high places. Quite a few dukes and earls, some admirals and some high civil servants. Your name was on that list."

"Hess was mad. We found him mad. Hitler thought he was mad. His peace mission was a fantasy."

"He was found mad after he was interrogated by us. No propaganda was made of it. Were his English names too embarrassing?"

"Hess was always mad. His list of friends of Germany was a delusion."

"Germany had a lot of friends just before the war. Even Red Rupert and Putney Bowles. Don't you remember Prague?"

"I have never been there."

"I saw you there. In a magic show in a club called the Alhambra. You went off with Maire."

If Magog were not sipping his tea, he would have laughed and choked. As it is, he carefully puts down his cup and saucer and looks Gog in the eye with the straight stare of deceit.

"I was never in Prague. I have never been off with Maire – and I am so glad the dear girl got out of France just before it fell. How *is* she?"

"You know, Magog. She's seeing you all the time. She hardly ever sees me, even when I get up to London."

"Another fantasy. Oh dear, oh dear, the war seems to be deranging your intelligence faster than everyone else's. And you are in Intelligence, too, which is one of the wonders of the western world."

Gog will not rise to the taunt. He has an enquiry.

"So if you're not planning the invasion of England, you're planning the invasion of France. Just like the Germans did."

"We are planning to liberate France from the German invaders." Magog speaks as slowly as to a backward child. "I therefore have access to some of Boniface, which reaches my committee, where alas, some of our American friends have just joined us."

"You just called them invaders."

"Did I? Surely not. Our dear allies." Magog takes a biscuit, nibbles its edge delicately, then puts it back on his plate. "One might as well eat unrefined dirt. But Boniface, I gather, is getting even better. Some new machine. You wouldn't have seen it?"

"You know how stupid I am," Gog says. "They wouldn't let me see anything important, would they now?"

"Oh, Graveling's a great friend of yours. He's a queen bee there."

"He was a friend of Rupert's. Does he know about the accident?"

Magog's voice is shocking in its clipped severity.

"Too much."

"What does he know?"

"Have a biscuit, George? They're excellent."

"You only nibbled yours."

"Our tastes differ. You would like it."

Gog tastes the biscuit. It is dry dust in his mouth, but he chews it and swallows. Waste not, want not. He decides to chance a reference.

"Maximilian Mann, he's in Oxford, too. So was Rupert. And now you. It seems all the Cognoscenti are here, at least all the friends of Russia and Germany before the war."

"We all have work here. Intelligence. And I came to visit Rupert."

"Who was burned here. Why? By whom?"

"I wish I knew, George. And I intend to find out."

"If Rupert was doing what he seemed to be doing in the late 'thirties," Gog says, "anyone could have wanted him dead. He was very convincing when he pretended to be pro-German. If he's gone on sending intelligence to Moscow all the time through the Stalin-Hitler Pact – though Stalin's now our beloved and trusted ally – I can think of hundreds of people he might have offended. The Abewehr, the Comintern, our own MI Five and Six. Black fire. Red fire. Our own blue fire. He was sure to get scorched."

"You tasteless bugger," Magog says. "Rupert is dying."

"What for?" Gog asks. "I know what I'm dying for."

"You're still alive," Magog says, "and this tea is terminated."

"Good," Gog says and stands up. "I must be going."

"Good." Magog also stands up. "Oh, I saw your son Arthur. He was outside the hospital in his school uniform when we wheeled Rupert out. He ran away."

"I'm not surprised."

"You'll be visiting him?"

"Among others. When I can. He's a boarder at the Dragon School. Visitors aren't often allowed."

"But you must have a reason to leave your vital war-work and come in to Oxford."

"To see you, dear brother. Only to communicate with you."

Maximilian Mann is so much under cover that he is almost underground. Gog looks past a hundred snails and glistening slug trails down a concrete ditch to the dark barred windows of the basement where Mann is said to live in Polstead Road. The lines of the old nursery rhyme pass through his head:

> Slugs and snails
> And puppydog tails,
> That's what little boys are made of.

And then Gog finds himself saying the words aloud, as Mann opens the front door to him after the code signal is pressed on the bell, two short buzzes, one long, two short.

"There are no little boys here," Mann says.

"Surprising," Gog says.

"How did you know the bell code? And my address?"

"Bletchley," Gog says. "It came up."

A twitch of surprise that may be irony puckers Mann's forehead. His plucked eyebrows and sleek hair are now silvery white and shine like the snail's trails outside the basement.

"Come down," Mann says. "It has been a long time since we parted company."

He leads the way down poky curling stairs to a dark room, where books lie in piles on the carpet and papers litter an old deal table. It is the room of a lumberjack student, not of an exquisite don. Mann appears to have reverted to the primeval and to be unaware of it.

"Take a pew," Mann says. "Wherever."

Gog removes a pile of newspaper clippings from an armchair with concave springs and sags deeply into the seat.

"Have you seen Rupert?" Gog asks, scrutinising Mann's face, which remains as bland as junket. "My brother Magnus saw him today."

"You astonish me twice," Mann says, unastonished. "They should have told me they were here."

"Perhaps they don't know you are here."

"My work is very secret. Few people do know my whereabouts. Consequently, my surprise to see you, Griffin –"

"Is genuine. You don't know about Rupert's recent accident?"

"The poor boy. Really? Please tell me. How too ghastly."

Mann's mixture of wonder and concern is so convincing that Gog doubts Graveling's evidence against him.

"He seems to have been badly burned. In an explosion in Oxford. He's at the hospital in St Margaret's Road. You didn't know."

"If I did, I would have galloped round to see him. I must go at once. St Margaret's Road, surely it is round the corner? But only terminal cases go there."

"You must have known Rupert was in Oxford. He's one of the Cognoscenti like my brother. You always see each other."

A look of disapproval crosses Mann's mask of sorrow, a contradiction in display.

"You are not meant to know, Griffin, although you obviously do. The point of a secret society is that it is secret. But actually, as you do know, we only ever meet each other at Cambridge at the week-ends. Otherwise we never see one another. I never knew Rupert was in Oxford. His work must be as secret as my own. Even if we had met, we would never tell each other."

This last statement snaps the thread of Mann's credibility. But Gog only nods and seems to accept the implausible.

"I believe you. Just as I couldn't tell you exactly what I was doing at Bletchley, even though you were my superior at Cambridge."

"I have been there. I have security clearance."

"I know that. They told me how to contact you."

"Why?"

Mann poses the usual Cambridge monosyllable with the apparent assurance that this investigation of him is reversed. It is he who is merely holding another tutorial with another obtuse undergraduate. As Gog remains silent, Mann repeats the unspeakable question.

"Why?"

"I don't know," Gog says. "It's probable they want to get something across to you."

"What could that be? Should I not be invited back to Bletchley myself and be briefed? To send you as an errand-boy . . ."

Mann's voice tails away in weary incomprehension. Gog makes his instructed revelation.

"They don't want you back at Bletchley. But there is another reason for it. We want you outside. Because we now know there are spies there, double agents, moles."

"In that barbed-wire burrow?"

"If we want certain messages to go to the right quarters – to our allies – now engaged in a death struggle against the Nazis – and you know how anti-Nazi I am, and I know how anti-Nazi you are –"

Mann bites on his words, defining them.

"Are you suggesting I personally am in contact with Moscow?"

"No," Gog says. "But it is thought, if certain information came your way of desperate importance to our allies – and we needed to get it to them unofficially – you might be able to help."

"Who thought this?"

"I cannot say." Gog tosses the bait across to Mann, a sealed packet from his pocket. "These are the latest decrypts from KESTREL. They show the combined Wehrmacht and Luftwaffe plans for a joint operation in the Ukraine."

Mann lets the sealed packet rest on the litter on his table. He considers it as if it were contagious.

"Why give me this?"

"I told you. We thought you could help to get it to the Russians unofficially."

A slight disdain puckers Mann's lips.

"Such an obvious effort to trap me, Griffin, would only be possible from somebody of your blunt stupidity."

"I was told you would think that," Gog says. "But you have to take a chance. The Russian front may collapse without that information. It comes from our new Bombe. We call it Robinson." Gog pauses and strikes. "It is so secret that none of its intelligence goes to Hut Six."

Mann considers Gog as if he were a problem in mathematical logic.

"Hut Six. Where all the essential decoding is done. Why should that interest me?"

"Why?"

It is Gog's turn to pronounce the unspeakable monosyllable.

"I have no contacts there," Mann says. "Not since I became persona non grata in your establishment." He puts out his long fingers and pushes the package among the litter of papers. "I promise nothing. I will see what I can do. Let us take a walk along Aristotle Lane."

Gog shakes his head and smiles.

"There can't be a place in Oxford called Aristotle Lane."

"There is, Griffin. Hard by here, or how could I endure this coalhole? It leads over the canal and the railway to Port Meadow, where one may browse among the cows and forget this whole ghastly war." Mann's fingers slide round the edges of the sealed package and slip it into his coat pocket. "This information is vital for our allies?"

"Win or lose a battle," Gog says.

Mann rises. He has betrayed himself to Gog. He has not referred to Rupert's accident again. If he has heard of it for the first time, they would now be visiting the hospital, not walking down Aristotle Lane.

"I would emphasise," Mann says, "that I can do nothing about this information. Please inform your superiors that I have no contact whatsoever with the Russians. My prewar

Marxism was the mere mode of the time, a passing frailty. But I do remain sympathetic to the Russian war effort in its resistance against the Nazis. I do believe that they should have the benefit of our intelligence when it specifically refers to German operations on Russian soil. That is the limit of my contacts with and belief in Russia. But –" Here Mann beckons Gog to follow him out of the room. "I do believe I know somebody who can contact our allies. A boating friend of mine. And of yours."

Aristotle Lane is the other side of Walton Street at the end of Polstead Road. It is hardly a lane, but a muddy track between wooden fences. It leads over a humped redbrick bridge, where Maximilian Mann stops and looks down to the onyx of the canal beneath. He seems disappointed, then turns to Gog.

"We will toddle along to Port Meadow. It is good for the legs."

They walk between hedges and over a railway bridge with sides of corrugated iron. A troop train roars beneath, making the structure shudder under their feet, belching an architrave of smoke above their heads. The steam shreds, the two men follow the track towards the meadow at the end, where cows graze and swans glide among the reeds that border the Isis River.

"Would you agree with Morgan Forster," Mann asks, "that you would rather betray your country than your friend?"

"It's a difficult choice," Gog says. "Nearly impossible."

"But if it were your choice?"

"One cannot betray a friend."

Mann nods in gloomy satisfaction.

"Back to the canal. Our friend will be there."

The return down Aristotle Lane seems to be leading to a proposition, if not a paradox. And sure enough, moored by the redbrick bridge is a black barge, its bows and cabin painted in bright red, and its name – SYLLOGISM. A figure dressed in white dungarees, a red sash and a large straw hat stands at the stern. His lips are as vermilion as the ribbon round his hat. Putney Bowles.

"I brought a friend along you hardly expected to see," Mann calls down.

"Come aboard."

Gog follows Mann down to the towpath and across a narrow gangplank that Putney has dropped from the barge. Both men are kissed in turn by Putney and sat down on canvas cushions by the tiller.

"How very good to see you, Gog. I never knew you were round here."

"He brought me this." Mann takes out the sealed package and gives it to Putney. "Latest depositions of the Wehrmacht and the Luftwaffe in the Ukraine. Urgent this intelligence passed on *quam celerrime*."

"Ah." Putney takes the package and looks at Gog and at Mann and at Gog again. "You brought us this?"

"He brought this to me," Mann intervenes. "I bring it to you because you happen to be sailing by."

"Of course," Putney says.

"Griffin would never betray a friend," Mann says. "And you and he are great friends. Much more so than you and I."

"I see," Putney says, "and I hope."

He rises and walks to the steps down to the cabin. Gog also rises, but Putney shakes his head.

"Nobody is allowed into my box of tricks," he says. "Excuse me, but something pressing appears to press."

He vanishes down the cabin steps and closes the door. Gog looks across at Mann.

"He couldn't transmit from here. He would be picked up."

"By those amateurs on Radio Security Service?" Mann smiles. "I doubt it. All those millions of Morse Code messages. To pick up this particular one! It is like the difference between apples and an apple. And even if they did pick it up, it would hardly matter."

"Why?"

"That is my usual question. Why? Why did you do this?"

"Answer my why."

"Since the Russians became our allies," Mann says, "orders have gone out. All decrypting of messages from the United Kingdom to Russia or its agents have ceased. Even if they are recorded, nothing is done about them."

267

"Who gave these orders?"

"No matter. They are given. Now answer my why, please."

Gog looks Mann in the eye. He must be believed.

"I know there is a split in the intelligence services among those who believe Russia must get all information, because then it can win the war for us, and those who fear what Russia will do with the information after the war, if we win it. I happen to hate Germany. I think Russia should be helped at all costs."

"You always believed in the people, Griffin. Are you doing this for the Russian people?"

"Yes. Ten or twenty million may die before they defeat the Germans."

Down in the cabin of the black and red barge, Putney is hidden at his clandestine work. Gog remembers another black barge – or a dream of another black barge – where Crook took him to an exhibition of secret sexual delights. If he only dreamed of the barge, it was a prophecy of this barge, these secrets, this betrayal of his beloved Putney. Gog's loins tighten in fear and anticipation.

"You are silent," Mann says. "Are you considering what you are doing?"

"Yes," Gog says, "and what I have done."

"I trust I may count on your silence. And perhaps on more of this vital intelligence."

"On both," Gog says, saying to himself like a schoolboy – I'll be silent to *you*, but not to *them*. "I'll bring you more intelligence if I'm not transferred. But why should I be?"

"Mysterious are the ways of the military mind," Mann says.

"Amen," Gog says.

A sniper lies on a hillside aiming his Lee-Enfield, camouflage ribbons stuck over his tin hat. He shoots at the invisible sex of the naked blonde appearing from behind an old oak tree. Five Blenheim bombers fly in high formation above the clouds on reconnaissance, surveying a naked girl in stack-heeled sandals, who turns up from her lilo to look up at the voyeur aeroplanes. A light tank with a stubby cannon projecting from its turret grinds up a powdery hill about to plunge on to a naked girl lying beneath a net, her breasts escaping the meshes, ready to take on all comers: the caption on the opposite page is *Tank trap*. Gog is leafing through old copies of *Lilliput* while waiting for Maire at the Hungaria or the Nest or the Nut-house or the Paradise or another of the night-clubs (God or Gog don't know which) jammed with soldiers and sailors and riff-RAF, with WAAFs and ATS and Free Czechs and Free Estonians and Free Lithuanians, not to mention Free Letts, with Yanks and Diggers and odds and sods of the world, unite, there is nothing to lose but your pay and your lives as the blitz is on, with the halt and the maimed and the blind, with the wise and the foolish virgins, if any are still so, with the long and the short and the tall, with the old and the young and the not so young, with men and women and children and the indeterminate, for the true-blues and the pin-stripes and all shades of pink and yellow are down the Tubes or tucked up snug in their Anderson shelters, but up above at midnight, it's "Knees up Mother Brown" and anything else you can get up her, and it's "due back on duty tomorrow", the last night of leave and the last chance of love among the ruins, if that's all that's left of London, and that may well be.

Maire shoulders her way to Gog's table, losing the right top brass button of her black-and-white striped blazer to some amorous Pole she wouldn't touch a barge with, only he has touched her breast.

"Christ," she says, "what a scrum. I have the idiom, no?"

"You wouldn't get any English lessons here," Gog says. "It's Polyglot Unlimited. Cheers." He pulls a bottle of gin from under his table and fills the tumbler in front of Maire. "It's better to bring your own. Service here is strictly in the front line overseas. Thanks for suggesting we meet in such a private place – where is it, anyway? – I've forgotten."

"I meet you here, *mon* Gog, because you get sentimental in private. You say, there is a war on, so screw me now. Always, screw me now. A lady has her times of the month. She has her *raisons*. And this bugger of a war, men think, I die tomorrow, you give me tonight. Then they do not die tomorrow. They come back for more."

While Maire is speaking, Gog is watching the Woodbine smoke drift across the white moon cheeks and swelling lips of the woman and wife whom he loves. He does want her now. He has to have her.

"I am dying tomorrow," he says. "Perhaps tonight in the raid. I want to die holding you."

"Every night you can die of a raid in London. *Tricheur*. And why you die tomorrow?"

"I shouldn't tell you, Maire, but you're allowed to tell wives. Faithful wives. Wives you can trust."

"Like me." Maire laughs. "I love you, trust me."

"Just like you. I am being transferred. Flown to Egypt. I don't know for how long. I have to spend this night with you."

"Is true?"

"Is true. Cross my heart and hope to die, as we used to say, but don't any more. Where did you learn your English?"

"*Je ne sais pas. Tu m'emmerdes*."

"Don't go back to French, Maire. The only place really to learn a language is bed. With Magog, I presume. He speaks English perfectly. Civil Service supreme. An accent you could butter a royal ass with."

"Don't be silly, Gog. Your brother – I see him sometimes. You are always not here. I know him."

"She *knew* him. That's what the Bible says. And she knew him." Gog swallows the rest of his tumbler of gin and fills the glass to the top. "Let's get out of here, Maire. Walk in the blackout. Find each other again in the dark. Well-met by searchlight."

"OK, Gog. But it is not dark. Incendiaries, ack-ack. Fires in the City."

"At least the streets are empty. Where are you staying? At home in Hampstead?"

"You spend the night with me."

"Yes," Gog says, "yes. I'd have you in a doorway."

"I know a place," Maire says. She swigs down her gin and stands up to go. Two small Free Serbo-Croats grab at her, then drop her as they see the giant size of Gog loom above her and plough a way ahead of her through the crush of uniforms to the door and the streets of Soho outside.

Outside in Greek Street, they can see a geometry in the heavens. The blitz has proved Isaac Newton's mathematical universe. Lines of light bisect and grid the dark, they draw

270

triangles and rhomboids and dodecahedrons on the black-
board of the sky, while tracers bend in their brilliant arcs
and a dying flare inscribes its hypotenuse on the slate of the
night. Spitfires loop the loop drawn by aerial compasses and
the smoke trails of Hurricanes expand Euclid and insist that
the shortest distance between two points on the surface of a
sphere is a curve. This trigonometry of war is emphasised by
its language, the stutter of machine-guns and the hiccups of
ack-ack and the belching of batteries and the dry cough
of rockets and the cackle of incendiaries and the bellow of
bombs and the falling walls rubbing their dry hands and the
far infernos whistling out of tune as the fire-brigades douse
them and the high engines shrieking out their souls in torment
and the sirens wailing their melancholy requiems at the
killings that never stop.

Maire takes Gog's hand and leads him towards Soho
Square. They pass the Theatre Girls Club, where the girls
no longer live, they are sleeping in the green room at the
Windmill, which never closes because the girls never put on
their clothes, they doss down off-stage and only stick on their
one perfect rose when the patriotic tableaux of pure fresh
English flesh are wheeled on after Max Miller and the comics
have tickled the ribs and appetites of the boys in blue and
khaki out front. They never close, nor does the House of St
Barnabas opposite at No. 1 Greek Street, where William
Gladstone took his tarts for their salvation even when he was
prime minister, and where Thomas de Quincey, crazed with
eating opium, first met his noble doxy Ann under the portico.

"There," Gog says, "there. Let's make love on that door-
step. Danger's a drug, too. Far better than opium as an
aphrodisiac."

"*Tu parles*, Gog. You try my place."

She leads him to the iron railings that fence Soho Square,
which have not been cut down to melt for tank armour. They
trail round the planted pikes until they find a gate unlocked
at the north end of the square. They push their way inside
past a ghostly statue of King Charles II, masked with grime
like a highwayman, the crown and sceptres on his base eroded
to a skull and crossbones. Ahead of them down the stone
path across the grass is an unlikely fairy-tale Tudor cottage,
where babes in the wood and gardeners may take their rest.

Maire leans against the oak door, which swings open. There is the faint stink of old leaves and rotting fibre and grass mould turning to hay. Maire turns to Gog and pulls him down on her. She bites the lobe of his ear, almost severing it.

"Now," she says. "Now."

He struggles and wriggles and wrenches her skirt high, he yanks a button off his flies as he rips them open, his cock is bent back and springs forward, his thrust carries him fast and deep into the wet haven between Maire's naked thighs, she is wearing nothing underneath, she is expecting a quick bang tonight, what if she missed him, does she go out barebum and fancy free every night, don't ask, never ask why, plunge down the slippery well, heave-ho and jolly roger and spill guts into her scuppers, and as Gog groans in his coming, a bomb detonates in Oxford Street and shudders the eaves of their trysting-place.

"We nearly got it," Maire says.

"We did," says Gog.

The True History of King Ludd

(as shown to Putney Bowles in Egypt in September 1943)

London and Britain, 1926–36

Gog Griffin does not feel a scab. He is too young for that. The scabs he knows are those who strike at God, the snipers at the Pope, the saboteurs of the true faith called Anglicans, the mindless mob of agnostics, denounced by the priests and teachers of his Catholic public school. But in his second year of reading history at University College, London, Gog has downed tools to the Mass and thrown away the key to heaven; even so, at the age of twenty, he has not yet taken the communion of class consciousness. If he is aware of it, he thinks that his place is on the near side of the trenches between his sort and the workers. Chums man the machines that have been deserted in the General Strike. Comrades are preparing barricades.

Through the influence of his aunt Grace, the widow of the munitions manufacturer, Gog is where he wants to be, in the composing room of the *British Gazette*, the government broadsheet run by Winston Churchill. The cold type is being set by a super, a blackleg printer on loan from Lord Beaverbrook. He is filling the case with the lead letters and sliding up his stick to pinch the fullest line between the cheeks and the head so he may justify all the rest of the lines, until the page be out and ready to be inked and run on the printing machines. Nothing much has changed since Ned Ludd set up his pamphlets for Captain Swing according to the practices described in Moxon's *Mechanick Exercises*, which Gog has been reading.

"Watching, me boy," the super says. "Working's more like it. Get in the van and out on the streets. Let them see the colour of your eyes. Not pink, are they?"

"No, sir," Gog says and leaves the composing-room for the loading bay, where the red vans of the *Morning Post* wait at the end of the rollers from the presses. Two soldiers in khaki carrying rifles with fixed bayonets stand at the open mouth of the back of the print-works, where it disgorges its newspapers and bulletins into the streets. Pickets stand

275

outside, knots of men in caps and blue suits, all bags and shine. They shout incomprehensible slogans, but they do not threaten. Gog looks at the headlines of the newspaper on the top of the bale, ready to be loaded and taken away:

GENERAL STRIKE AN ATTEMPTED REBELLION
Ruin – Swift, Complete, Irresistible,
Says Lord Balfour

200,000 SPECIAL CONSTABLES RECRUITED EMERGENCY REGULATIONS IN FORCE
The Country Will Break the General Strike,
or the General Strike Will Break the Country.

GUARANTEE TO ALL RANKS OF THE ARMED FORCES
Any Action in Aid of the Civil Power Will
Receive Both Now and Afterwards, the Full Support
of His Majesty's Government.

Gog lifts the bale of copies of the *British Gazette* and dumps it on to the back of a van, already loaded down with a ton of newspapers. He slams the doors shut, turns the handle and the key in the lock. He removes the key and runs round to the passenger seat of the van. The driver looks at him and tries to start the engine. He and Gog peer through the wire mesh that covers the windscreen.

"Last time I saw anything like this," the driver says, "was Ireland. I was a Black and Tan. Bloody bogmen, you never saw the bricks coming out of the dark."

"My father died in Dublin," Gog says. "In the rebellion."

"That why you're here, posh?"

"Not exactly. Not at all. I'm all for the principle of free speech. The people must be able to get their information."

"You're a toff," the driver says, and engages gears and drives straight at the line of pickets. Men rise up in front of the bonnet of the van, they hover and throw themselves sideways as the vehicle charges on. Missiles fly through the air and bounce off the mesh. One projectile, flung by a scarecrow shrieking like an apparition from hell, lands on

Gog's lap through the side-window that he has left open. It is a leather-bound book closed by red twine. Gog looks at the title embossed on its spine: *The History of the Kings of Britain.*

"It can't be," Gog says to himself and turns to look back at the pickets, but the wild man has vanished behind the van careering along Fleet Street. Gog tugs the knot on the twine and opens the old volume. Under the name of the author, Geoffrey of Monmouth, is written in crimson, *You should know better. Evans the Latin.*

Now the van races along Fetter Lane past the pub called The Printer's Devil. From the windows in front of the type-faces set on the walls, ranging from Bodoni to William Morris, catcalls and jeers and taunts and imprecations hurtle in slugs and shrapnel round the ears of the news driver and his passenger Gog, who is leafing through the book and looking for a passage in it.

"Proper scholar you are," the driver says. "Your library hand-delivered. Nothing to pay neither."

"Listen," Gog says, "you know who founded London? King Ludd, I promise you. Or so said Geoffrey of Monmouth, if we can believe him."

Ah, Geoffrey of Monmouth, clerk and liar, chronicler extraordinary, maker of Merlin and magic for ever, your quill on your parchment and your tongue in our cheek, who made Gogmagog and the giants the original offspring of the daughters of Albion, who called Celtic 'corrupt Trojan' and named Britain after King Brutus, did you conjure up Ludd, too, in your History of Arthur and after, just to explain the name of the city, Ludd's Town or London? What's the worth of your words that ranted Lear into the Bard's brain and carved Camelot into Cadbury Hill? Your flame's fiercer than Nennius, your breath's brighter than Bede's, you tell of the History of the Kings of Britain as they never were and always will be the lie of the land without end, amen. Oh, Geoffrey, you should not have died seven centuries ago. The news-editor's desk above Fleet Ditch is still kept as hot as hell for you.

"There," Gog says, pointing as the van shoots beneath the railway bridge towards the City, "I can prove it. That pub. The King Ludd."

The driver scarcely glances aside as he changes down to mount the hill ahead.

"Good boozer, is it? Real ale?"

Gog does not answer him, but reads out his chosen passage from *The History of the Kings of Britain.*

King Ludd was famous as a planner of cities. He built again the walls of the Trojan city of Trinovantum and he circled it with more towers than could be counted. He ordered the citizens to set up houses and buildings there so beautiful that no city in all the kingdoms of the world could boast more of their palaces. King Ludd was a warrior who spent all on his feasts and cities. And this city of his was loved more than all other cities he had, and he spent most of the year within its walls. So it came to be called Caerlud and then, as the name was forgotten, Caerlundun. Still later, as the language grew, it was called London, and then, when the foreigners invaded and conquered the country, it was called Londres. When Ludd died, he was buried in the city of his name, near to the gateway which is called in Celtic Porthlud after him. In Saxon, it is called Ludgate.

"That's where we are right enough," the driver says. He grinds the van to a halt. "You hop off and get the papers out. A geezer's picking 'em up here."

Gog opens the side-door of the van and jumps down on to the tarmacadam that now covers Ludgate Hill. A solitary tram clanks by, the white face of its amateur driver suggesting that he does not know where the brake is. A pub sign creaks above Gog's head, a brown bare-breasted maiden in the painted forests, The Belle-Sauvage. Waiting, a plump costermonger with his empty barrow covered by a few coalsacks.

"Pull your finger out," he says to Gog, struggling with the van door. "Or you'll get your block knocked off. Pee-dee-queue, squire."

Gog wrenches open the back of the van and begins dropping the bales of the *British Gazette* on the barrow, while the costermonger covers them with the sacks.

"No bleedin' government never paid Morrie Mowler

before. What a laugh! Floggin' papers and not bleedin' apples. Bloody Baldwin needin' the costers to 'elp the toshes put out 'is pork pies. What's the country comin' to? Read all about it, and you won't know nothin' more."

Gog finishes dumping the bales of the government bulletin on the barrow. Coal-sacks hide the woodpulp and ink from sight. Gog looks up at Mowler the coster.

"People like you," he says, "always turn up at the right place at the right time."

"At the right price," Mowler says. "Ta-rah, tosh. And don't you never forget me."

"I won't," Gog says. "We'll meet again."

"Natch."

Gog does not remember any more of his past service in the General Strike, which is called off by the General Council of the Trades Union Congress after only ten days. The printers stay out for five days more, but after that, the Fleet Street presses resume their normal trade of turning forests into lies. There is no need for the *British Gazette*, which is as ephemeral as the threatened workers' revolution. And Gog goes back to his university, richer for the leather-bound copy of *The History of the Kings of Britain* and the reminder of how King Ludd built London town to celebrate his majesty, where his subjects the Luddites might rage against the royal government and all its works, yet might never tear them down.

Gog endeavours to return to Evans the Latin the book thrown into the news-van, but nine years pass before he can reach his old teacher of Celtic history. And when they meet again on Holy Island off Anglesey, Evans the Latin is furious to see his wayward pupil. His eyes blaze above his crooked back, his hair waves as in a storm while his voice is fierce with denunciation.

"How mean you," he says, "to ride with the spawn of the devil, Griffin bach, through the lines of the workers trying to stop the spreading of the false word? Shame on you, misbegotten child, but it is only half-born that you are, the other half being rotten limey, God save you, which He cannot do, given your shabby inheritance."

279

"I was wrong," Gog says. "I really regret what I did. The printers were right. They weren't machine-wreckers. They were stopping the government printing lies."

"London always does," Evans says. "And that lead type poisons the true word. I have seen the miners of lead, look you, die with their lungs as gasbags and their skin duller than pots of pewter. And the casters of lead type, they sweat the foul metal. In their last agonies, the drops roll off their dying skins in hard pellets like smallshot, you can cram a cartridge and shoot a pigeon with their droppings, ping-ping-ping on the stone flags as they expire. I tell you, Griffin, you know who the people are, you knew it, before those terrible Papists took you away into the wilderness and made you forget the land of your fathers."

"I remember it now," Gog says. "That is why I have come to find you."

And sitting beside the Welsh schoolmaster in his little cottage in Tre-Addwr Bay, Gog tells him of his studies for the past eight years, the knowledge he has learned so painfully in order that one future day he may begin to write a *True History of King Ludd* and of his family and himself. He has been a researcher for seven years for a *Complete Dictionary of Languages and Symbols*, in which all the ancient hieroglyphs and characters, pictographs and ideograms, signs and runes, notches and serrations are listed and cross-referenced in time and by structure in an attempt to find a common root for the dialects written and spoken by mankind. The endeavour has failed, the dictionary is incomplete, three editors are gone, one mad and one blind and one to Australia, and the project is bankrupt. Gog himself senses his own lack of formal training and has been sent by his aged Aunt Grace as a graduate student to Cambridge, that minor Aberystwyth of the Fens. But in his heart of hearts, he still searches for a basic script, the most ancient of them all, the lost language of the Druids whom St John Chrysostom confirmed were wiser than the Magi and the Brahmins, the Celtic springs of all writing and all speaking. But the Druids worshipped the oak tree, and they wrote on tablets of beech meaning book, and the woodworm and the maggot and the deathwatch beetle have eaten their learning, and how shall Gog find the original fount of the true word?

Evans the Latin hears Gog talk himself dry, then he smiles a privy smile and speaks as to a child.

"You know what you think is knowledge, mark you, but you know nothing. Yet surely you know of the tree-alphabet of the *Ogygia*, where each letter means a tree as well as a letter, and the Druids gave it to us all?"

"I have heard of it," Gog says. "The Beth-Luis-Nion alphabet and the Boibel-Loth. Each letter is a tree, B is Beth is Birch, L is Luis is Rowan, N is Nion is Ash, that is the ABC of the tree language, and so on to U which is Ur which is Heather."

Evans the Latin rakes his long fingernails through his tangled hair, making an undergrowth sprout from his skull.

"There are Druids and Druids, mark you, and I would not always say all Druids are true Druids, if the meaning is to you. Only after a Druid is known shall he be called a Druid. And that tree-alphabet, it was passed from bard to bard, it was never graven on stone or wood or parchment until a certain Mister O'Flaherty set it down, and you know what the Irish can do in their infinite inventions and lucubrations which they miscall their literature. No, Griffin bach, there is a true Druid language from which all others are inscribed, writ upon stone that has endured all the ages of persecution and damnation since that bloody Conqueror came from London to assault the Kings of Cymru and the Word of the Lord."

"You mean the Ogam script," Gog says. "But that is only a translation of the Nordic Runes. Instead of symbols, dashes and dots are scratched either side of a horizontal line."

"Fool," Evans the Latin hisses. "May Ogmios himself, god of the mouths of the Celts, come down in his lion-skin and break your numbskull with his club that you may see the truth of his language. For he gave the secret of the notches and the holes to the Druids, and from them the ruffians of the north took their inferior runes. And how do I know it, Griffin bach, and where was it revealed to me?"

Evans jerks upright from his oak chair and rips a green velvet cloth off an object that Gog has presumed to be a spinning-wheel. It is no such thing, but a stone shaped like the sun and mounted on a spindle of rock. On one side of the stone is the grille-work of the lines of the Ogam script, on the other side are scrawlings of the Viking runes, while on the spindle are engraved characters that appear to Gog to be Babylonian and Egyptian, Minoan and Cadmean, Sanskrit and Hebrew, Etruscan and Chinese, a scrabble of inscriptions signifying nothing.

"You have heard, have you," Evans the Latin expounds, "of the Rosetta Stone, that silly three-sided thing which deciphered three elder languages in Egypt? This is the Evans Stone, mark you, that is the most ancient holy dictionary of them all, with the Druid script that is called Ogam scratched on one side of the sun which the Druids knew as Ludd, the god of the sun and of intelligence – and the Norse script that is called the Runes scratched on the other side of the sun – and on the tree of life and meaning that holds up the heaven from the earth are graven all the other lesser signs and symbols and scribblings that pass for classical languages, yet are but the poor relations and pale imitations of the first writings of all, given by the god Ogmios to the Druids that they might instruct the Northmen in their magic runes and the Mediterranean peoples in their pictographs and mere accountancy of battles and dynasties which they chose to call their history. The Evans Stone is the Tree of Knowledge in the Eden of the Druids. To him who shall taste its fruit, shall all be discovered. To you Griffin bach, who is called the giant Gog of our legends, and who seeks the history of the Ludd of our old gods, to you is given the secrets of the stone. When you shall read the inscription on the sun, you shall discover that it foretells your coming up and your going down."

Gog stays with Evans the Latin for fifteen days and fifteen nights while learning the secrets of the stone. He copies the Ogam script and the runes that translate it and the correspondences with other ancient hieroglyphs and characters. They become the basis for his later work on the script that will be called Gogam and on the roots of all writings. As for the inscription on the sun stone, it may not be revealed until Gog's dying, for so he swears to Evans the Latin. It must be his last message. And thus *The True History of King Ludd* may be completed in Egypt by the hand of Gog Griffin, finally sent to the land of the pyramids in search of the mystery of truth and falsehood, brotherhood and enmity, peace and war, loyalty and treachery, sunlight and darkness, Ludd and death.

PART FIVE

Egypt, 1943

London, Venice, the North Sea, 1944–45

18

Now Putney has read the whole of *The True History of King Ludd*, Gog tries to explain the fragmented chapters of his history of the Luddites and his family and himself. He wants to give his work a literary provenance. Most writers do. They are afraid of scribbling alone. So he says:

"Laurence Sterne, of course, knew how a book *looked*. He wanted the reader to *see* the shape of *Tristram Shandy*, all squiggles and angles and loops. So he drew the plot of his novel on a page as five separate snakes suffering from convulsions. He was wiser about describing a pretty widow. He wrote: 'Tis all one to me – please put your own fancy in it –' and left a blank space. But his best description was his Corporal commenting to Uncle Toby on the freedom of not being married, which he did by flourishing his stick in the air – the flourish was drawn by Sterne in declining curves like a clothesline falling.

"Myself, I think *The True History of King Ludd*, as I see it, looks like the spirals inscribed on the entrance slab of the ancient burial tomb at Newgrange in the cemetery of Brug-Na-Boinne in Meath, where the kings of Tara and the Irish sun-god Lug were buried. Each episode of King Ludd is an intricate maze or involuted whirlpool ingesting itself, yet linked in a design – so –"

Gog shows to Putney his drawing of the carvings on the stone door to the Celtic burial tomb, then he continues with his lecture of explanation, mystification and justification.

"That ancient design is the prophecy of the history of the

287

British people and the Luddites, who are doomed endlessly to revolt and fail, revolt and fail, from their own inner contradictions. They are defective at the hub, because their leader must betray them. Their wheels of change rust. People's power corrupts absolutely. Yet there is a design in all these separate risings and movements. And there is a grander design, the pattern of revolt of man against his intolerable fate, against his ruler Magog, against his God and his universe. And so I would show you the second prophetic picture of *The True History of King Ludd* and of Gog and of Magog – the prehistorical cup-and-ring carvings on the stones at Old Bewick in Northumberland."

Gog shows to Putney his second drawing taken from the lines and grooves scratched on the rocks of northern Albion in time immemorial:

"As you can see, Putney, man's necessary rebellion, his fight for his liberty to be himself, is still ingrowing – self-defeating. But the spirals also spread outwards. They are linked in lines just as pistons link wheels in the engines of the industrial revolutions, and just as star maps link constellations to make figures and sketches in the heavens. Each episode of personal resistance, every little denial of injustice, each minor refutation of a lie – all incidents converge, join, declare a mighty concentration of random acts for freedom, committed in solitary despair."

Putney smiles and shakes his head in mock desperation.

"When will you ever learn, Gog? When will you ever learn?"

"When somebody can teach me better."

"The Celtic mania – and that's what makes Celtic folk such sweetie-pies to talk to – is not eccentricity – as the English fondly believe. It is the delusion that everything somehow connects, usually in a conspiracy."

"I thought that was Marxism."

"*Touché*, Gog – but we Marxists do believe in the underlying *science* of history. The Celtic mania is to get a bee in the bonnet – or sometimes the whole bloody swarm – and then try to clap a hive on all that buzzing and swarming to prove all is really in order. It doesn't matter if the bees don't fit the container – if the hive is an arbitrary prison for them. The Celtic mania says – look at the bees, they're real bees, real facts, touch them and you'll get stung. So if the bees are real, the hive we trap them in must be real, too. Only it isn't. It's imposed on the bees, who all want to get out."

"I don't claim all my facts are real," Gog says. "There's room for fantasy and imagination in history. That's what makes it true – humanly true. History is about humans with all their dreams."

"It's not what you invent, Gog, that worries me. It's the hold-all you carry all the bits and pieces in. It's debris as theory. You have a monomania for linking facts and myths wrongly. And you are not alone. Look at all the theories the British have taken out of Egypt and the Middle East. The endless speculation about the dimensions of the Great Pyramid – it is the golden mean, the divine model of all construction – if you sleep under a replica of it, you will live for ever and it will sharpen your razor-blades, too. And the British Israelites, what about them? They think Britain fulfilled God's prophecies about Israel by becoming the largest empire the world has ever seen. The Jews were simply too weak to be the Chosen People, who simply had to be the British. The proof: The British hold Israel now and call it Palestine. We don't even let the Jews back in there."

"Quite true," Gog says, smiling. "Rule Britannia must be Israel. We are the people whom God speaks of in the Psalms, who go down to the sea in ships, and do business in great waters."

"There," Putney says, "you can prove any delusion you want by quoting the Bible."

"You can do the same thing by quoting the Communist Manifesto. Or Mein Kampf."

Putney laughs, his red lips parting as a split plum.

"I have quoted both sources often and proved what was necessary at the time. Political necessity. But politics change. And so does the use and interpretation of political texts. Your mystic theories and ancient designs prophesying popular rebellion are presented as true and immutable. You have merely discovered them. They are there for all those who can see."

"Yes," Gog says, "I do feel like the Reverend Stukeley who first discovered at Stonehenge and Avebury the huge ideograms of the Druids. He saw our ancient priests had used writing – not only the Ogam script – but they wrote on the whole surface of Britain like on a page. Their vast hieroglyphs were much the same as the ancient Egyptians – and their monuments. He may have exaggerated, but he *saw* – writ over miles of hill and valley – circles of stones and grass, snakes of sinuous avenues, and the shapes of huge rings. The circle was the Father, the serpent the Son, and the wings the Holy Spirit. And so the sun worship and the winged snake gods of ancient Egypt were conveniently mixed up with the Christian Trinity, and the Druids were the prophets of that future religion, when it did come to Britain."

"But Stukeley was a dreamer much more than an archaeologist. He saw what he imagined he saw."

"I dreamt I flew over all the ley lines in the Vale of the White Horse," Gog says. "It was a real dream, and you can actually draw those ley lines on Ordnance Survey maps. They do exist, invisibly. What is certainly true is that the Druids did go in for the sculpture of the landscape. They wrote their lost language very large indeed upon the earth itself."

"But nobody can read it now."

"I try to."

"Just as nobody can solve the riddle of the Sphinx, the secrets of the Valley of the Kings, the meaning of all the hieroglyphs."

"That doesn't mean they don't have a meaning, Putney."

"Only the meaning you inflict upon them, Gog."

"Or you upon me with your dialectic history. I really think symbols – the swastika, for instance, that ancient Sanskrit and Celtic symbol signifying energy and eternity – is a very potent symbol still. Hitler thinks so and calls it Aryan. We now think so because of him."

"Hitler made the swastika powerful. The swastika didn't make Hitler powerful."

"It depends which way round you think of things. The symbol and the sign endure. People, even dictators, come and go. They may use a sign, but they will not own it or keep it."

"The hammer and the sickle," Putney says drily, "will continue as a sign as long as people use tools in their hands. That is as long as there are people. That is why the Bolsheviks chose a sign which would last as long as human society does. Man is a tool-using animal."

"Man is a dreamer, a myth-maker, a player with words, skilled at games. His true tools are his eye, so he can see signs, and his tongue, so he can use language. The hammer and the sickle are mere instruments of gain."

"Look."

Putney points out of the window of the rest-house. An orange moon is setting behind palm trees. A camel stands in silhouette against the night sky. A distant pyramid aligns the desert. The frame of the window presents the simple identifications of Egypt as brusquely as a postage stamp.

"You can see where we are, Gog."

"Exactly."

"It is real. Egypt. Now."

"Obviously the pyramid isn't," Gog says. "Anyway, I dreamed it. When I was a child, I had a postage-stamp which looked exactly like that view. Then I met a monk, who taught me geography as if he had been to every country on earth, but he never left Yorkshire. I asked him if I could do anything for him. 'Yes,' he said, 'send me foreign postage stamps, but only with views. When I can consider them and meditate, I travel there.'" Gog pauses and gazes at the framed sight of Egypt again. "That monk was here before I was. And this is the second time I have seen this. I was here as a child."

Putney stretches himself in his low-slung chair and yawns.

"Gog, you're incorrigible, thank the Lord. And thank you for showing me your true history. At least, it's true for you. Uniquely, you have absolute faith in your own self-deceit.

But let's kip now. We've got those duck to shoot in the morning."

"Yes," Gog says. "Oh, Putney, perhaps the last –"

Putney rises and puts out his hands towards Gog's hands to pull him to his feet. His lank fair hair falls over his forehead like a peaked hat askew.

"Never say last, Gog. It never is."

Gog smiles, but his sealed orders lie cold in his breast pocket against his heart.

"I was going on leave up to Jerusalem," he says, "but somehow I don't think I'll get there."

"You always told me," Putney says, "Jerusalem was in England. You would build it again."

"Not I. Not now."

19

The way to the shoot lies first along roads, where the dust is soot in the dawn, and then over causeways and beside canals, where wet mud gleams in spread sheets of silvery blackness. Frogs croak in a Greek chorus of despair, *Brek-kek-kek-coax-coax*. Hawks hover as if black brands have been burned on the early pallor of the sky, and a flight of flamingos trails long legs in gawky grace. Putney Bowles is at the wheel of the jeep taking Gog to a marsh near the Nile. Two Purdy shotguns lie in cases behind them, and a Webley service revolver in a hidden holster under Gog's left armpit. The bulge of the weapon is a tumour reminding him of his orders.

"You found me very easily," Putney says.

"Egypt is a small place."

"Not for the Egyptians."

Already fishermen are throwing hand-nets into the canals, briefly webbing the luminous horizon in filaments of phosphorescence. A child leads a blind man along the bank: the little snails of *bilharzia* have eaten out his eyes.

"They can't get their food without getting parasites," Gog says. "Just like our society. No rationing and equality without spivs and a black market."

"I'd rather not go home again," Putney says. "Somehow I think I never will. Thank you for telling me that Rupert died. Who burned him? Or will we never know?"

"Never," Gog says. "That's what war is. Death without accountability."

The jeep lurches. It has run over a dead dog on the track, spreading its carcass in a black waterlily on the dirt.

"I would like that," Putney says. "To leave a void. To cease upon the midnight with no trace. One feels too confused to continue. Even in Cairo and Alexandria, such opposites. Blimps like old Evelyn Waugh and real Marxists from Trinity like James Klugmann – both conspiring how to get weapons to resistance groups, Nationalists or Communists, who cares as long as they kill dozens of Jerries. Red or black, the enemy of our enemy is our friend. But then, my dear Gog, where

293

does it leave us with our friends? Are they our friends only because we have a common enemy? Are they our secret enemies when we have defeated the common enemy?" Putney pauses and turns a corner over a causeway that traverses the glistening irrigation of the earth. "You remember the last poem of Wilfred Owen? That line – 'I am the enemy you killed, my friend . . .'"

Gog's heart is cold within his chest. His tongue is swollen in his mouth. If Putney knows, why is he playing this voluntary as he moves towards his tomb?

"I remember," Gog says thickly.

"Good. Then how did you find me in Egypt?"

Gog swallows.

"Max Mann told me where you were. You remember, I brought you that stuff from Bletchley to the canal down Aristotle Lane."

"You didn't bring us any more."

"I came across nothing to interest you. The stuff I brought was important. And secret. And valid. The Russians won at Stalingrad. They knew where the Germans were."

"They won for us all," Putney says. "They are winning for us all. What have we done? Won a piddling victory at El Alamein, with a two-to-one advantage over Rommel. We have not invaded France, only North Africa. No Second Front now. Let the Russians die in their millions and ignore their SOS or interpret it differently. Save Our Skins, not theirs."

The causeway ends in a small island set above the marsh. The roots of a few stunted trees hold the packed mud above the reeds and the surface of the scum. A hut is built among the tree trunks and matting hangs on poles driven into the water's edge. Putney kills the engine and turns to take out the shotguns.

"We'll get in the hides," he says. "We'll wait till the duck forget that we are there. We probably won't shoot any. The sport for me is the silent expectance. A time of truce before slaughter."

Gog takes his shotgun in its case and follows Putney down to the matting by the marsh. Mosquitoes and midges make clouds of whining specks about their heads, but the insects do not settle on their greased faces and hands, the oily camouflage of hunters in the early day.

"I wish I knew what you believed, Gog," Putney says softly. "Outside your manias about the roots of communication and King Ludd. I am sure of only one thing. You would not betray a friend."

"Would you?"

Putney smiles.

"If I was ordered."

"By whom?"

"By those I take my orders from."

"And they are?"

"You're like Ludwig," Putney says. "That time you were casting runes on the Backs, he asked the questions. I do not choose to answer."

"Why were you posted here? Who do you work for?"

"Theirs not to reason why. Theirs but to do and die." Putney smiles at Gog again. "Do you remember the old arguments about free will and predestination? Now we are posted. There's a war on. We obey."

"Yes," Gog says. "I know."

Putney reaches in the pocket of his khaki jacket. Gog tenses and waits. Putney does not bring out a pistol, but a piece of stone.

"I forgot to give you this. Some stray loot from some tomb. I thought you'd like it."

There is enough light for Gog to see the design on this peace offering. A naked woman is stretched out in the shape of a rainbow over the serpent that is the Nile. Her skin is marked with stars and her feet are backed with hieroglyphs. Her hair is black and cropped like the hair of Maire, and gods attend her.

"I love it," Gog says. "Thank you, Putney."

"Its meaning is so obscure, Gog, that only you could give it one. I have lost all sense of significance. This great game of intelligence we play has made me stupid. I don't know what I am doing, why I do it, where the information goes, or who makes use of it. And I do not want to know, and nobody wants to tell me. I have changed. I would rather be a pig satisfied than Socrates unsatisfied." Putney smiles his third and last smile. "Let's do something passing, but positive. Let's have a pee and try to shoot a duck."

Gog nods and watches Putney turn away and walk to stand facing a tree with his back to his friend. Gog puts his right hand inside his jacket and feels the butt of his revolver in its open holster under his armpit. He closes his fingers round the grip of the weapon and takes it out. He lays its cold barrel along the palm of his left hand and points it towards Putney's back. There is the faint rustle of pissing. This is the only chance of action. Gog cannot look Putney in the face and kill him. With a sick swiftness, Gog raises the revolver, takes three paces up behind Putney, pokes the barrel up and into the nape of his neck, presses the trigger, and blows off the top of Putney's head. A dark pudding explodes against the trunk of the tree. Putney's body slumps, knocking Gog aside. He drops the revolver and looks down at his friend, who has no face, but a stump where his face was.

Gog retches, but he has his orders. He must prove his friend a traitor. He kneels and goes through the pockets of Putney's jacket. There is little except a few Egyptian notes, an empty pad of paper, a pencil, the keys of the jeep. There is no sign that Putney has been passing on intelligence to the Kremlin. A search is now being conducted at Putney's quarters, but Gog already fears that nothing will be found. There will never be any proof that Putney committed treason, if it is treason to pass military secrets to a temporary ally who will be the next enemy. Gog has obeyed orders. Gog has killed his friend, because his friend is said to betray his country by those who claim that they defend Gog's country. These are official words, and Putney is dead by Gog's hand, and has no face.

"Never," Gog says. "I will never –"

He stands and feels the stone in his pocket. He takes it

out and studies the rainbow woman arching over the serpent river. The constellations and starbursts tattooed on her skin have no meaning. They are symbols without significance, as are the values of war. Never is too late to speak. You are the enemy I killed, Putney, my friend.

20

There are no roots at the Mandrake. It is the home of the transient, poets and painters, decadents and agents, civil servants pretending to be bohemians and bohemians pretending to go to work tomorrow, and above all, a refuge for people keeping out of a uniform, or in the case of the commissionaire, a uniform keeping out people. Magog sits with Maire at a table, drinking gin. An emaciated swarthy artist in a naval pea-jacket dances, clicking the bones of his fingers like castanets, his eyes more glutinous than an El Greco. At another table, a spoiled handsome drunk laughs and caresses the dapper pretty boy diplomat by his side. Burgess and Maclean, flaunting their indiscretion.

"You English are always pederasts at school," Maire says. "Then you stay schoolboys and stay home. You think it is funnier."

"Guy Burgess is funny," Magog says, "and an old friend of mine. You know what he said to me when he was arrested with another queer in a public lavatory? I am under a cloud, dear boy, no bigger than a man's hand."

"It is not funny, Magog. The war is finish. Germany is falling now you have your D-Day."

"And a good job I made of it."

"I do not see you on the beaches of Normandy, strangling tanks with your bare hands."

"They also serve, my dear Maire, who plot our strategy. You can go back to Paris now, all because of some spadework and inspiration from your lover, earning your ticket home."

"I don't want to go to Paris yet. Too soon for *la rentrée*. They will think I am a collaborator. Consorting with perfidious Albion who burned Jeanne d'Arc."

"Your old complaint. That bit of failed politics – creating martyrs is always the worst option – was seven centuries ago. Never forgetting is a cardinal sin and very boring. Oblivion is correct. One simply must wipe the slate, start again and think of the future."

"I am," Maire says, then she raises her glass of gin. "I have babies." She drains the glass in one swallow.

"Swallowing all that gin is the best way to get rid of babies," Magog observes. "And when you say, I have babies, does it mean you actually have babies? In which case, whose and where? Or does it mean, I *will* have babies? And ditto, whose and where – and when?"

"Hay-ho, you're my baby," Maire sings. "Babies. I will have babies. I feel, it is now, it is time. All those dead soldiers. We need some *petits poilus* for France, or who will defend her in the next war?"

"We haven't finished this one yet."

"So we start the next war." Maire gazes at Magog with the serious fixity of alcohol. "You have nobody dead you love? You do not wish a new life for a lost life?"

Over Maire's full cheeks and helmet of black hair, Magog's vision superimposes the mobile lines and golden curls of Rupert Fox. Only in her spread lips does he see Rupert's kiss.

"Rupert Fox. He was burned alive. And Putney Bowles murdered out in Egypt, when my brother George was out there. He said he knew nothing about it. Did he ever say anything to you?"

"Gog, he tell me nothing now. He knows I am with you. So he tell me nothing."

"You are not always with me, Maire. If I had to define a woman about town, I –"

A hand falls on Magog's shoulder, beats a staccato rhythm with fingertips, then clutches tight as if on to a life-preserver. Looking down is the flushed glossy face of Guy Burgess.

"Can I touch you for the King's Evil, Magnus – otherwise known as the Cognoscenti. And a fiver. I touch you for a fiver."

"Of course, Guy." Magog takes from his wallet a white note with the Gothic script, the Bank of England promises to pay the bearer the sum of five pounds. "Join us. We were talking about Putney Bowles, wondering how he actually ended."

Guy Burgess puts a finger alongside one nostril, then up it.

"A little bird told me – of the genus Maximilianus Mannerist – that your relative Gog Griffin was not a hundred miles or yards or inches from the scene of the crime. A shooting accident while pursuing ducks, and ducky, doesn't one pursue ducks. The verdict was that our friend Putney – why wasn't he called Chelsea or Soho Bowles, somewhere habitable – dropped his gun which blew his head off accidentally and alone. The verdict and the coroner were hand-picked and despatched from London, which is why we naturally heard all about it. But having a homicidal brother – it must be thrilling – or don't you have him?"

"You're sure of that?"

"A rumour no larger than a fib. But for a fiver I'd tell you anything, ducks, wouldn't I?"

And Burgess is gone back to his table in the Mandrake, waving his five-pound note like a white flag of triumph. Magog stares over Maire's shoulder, unseeing.

"Gog kill him?"

"I can't believe it," Magog says, "even of Gog. I thought his violence was only mental. You know, bring me my bow of burning gold, bring me my arrows of desire. But he could have. He works for that part of the service that is obsessed by secrecy. And Putney – Maire, never mention it to my brother. I will deal with it."

"How? You will not kill Gog."

"Of course not. I do not think Cain is quite my forte. I will check out the truth of it, and in time . . ." Magog shakes his head. "I suppose the same lunatic fringe in the service burned Rupert, too, in the name of their God and their country."

"You appeal to me tonight, Magog. You look a little boy, vulnerable. You see, you remember your schoolboy friend. Come back now. To Hampstead."

"And sleep in my brother's bed?"

"And kill him through me," Maire says. "I like that. I like an angry man who want to hurt another man in me."

In liberated Venice, it is the time of illusion. The luminous haze on the lagoon confuses water and sky. Churches and *palazzi* are shadows in the mist, dark clouds in the shapes of vague structures. The occasional gondola glides past appearing as a lazy pterodactyl. Even the Piraeus lion beside Gog seems to be a legendary beast rather than a classical Greek copy of a big cat. Gog pinches his own arm to check whether he is insubstantial, but the pain persuades him that he is real, if reality has any meaning in this miasma of mother of pearl.

The runes carved on the hide of the lion exist all right. Gog runs his fingernail inside the grooves and translates the magic symbols that also serve as letters in the old Norse language.

> *They fared like men*
> *Far after gold*
> *And in the East*
> *Gave the eagle food*
> *Ravens were glad*
> *The wolf was sated*
> *Music of the harp*
> *Will not wake heroes*
> *They died southward*
> *In Serkland.*

But on to the tail of the ancient runes ending *Dou sunnarla a Særklandi*, new runes have been scratched and dirtied down to blend with the old memorial inscription that the Vikings carved after they had ventured down the Volga and the Don to the Black Sea and Byzantium and met their fate in bloody battles in the Aegean sea. A directive has been added for Gog on his next assignment. He traces out the symbols that now signify English letters, which are inscribed in their modern form where the original runes do not exist.

301

ᚠᛋᛏᚢᛉᛏ ᛒᛉᛁᛏᚠᛁᛏ

ᛒᛋᚹᚠᛉᛋ ᚠᚠᚠᛁᛋᛦ

ᛦᚲᛁᛋᛏᚲᛋ ᛇᚢᚠᛋᛦ

ᚹᛉᛇᚠᛞ ᚲᛉᛦᛏᚹᚠᛇ

Gog speaks to himself these new instructions for Viking Gog to strike north as Germany is falling. He must loot the land, not of vain gold, but of the heavy metal of trained minds:

> Go northward
> Operation Backfire
> Gain Germans
> Guidance Systems
> V2 Rockets
> Flight-Test Recorders . . .

Gog's fingernail sticks in the dots and dashes and circles of the next line inscribed on the Piraeus lion until he remembers that the runes have no numbers or symbols for mathematics. The Vikings took, they did not count. Graveling has sent this line of his instructions in the Gogam script. Gog's fingernail traces:

> 0   1   10   11

While his lips mutter to himself:

> 'Binary System Computers'.

Then he translates the remaining runes which tell him where to go and what to do.

> Peenemunde
> Nordhausen
> Volkenrode
> Return Britain
> Beware Allies
> Science Rules
> World Postwar.

Gog lays his cheek against the stone curls of the crouched lion. The northmen have plundered south and will be plundered in their turn. Ludd, Celtic god of the sun and warrior and sorcerer and seer, will send his servant Gog to steal the minds of the Germans and loot their secret thinking, while the Luddite allies will strip the machines from the enemy factories and break the Mammon and Moloch of the Third Reich into rubble and reparations. But the new world will be for the wise and the wizards of science, the boffins and the eggheads mocked by the people, who use the creations and despise the creators. That is the prophecy of the new runes cast on the skin of the Greek lion in Venice, that Gog translates on this morning of illusion.

The Viking ship that Gog takes with his living plunder from Germany to Britain is ironclad and decked over. Confined to a metal box that is called a cabin, Gog sits with Wolfgang zu Mayerlin, the human piece of intelligence abstracted from the Allied kidnappers of Nazi expertise, the Americans and the Russians, the French and the other branches of the British forces. The battle for the great minds of the Reich has been bitter, but Gog has absconded with one Frankenstein to aid Graveling in his construction of a super-Colossus called Ace One and the computer monsters of the future.

"You would lose the war," Mayerlin says in his precise and impeccable English, "if Hitler did not win it for you. He did not give us the right resources. Our rockets, our submarines, our jet aircraft, our fission bomb – these would have destroyed you, if we had the means to make them sooner. But all Hitler wanted was the Tiger tank, which did destroy you, and the Messerschmitt, which did not."

"Our weapons may have been worse than yours," Gog says, "but our intelligence was better."

"So you say." Mayerlin locks his fingers together in a complex cat's cradle and rests his handlebar moustache upon it. "Yet what are your Oxford and Cambridge, where I studied briefly under Lord Rutherford, to our Heidelburg and Göttingen? You do not respect scientists, you think they are unfortunate necessities."

"You may be right," Gog says, "but all is changing. Why do you think I came to get you?"

Mayerlin shakes his bald skull which his taut skin overlays as an intestine is stretched by a haggis.

"You came for my knowledge of guidance systems and our Askania flight-test recorders. You are still in the age of the abacus while we are electronic."

"We may surprise you," Gog says. "You'll be meeting a friend of mine, Colin Graveling. Perhaps you know of his work on computers and the random factor in numbers."

"I know all his work, at least before the war, Doctor Griffin. I am sure he was of great use to you – decrypting machines, I suppose, although I doubt if his random factor could solve our Enigma code."

"We may surprise you yet," Gog says. "I am not quite a doctor as you are. My thesis has only been accepted in Iowa, and it is not scientific. It is historical, if history is what I think it is. *The True History of King Ludd*. There's a lot of the random factor in that. On my last leave, I gave a few lectures on mythology and folklore for an old colleague of mine, Doctor Miniver, who now has the Chair at Durham. I ended by throwing a bottle of wine at his head. Do you know him?"

"I do," Mayerlin says. "I met him before the war in München, I believe, your Munich, where your sensible prime minister, Mister Chamberlain, came to declare peace with Herr Hitler. Doctor Miniver was at a conference and some others from Cambridge. It was on scientific co-operation between the Third Reich and England. I supported it."

Gog still searches for the proof that may make the murder of his friend in Egypt really necessary. Otherwise, all is guilt and doubt, suspicion and paranoia.

"Those other people from Cambridge wanting scientific exchanges – exchange visits to your secret research establishments. Do you remember two young men, both exceptionally good looking – Putney Bowles? Rupert Fox?"

"Bowles, I remember Putney Bowles," Mayerlin says. "A name I would not forget. Putney Bowles. A most charming and intelligent young man."

"Pretending to be a Nazi sympathiser," Gog says. "In fact he was a Russian agent. He's dead. I can tell you that now."

"You surprise me. We would not have guessed."

"Nor would we. And at that Munich conference, was there not a Ministry of Defence official, Magnus Ponsonby? Or even one of Cambridge's top professors, Maximilian Mann?"

"Not Mann, like our Thomas or Heinrich. I would remember that. But Magnus Ponsonby, yes. Another name I would not forget. And his position – it was extraordinary that somebody from your Ministry of Defence should be encouraging scientific co-operation. And so good a friend of Germany."

"Yes," Gog says, "wasn't he? Was he still a good friend after the war started?"

"Not bad," Mayerlin says. "As you know, many of us, including our Deputy Führer Hess, had many good and important friends in England. They believed and we believed in the German-English alliance against Communist Russia. It was right, and I still believe in it. It is now possible, if it is not too late. But after we invaded Russia to help you, to help western values against those Mongols and Bolsheviks in the East, we lost our good friends in England. They did not exchange information any more."

"It's very difficult," Gog says. "Those who wanted peace with Germany were called traitors. Those who gave sensitive information to Russia when it was allied with Germany were traitors. When Russia joined our side, Russian agents among us were still sort of traitors, but how can giving information to an ally be treachery? I do not know. A friend of mine – dead now – said that being in Intelligence made him know he knew nothing and believed in nothing. He was right. I wish he was alive. I would agree with him."

"Then why do you come to Germany to get me?" Mayerlin asks. "Why give me to your Intelligence to pick my brains? What is the good?"

"Indeed," Gog says, "what is the good? I talked to your great Austrian philosopher Ludwig Wittgenstein once. He would have said that the statement, 'What is the good?' was a meaningless proposition."

"Exactly."

"I would like to go mad," Gog says, "but I do not exactly know how. I certainly want complete oblivion. Shall we play chess instead? At least until we get to Edinburgh? I think that's where we're landing. Chess is a war game, after all, and it is the only one I feel capable of playing till I do forget everything."

Gog is just putting the last black pawn on to his travelling chessboard when he finds himself deaf and a fathom under the water. A stray mine has exploded against the troopship and has broken its back. A chill gulf enfolds Gog in choking brine. Intolerable weight presses on his lungs and skull. His brain implodes in a cold explosion. He knows he is dead, but as he knows he is dead, his body is spewed upwards and breaks the surface of the Scots sea. It is a log that rolls with the tide towards Albion.

PART SIX

The Story of Arthur
1952–87

21

There is only one Wall, and Arthur Griffin is First Wall and the Keeper of the Wall. Red bricks rubbed smooth by the downy cheeks of dead Etonians support his flank as he knuckles the Oppidan First Wall, grinding his fist into the pale face of privilege that is paying for this pain. Arthur inches forward along the Wall. At his feet in the bully, his Second Luke is crouched on the thick mud, his body hunched over the small leather cannonball that he is trying to move forward to Bad Calx. The studs of boots indent the back of Luke Lucan's gloved hands, the khaki knee-caps of the opposing Walls batter his head. But he must hold up. If his shins slip down to the mud, the bully breaks up and there is no gain for College. He holds on the ball, taking the pressure and the pain. The stench of gluey dirt, the reek of sweat, the wrench of sinew and tendon – his body begins to fail, extend, yield.

"Furk it, Luke."

Arthur shouts down for Luke to furk the ball sideways for the Fly to kick out of play. But there is no movement below. Entombed in a slow thrash of legs and tread of boots and suck of mud, the Second cannot move the ball. Arthur struggles on against the wall, pushing sideways into the enemy. The bricks scrape him through his padded helmet and jacket, the heavier Oppidan Walls claw at his exposed nose with the fives' gloves on their hands, they grind their thumbs into his eye-sockets until he has to turn face to the friendly Wall to save his sight. Above him, boys in white ties and tail-coats sit, dangling their shoes over the Wall, watching the steam rise from the game below. The minutes pass. The bully does not budge. Arthur is treading on something harder than earth, softer than mud. It does not move. No humpback of the Second supports his knees. Luke is down. He has been down a long time. His body is their playing ground.

"Air," Arthur says to the Wall, then swings his face round into the knuckles of the Oppidan Wall. "Air! Air!"

At the shout, the bully slowly breaks up. The lurking Thirds move back, the four-legged Seconds rise to reveal their front two legs are arms, the three Walls on either side shamble apart. Luke is lying spread-eagled on his face, the ball between his thighs. He does not stir. Arthur kneels down and puts his gloves under Luke's right arm and heaves him on to his back away from the Wall. In the mud, a death-mask is cast, an impression in wet clay of Luke's forehead and eye-sockets and nose and mouth and chin.

Luke coughs, then he begins to whimper. Dry sobs rack him. He sits up and puts his face in his soiled gloves, but the touch of the mud makes him gag and drop his hands. He is weeping now, the tears making furrows through the grime on his cheeks. The other players, the Oppidan and the Tugs, stand round, embarrassed. Nobody cries at games, certainly not on St Andrew's Day, when the best of the seventy poor scholars meet the best of the eleven hundred fee-paying Oppidans, and mean intelligence confronts the arrogant weight of wealth.

"Take him off," Arthur says. "Ten of us play. We don't need more."

Luke is taken off back to college. The bully forms again over his death-mask. There are twelve minutes to play, if this be play. Arthur knows what he must do. He is the strongest of the Tugs, the Keeper of the Wall. He will hold, taking the punishment, keeping the ball from Good Calx, only ten yards behind him along the Wall. There the Oppidans may score a shy and break the deadlock 0–0. 0–0. 0–0. Nought-nought. That is always the result on St Andrew's Day. Once upon a time, goals were scored, thrown against the green door of Good Calx and the rectangle outlined on the elm tree of Bad Calx. But that was a time before mind. Arthur must endure for a draw.

The dozen minutes that Arthur spends squatting on the ball, taking the knuckles and the elbows and the knees, the studs and the toecaps and the heels, the bodyweight that puts a vice and a tourniquet on his arms and legs, they are to become a college legend, second only to J. K. Stephens, who sat on the ball even longer, and whose health is drunk from a silver cup every St Andrew's night, *In piam memoriam J.K.S.* But as he suffers and resists and will not go down,

Arthur knows the battle of Waterloo was not won on the playing-fields of Eton. Passchendaele, Ypres, the Somme, these battles were *not lost* in the glutinous trenches, in the swamp of no-man's-land, during the months of survival or slow dying in soaking burrow and drenched hole. However hellish, never go down. Taking it is all. So Arthur takes it as the Tommies did for twelve minutes against their four years of war, and he learns the first lesson of the class he will oppose: Endure.

In the slough of despond after the game, the terminal tiredness when the gunpowder has run out of the heels of his shoes, Arthur slumps in his room in the New Buildings. His bed is hinged shut behind a curtain: he is too weary to undo it. Nobody is visiting him on his holiday of glory. No one in his family comes to admire the sponge-bag check trousers and pink silk waistcoat which prove him to have joined the society of all societies, the ruling group at Eton called Pop. His wealthy father Gog sometimes comes, but since he was washed up from the North Sea at the end of the war, amnesia and sheer bloody forgetfulness have made him unpredictable, a man whose manias drag him wandering and willy-nilly over the byways of Britain. Arthur's uncle Magnus Ponsonby is far too busy with his property deals and his film finance to visit his nephew except on the Fourth of June, when the need to be seen in the over-decorated company of the fashionable visitors involves finding someone at the school to pretend to visit. As for his mother, Arthur prefers to forget about her as she has forgotten about him. With shame he remembers a blowsy coarse corpulent creature whom he has hardly seen after Gog sent him to board at prep school at the age of eight, and who disappeared at the end of the war into the East End of London. The cousins who put up with him in the holidays, the Ponsonbys and the Griffins, and his grandmother Merry treat him as if he were not really Gog's son, which he knows he is, because Gog always tells him so. "In love," Gog tells him, "you choose or are chosen. Who can refuse the love of a child who chooses to love you?"

His room in college is Arthur's home. The other thirteen King's Scholars in his Election and the other members of Pop are his friends. Some of them are effectively abandoned as he is, the last of the colonial children, their fathers away on tours of duty in Africa and India, China and the Pacific Isles, their holidays a matter of cold welcome by indifferent relations. Once Arthur took twenty pounds out of his Post Office Savings Account and spent the four-week break after the Lent Half bumming around Bayswater, where he had many louche encounters and something approaching an affair. He did not starve because he spent the week-ends in great country houses owned by the parents of his friends in Pop, where he could not tell which knife and fork to use from the armoury of cutlery on either side of the plate, and called the butler, "Sir." His reputation as a Bohemian and an aesthete was matched by his toughness as an athlete. Prestige at Eton was a matter for Mesopotamia or Agar's Plough or the fives' courts or the river. The classroom hardly mattered. Learning lay outside.

One lesson Arthur never forgets. His classics beak is teaching them of the trial and death of Socrates. They are construing the *Memorabilia* of Xenophon. The Greek letters are alien and without meaning, α β γ δ . . . φ π. Alpha, beta, gamma, delta . . . fie, pie. The sun veils the classroom windows in golden silk. The beak drones on about the goodness of Socrates and how the philosopher is unjustly condemned to drink hemlock and die. Suddenly there is a command, "Griffin, you will do me four Eclogues by first division tomorrow." Arthur's heart stops. Injustice fills his throat. Two thousand lines of Latin to write out. He will have to stay up all night. "But I haven't done anything, sir."

"Exactly," the beak replies. "You are doing nothing about learning of the condemnation of Socrates, who hadn't done anything either."

Arthur rebels. "It's not fair," he says.

"You will have to learn about injustice," the beak says. "It rules the world. I am punishing you unjustly."

"I understand," Arthur says, "now I don't have to do the Eclogues."

"You do," the beak says, "or you won't understand about injustice."

"It's a stupid punishment," Arthur says. "Latin is a dead language."

"All punishment is stupid," the beak says, "and usually

unjust. Anyway, you may have to work in the Vatican where Latin is spoken all the time."

So Arthur learns of summary injustice. He also learns of death, lining the route one cold morning dressed in his Eton Corps khaki uniform, leaning forward on the butt of his old Lee-Enfield, its muzzle reversed into the gutter, as the black carriage is drawn past to Windsor Castle chapel, where King George's body will lie, long live Queen Elizabeth. He will be called up soon for National Service, he cannot avoid it before going up to Trinity College, Cambridge, where he hopes to win another scholarship in history. He would desert if he could, but he does not know how. His life seems ordained. He has slipped into privilege and opportunity through the chance of his birth and the luck of his brains. He accepts his fortune, for he has not learned to question it. He is still the child of rationing and of war, when orders had to be obeyed without thinking, when authority wore uniform and was never gainsaid.

Arthur goes to Chamber to look for his fag, a blond imp called Curtis. But Chamber is empty, the young Tugs all out, the curtains drawn across the doors of their wooden cubicles. The old round oak table still stands on its four stubby legs in the centre of Chamber, its surface pitted and marked by erosion and the knives of the young scholars over the centuries. Arthur walks to his Stall, where he first lived when he came to college. He wants to see that he has left his name behind him. And there on the black wood of the partition, he has carved *Arthur G.* somewhere near the *Percy Bysshe S.* of the dead poet. A new carving has appeared by theirs. It is in a script that Arthur does not understand, but must be the handiwork of his father. ✕ ⋨ ✕. Gog has watched his son at the Wall and has left his magic mark.

22

Arthur feels for his legs down the bed and cannot touch them. He can tap the bare skin on his chest, but his legs are swathed in a linen bandage. His head should be. It is an old Chianti bottle swilling with the lees of the night before. Brain damage has set in. His skull needs to be wrapped up, but only his feet are. He must have thrust them through a hole in the sheet. Shifting his body, he hears a small tearing sound. His diagnosis is correct. He is a terminal burns case like the dying mummies he saw as a boy in the last war.

"War Office," Luke says, reading his friend's thought as he comes into the bedroom. He is emaciated above his baggy shorts. He can eat more pasta with less effect than any living creature since the Roi Soleil's tapeworm. "You've been called up."

"That's a bad joke. Anyway, there isn't a war on."

"We haven't read a paper in four weeks. How would we know?"

Arthur fingers the buff envelope that has followed the two of them round Italy. They have been trying to see every Michelangelo below the Po during the long vac from Cambridge. It is the golden summer of liberty and the Vespa. They can sit on their small twin-wheels and ride from piazza to palazzo more freely than Augustus progressing through the whole Roman *imperium*. And now the call to arms on a scrap of paper.

"I've been a deserter for three weeks," Arthur says. "I should have reported to Pirbright at the end of July. I'll be shot."

"They don't shoot you now," Luke says. "You get seven years inside Shepton Mallet. The military policemen whack you with their truncheons through copies of the *Oxford English Dictionary*. It spreads the bruises so they don't show on medical inspection."

"Thanks, Luke, you're a ray of gloom. What do I do?"

314

"Desert," Luke says. "You already have. Pretend you didn't get the summons."

"They'll know," Arthur says. "They always do."

He rolls out of bed, taking the sheet with him. It makes a long skirt round him, as he clutches the edge of the hole in it with his hands.

"That's a nice white kilt," Luke says. "You could join the Surrender Guards."

"Shut up. We've got to go to the consul. I'll telephone the adjutant of my old battalion. Say I'm sorry, but I'm reporting for duty."

"Spoken like an officer and a gentleman," Luke says. "I thought you were against imperialism and colonial wars. This must be about the Suez Canal. Probably Nasser's seized it. We obviously want to take it back."

Arthur drops the white sheet and begins to put on his pants.

"Do you mind if I report back first, then find who I'm meant to murder afterwards? It might be Serbo-Croat Nazis or something valid. First, keep myself out of gaol or the firing squad. Second, moral scruples."

"Your logic was always impeccable," Luke says, "though self-serving."

"Serving your country," Arthur says, "is hardly self-service."

The consul's office in Florence is elementary, my dear Griffin. A small draped Union Jack stands on a travelling desk, brass carrying handles ready to shift the oak and leather work-space of Her Majesty's representative to his next posting. He is amused at the situation, the two young men in corduroy trousers and sweat-stained shirts claiming to want to defend their country. He defies probability and the Italian telephone system, finding Arthur's old adjutant within five minutes. He hands the receiver over to Arthur, who does not notice that he has stiffened his spine and stands at attention as though on a parade-ground two years and a thousand miles away.

"Lieutenant Griffin reporting from Florence, sir. I'm a deserter officially, but I'll be back in twenty-four hours. I didn't get my call-up papers."

The voice at the far end of the thin red line crackles with tolerant condescension.

315

"Oh, is that you, Arthur? Is that you? A bit of a bore, not leaving us your address. If you are on the Reserve, you should tell us where you are at all times."

"I've been travelling around, sir, being a bit of a vagrant. But I'll come back now."

"Don't bother, Arthur. As you didn't turn up, we called up somebody else instead of you yesterday. Have a happy hols."

Arthur cannot believe the receiver against his ear.

"You mean I needn't come back?"

"We can just do without you."

"By the way, sir, I haven't read the papers. My Italian's very ropy. Which war are we fighting in? The Napoleonic?"

"Egypt, I believe. Nasser could have timed it better. We're going to miss the shooting."

Arthur looks at the calendar on the panelled wall of the consul's office. August 12th. The day the grouse charge over the top of the moors into the guns.

"I'm dreadfully sorry, Peregrine," Arthur says, remembering his adjutant's Christian name. "You'll miss all the sport."

"It's a shame," the voice says down the line. "Potting gippos won't be the same. But, Arthur, do leave your address next time. This isn't the end of the show."

"I will," Arthur says. "I will. Good-bye."

He puts down the receiver. He stands at ease. He locks his hands together, because they are shaking. His knees flutter. The moral crisis has become a mild joke. *Commedia dell 'arte, opera bouffe*, a whimper not a bang. Only the smiling Luke will know that Arthur has volunteered to fight for the Queen and the Empire in which he no longer believes, a turncoat ready to become a redcoat again.

"That will be seven thousand, eight hundred lire," the consul says. "As you are not called upon to do your duty, young man, you are called upon to pay for your call. Cheap at the price."

It is, and Arthur pays it.

"History may begin in farce," Maximilian Mann has told Arthur, "but it ends in choice." That is what has happened at the Suez Canal. Anthony Eden is lying in the House of

Commons that Britain and France are not in collusion with the Israelis, that they are sending in a peace-keeping force to take the Suez Canal and separate the warring Egyptians and the Jews, who are threatening to cross the Red Sea in the reverse direction to Moses. British bombers are dropping pamphlets telling civilians to run away before they get bombed. Hypocrisy precedes the flag. Seeing the western allies otherwise engaged in a confusing struggle over a sandy ditch, Russia has invaded rebellious Hungary, and street battles are blazing in Budapest. And Arthur Griffin is top of the call-up list on the Reserve and does not know what to do.

"I have to leave the country," he tells Maximilian Mann, his old supervisor who seems almost too interested in his problems. "I am top of the call-up list, and if I desert again, the Army won't let me go twice."

The white-haired sage of King's College places his finger-tips together and breathes lightly over them, as if the nail polish were not quite dry.

"You told me you did not protest your call-up the first time. You were ready to return from Italy and serve in Egypt."

"I have had months to think. It is wrong to fight at Suez. It's an imperialistic adventure. Gunboat diplomacy. Murder of the innocent."

"Griffin, you are learning something," Mann says, "which is more than your father ever did."

"I never knew you knew him."

As always, Mann answers with a question.

"He never told you that I knew him?"

"I see my father very rarely. He's a lonely man. Fish-farming in the north of Scotland. And dreaming that Jerusalem will come again to the white cliffs of Dover – that sort of thing."

Mann smiles and displays a greater interest.

"That sort of thing. Gog and Magog and King Ludd. I have not forgotten. Nor have I forgotten that your father went to Egypt, which you refuse to do. And he killed a man there, which you also refuse to do."

Arthur looks in surprise at his old supervisor.

"Gog killed a man in Egypt? He never told me that."

317

"He wouldn't, would he?" Mann stares over the pinnacles that make a cluster of lances along the roof of King's Chapel. "But like father, unlike son. *You* wouldn't kill a man in Egypt, just because your country said he was your enemy. Tell me, would you in Budapest?"

"Why do you ask me that?" Arthur says. "How do you know why I came to see you?"

Again there is no answer from Mann, only a query.

"Would you think the question was easier in the Spanish Civil War? Or in the Second World War? Why should the question ever change? Killing people is wrong. If your country says it is right, is your country right? And if you kill people for a revolution – if you believe Lenin that the only wrong is not aiding the revolution by any means – then what would you do if you went to Budapest? I presume you already have bought your ticket one way."

"How did you know?"

"Because the young are predictable. You hear there are freedom fighters in Budapest. You are not a pacifist. You do not wish to be thought a coward by refusing to fight at Suez. So you wish to fight for the gallant freedom fighters in Hungary against invading Russian hordes. I trust, my dear Griffin, this is an adequate description of your present state of confusion."

"How do you know, sir? I mean, I never said a word . . ."

"It has all been said before. The 'fifties are too often a tired replay of the 'thirties. It is like sweeping up the red streamers after the carnival is over. Would it occur to you, Griffin, as it would not have occurred to your father, that your freedom fighters in Hungary are probably neo-Fascist reactionaries? They want to put a dictator back, some contemporary Horthy. Or even the Habsburg emperor. Liberty is their cry, authority their intention."

"But the press says they are fighting for their freedom from the Russians . . ."

"The press says." Mann laughs. "That phrase is the definition of a lie. And as for Cambridge, to hate the Russians and despise the truth is our curriculum. Do you really want to change the world, Griffin? Most young people do. I once did. Nothing much comes of it. The world is very resistant to change."

318

"Yes, I would," Arthur says. "And I believe I can help to change it."

"Then ignore this petty crisis. Marxist progress will continue in Budapest. America and Russia will end this last pathetic colonial adventure in Egypt. Naturally, it will not be represented in this way by the press. We shall read, 'Russia Crushes Hungarian Freedom Fighters! Gallant Britons Keep the Peace in Suez!' Nothing will change, neither the futility of current events nor the misrepresentation of them. What is your analysis of this?"

Arthur does not know what Mann intends him to say.

"Do you mean that communications . . . if we want to change things, we will have to change communications first?"

"Excellent, Griffin." Mann is pleased. "I must say, it is a pleasure supervising you after your father, but these things sometimes skip a generation. Those who will change the world in the future will control communications."

"My father was very interested in that. He even invented a Druid script. He had a typewriter keyboard made of it – and he added the runes."

"I remember that," Mann says. "But he preferred to obscure things, not improve them scientifically. If ever a man *lowered* class-consciousness . . . but you, *Arthur*, may I . . ."

Arthur is flattered to be called by his Christian name. He is being recruited for another secret army.

"You know the future lies in the communicators. The scientific unions who will man the computers that are causing a new industrial revolution. The workers in electricity and technology. The print-workers. These are the people who will change mass consciousness by explaining the truth of history. And he who influences them changes the world."

"I would never be acceptable," Arthur says. "Eton and Cambridge hang like an albatross round my neck."

"It's not a bad camouflage," Mann says. "You'd be surprised how a privileged background is a perfect cover. But that is not your point. You feel you will not be accepted as a representative worker. That is nonsense. Intellectuals have no class. They are the vanguard of the proletariat."

It is Arthur's turn to laugh.

"Even Arthur Griffin, King's Scholar and Major Scholar of Trinity, Cambridge. Hardly."

"Even Arthur."

"Wouldn't I be better off with the knights and lords at Camelot than the comrades at Fleet Street?"

"It depends on your grail, Arthur. Your father was an incurable romantic and Manichaean. He believed in the struggle of the people against power – he called it Gog against Magog – until the people had smashed up all the machines in a great Luddite rising and created some golden anarchic age. We don't believe that. We believe the working people will create a strong state that will wither away, so ending the eternal conflict between classes. The machine will liberate man, not enslave him, once man owns the machines and the means of production. So the way to your grail, Arthur, lies there, among the men who work the machines, among the communicators of the message of the new age – Raise our consciousness to that which will set us free."

In later years, Arthur is to know that his life is changed after this conversation with Maximilian Mann. But at the time, he leaves Mann's rooms in a state of indecision. He does not flee from Cambridge. He does not go to Budapest. And he is not called up to fight in Suez. All comes to pass as Mann has predicted. The Russians suppress the Hungarian revolt, the Americans force the British and the French to retreat from the Canal. It is the signal of the end of empire and the beginning of a new consciousness in Britain.

That new consciousness leads Arthur to organise his first strike on home ground against the establishment. He persuades a group of the porters and kitchen workers in Trinity and King's to protest against their low wages and exploitation by the authorities. He mans his first picket-line inside his own college. The master threatens to send him down, but a mass rally of other undergraduates persuades the master to change his mind. The strikers win better conditions. Unfortunately, there is one serious incident. A porter carries Maximilian Mann's lavish dinner to his rooms and uses the heavy tray to smite the old professor, who loses consciousness after trying to raise the ditto of his aggressor. His subject is events in Budapest. The porter is a Hungarian Jew, who has been a professor, too. Mann does not prefer charges, but sees that the porter loses his job. Even Arthur cannot prevent this tiny pogrom. The history of the kitchen strike ends in farce and bad choice.

23

It befalls Gog in the years of his retiring to the northern seas that he hears tidings of the grievous hurt of his son Arthur, and of Arthur taking his left hand from the stone, and of Arthur being crowned by his countrymen, and of the many feats done by the king and his comrades in their conferences at their Round Table. The tidings are brought to Gog in the words of the knight Sir Thomas Malory, who once told how King Arthur was engendered and lived and died in ancient Albion, and now tells of a new Arthur.

And when the plates and the galleys were done, there was seen in the type foundry, against the machines, a great stone four-square, like unto a marble stone, and in the midst thereof was like an anvil of steel a foot on high, and therein between the two presses stuck a fair arm naked by the wrist, and oaths there were sworn in anger about the arm that said thus: "Whoso pulleth out this hand of this stone and anvil, is rightwise king of all Fleet Street." *Then the comrades marvelled, and told it to the press lord.* "I command," *said the press lord,* "that ye keep you within your chapel, and complete the plates; that no man touch the hand till the print run be all done." *So when all the plates were done all the comrades went to behold the stone and the arm. And when they heard the swearing, some essayed; such as would have been king. But none might stir the hand nor move it.*

Thus at the feast of Pentecost in the year of our Lord nineteen hundred and sixty-six all manner of men essayed to pull out the arm that would essay, but none might prevail but Arthur, whose hand it was stuck in the anvil. And lightly and fiercely Arthur pulled his arm out of the stone without any pain afore all the fathers of the chapels and the comrades that were there, wherefore all the comrades cried at once: "We will have Arthur unto our king, we will put him no more in delay, for we all see that it is God's will that he shall be our king, and who holdeth against it, we will slay him."

And there was Arthur sworn unto the fathers of the chapels and the comrades for to be a true king, to stand with true justice from thenceforth the days of this life. Also then he made all press lords that held of Fleet Street to come in, and do service as they ought to do. And many complaints were made unto King Arthur of great wrongs that were done since foreign gold had purchased The Times, *of many practices that were bereaved fathers, comrades, ladies, and gentlemen. Wherefore King Arthur made the practices to be given again unto them that used them. When this was done, that the king had stablished all the practices about Fleet Street, within a year, he won all the north through the noble prowess of himself and his comrades of the Round Table.*

Such were the glad tidings that Gog hears by the northern seas of his son Arthur. And as Merlin has foretold the deeds of the first King Arthur and so they came to pass, the words of Evans the Latin will come to pass of Arthur Griffin, who will be transported as King Bladud was in an aerial machine to the artificers of the city of Prague, there to be given a silver hand in place of the left hand that he has foregone in the stone, there to fulfil the prophecy that King Ludd will come again for the benefit of the peoples of this earth, to make them prevail over the machines.

Arthur does not know if he is the bride of Frankenstein or the evil robot Maria, forged by haloes of electricity in the film of *Metropolis*. He looks at the shining metal knuckles and joints, fingers and thumb on his left hand and feels at the metal joy-stick implanted in the small machine strapped over his heart. As he moves the lever with his right hand, a shining monstrous beetle flexes and crawls on the socket of his left wrist. There was another film, *The Beast with Five Fingers*. A lethal hand scuttled about committing murders on its own. His new hand.

The surgeon comes into Arthur's room in Prague, hesitant, nervous, his words jerking in fits and starts. "Cannot keep you . . . we wish . . . hooligan elements . . . no trouble but hospital full . . . fraternal assistance . . . we are all comrades . . . long live Czechoslovakia . . ." Arthur has heard the cannon in the streets, the screaming and the shooting, but these are his dreams. Now he is dressed and taken into the corridors of the hospital, and the wounded are lying as if they are evacuees in their own city, refugees from the Krakovska and the Staromestske, the Hradcanske and the Prasnabrana, the landmarks and routes that are familiar. Bleeding bodies are ranged in rows, mute as if shocked into silence or moaning in interminable despair. The nurses on either side of Arthur try to block off the shambles with their bodies, but he can see the evidence of the massacre, comrade killing comrade, the crime of another Kronstadt, the things that should never be and are, according to the logic of the revolution.

There is no transport to take Arthur to the airport. Tanks have blocked off the routes. He must walk over the medieval Charles bridge that ambles across the river towards the old town. An army car will meet him on the far side: every attention is being paid to fraternal delegates from foreign countries. Standing by the statues of black saints along the parapets, soldiers point their rifles and submachine-guns at the banks and the swans, floating royally indifferent on the green currents below.

Already the clearing has begun. There are dark stains on the sand and the cobbles, detergent or blood. There are groups of men in uniform on every corner, the red stars on their caps and collars simulating bullet wounds. The pavements are as empty as curfew. Only one column of smoke signals a burned building or a bonfire. Arthur knows that Prague, 1968, will be another Budapest, 1956; but how explain the new rebellion as another neo-Fascist uprising when Hitler himself put an end to Czech liberty? In the capitalist world, dog eats dog. That is what Arthur is trying to stop. But when comrade eats comrade, where will Arthur find his Round Table? He raises his left and mechanical hand to heaven, activates the joy-stick and makes his aluminium fingers clench in a mailed fist. "We who are about to die salute you, Lenin," he says to himself. "The international victory of the proletariat must be." Then he remembers the book on Czech history that he has read in hospital, while he was being given his new hand. Before he revolted from feudalism and was burned at the stake, John Hus preached a sermon, declaring that there was a universal ass. Indeed, Arthur thinks in Prague. It is myself.

*   *   *

The Albion triptych stands three feet high and is painted on beechwood. On the right hand there stands the figure of the Cerne Abbas Giant, naked and outlined in white against a green ground, brandishing his club and cock high. Round him is a bordering frieze of sickles and wheat sheaves, which also surrounds the tattoo of GOG on Gog's right hand. The middle picture of the triptych is of the leviathan King Ludd containing the bodies of his people within his own person and under his crowned head, towering over the city and the countryside below, a drawn sword in his right fist and a bishop's crook on fire in his left and silver fist. The frieze about him is a pattern of dots and dashes and circles, the Gogam script. And the third picture is of the Long Man of Wilmington, the chalk figure holding in either hand the rods of measurement or divination. He is contained within a series of wheels joined with a lever and crowns joined with a chain, which also surrounds the tattoo of MAGOG on Gog's left hand.

"It is my last gift to you," Gog says to Arthur, "before I disappear officially and shortly. Of course, you benefit from my will, as does Rosa, your surviving sort of sister. Have you met her?"

"Only once at school," Arthur says. "She was very beautiful."

"And unfortunate. So was her twin Josepha. She was killed in Cuba. But she did leave a daughter, Mary, who's still a child."

"So I heard. You must find it daft, having two revolutionaries in your small family."

"Not daft," Gog says. "Ordained, in a way, like a bad clergyman. I'd say that, but you'd say your revolution is ordained, too."

"We are only its midwives," Arthur says. "But after Prague, I wonder what a bloody mess we are giving birth to." He looks out over the grey River Thames that worries the back-door of his docklands house. "Why did you come and see me, Gog? You never do. You're really anxious about my hand?"

"It was ordained, too," Gog says. "Now you are Ludd, are you not?"

"It was one of many industrial accidents. You can say that

they are ordained, because the safety standards are so lousy. But I didn't stick my hand in the press for fun. Or to become a print-union martyr, like some rags have suggested. I saw an oilcloth drop on a plate and I tried to whip it out. Reverse sabotage, you could say. But the press came down too quick and printed the bloody headlines on my hand. Think of it, Gog, the banner type of *The Times* crushing your finger-bones. All the lies fit to print mashing the fortune-telling lines on your palm. I got good compensation, I will say. It bought this house. And metal claws gratis from the Czech comrades."

"You would never be King Ludd, the god of the Celts, without your silver hand. Look you, as my friend Evans the Latin used to say." Gog points at the leviathan figure in the middle of the triptych. "In you are all the members of your union, all the people who have the means to print the words that will go to all the people, and you will make of them a mighty machine that will give freedom to men from the machines, and you will do it through the language of the Druids and the computers that make up the sacred frieze around King Ludd."

Arthur does not know how to reply to the old man who says he is his father and has paid for his education. Sometimes he thinks his whole life is a rebellion from his father and what his father has paid for him to become, but when he sees the ancient stooped ruin of a person, wild and shaggy as an overgrown broch, he does not want to contradict him or seem not to understand.

"The Cerne Abbas Giant I know," Arthur says, "and I am sure you identify with him, but that figure on the left, who he?"

"The Dodman," Gog says. "The only other earth giant left cut on the face of Albion. He balances between measuring rods like Magog does, a terrible surveyor of all the ground. And round him are his weapons of peace and war. But you will comprehend him."

"Happen so," Arthur says. He puts his right hand to his heart, manipulates the joy-stick, opens his aluminium fingers and closes them round a glass of whisky, which he pushes towards Gog. "Take a wee dram from the robot arm. The service of the future. Automation replacing the need for human workers."

Gog takes the glass and looks at the jointed metal glove at the end of Arthur's arm.

"How do you feel about it?"

"You're not one for psychology," Arthur says. "You've always told me – describe a man. Judge him by his actions. By his work ye shall know him. And his industrial accidents."

"Don't you believe that?" Gog says. "Isn't industrial action your forte?"

"Yeah," Arthur says. "Right on the button." The Americanisms sound as acquired as his vague Midlands accent that comes and goes. "I say the unconscious should stay unconscious, a secret only revealed by joining in mass action. It is the individual consciousness we have to raise, and to hell with the rest of the psyche, which probably doesn't even exist. It's like the smile of the Cheshire Cat – now you see it, now you don't."

"That's how I am going to be," Gog says. "Now you see me, soon you won't." He looks out at the Thames that the evening has turned into darkling ripples on which snakes of light writhe and play. "I am going to take a last voyage soon. Join the sea. But I'll be here in a sense. Not in a sense you might recognise now, but in a sense you will recognise when I go."

"My dear Gog, a riddle wrapped in an enigma in a fiddle in a fudge. As always."

"When we said to die or drown," Gog says, "that is only in the material sense. The particles that make up our bodies do not die. They linger round if they are disordered or out of true. Some people call these ghosts, but they are not. Merely the sparks of life misfiring. But if the particles of the body are in order, then they fly out to the edge of the expanding universe that has no edge. They join in the *primum mobile*, the first big bang that started the universe, the infinite explosion that is still filling the ultimate void of the heavens. I believe that. I don't ask you to believe it. But when I seem to disappear, remember the lines in *The Tempest*. Nothing of him but doth change into something rich and strange. I'll still be changed five fathom deep down there. And when the prophecies are fulfilled, when you are King Ludd and have solved the perennial war of Gog and Magog, then you shall receive the last message of my particles as they fly for ever upwards for as long as always is."

Arthur smiles. The love of a father he does not have swells his heart.

"You are a bard," he says. "The last of the bards. I don't know what you mean. One day I hope I will know it."

"You will," Gog says, "for you are ordained to do so. From Ned Ludd who was the first George Griffin to Arthur Griffin who will be King Ludd, the great chain of the living and the undead binds you. Only recognise."

"My mother," Arthur says. "I have spent all my years as a union organiser denying you – who wants a rich father who sent him to Eton? And I was always saying how bloody wonderful my mother was because she was a proletarian – and she was bloody rotten to me. What happened to her? Did she really die?"

"She was buried ten years ago in a special coffin," Gog says. "She was so obese. She had forgotten you. If you need working-class credentials, praise her generosity, though it was to her own weight. I never really knew her or needed her. I am glad you need her now."

"Old Etonians don't thrive in the Movement," Arthur says. "Class traitors may betray twice."

"The ones I knew at Cambridge always did," Gog says.

"My old supervisor there was your old supervisor. Maximilian Mann. You never told me. Why?"

"He was a traitor to all classes. I want to forget him."

"He said you killed a man in Egypt. Did you?"

"Yes," Gog says. "He has never left me. His name was Putney Bowles. That is why I will never leave you until you can receive my last message."

Gog rises and looks at the ropes that caulk the wooden floorboards of Arthur's house as if it were a ship.

"You are very hard to find. You are never here. You live as clandestine a life as the spies I used to know and love. Why?"

"That's life in the union. We're bugged and followed and threatened. So we have to be careful. Do you know my particular bête noire, the new mega-proprietor? Lord Mowler."

Gog laughs.

"Morrie Mowler. He was a black marketeer in the war and a spiv after it. He rose and rose by dirty deals to the Wilson peerage list. Be careful, my son. That's a bad man."

"I can manage." Arthur also rises and comes towards his father. "Don't take so long before you come and see me again."

"I will not," Gog says, "will I?"

The two men embrace clumsily, holding each other as bears do, their bulk making them awkward. The bristles on their cheeks engage in prickles. Arthur's metal fingers stick in Gog's tweed jacket, and he has to rip loose his aluminium nails. Only when Gog is finally gone does Arthur reflect on the meaning of his last words. "I will not, will I?" Does that mean that Gog will not take so long before he comes again or that he will not come again? Will he?

Arthur shakes his head and speaks the statement of Gog that he will always remember. "There are no meaningful statements. There are only questions."

24

"We are not King Canutes," Arthur says, "to stop the tide of change in nineteen eighty-five with our wet feet. We are not King Ludds to bang out the new machines with our rules and rule book. But there will be no single keystroking. Where there is an electronic keyboard, our members will stroke those keys. We are the Puccinis of print and the Nijinskys of the newspapers – and no bloody journalist is going to get his fingers on our jobs." Arthur makes his metal hand become an aerial spider spinning invisible filaments with its glittering nailpoints. "The writer writes, the print-worker prints – this was the law of the Medes and the Persians when they inscribed their notes on clay. And this is the law of the media and the press barons – unless they want to go out of business."

Arthur is delivering his lines that are calculated to make headlines at the press conference called at union headquarters. He stands in the middle of the round desk that he has made his trademark, a hinged circle of wood with a hole in the middle for the speaker, who may arrange his papers like ripples spreading outwards from a stone flung into a pond, yet he may view the tele-prompter sunk in the forward arc of the wooden top. Arthur can see some of the journalists below already typing his instant quotations into the memories of their portable keyboards. Computers are here to stay. The problem is, how to contain their use for his members, the comrades that sit in rows on either side of his round table and flank the journalists like the ranks of Red Guards on a counter-revolution against the new message that must not be spread.

"What about the fat?" a woman's voice asks from the floor. "Your people pulling down thirty thou a year for showing up four nights a week for a job that's been automated out of existence."

"Every one of our members on a newspaper is a worker," Arthur says. "If new technology limits his use, he must be trained to use that new technology. The job of every member of every chapel is his right. It has been his right since the days of the first chapels of print-workers, which date from the original use of movable type by William Caxton five hundred years ago."

Arthur puts on his sonorous voice that makes him the organ of the union leaders.

> When printing first began,
> Who was the master, who the man?

"The answer, friends and comrades, is the chapel and its customs and its practices. We look after our members and we discipline our own. In the old days, a member of the chapel who went wrong was solaced, which meant he was held down on the correcting-stone and given eleven blows on his buttocks with a paper-board. Without us and our rules and practices, there will be no printing. For printing is our work. You press lords and barons, and you scribblers and hacks that are occasionally comrades and good journalists, you shall not get between the printer and his type. Without him, you will not be read."

"And freedom of the word?" the same woman asks from below. "Wouldn't you say that the new technology, the cheap word processor and printer, has given the person who creates the word – the actual *writer* – the power for the first time to print her own words directly and distribute them on the streets?"

"That's not what we're about here," Arthur says. "We're against the big proprietors. They take the profits from your words. What's freedom of speech got to do with fewer and fewer millionaires controlling more and more newspapers and forcing journalists to write the Fascist cant which they want?"

"We can give up our jobs," the woman's voice says – and now Arthur seems to recognise the handsome face of the speaker. "We have our own principles. We do not write Fascist cant. But if we wish to write against Fascist cant, must we still use a pen? Must you stroke the keyboards? Must our words be harnessed on the plate if the printers don't like them? Freedom for writers, Mister Griffin, may lie in the cheap processor and printer in the home. We don't want you to lose your historic jobs, but what about the freedom of our own craft?"

Through the mask of cosmetics that tries to hide the few lines on the full and ripe face of the questioner, Arthur sees another younger face, as if a blurred lithograph were pulled off a stone. It is Rosa, his sort of sister, Gog or Magog's child by the intolerable Maire, nobody seems to know who's the father.

"Freedom means recognising other people's jobs," he says. "Selfishness is demanding your own liberty to put your comrades on the streets. The writer and the printer should walk with fists clenched together against the true Luddites of our times, the proprietors who are determined to wreck our industry by forcing the introduction of new technology without customary bargaining procedures according to established codes and practices. We will stop the presses until we receive our just demands. We will not surrender. We will fight, fight, and fight again for our members. And we will struggle until we have won the victory. Ladies and gentlemen, the conference is terminated."

The headquarters of Lord Mowler's newspaper group resembles a congealed Union Jack. The gigantic frigate of a building is clad with plastic panels of red, white and blue. Oblongs of black glass make cannon-ports against any assailant. In a penthouse perched like a crow's nest on the roof, Lord Mowler sits with his consultant, Magnus Ponsonby. His rosewood desk is not spread with plans of attack: this is no Trafalgar or Waterloo, except for the presence of the self-appointed Napoleon of the print trades, Arthur Griffin of the silver hand, who sits on the far side of the desk. He has decided on the soft touch. His strategy will confuse theirs. He will pretend to the familiarity of their chosen class, which will try to include him.

"Uncle Magnus," Arthur says. "Long time no see. Whose side are you on?"

"The just side," Magog says. "Lord Mowler knows that I know you. And in my retirement, I am a consultant. Wisdom is the last refuge of the aged."

"You have a wise daughter," Arthur says. "Rosa gave me

a hard time at the press conference. She was confusing freedom of speech with working for you, Lord Mowler."

Mowler grins. His perfect rows of porcelain teeth that are attached to his last two rotting molars look as regular as far tombstones.

"She's got 'er 'ead screwed on a nice pair of knockers, and you can't say more for a bint than that. She's bloody well free to say what she bloody well likes, long as I like it or don't 'ear it. 'Andsome, dontcha think?"

"Very handsome," Magnus says. "You remember how the immortal Zanuck defined free speech? Don't say yes till I've stopped talking. We have stopped talking to you, Arthur, about generous redundancy for those of your superannuated members who don't want to spend their old age punching up green letters on tiny screens with arthritic fingers that can't do the job. How's your hand, by the way?"

"It can do the job." Arthur manipulates the joy-stick over his heart, making a fist out of his metal hand and raising it. "It does what I ask it to do. So do my members."

"The Fleet Street mafia," Mowler says, "and you're the Godfather. The Godfather of the chapels. Chapel in my young days meant godfearing, decent Welsh blokes what knew the difference between a day's work and an 'and-out."

"The only chapel you were ever in was Whitechapel," Arthur says. "On a barrow, I've heard, selling on the black market or flogging stuff that fell off a lorry on the way to the Palace."

Mowler laughs and Magog imitates his laugh.

"'Ere's a union bloke comes from soddin' Eton and tells a peer of the realm what worked 'is ticket to the 'ouse of Lords 'e didn't ought to done what 'e done. Cor, stone the crows and pass the sick-bag, Alice. I thought I'd 'eard it all, but you, my son, take the bleedin' biscuit."

"I must say, Arthur," Magog says, "it ill behoves you to make your old school tie into a noose to hang Lord Mowler with. What will the comrades say? What will the comrades?"

"The comrades are out tomorrow," Arthur says. "Down tools. No Stop Press, because we've stopped the presses. You will lose two million pounds a day, Mowler. And you can count, if it's the only thing you can do."

"I can count, Arthur, that I can. I've 'ad a bloke tottin'

up your strike fund. Between that piss and the reserves in
Mowler 'Oldings plc and Lichtenstein, you 'aven't got a free
fart at the moon. You can't 'old out two soddin' weeks.
Greedy, your boys. All them lovely semi-detacheds on the
never-never. Never worry about paying, do they, till there's
no pay day, and they've got to pay 'cos they forgot 'oo pays
the piper. Me. The old fiddler what now calls the tune. Tell
'im, Magnus, tell your relative. The notices."

"Dismissal notices have been sent to all your members,"
Magog says, "because they are voluntarily terminating their
own contracts of employment by refusing to co-operate with
the new technology."

"We don't need you," Mowler says.

"We'll picket," Arthur says. "We'll sit in. We'll fight and
we'll win. There won't be a newspaper printed in this country
until we've won. We're solid."

"Solid as a Swiss roll," Mowler says. "I knew a bloke 'ad
a greyhound once. Fancied it to win the Derby. Another
bloke I knew left the kennel door open. An inspired fit of
negligence, as the 'ound turned up later in Ireland as a ringer
lookin' like a tiger with all them stripes painted on, and
cleaned up. The bloke over 'ere, 'e should have backed the
electric 'are. It always comes in first and pisses on the dogs
what come after."

Arthur stands up.

"I don't know what you're saying, but there will be a
complete stoppage and no further negotiations until all the
dismissal notices are withdrawn."

Mowler barks. Arthur would like to hear "Mowler yelps."
But Mowler never yelps, alas.

"You won't listen, Arthur. You won't never catch the
electric bunny. And the bleedin' 'ound's slipped the kennel
bleedin' months back. Gone to the dogs, the Isle of Dogs,
where else, cock? No 'ard feelings. Nobody never said
Morrie Mowler ain't got a good nature what all the lads take
advantage of if 'e don't take it first. 'Ave a cigar." He
produces a Havana the size of a missile. "Shove that Cuban
up your gob and shut up. You're too late, cock, too bleedin'
late."

*   *   *

334

The low riot railings pen them back. They face the barbed-wire barricades piled in rolls twelve feet high across the street. Within the encampment is the new technology, manned by journalists and kids off the dole, and housed in the old warehouses of empire, the very bricks looking like scabs on the rotting walls where no cargo lies. For the wharves and piers beyond are empty of ships, the flood barrier has closed the Thames to the dockers as the spiked wire has shut out the computer terminals to the printers, it is the end of the age of iron ship and steel crane, it is the requiem of lead type and brass case, and all the shouting and the jeering and the flung cobbles and the broken coppers' helmets will not bring back the dirty British coasters and the Thames lighters, the composing-sticks and the galleys, the working tools of yesteryear when a job lay in a man's arm and in a man's long experience, in a man's mates and in a man's fellow-feeling, not in the lonely operator of the fork-lift truck nor in the monk sat by the green screen at his solitary setting of the words. The newspapers have come to dockland to fill in the vacant spaces there, and the mobs rage at the gates, the displaced, the despairing, the doomed. As in every peasants' and workers' revolt since John Bull and Wat Tyler and Keir Hardie, they will attack their way to defeat, powerless to the end, amen.

Arthur is in the front line of the comrades with the black knights on their police horses facing them. It is the final battle and Sir Mordred and the minions of Sir Magog and Lord Mowler confront the king of the Round Table and his flying pickets. And as the grim delivery lorries roll out with their armoured windscreens, the stones and the shouts fly, and as the black buses roll in bearing the strike-breakers, the rivets and the bolts and the curses are hurled at the barred windows. And the words writ by Malory of the death of King Arthur and set by Caxton's lead type at the beginning of printing are the prophecy of the downfall of King Arthur Ludd on the Isle of Dogs and the end of printing by lead type:

And never was there seen a more dolefuller battle in no Christian land; for there was but rushing and riding, foining and striking, and many a grim word was there spoken either to other, and many a deadly stroke. But ever King Arthur charged throughout the battle of Sir Mordred many times, and did full nobly as a noble king should, and at all times he fainted never; and Sir Mordred that day put him in devoir, and in great peril. And thus they fought all the long day, and never stinted till the noble knights and comrades were laid to the cold earth; and ever they fought till it was near night, and by that time was there a thousand laid upon the street. Then was Arthur wood wroth out of measure, when he saw his people so slain from him. Then the King looked about him, and then was he ware, of all his host and of all his good comrades, were left no more standing but two: that one was Sir Lucan the King's Scholar and old Companion, and the Lady Rosa the Scribe, and they were full sore wounded. "Jesu mercy," *said the King,* "where are all my noble comrades become? Alas that ever I should see this doleful day, for now," *said Arthur,* "I am come to mine end. But would to God that I wist where were those traitors Sir Mordred and Sir Magog and Lord Mowler, that have caused all this mischief."

Then was King Arthur ware where Sir Mordred sat upon his charger among a great heap of fallen men. "Now give me my wrecking-bar," *said Arthur unto Sir Lucan,* "for yonder I have espied the traitor that all this woe hath wrought." "Sir, let him be," *said Sir Lucan,* "for he is unhappy, and if you leave off now this wicked day of destiny is past." "Tide me death, betide me life," *saith the King,* "now I see him yonder alone he shall never escape mine hands." "God speed you well," *said the Lady Rosa. Then the King gat his bar in both his hands, and ran toward Sir Mordred, crying:* "Traitor, now is thy death-day come." *And when Sir Mordred heard King Arthur, he rode until him with his truncheon drawn in his hand. And there King Arthur smote Sir Mordred under his shield with a foin of his bar, throughout his body. And Sir Mordred smote the King with his truncheon held in his hand on the side of the head, and the noble Arthur fell in a swoon to the street. And the charger of Sir Mordred did place his hoof upon the left and silver hand of King Arthur, who gave a great cry to lose his hand and swooned ofttimes. And Sir Lucan and the Lady Rosa ran forwards and heaved him up and weakly led him to a little room where the chapel was wont* to meet. *And Sir Lucan departed anon for the battle and was grievously wounded, for the minions of Sir Magog and Lord Mowler pressed his face into the dark ground, yea, until the noble knight might not draw breath. For so it had been in the bygone days of his youth, and so it was to become again, in his noble service for King Arthur.*

And the Lady Rosa threw the bar of King Arthur in the dark waters of the River Thames, that there might be no evidence against him of the harm he had done to Sir Mordred, and she bore King Arthur away in a little barge at the waterside into the vale of Avallon for to heal him of his grievous wound. And so passed the final battle between Sir Mordred and the minions of Sir Magog and Lord Mowler against King Arthur Ludd and the comrades of the Round Table.

25

The gale sets the trees at odds. Outside the Gothic Temple, the cedars shake their high branches, which creak like the rafters of buildings in a blitz. The careful clumps of oak and beech, ash and chestnut set by Capability Brown among the meadows and the valleys and the vistas and the lakes of the landscape are writhing and lashing, straining and slashing at their neighbour trees in a wrestle to stay rooted. Here an oak groans and shudders and falls, throwing up a parasol of earth at the base of its trunk. A beech bough cracks and drops across a chestnut, scattering its green-spiked conkers on the ground. Leaves flail, bark shreds, twigs are hurled as slingshots. The thickets grapple and entwine, their kilts flying in a charge of highlanders. The wind skirls and screeches in the demented piping of the storm. And the greatest of the cedars, which Rosa calls the Tree of Life, splits asunder and crashes down, its topmost weather-vane broken on the iron railings that surround the red and yellow ironstone tower and dome of the folly within Stowe park.

Rosa holds Arthur's new beechwood hand as they look out from the window-seat through the arched panes of glass at the turmoil of the trees. The grey light dulls the purple balustrade that runs behind them under the golden heraldic devices on the dome to the yellow bedroom, shaped like an egg, where the couple sleeps. On the six cornices supporting the vaulted hemisphere of the ceiling, the gods of the compass-points and the winds have been sculpted, but no breath of breeze disturbs this still centre of the hurricane of 'eighty-seven, the worst tempest recorded for near on three hundred years.

"Gog must have known it was coming," Rosa says, "or he wouldn't have sent me that poem when Simon was born. That one you're using to make a computer game for Simon because you weren't there when he was born, and you feel you wanted to be."

"Gog knew everything was coming," Arthur says. "But he

didn't know how he knew. And we only know far too late that he knew." He looks down at the verses that Rosa had been sent by Gog, who claimed that they were a translation from the ancient Anglo-Saxon epic called *Ludgrove* or *The Battle of the Trees.*

"Let's sing it together, Rosa. We'll drown out the storm."

So Arthur and Rosa chant the last lay that Gog had discovered in the far north.

> Come, Ivy, wall-tearer
> Oak strangler, stone splitter
> Furze of ten thousand thousand
> Spearmen warriors
>
> Stand against alien vine
> Green-dark, drunk-maker
> All-enveloper on fir trunks
> Moon-bright and silver
>
> Pluck sucker, prick points
> Myriad mountings on Magog,
> Grape-grasping and cone-crushing
> Drag treetop downward
>
> But Vine smothers Ivy
> Two in one twinning
> Furze prickles fall fallow
> Faint below silver fir
>
> Now rides high the rowan
> The oak and the heather
> Trees of might and mercy
> Moor cloak and earth cover
>
> Struggle end at Ludgrove –
> And Rune and twig line
> Shall firespeak in Ludd's town
> Melt lead and letter
>
> Break press and crack case
> Cast iron in ruin
> In the end as beginning
> Words free as pine needles

"He knew we were going to lose the strike on the Isle of Dogs," Arthur says. "He knew it twenty years before it happened. He sent you that poem before you knew you were going to end up with me, your cousin Arthur. How did he know?"

"He's an archetype," Rosa says. "And a prophet and a bard. He expected us to play our roles willy-nilly in what is foreordained, what must be. And perhaps we do." She smiles the lovely smile that makes her full lips swell into an amused pattern of desire. "I think I chose you. Freely. When I knew who you really were."

"It took a police horse stepping on my bad hand for you to know who I really was. A loser who lost the biggest fight he was ever in and lost it for his members and got put out to grass on a grant to write his great work on another loser, who also took other people's money for something that never would work."

"Charles Babbage's computer did work in the end," Rosa says. "You told me, he invented those perforated rolls of paper that Gog said were used by Graveling in our first computers. It was just that Victorian technology wasn't up to the supporting bits."

"Babbage spent a quarter of a million pounds of government money in failing to make the first computer work. I lost my members about fifty million pounds in wages and redundancy payments in making them not work for Lord Mowler. Even our strike did not work. Babbage and I, we know each other. We make an art of things that don't work."

"Your biography will work. I know it will. Babbage was a pioneer. Misunderstood. You'll show that. And you are a pioneer. Misunderstood, but not by me."

"A pioneer in what?" Arthur says. "In industrial misunderstanding."

"In love," Rosa says, "before it's too late." She takes his wooden hand and puts it against the swell of her belly. "A year later, I wouldn't be able to have her. Or him, if it's a him, as you insist. I'd have left it too late. You were on time for having her."

"It's not pioneering to have a baby."

"It is," Rosa says, "and to take on somebody else's son."

"Simon," Arthur says. "I like the lad. He's a good boy

with his heart in the right place. Stopping up the nuclear waste pipe at Sellafield. That was bloody brave. And all that work for Greenpeace. You've got a firecracker there, Rosa. I'm proud to call him son."

"He's pleased to have you look after his mother," Rosa says. "He doesn't think you're a failure. He says your fight at the Isle of Dogs is a legend. And if you have to lose, it's what myths are made of. And martyrs."

"I hope he likes his computer game," Arthur says. "I can't show it to you. But I've started the instruction manual. Would you like to have a look at it? Take your mind off the storm."

"I don't understand computer games," Rosa says. "Little boys and girls terrify me now, like my niece, Mary. All those quick little fingers at the Sinclair Spectrum keys. All those darting thoughts. And the graffiti on the little green screen, symbols, signs, gibberish, calling up demons and dragons and lost worlds."

"They're fairy tales, computer games," Arthur says. "They are the myths of today – our Odyssey, our Beowulf, our Romance of the Rose. Do look at my manual. It's what Gog would have written if he could have distinguished a megabyte from a Medusa. Go on, look at it."

So Rosa reads and fails to understand Arthur's manual for Simon's game.

INSTRUCTION MANUAL

(1.1) INTRODUCTION
Welcome to the KING LUDDOGRAM CREATOR

(1.2) LOADING INSTRUCTIONS
The King Luddogram Creator (KLC) cassette contains four files, as follows:

1. "KLC"   – The Creator Itself
2. "FS"   – The Fastart File
3. "LATURE"   – The Ludd Adventure
4. "GOGMAGOG"   – A Gog and Magog Adventure

To load KLC, type "LOAD" and press "ENTER". Once loaded, FS or LATURE can be loaded by selecting KL from the Main Menu – these are data files.

FS – Fastart programmes you with the necessary words and messages.

LATURE gives you the manual to plot a Ludd Adventure.

GOGMAGOG is an example of a Ludd Adventure that resolves the permanent war between the giants Gog and Magog in a wood area.

(2.1) WRITING LUDDOGRAMS

The elements necessary to writing Luddograms are displayed on the Main Menu which will be seen after loading up. Each symbol based on the old runes will call up line keys on the Gogam twig alphabet keyboard. When keys are pressed, you will call up any part of KLC. You may write your Ludd Adventure in any sequence.

(2.2) SYMBOLS AND LINE KEYS

Symbol	Line Key	Roman Letter	Tree Equivalent
X		G	Ivy
◊		O	Furze
⋈		M	Vine
		(Majesty/King)	
Ⅎ		A	Silver Fir
Γ		L	Rowan
∩		U	Heather
⋈		D	Oak

The properties and powers of each rune symbol will derive from the tree equivalent listed on the menu. The tree alphabet is taken from the ancient Beth-Luis-Nion alphabet in Roderick O'Flaherty's *Ogygia*.

(2.3) WOOD DESCRIPTION

The term wood can be used to locate any area in your Ludd Adventure. You may use "copse", "spinney", "grove", "clearing", "park", "avenue", "square", "hedgerow", "fence", and so on. You must specify which trees use the area and how each area connects to another area. Each tree battles against another tree according to the ancient tree alphabet, namely:

	Roman Letter	Rune	Twig Alphabet
Alder	F	ᚹ	⊤
Ash	N	↑	⊤⊤⊤⊤
Birch	B	ᛒ	⊥⊥⊥⊥
Dwarf Elder	P	ᚲ	⊤⊤⊤
Elder	R	ᛦ	⊥⊥⊥⊥⊥
Furze	O	ᛩ	⊢⊢⊢
Hawthorn	H	ᚺ	⫽⫽⫽
Hazel	C	ᚲ	⫽⫽
Heather	U	∩	⊢⊢
Holly	T	↑	⊥⊥⊥
Ivy	G	ᚷ	⊥
Oak	D	ᛝ	⊥⊥
Rowan	L	ᚱ	⊤⊤
Silver Fir	A	ᚠ	⊢
Vine	M	ᛗ	⟋
White Poplar	E	ᛊ	⊬⊬⊬
Willow	S	ᛉ	⊤⊤⊤
Yew	I	ᛁ	⊬⊬⊬⊬

Each tree has properties and magic associated with it, which may be chosen for each Luddogram adventure up to the value of 150 Gogam twig lines. All trees and runes and letters are associated with Gog or Magog, but must give place to the trees of Ludd himself, the rowan and the oak and the heather.

(3.1) GOGMAGOG EXAMPLE LUDD ADVENTURE

Word Description

1. You are in a copse of hazel, ivy and oak. There is a gate to the east and a tunnel to the west.
2. Hazel has qualities of wisdom. It harbours ravens and vultures, which prophesy the future. It has a poisonous milk that counteracts mistletoe.
3. Ivy is a tree of celebration and ecstasy. Its juice brewed with silver fir creates a magic potion which makes the drinker irresistible. It survives death and always returns, as does its enemy, the other spiral tree, the vine.
4. The oak is the tree of strength and endurance. Its branches burned in a midsummer fire are invincible. With mistletoe, it will destroy all enemies except the hazel and the ivy.

5. Choose the quantities of each property belonging to each
   tree up to 150 on the twig alphabet. Press "ENTER" and
   "COPSE" and let the Luddogram adventure begin in a
   battle of trees and use escape routes to the next wood . . .

Rosa returns the Instruction Manual for the Luddograms
back to Arthur.
  "I read, I try to understand, I do not."
  "Any kid would."
  "I am not a kid. I am a grown woman."
  "Thank God."
Arthur leans across the window-seat and kisses Rosa on
the curve of her neck. The hollow of skin contains his
questing face. He feels like warm milk in a cup.
  "I am everything you used to denounce," Rosa says. "A
lay-about flower-child of the 'sixties with a son by a black
rock musician, Sweetass Brown. The heir to a vast fortune
through Magnus Ponsonby, my father if Gog isn't. Working
as a journalist through a fix, but really living on an allowance
and dividends sweated from the workers' backs. I don't know
what you see in me, Arthur Griffin, but I like your head in
my neck."
  Arthur does not reply, but leaves his mouth and eyes
buried in her nape. He cannot even hear the gale. He will
stay here for ever, in the blind centre of the world.
  "I give up," his lips mutter inaudibly. "Surrender. Give
me back to me."

After the storm, Arthur and Rosa walk out of the oak door
of the folly. Behind them, lead masks of Dionysus leer above
the keyhole. The trunks of the fallen cedars block the gravel
path down the hill through the meadow to the lake, where
a stone Palladian bridge leap-frogs the water. Jacob's sheep,
the dark ones cast out from the flock, huddle under fallen
branches, some of the lambs as big as their mother trying to
jerk at the ewe's udder in search of comfort. One shorn
sheep is lying beside a sprawling tree, its four legs stuck out
from the gasbag of its belly. So swollen is it that it might
float in air but it is laid on earth. Rosa and Arthur skirt its
body on the far side of the gravel path, fearing a contagion

where there is none, wanting no pain after the storm, or responsibility.

"We must get help," Rosa says. "Is it dead?"

"I don't know. We'll find a farmer."

But none of the Stowe schoolboys is on the tennis courts after the storm. Only moorhens skip across the water on the lily pads. Rosa and Arthur pass a grotto where bright pebbles and seashells set in stucco make a Brighton beach of a country seat. Then they pass across some rotten logs to a wooded island, where the trees have bent to the gale and sprung upright. They find Kent's memorial to the playwright Congreve, a monkey considering itself in a mirror on a plinth.

"He was nasty about society," Arthur says. "He made jokes at how rotten we all were. So Kent made him a monument where he's a monkey. The faults that Congreve mocks are his own. He is the ugly face of his own world." Arthur pauses and takes Rosa's face between his good and his wooden hands. "Look at me. What do you see?"

Rosa kisses the deep line that runs down from Arthur's nose beside his mouth to the chin.

"I see the face of the man I love."

"Not just an ugly face."

"Oh, you've learned, Arthur. You've seen the ugly face of the world and it isn't your own. When I met you, all the bitter experience, it marked you. But not now. Or not so much."

"I just love you."

"That's what Camus said in *La Peste*. When the plague's on, one's job can be just to love one woman. The plague's on. And look into my face, Arthur. Your mirror. What do you see?"

"Someone who loves me. Who looked after me."

"More."

"Someone who gives me back to myself. Better than I am."

"More."

"My only love. My whole life."

"More. Mirror, mirror, on the wall, who is the fairest of them all?"

"You."

"Both of us."

Treading the far bank of the lake by reed and cow-parsley, approaching the Temple of Venus ahead, Rosa and Arthur come to view the great house of Stowe across the water, its long lawn lounging up to the pillars of the broad low stone front of dull gold that Vanbrugh began and Robert Adam ended. The mansion completes the slope, as inevitable as the views sketched on the crooked compass of the landscape, wrought by the generations of the working of men and the growing of trees, fallen, fallen from their high estate, and cancelling the planned geometry of the centuries.

"You know what they wrote on Vanbrugh's grave, Rosa? Lie heavy on him, Earth, because he hath laid many a heavy load on thee."

"The trees are down now. Poor old earth. All that weight."

"And the stock markets," Arthur says. "The great crash of 'eighty-seven. You must be poorer."

"I don't care," Rosa says. "I don't know what I'm going to get and I don't care. It's quite Shakespearean, isn't it? As though there were portents. The storms of nature leading to the tempests of money and men. Like the apparitions before the murder of Julius Caesar or that stage direction in *A Winter's Tale* – Exit, Pursued by a Bear Market."

Arthur laughs.

"All the seven oaks in Sevenoaks have crashed, bar one. It probably means that capitalism isn't quite finished. The stock market will rise again. Enter, Pursued by a Bull."

Rosa and Arthur cross over a bridge built in deliberate ruins to make the illusion of crossing a weir, and they reach the near side of the lake and the stroll home. They remember the distended sheep and do not say why they take the long way back to their Gothic folly. They walk by the meander of a little river to the Temple of the Worthies whose great deeds have honoured great names. In an arc of stone, busts are set. Rysbrack carved Queen Elizabeth the First and King William the Third, the Protestant heroes: then he wrought William Shakespeare and Francis Bacon, Isaac Newton and the three intellectual Johns, Milton and Hampden and Locke. Scheemakers made the rest of the busts: King Alfred the Great and the Black Prince, commemorated here as "The Terror of Europe": then Gresham the merchant and Bernard, the enemy of stock-jobbers and the National Debt:

then Francis Drake and Walter Raleigh, more pirate than poet: then Ignatius and Inigo Jones and Alexander Pope, the avatars of the Augustan age that tried to perfect Nature and could not deny its disturbance.

"Pose among the worthies," Rosa says. "The light is right. And the dialectic – that tree that has crashed behind the monument."

Arthur strikes a pose among the stone luminaries of history, arms crossed, brows knit, stare fixed on the miniature Roman rotunda across the river. Click on the image, caught on celluloid as immutable in picture as any statue. Then they go over the meadow between the curious bullocks, taking the back way to the Gothic temple. A Jacob's lamb jerks bleating past, as if it were a black sheep driven out. *Ma-ma, ma-ma*, it complains, then *me-me, ma-maire*.

"Did you hear that?" Rosa says. "Mama. Maire. Mummy's name. I always told her that she was maternal – the last thing she wanted to be. She could not totally ignore me and my dead sister Josepha – or Josepha's daughter. She treated us like scapegoats. Sort of beings who came out of a woman and were all the father's fault. Do you know, Arthur, I still don't know who my father is. Gog or Magog, either of the brothers. Griffin or Ponsonby. It's not clear."

"It doesn't matter," Arthur says. "A child is. Despite its mother or father. To hell with all families. We start again. What will Maire feel, being a grandmother again so soon. It will age her, I suppose. She'll hate it."

Rosa and Arthur go back into the folly that they have rented. The oak door closes behind them. They look up at the golden dome that houses them briefly. As far as they have ever been secure, so they are now.

"My mother, Maire," Rosa says, "she always astonishes me. Totally egocentric, yet she can love. She will probably decide that a new child, by someone respectable –" Arthur begins to laugh, but Rosa stops him. "Don't laugh, by a respectable father – don't forget, Arthur, Maire fought in the 'thirties. She was an artist's girl. Picasso and Guernica, the Spanish Civil War, anti-Fascist. You knew where you were then. Right and wrong. It's more difficult now. She'll respect you. At least, you fought for your cause, the workers, and you lost, like Charlie Chaplin lost in *Modern Times*.

She'll love our love child, and because of Magog, it'll be very rich."

"The worst legacy – money."

"Unavoidable. But it will be wasted."

"Unless it is spent right."

"That is for you to say."

"If he or she listens."

"They rarely do."

Arthur goes back to the computer screen and keyboard that he has set up in the folly. Rosa goes upstairs to the womb bedroom under the dome and puts on her Japanese kimono. Both are thinking about the sheep with its swollen belly, but neither will mention it. There is a knock on the oak door with its leaden Dionysiac masks. Arthur opens it to find two school prefects from Stowe on their nightly rounds to check the far pavilions. The blond angel of the two of them holds a black book.

"We found a sheep down the path, sir," the angel with the book says. "It's ill. Do you know anything about sheep?"

"Where sheep may safely graze," Arthur says. "Jerusalem. What's wrong with it?"

"It's got a swollen stomach. It isn't moving."

Cinema memory is better than one's own in the age of pictures and signs and semiotics. So Arthur remembers the film rather than the book. Such is the quality of communications now.

"Did you see a film called *Far From the Madding Crowd*? A whole flock of sheep eats the wrong weed and they swell up with gas and fall over. Alan Bates comes along and saves the day. He punctures their stomachs with a round knife to let the gas out. I've got a carving knife here, but I haven't got the guts to do it."

"Thank you for your advice, sir," the recording boy says. "We'll go back to the school. There's a farmer's son on duty. He'll know what to do."

The boys leave on their errand of mercy. Arthur turns back to Rosa. There is nothing to say about their callousness, their casualness, their lack of care. She floats down the gravel path by the fallen cedar, as pale in her kimono as a ghost from *Kwaidan*. Arthur stands guilty until she returns.

"I'll find the farmer," he says. "Don't worry."

He walks down the interminable gravel path to the two Boycott pavilions, where the caretakers live. One is dark, the other studded with light. Parked cars graze safely around it. Three squat small boys in shorts run out to face him.

"There's a sheep in the pasture," Arthur says. "Very ill with a stomach as big as a balloon. What can we do about it? It wasn't killed by the trees."

"The revolver," one of the small boys says with pleasure. "My dad will get his revolver."

Three country wives come from the pavilion to stand behind their boys, who run away. Arthur tells them his story, and one woman shakes her head with conviction.

"The bloat," she says. "You can't do nothing for them when they've got the bloat. Was it shorn?"

"Yes, it was shorn."

"It's the shock. Losing the wool. Sometimes they get the bloat."

The caretaker arrives, bearded, matter-of-fact. He takes directions, thanks Arthur for the news, says he will do something about it. Again he thanks Arthur for bothering, but Arthur feels like a Judas with the lamb at the Passover feast. He doubts if Judas enjoyed his meal.

In the Gothic temple, Rosa is lying in their small round yellow bedroom. The door is open, so that they can look out across the inner circle of the vast room to the pointed window, no longer filled by the branches of the cedar tree outside. The dome of the building contains a great hush, a silence in suspension.

"We could have done nothing," Arthur says to Rosa. "It was the bloat. Nothing lives if it has the bloat."

"We don't really care about animals," Rosa says. "Only humans. It's a weakness in us."

"We can't do anything about the bloat," Arthur says, and takes Rosa in his arms.

Beyond the empty arches of the windows where no cedar branches now pattern the night sky, the sound of a shot. And a second shot. A little execution for Rosa and Arthur. They know they have the bloat too, the bloat of their privacy and their pleasure, the bloat of their indifference, the bloat of being a woman and a man together separate from the world.

"We will care more," Rosa says. "Always."

"Now," Arthur says. "We will care now."

"We can start with the trees," Rosa says. "We must plant them. Hundreds of thousands are down. And it will take hundreds of years for all those oaks and elms and beeches and ash trees to grow fully again. Do you know what I heard on the wireless when you were away? All the trees on the Gogmagog hills are blown down. And those chalk figures of earth giants near Cambridge – they're uncovered, but there's such damage from the tree roots that they're all spoiled. Their outlines can't be seen. They're undecipherable."

"Poor Gog," Arthur says. "That would disappoint him, if he's still here."

"Vanished, presumed drowned," Rosa says. "But he's still here. He'd want us to plant the trees again. And we will."

"There's another thing he'd want us to do," Arthur says. "And I will do it. I never told you, but I'm seeing a genius called Woyka. He applied his work on metaphor in Greek drama to programming computers for languages in a different way. Instead of putting one letter of the Greek alphabet on one byte – that's eight 0s and 1s – he got whole texts on one byte, and sixteen thousand words on to a sixteen digit binary sequence, sixteen 0s and 1s. It's possible now to store all those hieroglyphs and signs and characters and Gogam twig-scripts and runes on to a computer and compare them all against each other, to hunt for correspondences a million times faster than our minds can. We can finally crack the secret codes and ciphers and symbols behind all our prim-eval scratchings on stone and wood and paper."

"That's weird," Rosa says. "The computer solving all those ancient riddles."

"It feeds on signs and symbols. It conjures up things. It makes comparisons faster than light. Then it displays its findings on a screen in graphics and patterns. And we can have our own computers and they don't cost much. We have free access to all the pictures and information of our age. Even savages and peasants didn't have that in the audio-visual age before the age of print and the machine – and now the computer has restored to us the freedom of all the data of the senses –"

"Not smell," Rosa says. "I like your smell. And the taste of your skin. But your keyboard isn't the same."

"All right," Arthur says. "All the data of seeing and touch-ing and hearing, all the evidence presented to the mind through those senses, that is what the computer shows through its bytes, its 01, 10, 11, 100, the dots and dashes and circles Gog always said came from the Druid scripts and before.''

"I touch you," Rosa says and does. "I see you," Rosa says and does. "I hear you," Rosa says, but does not. "I taste you," Rosa says and kisses Arthur. "I smell you," Rosa says and rubs her nose against his good hand. "Come to bed.''

"Yes," Arthur says. He looks out of the bedroom door across the hollow beneath the golden dome of the folly that might grace a Church of the Sepulchre in Jerusalem. There is a flash outside. A streak of fire. It may be lightning, but there is no thunder.

"Gog," Rosa says. "Gog's away.''

"He heard us then.''

"He heard us at last.''

Indeed, a radar screen set in a Nimrod aeroplane patrolling 30,000 feet above Orkney records a blip that may have been a detonation in the Hebrides. Even stranger is the interference on the radio waves, which snort with a series of dots and dashes, the Gog code of his transference from earth to sky, the final transmission, pulsars and quarks. The message, if such it be, is recorded, but it cannot be deciphered. To look at, these patterns appear:

By chance or destiny, inadvertence or happenstance, a transcript of the curious symbols is sent to Arthur by an old friend from the printers' union who has secured a job in GCHQ, decoding foreign and alien messages. Arthur recognises a pattern from the old Benin bronze plaque that has descended to him from his grandfather George Griffin. When the eroded and missing grooves and ridges are drawn on the Benin patterns, they correspond exactly with the radio intercept. The language is the Gogam script, which Arthur's father has always claimed to be the ancient language of the Druids and the trees. If it reached the peoples of the rain forests of Africa, it suggests a lost universal language of notches and points that was not preserved on wood, but only on metal. Arthur can read the completed transcript with ease, although he cannot understand how the Benin plaque has prophesied the wireless message, which signifies:

FLESH	IS	EARTH	IS . . . .
SEA	IS	SKY	AND . . . .
ALL	IS	FIRE	AND . . . .
LIGHT	AND	SPIRIT	AS . . . .
LONG	AS	FOREVER	IS . . . .
AND	GOG	WAS	IS . . . .
WILL	BE	0 1 10	11 . . . .